CEN 02/10

Camilla Way lives in London and when not writing fiction works as a journalist. This is her second novel.

LITTLE BIRD

Just one-year-old, snatched from her push-chair by a troubled man who was mute. She grew up in the forest in France, without speech. All she learnt was bird song. She was a teenager when she was found . . . The media frenzy brings her to an American psychiatrist, challenged to teach her to speak — another country, environment and identity for Elodie in which to grow up. But Elodie flees from being a guinea pig when violence flares. Alone in a city she doesn't understand, she leaves, assuming a third identity in London as Kate. Seeking a life without relationships or obligations, she slips through the cracks in society. But what happens if she learns to love someone? What if someone from her past won't let her go?

Books by Camilla Way
Published by The House of Ulverscroft:

THE DEAD OF SUMMER

CAMILLA WAY

LITTLE BIRD

Complete and Unabridged

CHARNWOOD
Leicester

First published in Great Britain in 2008 by
Harper, an imprint of
HarperCollins*Publishers*
London

First Charnwood Edition
published 2010
by arrangement with
HarperCollins*Publishers*
London

The moral right of the author has been asserted

This novel is entirely a work of fiction. The names, characters and incidents portrayed in it are the work of the author's imagination. Any resemblance to actual persons, living or dead, events or localities is entirely coincidental.

British Library CIP Data

Way, Camilla.
  Little bird.
  1. Kidnapping- -Fiction. 2. Secrecy- -Fiction.
  3. London (England)- -Fiction. 4. Psychological
  fiction. 5. Large type books.
  I. Title
  823.9'2–dc22

  ISBN 978–1–44480–011–1

Published by
F. A. Thorpe (Publishing)
Anstey, Leicestershire

Set by Words & Graphics Ltd.
Anstey, Leicestershire
Printed and bound in Great Britain by
T. J. International Ltd., Padstow, Cornwall

This book is printed on acid-free paper

For Dave

PART ONE

1

Le Ferté-Macé, Normandy, France,
24 May 1985

It took one second to snatch the child. One silent, unseen moment to pluck her from the world. In a click of a finger, a blink of an eye she was gone. As if, like a bird, she had just flown away.

Georges Preton had seen no strangers in the square that morning, no unfamiliar vehicles in the street outside his shop. He had opened up at eight as usual, smoked a cigarette as he always did. He'd unloaded the first bread from the ovens, arranged his display of pastries, had wiped down the counter then flicked through his paper. At around eight-forty he had seen Thérèse approach from the furthest corner of the square, pushing an old-fashioned pram, and smiling down at her daughter as she walked.

In the white-tiled warmth of his boulangerie Georges had looked out at the morning. A beautiful day: clouds like scattered bread crumbs, the sun round and yellow as a custard tart. Through his window he'd watched Thérèse leave the child sleeping in her pram in the shadow of his canapé. They'd chatted, as they always did, she'd asked for some croissants and then she'd paid and left. An ordinary start to an ordinary day. The bell above his door had jangled as it closed behind her. A minute, that was all. A minute's worth of seconds and a second was all it took.

When Georges Preton, in the days and months and years to come, was to think back to the sound of Thérèse's scream, he would recall, simply, that it had been the sound of every nightmare, every hell. And when he remembered the eyes of Thérèse, as she hurtled back through his door, yanking the empty pram behind her, bashing it against the door frame, holding in her hand the pink, woollen, baby-less blanket limp and useless as a flap of blistered skin, he would remember the moment in which their eyes had met: the awful, mutual understanding; a shared, desolate premonition that no matter how many searches there would be in the days and weeks to come, no matter how many appeals made to the public or the number of policemen assigned to the case, the truth was the child was gone; she was gone and she would never be seen again.

Preton would always know that in that same brief moment, he had witnessed the end to the young woman's life — that in the second it had taken to snatch her child, Thérèse and all she was and might yet still have been had been taken, too.

2

The Mermaid, Dalston, north London,
21 September 2003
A rat's nest of a place. Men lining the walls
clasping cigarettes and gulping down pints, their
shouted conversations like the barking of dogs.
Eyeing the door, eyeing the talent, fingering their
mobiles and wraps of cocaine. Into that she
walked; Frank saw her above the record he'd just
raised, glimpsed her between his two friends'
shoulders as they huddled there with him in the
DJ booth. A girl walks into a bar.

'Frank? Frankie old son?'

But a girl had walked into the bar and Frank
could see or hear or think of nothing else.

'Look lively. Track's about to end.'

Another record on the turntable. Craning his
neck so he could watch her between the dancers.
There she was, getting a drink from the bar. Thin
shoulders, a flash of short yellow hair, turning
back into the crowd then vanishing again into
the clouds of pale-blue smoke, between the
leather jackets, the fake tanned skin, the pints of
piss-weak beer, swallowed up by yet another
Friday night in London as if she had never been
there at all.

He became aware of a swarm of eyes staring
reproachfully from the dance floor. He elbowed
his friend who looked round at him with a
bleary, five-pints smile. 'Take over for a minute,'

he said and began fighting his way to the bar, to where she'd stood, this moment in his life soundtracked, after an initial screech of needle on vinyl, by a Gary Glitter track set at the wrong speed. And there she was. There she was, thank fuck.

Small. She'd barely reach his shoulder. Short tufts of bleached hair. Dark eyes, blue and quick. A delicate chin. So slim that he knew that if he were to trace a finger along her spine he would feel every tendon and bone and muscle of her. Knew the touch, already, of her skin.

'Love? What do you want, Love?' The barmaid stuck her bearded chin in Frank's direction and he asked her for three pints. By the cigarette machine she stood amongst the barking crowds as if in an empty room and somewhere, somehow, a glam-rock paedo screamed on too fast. Frank sipped his pint and watched as she was approached by a tall, spiky looking redhead and a chubby brunette. She smiled, then, the girl. A smile that seemed to flood her face with light.

The hiss and thump of the needle in the grooves.

Time to go back. Put another record on. Sort it out, Frank. *Not till she looks at me. Not till she turns round and looks at me.* Tony the Turk with his sick, dwarfy legs steaming towards him, oily hair glistening red, blue, green in the disco lights. This is not what he paid Frank for, no way. Come on Frankie, gotta get going, move it. (*But just . . . look at me. Look at me first.*) In mid conversation she half turned her shoulders, this stranger, lifted her chin, scanned the bar, searching for something. Searching for someone. Found him. Found his eyes, lifted her chin. Held him. Held him there, right there, in her gaze. When does love start?

Back at the decks Jim and Eugene, pissed and stoned and deep in inane conversation and fucking useless as they always were had not noticed, were the only people who had not noticed that the evening's musical entertainment was, and had been for some minutes, absent. Frank fought his way through the crowd again, past two kids swapping cash for drugs and a middle-aged woman passed out upon a table, and dropped a Beyoncé track on the turntable. The dance floor refilled instantly. Easily pleased, was the Mermaid's clientele. The night sped on, the place filled out, Frank's records keeping the dance floor rammed and the atmosphere about as good as the atmosphere ever got there. The three girls stayed by the bar meanwhile, a hundred eyes landing on them like rain, the brunette and the redhead porous, thirsty.

As he watched her, the hectic squalor of the Mermaid seemed to recede to a meaningless blur. She was dressed in a simple skirt and T-shirt, unfashionable plimsolls on her feet, her closely cropped hair a yellow cap. The hard-faced pair next to her, the noise and flashing lights were just a monochrome haze against which she stood out in sharp, vivid relief. And as his gaze traveled over the small triangle of her face, the almost supernaturally large blue eyes, the slender neck, he felt almost as if her were touching her.

7

It didn't take her friends long to notice Eugene. It rarely took any woman long to notice Eugene. The effect was instant, like kindling under flame and Frank smiled at their sudden animation, the volley of glances that flew past him to where Euge stood, oblivious and drunk, with Jimmy. For the next hour, Frank played his records, keeping one eye on the girl, the other on the ebb and flow of the pub. The usual Friday-night mess of East-End geezers with their shit coke and their mean-eyed women drinking cheap cocktails, and he wondered what she was doing there, what it meant. After a while he spotted his friends amongst the dancers, Jimmy pogo-ing out of time to the music, bellowing happily at the brunette's chest. Eugene chatting up the red-head, his eyes gleaming with either lust or booze. Frank wondered what had taken them so long.

And there she was, his girl. Stood slightly apart, a half-smile on her lips. And when suddenly she looked up and turned her eyes on him again he knew with a shock of certainty that he would hold that image of her, in the smoky flashing gloom of the Mermaid, glass half raised, the sudden, full, frank, petrol-blue gaze of her eyes on his. He knew he would look back on that image one day many years from now as the night he first saw the girl whose name he didn't yet know.

★   ★   ★

'How's it going old son?' It was 2 a.m., the Mermaid almost empty. Frank knelt on the floor

8

packing up his records. He looked up to see Jimmy's flushed face peering down at him.

'Those birds are coming back with us,' he grinned. 'That dark-haired one's a right laugh. Eugene's tucking into the ginge already, lucky bastard. Think you might be stuck with their mate though is the only thing. She don't say fuck all, but as you know,' he winked, 'that usually means they go like a frog in a sock.'

Frank nodded, but continued kneeling for a moment, staring needlessly into his record bag, the realization that he was seconds away from talking to her freezing him to the spot. Finally he hauled his gear onto his shoulder and then reached down again to pick up his headphones. When he straightened, she was standing in front of him.

She smiled. 'I'm Kate,' she said. 'Do you want some help with that?'

* * *

The driver who took them home to south-east London turned the volume up on his radio, trying to drown his passengers out with LBC. Kate and Frank sat alone in the back seat of the people carrier, a silent audience to their friends in front who were noisily making their way through a hefty spliff and a bottle of whisky blagged from the bar.

And there they were, as simple as that. He could feel the soft weight of her leg against his, the heat of her shoulder on his arm. She continued to stare straight ahead, the same

9

half-smile fluttering across her mouth, the air between them taut with possibility. Desperately he searched his mind for a topic of conversation but it remained blank. The silence lengthened. Panic shifted queasily in his gut. He was never normally like this with girls. Bit by bit that brief, sweet moment when their eyes had met in the bar receded. Why could he think of *absolutely nothing* to say?

She shifted her weight slightly and now her thigh burned through his jeans. His gaze fell to her hands, folded in her lap. The cab stopped at a light and he looked out at the black and yellow street, fighting the impulse to open the door and throw himself under the wheels of the nearest night bus — anything but this. The light turned green. The car growled and lurched. *Come on, Frank: say something.* She continued to stare ahead, her eyes revealing nothing. *Anything, say anything.* Frank pushed his hands beneath his knees and wondered when it was exactly that he'd turned into such a prick.

The cab sped on across Waterloo Bridge. He cleared his throat as if to speak and she turned to him expectantly, while the words died instantly in his throat. The air between them thickened, the world seemed to hold its breath in anticipation. But the silence lengthened, the tension withered and at last she looked away. With a sinking heart he watched her gaze out at the floodlit buildings of the South Bank, the fuzzy, neon reflections strewn across the black river like the trails of fireworks. Soon they would be there and his chance would have passed. He was an idiot.

The car approached the Elephant. In no time they were in Deptford.

Too late. Too late.

He called to the driver to stop. Clambered awkwardly through the car, treading on the foot of the redhead who was sprawled across Eugene's lap, and almost falling onto the brunette, her hand on Jimmy's thigh. 'I'll see you later, yeah?' he said. He had bottled it and he couldn't bear to look at her now.

'What you doing?' protested Jimmy. 'Come back to mine!'

Eugene nodded through a cloud of smoke. 'You gotta come back, man. Come and party.'

'I'm just dropping my records off,' he lied soothingly. 'I'll come round after.' He got out of the car, tried to think of how to say goodbye to her, could only manage a brief smile, disappointment clutching at his throat. *Fuck it.* It was only after he'd unloaded his bags and the car had sped away that he turned and saw her standing beneath the fuzzy orange glow of a street lamp.

'I thought I might keep you company,' she said, her voice quiet, precise.

She had the most vivid face he'd ever seen, he thought. No make-up but full, red lips, a patch of pink high on each cheek, her eyes dark blue, speckled black. Dense and quick, like water running over rocks.

'Are we going in, then?' Amused, expectant.

'Oh,' said Frank. 'Yeah. Sorry. It's this one.'

He unlocked his front door and realized by the smell that he'd forgotten to take the bins out again. She followed him along the dark, cramped

11

hallway to the lounge. The overhead bulb had gone, and he crashed around for a few seconds trying to locate the lamp.

He cringed when the light eventually revealed the chaos of his lounge. He hadn't done anything to the house since moving in three years ago apart from install a large sound system. There was a smell of damp, and leaky gas fire. A green, flowered carpet cringed beneath purple wallpaper. The furniture was sparse, had seen better days. But the worse thing, he decided, the very worse thing was that everything — every inch of space: the floor, the table, the sofa, the shelves — was covered in piles of records. Twelve-inch and seven-inch black, shiny orbs, naked or half-dressed in white paper sleeves or peeping out from colourful, cardboard covers. It was like a bizarre kind of record shop that had recently been burgled, he realised. He looked over at Kate, who stood surveying the room from the door.

'Interesting . . . décor,' she said, a smile like a bird's wing brushing her lips.

'Yeah,' said Frank. 'Sorry. Bit of a dump. It was my Aunt Joanie's. I inherited it from her a few years back and I never got round to, er — ' He rubbed his face and glancing at her, fell silent.

'You've done wonders with the place,' she laughed, and watched as he began picking up records from the floor and the sofa, making space for her to sit.

'You like music.'

He smiled. 'Yeah,' he agreed. 'I like music.'

12

What was he going to do with her now, now that she was here?

'I'm sorry,' she said, after a short silence. 'About your aunt. Were you close?'

Frank shrugged, nodded. 'I suppose we were.' He continued to shift piles of records from one space to the next.

'Come and sit down.' She'd taken her jacket off, and he could see the goose pimples on her thin arms. He could not remember when he had last felt so nervous. And what was it about her voice? It was incredible, he thought, like music. When she stopped talking it was as if that final word hung in the air afterwards like the last note of a song, his ears stretching after it in the silence that followed.

They stared at each other for a moment. 'Coffee,' he said abruptly, and left the room.

In the pitch-black hall on the way to the kitchen, he tripped over another box of records and told it he was sorry. As he made the coffee and crashed through some washing up, his mobile buzzed repeatedly in his back pocket. Jimmy and Eugene, he supposed, and turned it off. His kitchen smelt of bad fridge. From the next room, he heard her put a record on. A Bowie track, Life On Mars.

When he returned she was standing by the window. She didn't notice him for a second or two, and he stood, poised in the threshold, looking at her slender neck bent over the record sleeve she held. He wondered what her skin smelt like. She turned to him then, and he felt himself flush with pleasure at her smile, momentarily dazzled. She put down the record and walked towards him.

Carefully, she took the mugs from his hands and put them on the table. She led him to the sofa, gently pulling him until he was sitting next to her. She reached for his face and drew it closer to hers and then grazed his mouth with her lips. Frank scarcely breathed. Next she kissed his brow, his cheek, his eyes, and, finally, his mouth again, her tongue flickering between his lips. Frank put his hand on her back, his long fingers tracing the dips and hollows of her ribs, pulling her closer to him. In the silence they kissed and he felt himself respond with a mad exhilaration as if he'd just stepped off a cliff.

The coffee went cold, the record came to an end. She took his hand and led him into the dark hall, then up the narrow staircase as if she'd been there many times before. In the doorway of his bedroom they stopped to gaze in at the room that like his lounge was strewn with records. Kate moved first. Lightly kicking the Stones from her path she led him to the bed, still holding Frank's hand she stepped neatly over the Kinks. With one arm she swept Aretha Franklin off the duvet, and sitting down next to John Coltrane she pulled Frank towards her. Letting go of his hand, she tugged her T-shirt over her head, and pushing Frank back onto the bed, she kissed him again.

3

Nobody really knew the man who lived in the forest, and the few who were acquainted with him knew him only as 'the mute'. He would arrive in his rusty blue pick-up truck at a store in one of the villages some distance from the Forêt de Breteuil, and the shop owners who served him would be struck by a distant memory of the peculiar weight of his silence. And as they helped him take his provisions to the truck or collected money for his petrol, they would feel sure, suddenly, that they had served him once before, one day long ago.

Their conversation would be met with a pleasant, apologetic smile and the silent man would raise a single, bony finger to his mouth and sadly shake his head. Then he would pull from his pocket a note pad and write down his order, and the shop keeper would be struck by the frank sweetness of his gaze, would watch him drive away, wonder briefly who he was and where he lived, before shrugging and turning back to their day.

The young woman who worked in the charity shop in Argentan, however, had never seen the man before. Wham blared loudly from the radio and she was busy on the phone when the tall, grave stranger with the shy smile and slight stoop handed her the amount she had absent-mindedly

15

rung up on the till. And so, ten years later, when the same man's body had been found in a forest twenty miles away, and when a picture of his face flashed across TV screens around the world, the young woman, whose name was Laure, would not remember that this was the same, silent person who had once bought bags and bags of clothes one afternoon a decade ago, for a toddler, for a child, for a young girl.

4

Forêt de Breteuil, Normandy, 1985
Her old life is soon forgotten, here amongst the trees. She's almost three. At first she babbles the few baby sentences she has learnt, but when the man does not reply, language too, is lost. There are no words in the forest. Hot sun and cool rain and freezing ice come and go and then return again, and her mother's smell and touch and voice, her home, everything is forgotten, the wind takes all that with it as it rushes and bellows and whips between the beeches and oaks, over the river, escaping through the snatching leaves, out, out of the forest, leaving her behind.

The small stone cottage is little bigger than a shack with two small rooms, a leaking roof, a narrow bed on either side of the wide hearth. Dense woodlands surround it, the nearest road eight miles away is only rarely used by passing truckers on their way to somewhere else.

The years pass. In the winter the forest is still and melancholy. The tree trunks rise black and gaunt from the snow like bones, only a few desiccated leaves remain, dead but not fallen. In the winter the cottage is thick with heat from the fire and the smell of stew cooking above the flames. They sit and eat and watch the burning wood, while outside, dense and black, the night sits and waits, sits and waits.

Spring returns and a new softness begins to creep across the shadows. Saplings rise from the barren ground. The trees, slowly at first, begin to sprout their buds. And then the pulse of the forest begins to gather speed, beating louder and stronger until almost all at once the trees are alive with noise and colour. A pale, green light creeps between the trees. The river flows thick with fish and the bracken rustles with deer, hares, squirrels, badgers, boar. The branches stir with birdsong.

When she is five the man makes a fishing rod for the child and teaches her to fish. Side by side they sit on the riverbank, waiting patiently for the tell-tale tug on the end of their lines. He shows her where to look for berries and where the wild garlic grows. She watches, delighted, as effortlessly he splits logs with his axe and builds for her a see-saw. He is stronger and taller than all the trees.

★　★　★

Soon she's entrusted with her own chores and each morning she tends the vegetable patch, checks the animal traps and fetches eggs from the coop, proudly bringing him her spoils. Later, she will watch in unblinking admiration as his quick, agile fingers expertly skin a rabbit, making light work of its glistening pink flesh and transforming the once hopping, furry thing into a hot and tasty meal. At night after they have eaten and she has grown sleepy by the fire, she hugs him tightly before she goes to bed and his beloved woody, smoky smell lingers in her nostrils as she drifts into sleep.

The man has shown the girl how far she's permitted to roam. No further than the river, nor past the very end of the third clearing, behind the cottage where their vegetables grow. She could disobey him. On the rare days that he sets off in his truck and doesn't return until after the sun has set, on these days she could run without him ever finding her. But where to, and why? Instead the hours of his absence are waited out anxiously; no sooner has the rusty blue truck disappeared from view than she begins to listen impatiently for the rumbling splutter of its return. Perched on the narrow front step or with her face pressed against the window pane she strains her ears and eyes for him, her hands clasped tightly to her chest to calm the twisting, gnawing there.

Once, when the man has been gone much longer than usual and the sun has long since set, the little girl stares out with growing dismay at the forest that seems to get blacker and denser with every passing second. At last she decides that he is never coming back for her. Panic-stricken she imagines setting out alone through the trees to look for him but she can no more picture a world beyond the forest than she can imagine a life without the man.

Eventually her anxiety forces her from the cottage and beneath the cold, silent moon she paces back and forth between the path and the river, insensible to the rain that has begun to soak her clothes and hair. And when finally he appears, struggling towards her through the darkness with a heavy sack of supplies on his shoulder, her relief is so great that it takes him some time to prise her arms from his legs, to calm her anguished sobs. He picks her up and carries her into the house, rocking her gently on his lap until at last her tears subside and she falls into an uneasy, clinging sleep.

★ ★ ★

Only once do strangers come. She is eight. The man and the little girl are by the river when voices curl their way through the trees. It's the child who hears them first. She lifts her chin, alert suddenly, her ears straining to identify the strange new sound as words drift towards her like dandelion seeds on a breeze. And all at once something in her remembers; some small part of her stirs: a distant, half-forgotten longing rises inside her. Instinctively she gets up and moves towards the voices, towards something she hadn't even known she'd hungered for till then. And then the man has snatched her up, is running with her towards the cottage, his hand silencing her sharp yelp of shock. Inside the tiny house he wraps a shirt around her mouth, tying it so tightly that the tears choke in her throat. He pushes her beneath the small wooden bed and pulls the blanket down until she's in darkness, shivering on the cold stone floor. And then she hears him leave, the bolt of the door sliding heavily in its lock.

* * *

Later, when the fire's burning in the grate and the sky outside is dark, the man sits and holds her to him and wipes away her tears. Whatever lies beyond the forest is to be feared, she's certain of that now. She gazes up at him until the anger and hurt gradually leaves her. After a while, she reaches for his wrist and turns it to its white, fleshy underside. It's something she has done since she was very small, has always been drawn to the soft, white skin there, such a contrast to the rest of him that is so rough and tanned or covered in swirls of hair. She traces her finger along the delicate flesh, where pale blue veins pulse beneath the whiteness. He smiles down at her. All is well again.

* * *

Every night the girl lies on her narrow bed and listens to the sound of the man sleeping on the other side of the hearth, his slow steady breath mingling with the 'hee-wiiit' and 'oooo' of the owls as they move outside on silent wings. Each morning she wakes before the first light. Quietly, while the man sleeps, she slips out of the cottage and sits on the step, waiting patiently. As soon as the first light appears the forest seems to stretch and sigh expectantly. Mist hangs heavy between the trees; a warm muskiness rises from the bracken, foxes cease their dissolute shrieking and even the gurgling river seems to pause awhile. And then, at last, it begins.

21

Each first, tentative note is answered by another and then another. Gradually, the simple calls are replaced by a thousand complex melodies that weave and wind around each other, building layer upon layer until the forest is swollen with sound, the trees are heavy with song, and music falls like rain from the branches of each one. The sun floats higher in the sky bathing each leaf in a soft, pink light. And the forest is transformed by birdsong: it is saturated with music and it's magical, it's hers. The sound grows louder and louder until it feels to the child that the whole world is drenched in melody. But then, finally, suddenly: nothing. Only a silence that is as dramatic as the symphony it has replaced. The child rouses herself and returns, satisfied, to the house and the sleeping man.

★ ★ ★

At dusk on summer's evenings, the man and the girl sit together on a little bench in front of the cottage. While he smokes and stares thoughtfully at the fading evening light, the child performs for him the music she has learnt. From the loud, mewing 'pee-uuu, pee-uuu' of the buzzard, to the jangling warble of the redstart, to the warm cooing of the cuckoo and the 'chink-chink, chink-chink' of the blackbird, the child is able to mimic each one perfectly. Tika-tika-tika, she sings. Chiiiiiiiiiii-ew. She knows the music of every bird from the whitethroat to the kestrel to the guillemot to the lark. And the man smokes and listens, while he carves his gift to her: a little wooden starling whittled from a fallen branch.

They are happy together, the silent man and the wordless child. The days and months come and go, as the seasons attack, take hold, and then recede. But in the same way that night banishes the sun, and winter crushes summer in its fist, so too does darkness come to the man. It arrives without warning and lasts sometimes days, sometimes weeks, but it seems to her that when it comes it falls with such heavy finality there will never be light again. It is as if the mud from the riverbed has crept up on him while he slept, as if its thick, black muck has seeped into his ears, his nostrils, through his mouth to choke him on its wretchedness.

At these times, the child can do nothing but watch and wait. When night falls she builds a fire and perches miserably at the man's side while he sits, immobile in his chair, with heavy, brooding eyes. Sometimes she creeps towards him and, lifting his arm, she brings the naked underbelly of his wrist to her cheek, but when he doesn't respond, she lets it drop listlessly to his side and returns to crouch by the fire alone. Some mornings he will not rise from his bed at all but will continue just to lie there, his knees bent almost to his chest, his face staring sightlessly at the wall.

And when finally he returns to her, emerging blinking into the sunlight as if bewildered to find the world exactly as he left it, she will go to him and take his hand and lead him to the river to fish. Later they will tend the vegetables and chickens together, and eat their supper side by side on the little bench beside the cottage while the birds begin again their evening song.

5

The Mermaid, Dalston, north London,
21 September 2003
Into the bar she walks, winding between the
bodies like cigarette smoke. She's here to
celebrate her last day at the insurance firm where
she's temped for the past six months. She's tired,
would prefer to go home, but Candice and
Carmen have insisted: they want to see her off in
style. A Gary Glitter song screams suddenly
through the room at high-speed like a rampaging
gatecrasher. Kate stands by the cigarette
machine and waits.

The Mermaid is packed with the sort of
people discouraged from patronizing the bars
and restaurants a few miles away on Upper
Street where Kate, Carmen and Candice plan to
head after they've taken advantage of the
Mermaid's 3-for-1 cocktail offer. She has never
been here before. It is one of those bars that has
tinted windows and CCTV. Disco lights flash
encouragingly from the dance floor: red, blue,
yellow and green. She looks at the various
groups of drinkers: the shaven-headed men in
their tan leather jackets and their orange,
wrinkly-cleavaged women. They each drink and
talk in short sharp bursts, all the while scanning
the room with restless, flickering eyes. She buys a
drink and stands by the cigarette machine,
waiting for her friends.

And by the bar a young man stands alone, staring at her, as if she has just called out his name.

Candice and Carmen arrive. They are fond of Kate; girls like them always are. She's the quiet type and therefore impressed, they're sure, by their confidence and bravado. She is unfashionably dressed, so must be envious of their TopShop clothes and long flat hair. She has no man of her own so hangs (bless her) on their tales of flirting and fucking, their one-night stands with rich city boys. She is the blank canvas on which they paint themselves in the most flattering of lights. They will miss her when she's gone and feel vaguely outraged when she doesn't keep in touch.

★   ★   ★

The hissing and scratching of the grooves.

★   ★   ★

She notices that the man at the bar has returned to the DJ booth and put another record on. The dance floor refills and, between the swaying bodies, she examines the three men by the decks. The tall, dark-skinned man is very beautiful; his eyes cat-like, his lips full and mournful, his fingers long and graceful. Every so often he pulls a tiny plastic vial from the pocket of his jacket and takes a sniff in a sly, furtive gesture that belies the slow, sleepy sensuousness of his face.

The man next to him is stocky, solid, and has

a large, open countenance with smiling eyes. He moves in big, expansive gestures and rarely stops talking, laughs a lot and loudly and is very tactile, slapping his friends on the back or ruffling their hair. He is very sure of himself; very comfortable in his skin. He's the sort of man, she thinks, who has probably changed little since boyhood, except perhaps for an almost imperceptible glimmer of doubt that slides at odd moments behind those keen, laughing eyes.

The third man is the man who had been staring at her by the bar and who is staring at her still. He's dressed in shabby jeans and a pale green sweatshirt. He has an attractive, sensitive face and his slim frame is tall and slightly awkward. She sees that while his friends become increasingly drunk, there is something contained, something infinitely calm about him. She notices that his friends glance at him often, as if to reassure themselves that he is still there, that everything is as it should be. After a while, she finds herself beginning to do the same.

'Fucking hell, Car, have you seen that bloke, there?' Candice clutches Carmen's arm and the two look over at the beautiful mixed-race man. Kate wonders what has taken them so long.

The night speeds up, bodies fill the dance floor, the man in the green sweatshirt upping the tempo with each song. She sees how lovingly he handles his records, how expertly he gauges the dancers' mood. His movements are fluid, sure. In this at least, she sees, he is sure. His two friends approach Kate and her colleagues. The beautiful man tells them his name is Eugene, the stocky, smiling one is Jimmy, and he offers to buy them drinks. Kate hangs back and watches the four of them dance. She raises her glass to her lips and turns to the DJ booth to meet the third man's soft, brown gaze full on. She holds his eyes for a long time.

★　★　★

In the taxi that takes them to south-east London she sees that his hands are large with bitten nails. She's sorry when he pushes them beneath his knees, out of sight.

★　★　★

Standing in the doorway of his lounge in the tiny Deptford house she watches him across the chaos of the shabby, record-strewn room. As he blunders around shifting piles of vinyl she notices how the words bubble behind his eyes, come briefly to the surface only to be dismissed immediately with an uncertain smile. He clears a space for her on the sofa and she sits.

'You like music,' she says, after a moment or two.

'Yeah,' he shrugs and rubs his face. 'I play any old shit in the Mermaid. As long as they can dance to it they don't give a fuck. But, yeah — ' he looks around at the mess of records as if noticing them for the first time and laughs apologetically ' — yeah,' he says softly, 'I like music.'

Her arms goose-pimple in the cold room. She

28

watches him, as he hangs there awkwardly before her, trying to think of what to say next. His entire body leans forward, as if desperate for her. She senses that he wants to touch her; that every speck of him longs for that. Abruptly, though, he leaves the room, muttering something about coffee.

She goes to the sound system and picks up a record at random from one of the boxes on the floor. She doesn't look at it as she places it on the turntable and raises the needle: she knows nothing about music. By coincidence, it's a song she recognises. Life on Mars. She freezes, immediately shoved by the familiar tune back to a different time and place. A small, cramped room in a New York apartment. A pink nylon bedspread. A young Vietnamese boy named Bobby who is covered in bruises and who still smells of his last customer's semen, a cheap cassette player that rattles as it plays the words, Is there life on Mars? Is there life on Mars?. Unexpected tears spring to her eyes.

She bends her head over the record sleeve and seconds later turns to see Frank standing in the door, the coffee mugs in his hands. They smile at each other and as she stands there gazing at him, she feels for the first time in a very long while that perhaps she might find peace, here, in this dark, messy house, with this tall, shy stranger, if only for one night. She feels as if she might perhaps sleep and not dream for once the same, old, terrible dream.

6

Forêt de Breteuil, Normandy, 1995
The child grows taller. Her light-brown hair with
its strands of red and copper falls almost to her
waist. There is a new restlessness within her that
was not there before. Now, when the man gets
into his truck she will try to jump in too, holding
on tightly to the handle until he pulls away. And
when he has gone she will roam further than she
ever has before, looking for something, for
somewhere else, but not quite daring — not yet
— to wander too far.

She is almost thirteen. In recent months
something has changed between them, a shadow
has crept over their contentment. Sometimes,
when they sit together in front of the fire at night
she will turn and catch him looking at her in a
way he never has before and although the
moment passes an uneasiness will continue to
linger in the air between them for a little while
longer, like a slithering in the undergrowth on a
dark and silent night.

One evening at the end of summer she returns
from the river to find the man sitting by the
hearth. A small fire flickers in the grate. She
pauses at the threshold of the cottage, aware
immediately that something is terribly wrong.
Outside in the dusk, the birds have begun their
plaintive evening song and she looks longingly
behind her to the twilit forest. The man turns

and sees her, and motions for her to come.

When she's seated next to him she notices that on his lap is a large wooden box she has never seen before. She wonders where it has been hidden for so long. The man's long silent fingers rest motionless on top of it for a long moment until abruptly and without looking at her he raises the lid and pulls from it a photograph of a young woman. The child cranes forward to see it, her heart skipping with excitement at this sudden, incredible image of another human being. He passes it to her and she takes it eagerly, marvelling over the square of grainy, faded paper, scrutinizing every detail as it lies there in her hands.

The woman is wearing a long green dress and her hair is thick and dark with a heavy fringe. Her smile is shy, secretive; her eyes are lowered to her hands which are clasped neatly together in her lap. The girl takes all this in with wonder until at last she is distracted by the man opening the box for a second time.

Next he pulls out the green dress itself. It's folded carefully, the fabric faded at the creases and it has a faint whiff of age. He hands it to the girl and indicates for her to put it on. But for a while she just sits with the dress in her lap staring down at the material as if hypnotized, her fingers absently, nervously, stroking the buttons at its neck. And though she doesn't raise her eyes she feels the air between the two of them crackle with something she cannot begin to understand. At last she turns to him and sees that he is unnaturally still: he doesn't tremble, doesn't breathe, doesn't drop his gaze from hers.

Obediently, she stands and pulls the garment over her head, smoothing it down over her T-shirt and shorts, hoping that the gnawing, twisting feeling beneath her ribs might disappear if she pleases him and does as he asks. But once the dress is on (the sleeves too long, the hem tumbling over her toes) and she is standing before him, her cheeks burning with something she has never felt before, she sees an expression of such pain flood his face that involuntary she gives a little cry and takes a step towards him. Just as she is about to reach for him however she falters and, confused, withdraws and takes her seat again.

A long moment passes before he gets to his feet once more and fetches the large workman scissors from his tool kit. Before she can understand what is happening he has begun to carefully chop at her hair until it matches the woman's in the picture. He sits back down while she cautiously strokes her newly shorn locks. He continues to stare at her for a long time, and then without warning he begins to cry. She has never seen his tears before and the sight horrifies her.

They sit there, the two of them, and the minutes, the hours pass. The man does not take his eyes from her and she, in turn, does not move, can neither abandon him to his pain nor think of how to comfort him. His tears are awful to her. Night falls; the fire dies in the hearth, and still they sit. Finally, when the cottage is completely dark and she can no longer tell where he begins and the night ends, she creeps into her little bed and lies awake, her heart thumping, while the man and the night sits and waits, sits and waits.

The next morning she rises before the sun and slips from the cottage to wait for the birds. But she takes no pleasure in their song today. She remains there for a long time, long after the sun has climbed above the forest. The small carved bird sits as usual in her lap, her thumb moving over the smooth contours of its head in slow, comforting circles.

When at last she ventures back to the cottage the stone floor is streaked in sunshine. A cloud of midges hangs in the doorway. All is still. She notices that the man is stretched out upon the bed. By his side lie the scissors, their large, clumsy blades streaked in red. She creeps closer. His eyes are open, staring at the ceiling. His left arm is wrist-side up and flung almost nonchalantly from his body. There is a deep, long wound that runs the length of his inner forearm, from wrist to elbow, the flesh and the tendons torn with force by the heavy blades. The wound is so deep she can see the bone. The bed is drenched in blood. The man's face is blue-white; he does not breathe.

She backs away to the farthest corner of the room and crouches there, her mouth wide with terror until, finally, she begins to scream. Outside, a flock of birds takes sudden flight and her cry rushes after them. Suddenly she springs from her corner, the little carved bird still clasped tightly in her fist, and she flees. Through miles of dense woodland she runs, further and further, long into the night, and the forest screams on around her.

7

The *New York Times*
Monday, 15 August 1995
International News — *France, Europe (Reuters)*

The Bird Child Of Normandy

A female estimated to be 12 or 13 years old has been found in the Forêt de Breteuil area of Normandy, northern France. It is thought that she is Elodie Brun, who was abducted aged two from the nearby town of Le Ferté-Macé and has been missing since 1985.

Lorry driver Marcel Collet spotted the child lying in a ditch as he was driving along the edge of the 20,000-hectare woodlands at 5 a.m. Thursday.

'I thought at first she was roadkill,' recalls Collet. 'When I realised it was a little girl I stopped. She was in a bad way. Her feet and legs were bare and bleeding and she was filthy. She seemed very frightened and would not answer my questions. I thought she must have been thrown from a car. It was very surprising, very upsetting, I didn't know what to do.'

Collet eventually coaxed the child into his lorry so he could take her to hospital in the nearby town of Evreux. 'My wife had

35

packed some cheese and ham for me,' he says. 'That eventually did the trick.'

After two days the child was transferred to L'Hôpital des Enfants in Rouen. 'It's an unusual case,' admits Doctor Bernard Dumas, chief paediatrician. 'She has been with us for five days and although she appears to be physically well, she has not yet uttered one word.'

Psychiatrist Doctor Cecile Philipe has been monitoring the child closely. 'We first assumed that her lack of speech was a reaction to some kind of trauma,' she explains. 'But it now appears that the child does not recognise human language at all. Instead she tries to communicate by making bird noises. Her range is quite extraordinary — it seems that she has learnt to mimic many different species. When she arrived she was holding a small, wooden bird and became hysterical when we tried to take it from her.'

Despite her lack of speech, the hospital staff have already become fond of their mysterious charge. 'She's a lovely kid,' says Helene Duchamp, head nurse. 'She's enchanting. She can become withdrawn and upset sometimes, but often she's responsive, even affectionate. The noises she makes are fascinating.'

The staff at the hospital call her 'Little Bird.'

The police investigation continues. If the child is indeed Elodie Brun, the question of where she has been held for the past ten years — and by whom — remains as yet unanswered.

The Sun
14 September 1995

Kidnap girl 'like wild animal'

As more SICKENING details of the Elodie Brun case emerge, *The Sun* has learnt that Brun, 12, can only communicate in GRUNTS AND WHISTLES. After 10 years in captivity she is more wild animal than human, experts say. Evil Mathias Bresson, 42, swiped the TRAGIC TOT in 1985 and kept her prisoner in his secret woodland lair. FULL STORY ON PGS 4,5,6,7

Pictured: Deserted foresters' shack where depraved Bresson trapped Brun for decade.

Science Tomorrow magazine
October 1995

'Little Bird' takes flight amid storm of controversy
The extraordinary case of Elodie Brun, the child found in a Normandy forest last month, has taken a new twist that looks set to reignite one of the most fiercely debated issues in cognitive science — how we learn to speak.

The twelve-year-old, nicknamed 'Little Bird' due to her astounding ability to mimic birdsong, was abducted in 1985 by Mathias Bresson. A mute since birth, Bresson took the child to a remote hideaway in the heart of the 20,000-hectare Forest de Breteuil, where the two lived for ten years until Bresson's suicide last month.

Since it emerged that the girl has no knowledge of language, she has been attracting attention from scientists and linguists worldwide. Until now, our knowledge of how the brain acquires language has stemmed largely from theoretical arguments. Experts from Noam Chomsky to Steven Pinker have long debated the extent to which it is innate or learnt and how far is it affected by environment, brain lateralization or other cognitive factors.

No definitive answer has yet been reached because cases of 'feral' or 'isolated' children — children who have grown up without language — are extremely rare. But, for Elodie Brun, at least, a glimmer of hope has arrived in the shape of Doctor Ingrid Klein, head of cognitive science at New York University. Klein, an acclaimed expert in psycholinguistics and author of three seminal books on the subject, has been granted permission to take Elodie back to her home in Long Island, New York, in what could be one of the most important studies in this field in recent times.

In an exclusive interview, Doctor Klein told *Science Tomorrow*, 'Speech is fundamental to what makes us human and I believe I will be successful in teaching Elodie to speak as well as you or I. Although she has led an extraordinary life, she is a happy, healthy and bright child with no evidence of having suffered any physical or emotional damage. My work with Elodie with the help of US government funding and with adequate scientific monitoring will, I hope, prove that not only is it possible to rehabilitate such a child but that she will be able eventually to live a normal life and integrate fully with society.'

The decision to move Elodie so far from her homeland and family has been met with controversy in France, however. But as Elodie's mother is now unable to care for the child herself she has reportedly given the plan her full approval.

'This is not just a scientific experiment,' says Klein. 'I have Elodie's mother's support and I am a mother myself. I believe that the best place for Elodie is in a nurturing environment where she can be helped by experts at the top of their field. That place is with me and my team in the US.'

The notion of the 'wild child' has captured the public imagination since the legend of Romulus and Remus. The idea of the uncivilised being taught to function normally in society is the stuff of both myth and romance. However, it's a sad fact that such cases rarely end well. If an isolated, confined or feral child has not learnt to speak during the so-called 'Critical Period' outlined by Lenneberg and supported by most neurologists (see box, left) they will never learn to do so. Once rescued, nearly all such children fail to be successfully integrated into society and remain forever institutionalised.

If Klein is successful her findings will not only mean a happy ending for 'the bird child of Normandy', but also significantly increase our understanding of how the human brain acquires language, in what could be one of the most important experiments in cognitive science for some time.

8

When Frank woke with Kate in his bed he watched her sleep for a while and willed the moment to last a little longer. Sunlight shone through dirty windows throwing the shadow of a dead geranium across the sleeping girl's cheek. He dreaded her waking up — the inevitable moment when she opened her eyes and realised where she was and made embarrassed excuses about having to leave, how she never does this sort of thing, how she's actually seeing someone else and then the hurried lies that she'll phone him. The bullshit he usually gave, he realized, and wondered when it was that he'd last cared about a girl.

A crow swooped past the window, cawing noisily. Kate woke with a start, her eyes fixed at once on his. After a second or two she smiled and cupping Frank's face, drew him towards her and kissed him. Relief flooded his veins.

'Tell me,' he asked later, when they were contemplating each other across the tangled sheets. 'Where are you from? You're not from London, are you? Are you American? What were you . . .'

She touched his lips to quieten him. 'Later,'

41

she said. 'Another day.' And then she said, 'I have to go.'

'When can I see you again?'

'Soon.'

'Tomorrow?'

★ ★ ★

It was gone five by the time he walked the twenty-minute journey to his mother's flat. A late-September day when the first cool tendrils of autumn begin to unfurl and creep through the last watery sunlit warmth of the year. The sky was pale and damp, nicotine stained. Kids yelled to each other in the remaining hours of the weekend, lone cars approached then growled on past, cats blinked at him from windowsills. And it felt like his blood sang. Like every smell and sight and sound was new and improved and unbeatable quality and he had never felt so real and certain before, never felt so sure of himself and his place in the world and it was all because of her.

At Chrysanthemum House Frank whistled as he sprang up the eight flights of stairs to his mother's floor. Outside her door he paused on the narrow landing and looked out at the familiar view. Beyond the estate he could see southeast London spread out before him. New Cross, Lewisham, Deptford, Greenwich: a vast grey sea turning and tugging in the twilight, while in the distance the towers of Canary Wharf gazed down upon it all, unmoved.

Directly opposite, Gladioli House and Hyacinth squared up to each other in the failing light. From one lone window a white and red flag of St George fluttered resentfully in the breeze. In the scrubland below a few skunk-dazed kids lounged upon a bench, mumbling to each other from beneath their hoods while a girl dragged her screaming pushchair past a sign that said No Ball Games. Frank turned to unlock the door with his spare key. Next to it, uneven letters scratched into the brickwork said, 'Eugene Rules', and 'Jimmy is a bender'. He grinned as he let himself in.

'Mum?' The familiar bleachy heat of his mother's flat hit him full in the throat. He found her on the sofa, boredom and loneliness draped around her shoulders like a favourite cardigan and he felt his spirits nosedive. If it hadn't been for the fact that she was dressed in different clothes, he would have sworn that she hadn't moved a muscle since he'd last been there two days ago.

'You all right then?' he asked, sinking into the sofa next to her while the TV blared in the stuffy lounge.

She nodded without looking up.

'Been up to much?'

She stabbed the remote at the TV set until David Dickinson loomed orange on the screen. They both knew she didn't need to answer that: she hadn't been outside for almost a decade. She had not once left this flat for nearly ten years. Restlessly he got up to fiddle with things around the room. On the coffee table, by a pile of Tarot cards, sat a variety of unopened aromatherapy bottles. Along the mantelpiece was a selection of runes gathering dust. The shelves were full of various self-help books ordered from the pages of a Sunday supplement. Frank scanned their spines and knew without having to look that each one would be bookmarked a few chapters in, showing the point where his mother had given up and gone back to the sofa and the telly. He sat back down. 'Any good?' he asked, nodding at the screen.

'Nah. Load of bollocks.'

He sighed. Outside, a train rattled and roared along nearby tracks, a familiar sound from his childhood — the noise of strangers hurtling onward somewhere beneath him, while up here, in this flat, nothing changed and nothing moved. He went to the window and tried to relive the moment when he had kissed Kate goodbye that morning. From his doorstep he had watched her walk the whole length of his street (she wouldn't let him call a cab or even walk her to the station), until all he could see was the yellow cap of her hair disappearing around the corner, and he'd finally closed the door and sat on his sofa for twenty minutes, grinning into space. He smiled again at the memory and went to make some tea.

On the way to the kitchen he stopped at his old bedroom and gazed in at the peeling FHM posters, the queue of plastic dinosaurs on the window sill, the cork board cluttered with pictures of him, Eugene and Jimmy as teenagers, a collection of ancient gig tickets, flyers for all-night raves, line-ups for long-forgotten

Glastonburys. Sitting on the single bed he slipped his hand beneath the mattress to pull out an old photograph hidden there. He hadn't looked at it for years, but now he stared at the familiar picture, absentmindedly smoothing out the creases with his finger. A summer's day in some long-forgotten pub garden, his mum and dad clutching drinks and smiling shyly at the camera. He was aged nine or ten, sat between them on a bench eating ice cream. Frank's eyes rested on his father's face. A few weeks later he'd gone out for cigarettes one morning and never come back.

Out of habit, Frank searched the sun-dazzled eyes for clues, but not too intensely, not anymore. The old grief had faded to almost nothing now, just a faint scar, albeit one that flared occasionally at odd perplexing moments, or when he spotted, fleetingly, his father's vanished face in his own. Mentally he sifted through the memories: a smell of tobacco and soap, a croaky laugh, a red tartan shirt, huge hands around him, throwing him into the sky. Memories of memories perhaps, rather than the real thing; he didn't entirely trust them. Since that morning fifteen years ago, his mother had not once mentioned his father to him again. He pushed the photograph back beneath the mattress and went to the kitchen.

★ ★ ★

Leaving Chrysanthemum House an hour later, Frank felt his mood lighten as he checked the

45

time on his mobile: 6.30 p.m. Twenty-five hours exactly until he saw Kate again. He headed in the direction of the Hope and Anchor where he was due to meet Eugene and Jimmy and smiled as he wondered how they'd got on the night before.

He had met Jimmy within minutes of his first day at Morden Comprehensive. White-faced, Frank had sat gripping his Star Wars pencil case and trying not to make eye contact with any of the other terrified eleven-year-olds in the unfamiliar classroom. He hadn't even noticed the large, stocky boy on his left. Their teacher, Mr Jacobs, had just begun bellowing the register when suddenly the kid had elbowed him in the ribs. 'Oi,' he'd hissed. 'Got any fags?' Frank had turned to see a fat face covered in freckles with two small round eyes staring back at him.

'Nah,' he'd whispered. 'Don't smoke.'

He'd turned his attention back to the front. A moment later the boy had nudged Frank again. 'Do us a favour, mate?' he'd asked. 'Tell the teacher you feel sick and need the bog.'

Frank stared back at him, horrified, and shook his head. 'Nah,' he said. 'No way.'

Immediately, the kid had waved his arm in the air. 'Oi, Sir!' he shouted, pointing at Frank. 'Says he feels sick, Sir. Wants me to take him to the bogs, Sir.' Thirty heads had swivelled in Frank's direction and, mortified, he'd ducked his head.

The teacher peered at him. 'That true?' he'd asked suspiciously. Frank had swallowed hard, and shrugged, while his new classmates looked mockingly back at him. 'All right,' Mr Jacobs had sighed. 'Off you go then. Hurry up.' Jimmy grinned and dragged Frank to his feet.

'Cheers mate, I owe you one,' Jimmy had said, once they'd reached the toilets and he'd fished a crumpled fag out of his pocket. 'I was gasping. Want one?'

Frank glanced anxiously at the door. In five minutes the bell would go and someone would come in. He was going to get caught bunking off on his first day and it wasn't even half-past nine yet. He shook his head, leant against a blue radiator and stared through wired glass to the empty playing fields below. He couldn't even remember his way back to the classroom.

'You all right?'

Frank suddenly realised the boy was peering at him intently.

He'd shrugged. 'Yeh.'

Jimmy finished his cigarette and contemplated him for a few moments, his brows furrowed. Finally the penny had dropped. 'You're not worried about *this* place are you?' he'd asked, amazed.

Frank stared at his shoes and shook his head unconvincingly. 'Nah,' he said. 'Course not.'

Jimmy chucked his fag butt into the urinal and slapped him hard on the back. 'You'll be all right,' he grinned. 'Stick with me, mate. You'll see: this place is going to be a fucking breeze.' He held out his hand and Frank reached for it, doubtfully. 'Jimmy Skinner,' said Jimmy, grasping Frank's hand.

'Frank Auvrey,' said Frank.

Their friendship had been an unlikely one. By the end of that first week it was abundantly clear not only to Frank, but to the other kids and to the teachers too that in the pecking order of Morden Comprehensive, among the bullies and the geeks, the popular and the hated, the invisible and the lunatics, Jimmy would rule: Jimmy would be top dog. He wasn't particularly cool or good-looking, but he possessed such an endearing combination of charm, confidence and wit (not to mention two notorious older brothers in the years above), that he was respected and liked by almost everyone he met.

It was typical of Jimmy's personality that while others might have been surprised by their friendship, it hadn't crossed his mind for a second that it should be any other way. And while everyone else might have assumed that the benefits were all Frank's, they were missing a crucial factor of the partnership: Jimmy needed Frank as much as Frank needed Jimmy. Whereas Frank's fears and insecurities were on an impressively mammoth scale, encompassing as they did: accidental death, other people, nuclear war, unspecified future tragedy (including unemployment and homelessness), being murdered by a burglar while he slept, and his mother's probable, eventual suicide, such things did not feature in Jimmy's somewhat simpler outlook on life. Instead, his secret anxieties were more straightforward, and included such things as spiders, strange-looking food, and ghosts.

Thus, Frank could afford to be admirably, reassuringly laissez-faire about his friend's more manageable concerns while at the same time basking in the novelty of Jimmy's absolute refusal to take anything much very seriously. Above all, however, the key to their friendship was a simple one: they made each other laugh.

They'd met Eugene a few weeks later. They'd found him hanging by the hood of his jacket from a fence post not long after the last bell had rung one Tuesday afternoon. He had been trussed like a mental patient, his coat arms tied behind his back, his face a red, spitting ball of rage as he'd writhed and wriggled up there on the post, trying in vain to free himself. Jimmy and Frank had watched the kid struggle for a bit while they sucked on blueberry ice poles. Eventually they'd looked at each other, shrugged, and gently lowered him to the ground. The boy had stood before them, hiccuping and sniffing furiously, scrubbing at his eyes and nose with his stretched-out sleeves.

They'd recognised him as the skinny, mixed-race kid who'd joined a different class to theirs at the start of term. He had a staggeringly uncool afro, and huge brown eyes with long lashes like a girl's. There was something a bit pikey about him too — the sort of kid who Had Problems. He wore shit clothes and had an uncared-for look and there was something a bit mad and angry in his eyes, like he'd be a good laugh to wind up. In other words, he was the sort of kid who walked around practically begging to be hung by his hood from a fence post.

'What's your name?' Jimmy had asked eventually.

'Eugene Jones.' Nobody said anything for a bit, and the kid had gazed at his shoes, his eyes filling with tears again. Frank had looked away, embarrassed.

Finally Jimmy had gone over and patted him clumsily on the shoulder. 'All right then,' he'd said. 'Pack it in now.'

And to Frank's surprise, Eugene did.

'State of you,' remarked Jimmy, impressed.

The three boys looked down at Eugene's stretched-out sleeves, the hole in his trouser knee, the skuffs of dirt and blood on his hands and face.

'Yeh,' agreed Eugene. 'This kid called me a coon so I spat in his face. Then all his mates jumped me.'

Jimmy emptied half a bag of Skips into his mouth and thought for a bit. 'Your mum give you grief, will she?' he asked, conversationally.

'Ain't got a mum,' said Eugene. 'Live at Eglington Lodge don't I?'

Oh. Foster kid, then. Probably a trick, thought Frank. Probably got a gang of mates round the corner who're going to jump us any second. Frank wondered when they were going to get a move on. But Jimmy had stood rocking on his heels for a while, considering the situation. 'Come on then,' he'd said at last. 'Might as well come back with us. *My* mum will sort you out.'

The three had trailed out of the gates and just like that, on the walk over to Jimmy's, it had happened, the way friendship does when you're a kid; instantly and irrevocably. Jimmy and Frank were stuck with Eugene now, and he was stuck with them, and an understanding settled over them without them ever really thinking about it; an unspoken acceptance that it was the three of them now. Eugene dried his tears and followed them back to Jimmy's house, back to the first and last real home he'd ever really love.

★ ★ ★

Frank smiled as he rounded the corner onto the New Cross Road, the Hope and Anchor just visible in the distance. He stopped and found something to listen to on his iPod, then continued on his way.

For Frank too, going round to the Skinner family's pebble-dashed semi after school had been like stepping into a kind of heaven. Jimmy's dad was a taxi driver, and outside their front door the black curves of his hackney cab had gleamed proudly from the kerb, infusing number 11 with a kind of authority and glamour cruelly lacking at Chrysanthemum House. Inside, it was noisy and messy and smelt of gravy. Jimmy and his five brothers and sisters all looked identical, with broad, good-natured faces, the same sandy hair, freckles, and small, keen blue eyes. Into the front room they would all pile, every day after school, all the brothers and the sisters and their assorted friends, squashed onto the three enormous sofas that lined the walls or sprawled out on the tufty orange rug, arguing and yelling and shoving each other out of the way. Jimmy's mum would hand out endless plates of fish fingers and beans, and while he ate Frank would stare adoringly, from the corner of his eye, at Jimmy's dad, immense and silent in his armchair after a hard day's cabbying, his arms enormous and tattooed, his lips pursed and his eyes impenetrable while the telly blared and the gas fire burned.

At 7 p.m. exactly, Jimmy's mum would rouse herself and say, 'Right then, whoever ain't one of mine can bugger off home now.' The various friends and visitors and hangers-on would reluctantly peel themselves from the sofas and drift off into the night, back to wherever they'd come from, to somewhere else they'd much less rather be.

And the same thing would happen every evening. Frank would wait patiently by the front door in his Parka while the hunt began. Because as soon as it got to five to seven Eugene would silently slip from the lounge to loiter somewhere else, hoping that the Skinners would forget all about sending him back to Eglington Lodge. It became a nightly ritual. All the brothers and sisters would tear around the house looking for him until finally he'd be found, wedged behind the kitchen door, or standing in the bath behind the shower curtain, or lying still and silent under Jimmy's bed. Mrs Skinner would be called to haul him out from wherever he was and frogmarch him to the door to make sure he finally went. But then she would always hug him tightly, Jimmy's mum. 'You go straight on home now, love,' she'd say, as she watched Eugene drag his feet down the front path. 'I'll see you tomorrow, OK? You'll come back tomorrow, won't you?' And there'd be something anxious in the way she asked, as if she was afraid of never seeing him again. He'd had that affect on women, Eugene, even then.

★ ★ ★

When Frank walked into the Anchor and saw Eugene standing alone at the bar he felt a brief and unnerving flash of shock at the disparity between the twelve-year-old kid he'd just been remembering, and the reality of the 25-year-old man he now saw before him. The intervening years had been good to Eugene, physically. The small, messy kid was now over six foot tall, his limbs grown lean and muscular, his face angular and handsome. But there was something about the difference between the two images, something that Frank suddenly realised had been lost from his friend's countenance that, when he reached him at the bar, moved him to grip his hand a little tighter than usual, to hold his shoulder a little longer than was necessary when they greeted each other.

'Easy, man,' Eugene complained. 'Nearly spilt my fucking pint.'

Frank smiled. He saw Jimmy emerge from the gents, still doing up his fly. 'Mr Auvrey, the man himself,' he slurred enthusiastically, already pissed, launching himself at Frank and pulling him to him into a beery, smoky hug. 'All right, sunbeam? How's it going?'

'Not so bad,' Frank laughed, and ordered a new round for the three of them.

Jimmy contemplated his friend while he sipped his pint. 'Fucking happened to you last night then? Eh? Got that little whatsername bird back to yours pretty sharpish didn't yer?' He gave Frank a congratulatory pat on the back and didn't wait for an answer. 'Just goes to fucking show. Always the quiet ones. Bet she went like a good 'un too, didn't she?' He nodded his head sagely. 'Mine was a dead loss. I should have stuck with the mousey one. Mind you, your bird was almost catatonic, weren't she? Thought she was fucking you know, what's the word, deaf and dumb at one point, didn't open her trap once. Those two me and Euge had, oh dear me. Sniffed all our gak, didn't they? Went through the whole fucking lot, so spangled in the end my one was good for nothing. Did my Elvis number for them and everything, fucking passed out, didn't she? Total waste of time.'

He finally noticed that Frank hadn't said anything. 'What happened, then? Any good?'

Frank looked down at his pint, struggled for a few moments to keep his face straight and lasted exactly four seconds. Jimmy gazed back at his friend, taking in his shiny eyes, the wide grin, the way he suddenly seemed taller and surer and better looking. 'Oh dear,' said Jimmy, shaking his head sorrowfully. 'Oh dear, oh dear, oh dear.'

PART TWO

9

L'Hôpital des Enfants, Rouen, Normandy,
5 November 1995
In the hushed white room the people come
and go. At first fear lies heavy upon her
senses, like a thick layer of snow, and she's
scarcely aware of the sharp, acrid smell, the
bright lights, the repetitive swish and whine of
the swing door through which emerge yet
more faces and footsteps and hands and eyes
that probe and stare, probe and stare. And so
she sits on the little, white bed, dressed in
crisp, white pyjamas, the small, carved bird
gripped tightly in her fist. She sits, motionless
and calm but in the depths of her, behind that
still, quiet gaze, she has returned to the forest
and sees only the leaves, smells only the
bracken and the river, hears only the birds
that call to each other from the trees.

At night, from somewhere behind the now-still
door, shoes squeak upon linoleum, machines
bleep, urgent trolleys trundle past. And beyond
her window, from out of the orange-tinged
blackness where the grey buildings loom and
sulk across the street, drifts the distant noise of a
world she can't even begin to fathom; the sounds
of growling, mumbling traffic, of unimaginable
lives being lived beneath an unimaginable sky.
And when sleep at last comes for her, it takes her
on its soft, silent wings, back, back to the forest,

57

where she flies and swoops and soars, to rest once again within its leafy arms.

★   ★   ★

And yet she has a brave heart, this child that has emerged from the woods like a hatchling from its egg. Slowly, gradually, beneath that thick, freezing fear there begins to stir the first tentative shoots of something else: a strange long-dormant impulse that grows ever more insistent. Gradually, she becomes accustomed to the faces that appear to her each day, and her ears begin to tune into the sounds that they make, a strange but infinitely seductive sound that seems to pierce the fear and confusion like sunlight through leaves.

And then: something else. Like the dragonflies that used to flit across the surface of the river, long-forgotten images begin to land briefly upon her memory: a woman's face, a certain smell, and, stranger still, snatches of a nursery rhyme, words spoken by her and understood; a woman's voice responding to her own. But they are impossible to hold onto for very long; too soon they take flight, disappearing once more into the sky. Nevertheless, some deep, instinctive part of her begins to respond to the voices of these white-coated strangers, to unfurl and reach towards them like a seedling towards the sun.

At first she tries to offer the birdcalls that had once given her such pleasure in the woods. But although the people smile and nod their encouragement at her whistles and her coos, her chirrups and her twitters, she knows that they're not right, are not what's needed now. Sometimes she feels as if a flock of frantic sparrows are trapped inside her chest. In vain she tries to free them, but her throat will not obey her, will only allow, at best, meaningless gurgles and grunts. Her frustration grows until, from out of the strange, dark world that lies beyond her window, into the white, hushed room walks the woman with the pale blue eyes.

10

Locust Valley, Long Island, New York,
7 January 1996

High Barn is very large and made of wood and glass. It stands alone on a hill and from her bedroom window she can see the garden's well-kept lawns, a winding road, a copse of trees and then in the distance, the quiet roofs of a small town. She remembers little of her journey here. A meal at the hospital, a car ride through dark streets where exhaustion had come from nowhere, filling her eyes and nostrils like mud. She recalls being led through a large, frightening place full of light and people, walls of glass through which she could see monstrous metal birds roaring to the sky. Later she had woken only once, groggy and confused in a small narrow bed, a low drone all around her, a row of closed white shutters, a pale, cold light. And then, oblivion again.

She understands only that she's very far from home, that her old life and everything familiar and loved is far behind her now. This bedroom has sloping ceilings and a pattern of rose buds on the walls. Each night she dreams of the silent man, the stone cottage, the forest. Each morning she wakes in this strange, new bed and waits for the woman to lead her down to breakfast.

The woman is very tall and has yellow-white hair tied tightly back from a face that's long and pointed as a whittled stick. Her pale eyes are rimmed in pink as if perpetually sore and sometimes the girl will catch little glimpses of the skin on her arms, patches of flaky redness. It's this tenderness, this rawness that Elodie at once and will always associate with the woman whose name she understands is Ingrid long before she can say the word.

And from the beginning she understands that Ingrid is all she has now: the one constant amidst the strangeness, the one link to her old life and her only means of navigating this new one. Ingrid's hands are very white, cool and dry to the touch, and in those first few days, the girl, Elodie, clings to those slender fingers as if to a twig dangling from the highest branch.

★　★　★

The house has many rooms filled with soft, elegant furniture very different from the few crude pieces left behind in the cottage. On the gleaming wooden floors lie thick, muted rugs. Slowly, under Ingrid's patient, pink-eyed gaze, the child begins to explore her new surroundings. The shelves full of books, the strange box that fires shockingly into noisy, colourful life at the touch of a button, a large blue bowl filled with dead, perfumed leaves. Each new object she explores tactilely, sniffing and touching until it's known to her. And wherever she goes she takes the little carved bird with her, her fingers always circling its smooth round head or tracing the delicate grooves of its wings.

On the kitchen table where they eat their meals, a large silver eagle stands, its half-raised wings perpetually poised for flight. In the window, a glass mobile throws squares of blue, green and red light upon the floor. There's a framed photograph of a little boy hanging upon the wall. Nothing escapes Elodie's careful examination. Even Ingrid must sit patiently while the child explores her with slow and careful fingertips. Every day, fastened to her blouse or sweater Ingrid wears a brooch. It's in the shape of a cat and Elodie likes to trace its sharp, sparkly edges, to touch the eyes made from clusters of shiny red stones that glint and twinkle in the light. She notices that a few of them have come loose, leaving behind black, sightless craters. She wonders what became of them — those tiny lost specks of red.

At High Barn, meals are eaten from large white plates three times a day at the kitchen table. Elodie and Ingrid sit opposite each other, always in the same chairs, and as the small neat portions are doled out to her, she thinks about the man in the forest, of the steaming rabbit stew they would make together then eat from chipped bowls. Afterwards, she would wash them in the river, returning to find the man smiling, waiting for her to sing to him. She sees again his thick fingers nudging tobacco into flimsy squares of paper while he listens. The pain slams into her. On the long, polished table the reflection of the silver eagle gleams.

★ ★ ★

One evening when Elodie has been at High Barn for over a week, she follows Ingrid to the kitchen for dinner as usual but stops in her tracks to see a stranger sitting there, a large glass of wine in front of him, a suitcase by his feet. Ingrid's husband Robert is a thickset, stocky man with curly brown hair only lightly touched with grey. They consider each other for a moment or two and then he raises his eyebrows and smiles, an easy grin that pulls Elodie at once across the room towards him. Ignoring her usual place setting she takes the chair beside him, staring up at him with wide-eyed curiosity, while the man gives a short burst of laughter and Ingrid, her lips pinched into a tight, thin line, slides Elodie's plate across to her.

As Elodie eats she takes in the man's thick wrists, the heavy features of his face, the incongruously small chin. She watches the way he drinks with large rapid gulps, the way he bites at his bread; how when he finishes his meal he drops his cutlery with a clatter, stretches and gives a loud, satisfied sigh. She feels a nip of disappointment when he takes his plate to the sink and then, with a brief word to Ingrid and a smile and a wave to her, takes his suitcase and disappears up the stairs. Left alone Elodie ponders this surprising turn of events. She had thought that only she and Ingrid lived in this large, many roomed house, and is intrigued to discover her mistake.

It's some time before she sees Robert again. Every day he leaves early in the morning, often not returning until after she's in bed. At the weekends he keeps to his study and the only sign of him is the faint rumble of the radio or television seeping from under his door. Often he will disappear with his big suitcase for weeks at a time. And mostly she and Ingrid keep to the top floor of High Barn, in the little room full of mysterious equipment that she will one day refer to as 'the schoolroom'. Sometimes a whole month can pass where she doesn't see Robert at all.

On the rare occasions that the three of them do eat together, Elodie begins to sense something in the air between Ingrid and Robert that troubles her. Although their voices are calm and quiet when they speak, there is nevertheless a strange, shivery tension that hovers in the gaps between their words. Sometimes Elodie will wake in the night and hear angry, raised voices, the slamming of doors. Gradually she begins to sense that the raw tenderness of Ingrid, the sadness she sometimes sees in her is somehow worse when Robert is at home, and that there's a subtle loosening of tension when they hear his car disappearing down the long, gravel drive each morning.

But she has little time to dwell on it. Her new life is too full of new experiences, too overwhelming and all-consuming for Robert to feature very heavily in her thoughts.

★ ★ ★

'Cat.' 'Sky.' 'House.' 'Tree.' Elodie understands that everything in the world has a corresponding sound, and that everything she and Ingrid do together is with the aim of helping her decipher them. The instinctive hunger that had begun to take root in her at the hospital returns and gathers strength, and it's Ingrid, she understands, who holds the key. Wherever they go, whatever they do, whatever they see, everything is labelled for her. 'Chair.' 'Window.' 'Elodie.' 'Ingrid.' 'Bowl.' A constant stream of words accompanies their daily walks together. 'Car.' 'Tree.' 'House.' 'Man.' 'Cat.' She understands that the games they play in the room next to her bedroom — the picture cards, the puzzles, the books — are all somehow linked to this endeavour. And she sees, too, that Ingrid's determination to teach her is as intense as her own desire to learn.

'Eeeee.' 'Ooooo.' 'Essssss.' 'Tuh.' 'Puh-puh-puh.'. Over and over she tries to mimic the shapes Ingrid makes with her mouth, to produce the same sounds that come from her teacher's throat. Over and over she fails.

At night in her dreams the silent man waves to her from the window of his rusty blue pick-up truck, before slowly driving away, disappearing between the trees. Sometimes she half-wakes in the darkness and believes for a moment that she's back there, in the cottage in the woods. For a moment she hears the sound of the wind in the trees outside, the man's low snores. In her half slumber she smiles and thinks how, in a moment, she will rise and go to listen to the birds' dawn song. And then she wakes and even as the stone walls of the cottage melt away, she's reaching for the little wooden bird, clasping it tightly in her fist as if to squeeze what comfort she can from it.

★   ★   ★

Occasionally Ingrid will take Elodie with her on her errands to the nearby town. On their first visit to the food store while Ingrid pays at the checkout Elodie slips away to wander alone through the aisles, stopping now and then to marvel at the neat, colourful rows of boxes and tins. At the fruit counter she picks up a banana, biting into the hard, rubbery skin before throwing it to the floor with a grimace. Next she trails a bunch of grapes across her face, first sniffing and then nibbling at the little purple fruits, rolling her eyes at the sweet explosions on her tongue. She spies an elderly man staring at her, amazed, across the aisle and going to him she circles her arms around his waist and rests her head upon his belly. Moments later she finds herself being pulled gently away, and while a dozen astonished customers look on, Ingrid leads her quickly out of the store.

★   ★   ★

Every week Ingrid takes Elodie in the car to the big, redbricked building in the middle of the city. As they drive she stares out of the window and marvels at what she sees. What shocks her most about this new world is all the people in it. There seem to be as many people as there are blades of grass or stars. Everywhere she looks, there they are: smiling and talking and frowning and laughing, and each of them, somehow, connected, connecting.

Inside, the red-bricked building is exactly like the hospital she left behind in France and sometimes they spend the whole morning there. Often she must lie perfectly still while a white dome glides noiselessly over her head. She notices that the men and women who lead her down the long white corridors to this room and that, and who put her on this bed or that chair, who shine lights in her eyes and stare and point things out to each other on the flickering screens, all share the way in which they behave towards Ingrid. She sees how keenly they listen to her when she speaks, how careful they are to do as she asks. She sees that they are a little afraid of her. And a part of her recognises this nervousness, this fear of displeasing, of disappointing, of provoking that brief, flash of impatience in those pink-rimed eyes.

★　★　★

She has been at High Barn three weeks when Colin and Yaya arrive. Two strangers who walk into the schoolroom next to her bedroom one morning while she and Ingrid are looking at a picture book together. Later, she will understand that they are graduate students, handpicked by Ingrid to assist her in her work, to make the endless reports on her progress over the coming months. But on that morning she knows only that from the moment they arrive, with the smell of the wind on their coats, their arms full of boxes and files and their faces lit with curious, excited smiles, that they bring a sudden warmth and light to High Barn that hadn't been there before.

The man, Colin, is quiet and always busy setting up cameras or writing things down or fiddling with the tape recorder or laying out the games and books and cards, but he smiles at her a lot and pulls faces to make her laugh. It's Yaya she loves the most. Yaya with her soft, tinkling voice like rain on the river, her glowing, dark-brown skin the colour of the earth, her long skirts and the rainbow scarves wrapped around and around her head, her bracelet of little silver bells that jingle when she walks, the warm, natural ease of her. When Elodie makes a mistake Yaya smiles and says, 'Never mind, little one. Never mind.' And even before Elodie knows what these words mean, she understands the kindness of them.

Over the following weeks the four of them settle into a routine. Every day, after breakfast, Elodie watches eagerly from the schoolroom window while Ingrid sets up the equipment for the day. She notices that whatever they do is led, always, by Ingrid, and that Colin and Yaya treat her with the same careful respect as the people in the hospital.

★ ★ ★

The days pass, and then the weeks, the months. She has got better at mimicking the sounds the others make, of pushing her lips into the correct shapes. She understands that this is a picture of a cat, this is a bed, and that a chair. She understands, but still the words will not come. The sounds she offers are not right, she can tell by the almost imperceptible tightening of Ingrid's lips, the increasing disappointment in her eyes.

Each week, she and Ingrid make the trip to the hospital and every visit there is someone new to meet, some new stranger to be stared at by. Sometimes these strangers come to the house, and watch silently while she plays with Yaya and Colin. She knows that they have come to see her, that they, like everyone else are waiting for something. Once she tries to sing to them, the old calls and noises from the forest, hoping that they will make them happy, but they are not what's wanted now.

★　★　★

And then, a year after arriving at High Barn, it happens. She is standing by the schoolroom window when she sees Yaya approaching across the lawn below, carrying her big red bag with the tassels and laughing with Colin. Suddenly, something in that moment fuses in Elodie's brain. The image of Yaya and the sound of her name. 'Yaya.' It escapes her mouth before she's even aware what her tongue and lips are doing. 'Yaya.' As effortlessly as a breath.

She turns to Ingrid, who is staring at her open mouthed, the pen that she had been writing with poised in mid-air. 'Yaya,' she says again, pointing through the window to where she stands in the garden below. And seconds later she's in Ingrid's arms, being hugged so tightly it takes her breath away.

From that moment words grow and multiply on her lips like leaves on a vine. It's pure joy to her, this sudden mental unbolting and now that it has begun, she cannot, will not stop. Her hunger for new words is limitless. 'Sky.' 'Chair.' 'Me.' 'Ingrid,' she says. 'Table.' 'House.' 'Balloon.' The four of them work harder still, and even after Yaya and Colin have left for the day she and Ingrid will often continue until supper. As the words multiply and become sentences — 'Elodie go there' — as she begins to master plurals — 'One spoon, two spoons' — and negations — 'No! Don't want that' — and questions — 'Where Colin?' — as her grasp of grammar and syntax becomes ever more accomplished, she begins to let go, a little, of her old life.

Sometimes, alone in her room at night, she will allow herself to wander beneath the forest's ceiling, will linger in the cottage by the fire and smell the embers burning in the hearth. Sometimes she will let herself rest for a while by the man's side, smiling up at his sad, grey eyes. But then she will rouse herself, and push the memories away. More and more often now she will leave the little carved bird behind in her bedroom when she goes to the schoolroom each morning.

* * *

Each of Elodie's successes and accomplish-
ments binds her closer to Ingrid. Day by day,
a new warmth grows between them. Often she
will look up and find herself the focus of that
pale-blue gaze and sees a new softness there.
Now, when Elodie takes her hand or puts her
arms around her, the tiny resistance, the barely
perceptible tension she used to sense has gone.
Now, Ingrid returns her embraces freely, takes
her hand with a brief, reciprocal squeeze.

One morning the two of them take a trip to
Oyster Bay. Although they've been there many
times before, the sight of the ocean never fails
to amaze the child. As soon as they arrive
she heads as usual straight for the water,
impatiently shedding her shoes and socks as
she runs to jump in the shallow waves. Usually
Ingrid watches from the beach, calling her in
too soon to return to the house to work, or to
keep an appointment at the hospital. Today
however Elodie looks up in amazement to find
her standing next to her in the surf, her shoes
and socks dangling from her hand, an
unexpectedly shrill laugh escaping from her
lips.

And Elodie works hard to keep Ingrid's
affection, anxious not to provoke the flashes of
displeasure that her mistakes can sometimes
bring. At night, when she's woken by the sound
of slamming doors or raised voices, she awaits
the next day's lessons unhappily, immediately
scanning her teacher's face for the familiar,

tell-tale swollen eyes and creeping redness on her arms.

★ ★ ★

One afternoon she comes to the kitchen to fetch a glass of water when she finds Robert sitting at the table eating a sandwich.

'Hey, Elodie,' he says.

'Hello.' Shyly she sidles up to him and watches him eat for a while. One of his hands rests next to his plate and she silently admires how square and large it is. Somehow, Robert's broad shoulders, his scent, the stubble on his chin, the deepness of his voice seems focussed in that one hand lying so innocently upon the table top. On impulse she takes a step closer and rests her own upon it, comparing her pale, slender fingers with his. Quick as a flash he slides his hand out from beneath hers and brings it neatly down on her fingers, trapping them on the table. She giggles and does the same. Quicker and quicker they take it in turns to pounce upon the other. But, 'You win,' Robert says at last, ending the game with a smile. Abruptly he rises and puts his plate in the sink.

Disappointed, Elodie gazes around the room, anxious to keep him from leaving. At last she spots the picture of the little boy on the wall and carefully reaches up and lifts it down. Robert is still standing with his back to her when she brings it to him and taps him on the arm. 'Picture,' she says.

He turns to her and when he notices the photograph in her hand a look of such sadness falls upon his face that Elodie takes a step backwards in surprise. Wordlessly they stare at each other for a moment, and then, taking it from her hands, Robert crosses the room and gently puts the picture back on the wall.

At that moment, Ingrid comes into the room. 'We're waiting for you, Elodie,' she says, a hint of displeasure in her voice, and obediently, Elodie follows her from the kitchen.

* * *

The way the words multiply is mysterious, organic. Her understanding seems to work on a level below her consciousness, where language spreads instinctively like wild fire. But for all the natural ease with which she learns, she cherishes every new word, marvelling and crowing over them when she's alone at night. Each one a hard-won treasure.

The more she learns and the wider her vocabulary grows, the happier she becomes. From the moment she wakes until she goes to bed, she talks. Alone in her room she will name every object she can see, or open her window wide and call out to the trees. 'Come on now, chatter box,' Ingrid will say as she takes her down to breakfast. 'Hurry up.' But Elodie will notice that even as she scolds her, Ingrid's face shines with pride.

* * *

For some months Elodie's trips to the hospital have included regular visits to a Doctor Menzies. Unlike the other specialists, Ingrid and Doctor Menzies always greet each other warmly, with a hug and kisses. But these sessions are almost unbearably dull to Elodie. The activities she's made to do seem pointless. Often she'll be told to draw a picture, and will then be asked endless questions about it. Sometimes she'll be asked about her old life in the forest, and Elodie will answer as best she can, all the while staring restlessly out of the window. Other times the doctor will give her dolls to play with, while she watches and makes notes, scratching away with her pen in her notebook. When, at last, the hour finally drags to an end, she's made to sit outside, while Ingrid and the doctor murmur to each other behind the closed door.

It's after one of these sessions that Elodie firsts asks Ingrid about her mother. They are in the midst of reading a story about a family of bears when she interrupts and says, 'Do I have one?'

The anxiety that flashes across her teacher's eyes is brief and almost imperceptible. Ingrid sits down in the chair next to her, and it's a while before she answers. When she does, her voice is very careful. 'You do have a mother, yes, Elodie,' she says. 'But she's very far away and not very well. You will see her soon, when she's feeling a little better.'

Elodie nods, and turns the page. After a pause, Ingrid continues reading. 'Who has been sleeping in my bed?' she says.

★ ★ ★

Only one strange incident mars the contentment of this time; something confusing that happens one afternoon, shortly before they are about to finish work for the day. Ingrid has been called to the telephone and Colin is busy packing up his movie camera and files of notes when Elodie wanders from her desk to where Yaya sits. Putting her arms around her neck, she idly plays with a strand of black, springy hair that has come loose from the older woman's headscarf, tickling her ear with it until Yaya starts to laugh and pulls Elodie towards her in a hug.

But their laughter comes to an abrupt halt when a sound from the door distracts them and they both turn to see Ingrid staring in at them.

Elodie isn't sure what it is about the expression in Ingrid's eyes, only that both she and Yaya react to it instantly by jumping apart. It's brief, the look she shoots them before quickly turning away, but Elodie is seized by unaccustomed and confusing feelings of guilt. The moment passes. Quietly, Elodie goes back to her own chair and her books and the four of them continue with their work.

But still Ingrid's expression confuses her. Later that night when Elodie is getting ready for bed the little gnawing feeling of doubt returns. There had been something unrecognisable in Ingrid's eyes, a dark and painful thing she couldn't understand. That night, when Ingrid

75

comes to say good night, instead of the brief kiss on her cheek that she usually bestows, Elodie finds herself pulled into a tight embrace. And when Ingrid releases her, the sense of unease lingers.

11

Deptford, south-east London,
15 December 2003

Historically, Frank's track record with women wasn't great. At twenty-five, it wasn't that he ever really found it a problem attracting girls — it was the keeping hold of them he always seemed to struggle with. He had a habit of falling hook, line and sinker for a person, putting her so high upon a pedestal that the only inevitable direction they could go after that was down. All would be great for the first few months, but then, out of the blue, entirely without warning, everything he had once found so charming about her would start to sour. Her laugh would begin to grate, in mid conversation she'd say something dumb, he'd notice that when she stayed she'd leave her things all over the bathroom floor. Suddenly, reality would come screaming into focus and the relationship would become instantly and irretrievably intolerable. Pretty rich, he knew: he was hardly catch of the year. But there it was.

When he was ten, something happened to Frank that would stay with him forever. It was a few weeks after his dad had left and his Aunt Joanie had taken him and her spaniel Bongo to Greenwich Park. It was a beautiful day and the place had been full of sunbathing tourists, picnicking families, kids playing football. The dog had been running in circles at their feet as they walked, and Frank remembered thinking how strange it was that the sky was so blue and the air so warm when inside he felt so horribly cold, so horribly grey.

'You're going to have to be a big, brave boy now Frankie,' his aunt was saying as they tramped along. 'The thing is, sometimes grown-ups find life difficult . . . ' He tried his hardest to block out her voice but suddenly he couldn't bear it any more. Why was everyone talking like his dad wasn't coming back? Why had his mum not gotten out of bed for three weeks? It was disgusting, *stupid* the way they were all talking. He pulled his hand from Joanie's and throwing a stick for Bongo, began to run.

Ignoring his aunt's call he threw the stick further and further, tearing after Bongo up the steep hill, on and on until he'd left the crowds and Joanie far behind. Of course his dad was coming back. Of *course* he was. He ran until he was in a part of the park secluded from the rest, on the heath side, near the deer and the big oak trees. And then he'd seen her. Under a tree twenty yards away was a girl of about seventeen, her legs stretched out before her, a book resting upon her lap. Bongo was sitting next to her, his big stupid tongue lolling out. Both of them watched him as he approached.

'Hello,' she said, when he reached her.

He had opened his mouth to speak, but it seemed he'd forgotten how. The sun was low in the sky behind her and shone through her curls so her face was framed in a flaming halo of golden red. Her eyes were luminous; dragon-fly green. Never, never had he seen anything so beautiful. He could barely breathe, certain that if he even blinked she'd disappear, or he'd wake and find himself back in his bedroom, staring at his collection of dinosaurs. A feeling of perfect calm settled upon him.

She was very slender, across the pale skin of her chest was a faint sprinkling of freckles. Through the thin white cotton of her top he could just make out the swell of her breasts and he felt himself flush red as something unrecognisable began to stir in his underpants. He gazed at her. Everything — the green of her eyes, the golden red of her hair, the blue of the sky — was supernaturally bright. With a little sigh, Bongo had flopped down and rested his head in her lap, and Frank had almost groaned with jealousy when her small, white hand had reached over and stroked the dog's ears.

'Are you lost?' she'd asked.

And even though he wasn't, not really, he had nodded.

She'd smiled, and after considering him a while said, 'Don't worry. I'm sure you'll find your way back.'

He felt as if he could stand there looking at her for the rest of his life. The world was perfectly silent, perfectly still. The sun sank lower in the sky. Just at that moment he heard Joanie's voice calling him. 'Frank! Frank!' His name drifted to them like a sound from another world. He held his breath and willed her to go away.

'Who's that?' asked the girl.

'Auntie Joanie.'

'Ah.' She continued gazing at him for a while, and then smiled. 'Well then, Frank,' she said, 'give me a kiss and then you'd better go.'

As if she was an exotic bird that might take flight at any moment, very, very slowly he had knelt down and carefully kissed her cheek.

She smiled. 'Bye then, Frank. Be good.'

And then he had turned and run towards Joanie's voice, Bongo racing after him.

'Did you see her?' he asked urgently, when he reached his aunt. 'Did you see her?'

'Who?' Joanie had squinted over in the direction he'd run from, scanning the grass. 'No dear, I don't see anyone.'

He had turned and raised his hand to shield his eyes from the sun, but Joanie was right: there was nothing there. The girl had vanished.

Since that day he had tried to find her again, had got into the habit of searching for her in crowds, of scanning the faces of every passing woman, but nothing. Sometimes in his dreams he would find himself back there, under the tree the summer he was ten, but just as he was about to kneel down and kiss her, he'd wake. Occasionally, listening to music, he would come close to finding again that sense of beauty — there amongst the notes and melodies and beats — but it was never quite enough: the thing he was searching for was always just out of his reach. His whole life he had been trying to find that perfection again, and in Kate he knew he had found it; he had found her.

At first, their meetings were maddeningly

infrequent. Kate was the most evasive person he had ever met. She had no mobile phone, moved from job to job, avoided talking about her home (to which he was never invited). And yet, just when he was about to give up hope of ever seeing her again she would appear at his door or at the record shop where he worked, saying simply, 'Hello, Frank,' with that same, breathtaking smile of hers beneath that same, steady gaze.

But still she would offer nothing concrete for him to hold onto, and he was always under the impression she might disappear at any moment. Whenever they parted she would leave no trace of herself. And he had never met anyone who talked so little about themselves — women, in his experience, always liked to talk about themselves. For hours. In contrast, Kate's silence was like a blank sheet upon which people were invited to draw whatever version of her they wished.

'Your accent,' he said, the second time they met. 'Sometimes you sound American. Did you used to live there?' Her response — a short, blithe account of a New York childhood, a car crash that had killed her parents, her move to London to live with an aunt — was so brief and delivered with such a lack of detail that he had hardly been able to land on any part of it and, almost without him noticing, she had asked a question about the record they were listening to and he had been talking enthusiastically about it for a full ten minutes before he realised the original subject had been abandoned.

And he didn't press her. Frank was good with

mystery, with a feeling of being always slightly in the dark. He was used to it, knew where he stood with it. Ever since his father had disappeared — seemingly slipping between the gaps in the pavements one day without so much as a backward glance — he had spent much of his life since wondering what the hell had happened. It was how he loved his father now; in the absence of the physical man his affection had become coloured and finally replaced by a vague, persistent bafflement.

Once or twice he would come across Kate lost in thought and it was like glancing through a window at something he shouldn't see, something private. With her guard down, just for a second, he would see an altogether different girl looming into view behind those dark blue eyes, like something emerging suddenly from behind a tree. It was like catching sight of a fox streaking down a London street at night; an unexpected glimpse of something wild. But the moment would pass, she would sense his presence and alter instantly back into Kate. These moments would provoke in him an almost unbearable protectiveness, and yet a part of him would be relieved too, frightened of having to deal with something he wasn't sure he was ready for, something that might demand unknown, difficult things from him.

He was falling in love. Despite the strangeness of their relationship at the heart of it lay something true, he was certain. And when, two months after they met, she didn't turn up to meet him as planned his anxiety was unbearable.

Two days passed, and then two more, and still she didn't phone or come. Each hour without hearing from her was agony. He was certain that this time she had gone for good. Finally, sick to death of his dark thoughts he had gone to the pub in search of Jimmy and Eugene — anything to take his mind off her.

The Hope and Anchor is a vast Victorian hulk of a boozer that looms malevolently over the New Cross-Old Kent Road junction. Inside its cavernous interior the flock wallpaper is covered in photographs. Yellow, curling Edwardian prints show the neighbour-hood lit by gas lamp and patrolled by horse-drawn carriages. Others depict the pub in its sixties heyday: various monochrome gangsters, minor celebrities and glamour girls caught in frozen animation before the same flocked paper. In one, Ronnie and Reggie Kray leer into the camera with dead eyes and mephitic grins. Amongst the photos hang a selection of mysterious brass ornaments interspersed here and there by dead animals in glass cases. The wall above the bar meanwhile is dedicated to the landlord's boxing trophies, celebrating the now chain-smoking, balding cirrhotic despot's vainglorious past.

The three of them had been drinking here since their mid teens and the ancient juke box still played the same selection of tired eighties pop. As Frank walked through the door Madness sang One Step Beyond. The air was thick with cigarette smoke and he squinted in the dimness — thick maroon velvet curtains blocked out the afternoon sun. In the Hope and Anchor, it was always midnight.

He found Jimmy and Eugene playing pool and he fetched himself a drink, glad suddenly, that he didn't have to make conversation. Almost immediately he began to wish he hadn't come, that he'd stayed at home with the curtains drawn and the stereo on full blast. He barely had the energy to lift his pint he was so hacked-off. After a while, Jimmy potted the final ball and came over.

'Not seeing Kate tonight?' he asked after the hellos were over with and he'd sat down.

Frank winced. 'No.'

Jimmy glanced at him questioningly, but taking in Frank's face, merely nodded. Eugene began to shout loudly into his mobile phone.

'How're the savings coming?' asked Jimmy after a brief silence. 'You must be nearly there now.'

Frank had to think for a moment before he realised what Jimmy was talking about. He'd been saving for the past year, trying to get enough money together to go travelling, and it had, until he met Kate, been the subject uppermost in his thoughts. 'Oh,' he said vaguely. 'Yeah . . . you know. Still saving.'

Jimmy shot him a puzzled look, but Frank ignored him. How could he possibly explain how he felt? That he was half mad with thoughts of a girl he hardly knew? That nothing mattered at the moment apart from the one desperate hope that he would see her again. He knew exactly what his friends' response would be: *Stop being such a fanny, Auvrey.*

'You want a game?' asked Eugene, nodding over to the pool table.

'Nah, you're all right,' he said, continuing to stare into his pint. Now that he was here, he just couldn't be fucked to talk to them. 'You have another one.' He pretended not to notice the look that passed between them.

He watched them play for a minute or two, before sinking once again into his own thoughts. He felt with Kate as if he'd discovered a whole new country that he was desperate to explore if only he could find where to catch the boat from. How then, when Jimmy asked about his plans to travel could he even contemplate Greece, Turkey, Germany, France? What the fuck did he care about those places — boring, bland, flat compared to Kate — if they were somewhere she was not? He didn't even have a phone number for her. He hadn't seen her for nine days.

'Fancy a line?'

He suddenly realised that Eugene was talking to him.

'Might cheer you up a bit.'

'No. You know I don't do that shit.' He must have spoken more sharply than he'd meant, because Eugene was pulling a face.

'Suit yourself. Jim?'

Frank went to the bar and tried to think up an excuse to leave. When he returned he realised that Jimmy and Eugene were arguing about something and half-heartedly he tried to get the gist.

'Well, what's the point?' Jimmy was saying.

85

'It's Sunday for fuck's sake. Just chill out for a night — lay off it for a bit.'

'Yeah, yeah.' Grumpily, Eugene got up and moved off in the direction of the gents. 'Just say no, right? Thanks, Jim. Gotcha.'

When he'd gone, Jimmy turned to Frank and appealed to him. 'It's starting to do my head in. Seriously, Frank, I'm worried.'

He shrugged. 'He'll be all right. You know what he's like.' To be honest, the subject bored him. He'd never been into drugs himself, but everyone and their dog seemed to be coked up at the moment — it was a national sport. No big deal.

Jimmy nodded unhappily. 'Yeah. It's just that he's spending all his time with those wankers down the Feathers. Andy Mitchel and that. You know the kind of shit they're into.'

Inwardly, Frank groaned. Not this. Not now. He couldn't bear the thought of Eugene becoming one of those sad fucks whose lives revolved around the dole office, the pub, and his next fix. In fact the thought was so depressing he refused to allow it as a possibility.

He shrugged non-committedly. 'He's always been like that. We've had this conversation ever since we were kids. He's a grown up, Jimmy. It's not our job to rein him in all the time is it? And to be honest I've got enough to worry about other than Eugene's benders.'

He realised that Jimmy was looking at him strangely. 'Fair enough,' he said. A silence fell.

'Look, Jim,' Frank said, getting up. 'Sorry, but I'm feeling a bit gyp. I'm going to head on home.' Eugene had just re-emerged from the gents and he waved over at him. 'Have a good night, yeah? I'll give you a call in the week.'

★　★　★

On the edges of Deptford he passed vast sites of half-built apartment blocks. Bill boards boasting designer living with river views. White towers of little square rooms with the same dimensions and soullessness as the council flat he'd grown up in five minutes down the road, only with Italian-style taps and a £300K price tag. He felt his mood worsen.

And then, turning the corner, his spirits soared as he spied a familiar flash of yellow hair outside his door. She was sitting on his step smiling up at him as he approached. It was all he could do not to shout out with relief: the world sang.

12

She is fourteen when she firsts asks Ingrid about the photograph. They are eating breakfast one morning when her gaze happens to fall upon the image of the little, blond child and she asks, 'Who is that?' vaguely remembering Robert's reaction to it the summer before.

'Eat your breakfast, Elodie,' Ingrid pours more coffee, and looks pointedly at Elodie's bowl of cereal.

'Yes. Who is that?'

'That is my son, Elodie. Our son, Anton. When he was a little boy.'

Elodie continues to spoon Cheerios into her mouth. 'Anton. Where is Anton?'

Ingrid doesn't answer for a moment. In the silence Elodie stretches across the table to trail her fingers along the sharp lines of the silver eagle, its gleaming half-raised wings. She hums a tune she has learnt from a television advertisement for detergent.

Ingrid's voice, when she speaks, is very quiet. 'He lives in England, Elodie, in something called a boarding school.'

'Oh,' says Elodie, mulling this over. 'Why?'

It's the sound of creaking floorboards that alerts them to Robert's presence. In the forest there had been a stagnant pond in which the water had sat dank and green beneath a layer of

88

rotten leaves. Once, she had broken the stillness with the end of a stick and had recoiled in shock when a large, slime-covered toad had suddenly sprung out at her. This is what she thinks of when she sees the look that slithers between Ingrid and Robert at that moment.

Ingrid breaks the silence first. 'Was there something you wanted, Robert?'

A second, and then another, drips icily by, before Robert drops his eyes and turns away. 'No,' he says, quietly. 'Nothing.'

'Go and get dressed, now, Elodie,' Ingrid tells her. 'You have an appointment with Doctor Schultz at nine.'

★   ★   ★

Later, she will be able to recall this incident vividly, because it happens on the morning that the blood comes, an event that would render every detail of that day unforgettable. Ingrid had already prepared her for her first period. Only a few months before, soon after she had turned fourteen, she had sat Elodie down and carefully explained what would soon be happening to her. She had used unfamiliar words and though Elodie had nodded and said she understood, the subject had fallen from her mind in the time it had taken to turn the TV on again.

She is about to get into the shower when it happens. It's not until she's removed her pyjamas and is about to turn the tap on when she looks down and notices the smears of blood. 'Ingrid!' Her cry is so loud and panic-stricken that she hears her footsteps on the stairs almost immediately.

In the few seconds that it takes Ingrid to grasp the situation, she stands in the doorway, her startled face looking in at Elodie as she shivers, naked on the bath mat. Within moments she has fetched sanitary napkins and clean underwear, turning on the shower and gently pushing Elodie beneath the water. Afterwards, wrapping her in a towel she patiently explains what has happened to her. Soon, Elodie is back in her bedroom, dressed and reassured, a mug of cocoa in her hands.

But later that evening, alone in bed, something from the incident lingers in her mind, something quite separate from the shock of her first bleeding. In the moment that Ingrid had opened the door and gazed in at her, something had passed between the two of them that had reached Elodie even through her confusion and panic. She had been undressed in front of Ingrid before, but this was the first time that she had been conscious of her nakedness. In the few seconds before Ingrid had grasped the situation, Elodie had become acutely aware of her new, small breasts and the soft down of hair that had recently begun to sprout between her legs. And as she'd stood there, shivering on the bath mat, she had felt Ingrid's gaze linger on her body for a moment. She wasn't sure what she had seen there, in the other woman's eyes. Like a black crow landing briefly before quickly taking flight again. The moment passed, and almost immediately Ingrid had dropped her gaze and begun to busy herself with helping her.

Soon, Elodie grows accustomed to her monthly bleeding, but the strangeness that passed between them in the bathroom that morning stays with her, and for reasons she cannot even begin to explain to herself, she takes to locking the door now, whenever she undresses.

★   ★   ★

It's a few months later when Anton arrives. It's winter, Christmas time, and recently Elodie has been woken more frequently by the sound of angry, raised voices and the slamming of doors. One afternoon, not long after Yaya and Colin have left for the day and Elodie is sitting in the schoolroom finishing her lessons, Ingrid leaves her desk and comes to sit beside her.

'Elodie, do you remember I told you about my son, Anton?'

She nods. 'Yes.'

'Well, he's coming to stay with us for a little while.'

'Oh. Is he nice?'

'Elodie. He'll only be here for two weeks, but you will notice certain changes. You will eat your meals up here, that sort of thing. Things will be a bit different for a short time, just while Anton's here. Do you understand?'

'OK.'

The first change is the locked door. Although she's never been allowed to leave the house by herself, she's always had free range of all the rooms. Now, however, the door at the end of the landing which separates her top-floor quarters from the stairs to the rest of the house remains locked. Yaya and Colin are on vacation, and so her days are spent alone with Ingrid.

With each day, Ingrid seems to grow more distracted and unhappy, and Elodie notices that the flaky, raw patches on her arms have begun to flare again, sometimes into angry, red welts. One afternoon she looks up from her books and sees her absently scratching at herself, seemingly unaware of the tiny specks of blood that have begun to appear beneath her nails. Quietly, Elodie gets up from her seat and goes to her, gently taking the slim white hand in her own, while Ingrid looks up, startled, blinking in surprise at what she's done.

But often during the few weeks of Anton's visit, Elodie is left alone. In Ingrid's absence she whiles away the time staring out of the window, trying to catch a glimpse of the stranger who's so mysteriously kept apart from her in the house below. Mostly she watches the little TV set that Ingrid has recently allowed her to have in the corner of the schoolroom. Through endless cop shows and soap operas, romantic comedies and late-night thrillers, Elodie stares unblinking at a world beyond High Barn that she can barely comprehend. Jerry Springer and Oprah Winfrey,

The X-Files and Buffy The Vampire Slayer, Letterman and Larry Sanders, Hill Street Blues and America's Most Wanted. With no Ingrid to monitor what she sees, two or three hours will pass without her stirring, and she'll watch an infomercial for skin cleanser with the same open-mouthed incredulity that she'll watch a report from Death Row. There she sits, night after night, while love and death, sex and betrayal, murder and redemption in all their myriad variations are played out before her in a billion pixellated images upon a nine-inch screen.

Later, in bed, beneath the silent darkness, her fingers caress and stroke her new, changing body. And day by day, a nameless hunger grows.

★ ★ ★

Only twice does she catch a glimpse of Anton during his stay. The first time, she is standing at her bedroom window when Ingrid, Robert and a tall, slim teenage boy emerge from the house onto the drive. The boy has long messy hair that hides most of his face and a tense, tight way of holding himself, his fists clenched by his side. It's strange, watching the three of them without their knowledge; they seem small and far away somehow, like characters in a movie. She sees Ingrid speak to Anton, her pink, anxious eyes fixed nervously on her son's face. And though she can't hear them she sees that the words that escape the boy's barely open lips in reply make Ingrid flinch as if he'd struck her. She sees, also,

93

the quick flash of enjoyment that momentarily lights up Robert's face, even as he puts a remonstrative hand on Anton's shoulder.

The second time, she spies him standing alone at the very end of the garden, between the two cherry trees. And although he has his back to her, something strikes her about his bearing; the droop in his shoulders, the still, somehow defeated way he remains at the edge of the lawn as if reluctant to return to the house. Silently she wills him to turn, desperate suddenly to see his face. But just at that moment Ingrid returns to the schoolroom with her supper and Elodie obediently takes her seat, instinctively keeping quiet about what she's seen.

It's a few days later that the police come. She's woken in the night by Ingrid and Robert arguing more loudly and more passionately than usual. She is lying there in bed waiting for them to stop when the red and blue lights start flashing across the ceiling and she hears the sound of a car pulling up on the gravel outside. Going to her window she watches as a police officer leads Anton from the back seat up to the house. It's too dark to see clearly but she notices that he puts up no resistance and waits silently next to the policeman while his parents come to the door.

Elodie sits and waits in the dark, unable to hear anything but a low rumble of voices from the kitchen below. When after half an hour the policeman leaves, the shouting starts immediately. Elodie can't make out Anton's voice, only Ingrid's shrill pleading and Robert's exasperated bellow. But at last she hears the front door slam and from her window sees the boy running across the lawn. At the end of the drive he pauses and looks back at the house. For a split second his gaze falls upon her bedroom window and she retreats quickly back into the shadows.

She had fallen back to sleep and has no idea what time it is when she wakes again with a start to see through the darkness a figure standing at her door. 'Ingrid,' she says, sitting up, her heart thumping. Wordlessly Ingrid comes to her and takes a seat at the end of her bed. Her eyes gleam in the moonlight. 'Ingrid?' says Elodie nervously. 'What is it?'

When at last she replies her voice is strange and tight. 'I knew he shouldn't have come,' she says. 'I knew it would be a mistake.'

Elodie stares at her and after a while Ingrid gets up and goes to the window. The moon bathes her face in its cool, pale glow and her voice is so quiet now it's almost as if she were talking to herself. 'Nothing I did was good enough,' she murmurs. 'By the time we sent him away he'd made our lives a misery.' She pauses and then in a small, dull little voice adds, 'He even hit me once.'

She returns to the bed and stares at Elodie imploringly. 'I did my best,' she says. 'I sent him to school in England because I have relatives there. And Robert agreed! He agreed!'

Elodie nods. 'Yes,' she whispers.

Ingrid swipes angrily at her tears. 'I've failed him, I know I have. But it was my idea to have him here for the holidays, even though I'm so

95

busy. And now this! Picked up by the police for stealing a car.' She shakes her head bitterly. 'He does it just to punish me.'

Tentatively Elodie reaches over and touches her on the shoulder and almost instantly she finds herself in Ingrid's arms, wrapped in an embrace so tight she could hardly breathe. Eventually she's released and Ingrid picks up one of her hands between her own, thin white fingers. Elodie shrinks a little beneath the intensity of her gaze. At last Ingrid whispers, 'I haven't failed you though, have I, Elodie?'

Elodie opens her mouth to answer and feels the fingers tighten their hold. 'No,' she says quickly.

'I love you, Elodie,' Ingrid says then, with a final squeeze of her hand. At last she gets to her feet. Moments later the door closes softly behind her and, left alone, Elodie lies awake for a long time, staring up at the ceiling.

★   ★   ★

A week later, when she returns with Yaya from a day of examinations and tests at the hospital, she finds Ingrid in the schoolroom, staring out of the window. 'He's gone,' is all she says, not shifting her gaze from the garden below. 'It's for the best.' They do not mention him again. She finds the door to the rest of the house remains open now, whenever Ingrid leaves her by herself.

★   ★   ★

96

She isn't sure exactly when it is that the conference begins to take over their lives, only that from the moment Ingrid mentions it, it slowly begins to dominate everything they do. Some weeks after her fifteenth birthday, she's in the schoolroom with Yaya and Colin when Ingrid makes her announcement. She stands behind her desk, her white-blonde hair fastened tightly back from her face as usual, the paleness of her skin and eyes in stark contrast to the severe, black, high-necked blouse she wears.

'There'll be many important people there,' she tells them, twin red patches of excitement high on her cheeks. 'Scientists and doctors from all over the world.' She smiles at Elodie, 'And you, of course, will be the guest of honour.'

It's not the prospect of the event itself that alarms Elodie — soon, Ingrid has explained so many times what will be expected of her that she only feels mildly nervous about her part in it. Rather it's the change she detects in Ingrid that begins to breed the small flutters of anxiety in her chest. Their lessons take on a renewed zeal and as the conference draws closer, the hours they spend preparing for it increase. Sometimes the two of them remain at their desks long after Yaya and Colin have left for the day and their outings, their trips to the beach or to the park all but stop. There's a subdued, anxious edge to the schoolroom now.

For months the little carved wooden bird has sat untouched on her bedside table. But now Elodie finds herself reaching for it more and more frequently, holding it in her hand during

97

lessons, her finger stroking it in comforting circles whenever her mistakes provoke Ingrid's displeasure.

★ ★ ★

During these long, tense days, only one shines out from the others. 'Today we're going to do something a little different,' says Yaya, turning from the window from where she'd been watching Ingrid's car disappear down the drive. 'Put your book down, Elodie,' she tells her.

Outside, the afternoon sun hangs heavy in the sky. Fallen cherry blossoms drift over the freshly mown lawn and the air smells of cut grass, new buds and damp earth. The three of them stand beneath the pear tree, while far above them an aeroplane trails a silent line of white.

'You ever played baseball before?' Yaya asks her. Her eyes sparkle and Elodie's heart skips at the flicker of rebellion in the air.

'No,' she says, staring down with curiosity at the bag at their feet. 'But I've seen it on the television.'

Yaya laughs dryly. 'There anything you *haven't* seen on television, honey?' She bends down and takes out a leather mitt, a wooden bat and a red ball. 'OK, you can bat, I'll pitch, and Colin can field. Let's go!'

After a few wild swings of the bat, with Colin's guidance Elodie eventually gets the hang of it and soon the three of them are running and shouting excitedly, entirely caught up in their makeshift game for three. Elodie kicks off her shoes and as she feels the satisfying crack of the bat against the ball and the damp grass beneath her feet, the conference, the long, frustrating hours in the schoolroom, the pressure of trying and trying to please Ingrid, all entirely melt away.

An hour or so later the three of them throw themselves, panting and laughing, to the grass. After a while, Elodie rolls onto her back and stares up at the sky. From the corner of her eye she can see Colin's pale, thin wrist and the sleeve of his favourite brown cardigan, a few blades of grass in his open palm. A feeling of total peace drifts over her.

'Come here, sweetie,' Yaya calls to her after a while.

Obediently Elodie goes to her and sits patiently while Yaya braids her hair. In the silence Elodie leans against her shoulder and looks out across the lawn. The thought strikes her that soon, Colin and Yaya will pack up their things and go home, leaving her at High Barn alone. She closes her eyes tight against the thought, wishing that the afternoon could last forever.

'Let's have a look at you.' Yaya pulls Elodie round to face her and, holding her chin in her hand says thoughtfully, 'Gorgeous.' She smiles. 'You really are such a pretty girl.'

They are interrupted by the sound of Robert's car approaching up the drive and the three of them jump instantly to their feet, glancing nervously at each other.

'Hi,' he calls to them. 'Having yourselves a little field trip, I see.' His smile is friendly, and she feels the others relax a little.

'Hello, Mr Klein,' Yaya calls back. 'Just a game of baseball.'

'Good for you.' He nods and smiles again, then turns towards the house. But then, at the door he stops. 'Used to be pretty good at baseball in high school,' he says, raising his hand to shield his eyes from the sinking sun.

'Would you like to join us?' Colin asks politely, after a pause.

And to Elodie's delight Robert shrugs, grins, takes off his jacket and makes his way across the lawn towards them.

The four of them play for nearly an hour, until the sun has almost dropped below the hill. While Elodie fields she watches Robert run around the lawn, his shirtsleeves rolled up, his face flushed with exertion. She shrieks with pleasure when they both hurtle toward a base and collide in a heap on the grass. They lie there for a second or two, laughing, before Robert gets up and reaching for her, pulls Elodie to her feet.

At that moment they hear Ingrid's car returning up the hill. The four of them freeze and look towards the bottom gate.

'Well,' says Robert, his smile fading instantly. 'Guess we should . . . '

Yaya nods and begins packing up their things. 'Yeah,' she says. 'Come on Elodie. Time to go in now.'

That night in bed Elodie smiles in the darkness as she relives each moment of that afternoon. Just before she goes to sleep she thinks about Robert, of how his body had slammed into hers, of how his arms had briefly circled her waist as they fell.

★ ★ ★

And then, a few weeks later, something terrible. It's not long before the conference and she, Yaya, Colin and Ingrid have spent the morning working without pause on a particularly difficult exercise, when Ingrid leaves the room to start lunch, nodding at Yaya to continue.

'Elodie,' Yaya says, picking up the book. 'What is the man in this picture doing?'

Elodie tells her, but stumbles over her grammar.

'No, Elodie,' says Yaya gently. 'Try again.'

But she makes the same mistake and looks anxiously up at Yaya, unable to continue.

'Never mind, honey,' Yaya smiles, wearily rubbing her temples. 'We'll come back to it later.'

'Yaya, can I have a word?'

They hadn't noticed that Ingrid had returned and her voice makes all three of them jump.

After the door has closed behind them, she and Colin go back to the book. 'Elodie,' says Colin, after a while. 'Concentrate, please.' But the voices on the other side of the door have grown so loud they're impossible to ignore.

'It's just not good enough,' she hears Ingrid say.

And when Yaya replies, Elodie is amazed at the defiance in her voice.

'You work her too hard,' she says. 'It's ridiculous to keep up this pressure.' Her voice

101

rises higher still. 'Doctor Klein, the child's exhausted. She needs a break. When's the last time she spent more than a few hours away from this place? Aside from the neurology ward, I mean? She should be outside having fun, meeting other kids, not cooped up in here.'

At that moment, Colin puts down his book and leaves the room too, and Elodie hears the three of them move away from the door, further off down the corridor. She can still hear Yaya and Ingrid arguing, and now Colin's deeper tones joining their voices, but she can no longer make out what they're saying. She stares down at the book in her hands but the images swim in front of her eyes, and her gaze keeps returning to the closed door.

★ ★ ★

The next day is a Saturday and when on Monday morning, Yaya and Colin fail to arrive, Elodie says nothing. She glances anxiously from the door to Ingrid's face, but when Ingrid starts the lesson without them, as if nothing were amiss, she begins to feel a strange, gnawing doubt. But there's something in the set of Ingrid's jaw, the expression in her eyes, her brisk, no-nonsense manner that warns her not to broach the subject.

On the second day, however, when still they don't appear, she steals herself to ask, 'Where is Yaya, Ingrid? And Colin?'

'They'll no longer be working with us,' is the brief, terse reply.

Elodie's guts turn over uncomfortably, and although she knows she shouldn't, she can't stop herself from asking, 'But why, Ingrid? Why not? When will I see them?'

The distress is plain in her voice, and Ingrid's head rises sharply. But she merely says lightly, 'Oh, soon, no doubt. They have other work to do right now. You'll have to put up with me for the time being, I'm afraid.' And though she smiles brightly, her tone tells Elodie that the conversation is over. She bows her head again, but privately she thinks about being alone every day with Ingrid, cut adrift from the outside world, and her heart sinks. With Ingrid's watchful gaze still upon her, she busies herself with her work, but still the sense of foreboding laps queasily in the pit of her stomach.

The next day, a small, insipid young woman named Claire arrives at the schoolroom. She's shy and meek and jumps whenever Ingrid speaks. She turns up again the next day, and then the one after that, and soon Elodie understands that there had never been any question of Yaya and Colin returning to High Barn.

* * *

Soon the conference is almost upon them. She finds herself waking at odd times during the night, a nameless, restless anxiety forcing her awake, her mind spinning with a million nonsensical sentences. Sometimes she dreams that she's about to speak in front of a vast crowd of people, but when she opens her mouth all that emerges is an endless stream of feathers. Now, when she makes a mistake — and she seems to make them more and more frequently — Ingrid's exasperation is immediate. 'No, Elodie!' she says through tight lips. 'Start again.'

Most days, they work together long into the evening, repeating and repeating the day's exercises until Elodie aches with tiredness. She feels the air between them grow tauter and tauter.

And then, two days before the conference something snaps. Ingrid has left her to make some lunch, and she's staring out of the window, watching a pair of jays build a nest in the branches of a nearby tree. And almost without knowing she's doing it, she begins to call to them. It has been a long time since she's uttered the old, comforting sounds, and, softly at first, but soon growing in conviction, she slowly works her way through her old repertoire.

At first her throat — unused now to making the sounds once so familiar to her — resists. She can only manage odd, discordant rasps and weak whistles. But soon her larynx, throat, tongue and lips obey, like a dancer's body remembering old steps from decades ago, and soon the almost supernaturally high sounds emerge from some-where deep inside her, the low notes vibrating against her tonsils. The back of her throat seems to expand to channel the sounds. It is a strange magic, and she luxuriates in her ability, caught up in a sort of blissful trance.

Soon she can no longer see the schoolroom, or

even the window and the garden beyond it. She is back there, in the forest, surrounded by green trees, the late afternoon sun streaming through the leaves, the evening chorus mingling with her own voice. So caught up in it is she, so profoundly comforted, that she doesn't hear Ingrid's footsteps as she mounts the stairs and approaches down the corridor, until there she is, standing in the threshold of the schoolroom. And mid arpeggio, Elodie turns to meet her gaze.

Her mouth snaps shut.

'Why must you persist in making those wretched sounds?' asks Ingrid, striding across the room towards her. 'When I have dedicated nearly three years of my life to helping you?' She shakes her head in bewilderment.

Elodie says nothing.

'Is this what you want?' Ingrid continues, her voice rising. 'When you stand in front of all those people on Thursday, is this what you want them to see?' Going over to Elodie's desk she snatches up the little wooden bird. 'And this!' she says. 'This hunk of wood you insist on carrying around with you still, like a *souvenir*. Why would you want to be reminded of that man? Of that place? When I have done so much for you? Do you understand, Elodie, the money and hard work that has gone into helping you? Do you?' Abruptly she leaves the room, taking the wooden bird with her. The door slams shut behind her.

13

Long Island, New York, 20 August 1998
She stands in the wings of the university's main
theatre and is overwhelmed by what she sees.
The auditorium is filled with people and the air
seems to bulge and sag with their voices. Elodie
notices that right at the back, behind the last row
of seats, a couple of men stand behind enormous
cameras on tripods, far larger than the one Colin
used to film her with at High Barn. As she
watches, the lights begin to fade, leaving the
stage itself illuminated. A hush falls.

At that moment Ingrid walks across the stage
and takes her place beneath the spotlight. Her
appearance is met instantly with a sudden burst
of applause like heavy rain. There in the shadows
Elodie wipes her damp palms on the new green
dress bought specially for the occasion. When
Ingrid begins to talk into the microphone her
voice rings out loud and shrill across the rows
and rows of people. A series of diagrams and
pictures flash up upon a large white screen behind
her, and as she points to them she uses many
long, unfamiliar phrases that Elodie doesn't understand — hemispheric specialization, neurological
laterization, linguistic acquisition, cognitive devel-
opment. On and on she talks: an unceasing wall
of words.

And then it happens. With the press of a
button, the static images on the screen are

replaced by moving film and the large speakers that hang above the stage crackle into life. Elodie gives a little gasp of surprise, because there she is, suddenly, for all to see, sitting at her desk in the schoolroom at High Barn.

She can tell by the way she looks and speaks that it must have been made some time ago. In the film, Yaya is sitting next to her, pointing to a picture book and asking, 'Elodie, what is this?'

'Dog!'

'And where is the dog, Elodie?' Yaya continues. 'Is he sitting on the table, or is he sitting under the table?'

The strange, film version of herself replies, 'Under the table!'

From where she stands at the side of the stage, Elodie gazes longingly at the image of Yaya, and feels her eyes begin to prickle. It's a peculiar sensation, watching herself like this, and she gazes, fascinated, as the film cuts to a new shot of her in the hospital where the machine that Ingrid calls an MRI glides noiselessly over her head. Next, the camera focuses on Doctor Irving, one of the specialists. He's talking to Ingrid, and pointing at a computer screen upon which she recognises the black and white, soft scale images of her brain.

Ingrid freezes the film and turns back to the audience. It seems to go on forever, this part of the talk, and after a while Elodie feels her legs begin to ache and she claps a hand over her mouth to stifle a yawn. At last, however, Ingrid turns once more to the screen.

And there she is again, back in the

107

schoolroom. But this time the film is older, and shows Elodie as she was when she first arrived in America. Now, when she looks up at herself, a strange emotion floods her. Her hand flies to her mouth in a kind of horror, and though she can't tear her eyes away, she longs for it to stop.

She hardly recognises her; this small, thin, wide-eyed child with the long wild hair. Worst of all though are the noises she makes, the whistles and the grunts, the slack-jawed babbling. It's awful to see; grotesque. The camera turns to Ingrid. 'A' 'E' 'I' 'O' 'U' she says, over and over, 'Tuh, Ess, Ruh, Puh,' she repeats, emphasising each sound, her lips exaggerating their shapes. The camera returns to Elodie, to her pitiful attempts at aping her. As she watches unseen from the wings, she feels her cheeks burn with shame.

On the stage, the screen fades to black, and once again Ingrid addresses the audience. 'And now,' she says, 'I'd like you to meet a very special person indeed.' She turns to where Elodie stands, waiting in the shadows. She raises her hand in an encouraging, beckoning gesture and smiles warmly as she says, 'Ladies and gentlemen, I give you Elodie Brun.'

There's an expectant murmur from the audience. It's only a few metres, the distance she has to walk, but each one feels like a mile, every second an hour. At last she stands beside Ingrid, flinching from the bright spotlight. A cold panic engulfs her. After watching herself as she once was, she is now desperate to show how much she's progressed, to prove to all these strangers that she's no longer that same, grunting little girl. She opens her mouth, acutely conscious too of the need to not let Ingrid down, but her mind is entirely blank, her throat as dry as sand.

Taking a deep breath, she begins to speak. 'My name is Elodie Brun,' she says, 'and I am fifteen years old.' It is not very long, the speech they have rehearsed, and as soon as she has begun, she finds her way through it easily. When she comes to the end she says, as she has been instructed, 'I would like to thank Doctor Ingrid Klein, and her colleagues at the hospital for everything they have done for me.'

She's shocked by the applause she receives. It seems to go on forever, filling the auditorium, growing louder and louder as she stands there, blinking back at all the faces. At last she turns to Ingrid, who takes her hand and leads her from the stage.

'Well done,' she says, when they reach the wings. 'You did very well.'

Elodie looks up at her teacher's approving smile and swallows hard, dizzy with relief.

★ ★ ★

It's strange, returning to High Barn alone after all the excitement. At first, after Claire has dropped her off, she wanders from room to room feeling flat and listless. At last she takes a seat on one of the large, elegant sofas in the living room, and switches on the TV, quickly becoming engrossed in an episode of Friends. It's only when Robert clears his throat and says

109

her name that she turns and sees him looking in at her from the door.

'Hi,' he says.

'Robert!'

'So how'd it go this morning?' he asks. He leans against the doorframe, dressed in jeans and a T-shirt. Her eyes flicker across his chest.

'Good, thank you.' She tries to think of something else to say, but her tongue feels heavy and shy.

He nods, and stares for a few moments at the TV screen. 'And where is my dear wife?' he asks then. 'Receiving her public I suppose?'

She hesitates, unsure of his tone.

He smiles and crosses the room, flopping down heavily in the seat beside her. She notices the way the hairs on his wrist catch around his metal watchstrap, the fine wrinkles around his eyes. If she reached out her hand, she could touch him.

They stare at the TV in silence for a while, but out of the corner of her eye, Elodie continues to watch him. She thinks about how nice he was to her, the day they all played baseball, how friendly his smile is whenever she sees him. But still, a little niggling doubt persists. Could this be the same man whose angry voice she hears so often, who causes Ingrid such sadness?

He breaks the silence first, saying, 'Tell me, Elodie, are you happy?'

'Yes,' she says, immediately.

He leans a little closer. 'Really?'

She smiles hesitantly, searching his face, unsure of what he wants her to say.

'You do know,' he says after a moment, 'that there is more to life than being my wife's performing monkey?' He stares at her, and then adds quietly, 'You do know that, right?'

She doesn't like talk like this. Where a person says one thing, but means another. 'I am not a monkey,' she says flatly.

He smiles apologetically. 'Of course not,' he tells her. 'No, of course you're not. Sorry.'

They turn back to the TV. After a while, Robert continues, 'I just meant, you shouldn't be cooped up in here all the time, that's all. You should be out, meeting other kids, going on dates, that kind of thing.' He winks at her then, and adds, 'pretty girl like you.'

She ducks her head, feeling her cheeks redden.

'You should be in France, with your mother,' he continues, his eyes on the TV once more.

The word hangs in the air. *Mother.* Elodie feels a confusing stab of longing as the two syllables float around and around her brain. Mother.

Robert shrugs, glancing at her. 'But what do I know?' he says, his voice cheerful again. 'Ingrid's the expert, right?' He gets up. 'I was going to make some coffee,' he adds, leaving the room. 'Want one?'

★ ★ ★

In the weeks that follow the conference, life at High Barn begins, slowly and subtly, to change. Ingrid is more frequently away from home, often leaving Claire to carry on with Elodie's lessons

111

without her. And Elodie begins to recognise a new fervour in Ingrid's manner, a new excitement and purpose in her eyes. 'I'm sorry to have to leave you again,' she tells Elodie one evening, when they are eating supper together. 'But life has become so incredibly busy lately.' She chews her food thoughtfully and then adds with a flush of pleasure, 'I have a series of radio and television interviews to give, more lectures than ever, and then there's the new book I've been asked to write.'

Elodie nods dully, and asks, 'Can we go out, tomorrow? To the beach?'

'Of course,' Ingrid replies. 'Or, if not tomorrow, then the day after.'

She notices that the more often Ingrid is away, the more Robert is to be found at High Barn. He tells her that he no longer needs to travel so much these days, that he can work from his offices in New York, or from home. Often, Elodie will watch Ingrid's car disappearing down the drive from her bedroom window, then wander down to the living room at almost exactly the same time Robert emerges from his study, which also has a window with a clear view of the drive.

'You want a coffee?' Robert will ask her, smiling broadly as if surprised to see her there. And the two of them will sit on the sofa together with their mugs, watching the television. Eventually, Robert will begin to talk.

What she loves, especially, is the way Robert talks to her. As if she were an adult, a friend. The confiding tone he uses, the little glances and touches of her arm to emphasise a point. A

112

conversation. Not watching other people on television, or listening to Claire's or Ingrid's instructions.

One morning he begins to talk about Anton, and her heart twists with pity.

'I blame myself, of course,' he tells her earnestly. 'Anton was always such a troubled boy. He and his mother . . . ' But he shakes his head without continuing.

'You know what he did, once? He stole all her clothes from her closet, took them out into the garden, and burnt them! I suppose you've got to admire his balls.' He laughs sheepishly. 'God knows where he gets them from.'

She waits.

'Another time he got high and stole a car and crashed it right into a pet store. Broken glass and squashed goldfish all over the sidewalk! Soon he was being picked up by the police almost every weekend.' A shadow falls across his face. 'But of course, when he hit his mother . . . that was, well. That was not smart. That was wrong. Very wrong.' He stares off into space and it strikes Elodie that Robert doesn't look very much like he thinks it was wrong. He looks rather like he thinks it was understandable.

A couple of weeks later, it's Ingrid who is the subject of their conversation. 'I guess you've heard us arguing,' he says, apologetically. Elodie looks at her hands, embarrassed. It's a warm afternoon, a Saturday. As Ingrid is spending the day at the hospital, the two of them are sitting on the lawn outside, sipping iced teas. Robert sighs, and lies down on his back. A faint breeze lifts the curls away from his forehead.

'She was so attractive when we met,' he tells her. 'And the complete opposite to me. So cool and clever and . . . ambitious.' He laughs. 'We met at university, were married by the time we were twenty.' He smiles his boyish, rueful smile. 'I think she was rebelling.' He turns on his side, propping his chin in his hand and gazing up intently at Elodie. 'She'd had a sheltered upbringing. Her father was very strict. And rich of course.' With a dismissive wave towards High Barn and its wide, sloping lawns, he adds, 'Hence all this.'

After a while he continues, 'I guess I can't blame her for the way Anton turned out. She never really wanted a child, not really. I talked her into it because I thought it would be good for us. Then, just after Anton was born, her career really took off. And there was this animosity between them from the start. Motherhood just didn't come naturally. And a child needs his mother.'

He does not notice the pain that lands fleetingly in Elodie's eyes. An embattled look crosses his face. 'I shouldn't have listened to her, perhaps,' he continues as if he's talking to himself. 'But she always knows best. I mean, she's trained in psychiatry, amongst everything else. Her quack friend Maria agreed it would be good for him to be sent away. I didn't know what else to do but agree — he was completely out of hand by that point.' He shrugs then, in a gesture now familiar to Elodie, a half despairing, half bewildered little movement. 'She's always told

114

me I was weak. I hadn't realised how right she was until I let her send our son away.'

He sits up then and smiles gratefully at her. 'You're such a great listener, Elodie.'

As she smiles back at him, her heart swells with pride. Just then, they hear Ingrid's car pulling up at the bottom gate. 'Well,' he says, jumping up abruptly. 'We'd better go in, hadn't we?'

She takes in the nervousness that flickers across his face, and as she follows him into the house and watches him disappear into his study, she feels a sharp tug of disappointment.

★ ★ ★

As usual their rare, shared mealtimes are fraught with tension, the initial few minutes of cool politeness soon giving way to a steady stream of needling and bickering. She notices that the more wine Robert drinks, the louder and more aggressive he becomes. It shocks her, the strength and speed of the anger that will infuse his face, instantly transforming his handsome, good-natured features into something ugly. Try as she might she cannot reconcile this person with the man who is so sweet to her when they're alone. And the more goading and belligerent he grows, the more icy and cutting becomes Ingrid. At these times Elodie will eat her meal as quickly as possible and escape upstairs, trying to block out the voices that grow steadily louder and angrier.

As Ingrid's absences from High Barn become

more frequent, Robert takes to visiting Elodie on the top floor, often sitting on one of the little chairs in the school room and talking to her over the sound of the television, filling the small, low-ceilinged room with his words. She notices that he rarely asks her about herself now, the way he once did. Never mentions his concern at her being cooped up too much alone. In fact, more and more these days it occurs to her that when Robert begins talking, it almost doesn't matter if she's sitting there or not. And sometimes it will strike her that he is rather like a fly, buzzing to and fro in a room, batting angrily against walls and glass, entirely ignoring the one, wide open window that would set it free. Almost as if it were enjoying itself. She thinks about how, when she's given a particularly difficult exercise or project by Ingrid, she tries and tries until she gets it right. As she watches his endlessly moving lips, she realises that she couldn't ever imagine Robert trying very hard at anything.

★   ★   ★

And slowly, a new restlessness begins to flap its wings within Elodie. The rooms of High Barn seem to have grown much smaller recently. Often she'll gaze out of the window to the world that lies beyond it. Questions begin to rise to the surface of her mind. Sometimes she'll feel a tightness in her throat as if the still, trapped air she breathes is slowly choking her.

One day at the end of summer she's in the schoolroom with Ingrid. It's very warm and the window has been left wide open. From where she sits, Elodie can see the lawn bathed in the mid-afternoon sun, and the edge of one of the apple trees, its lower branches bowing with the weight of its fruit; golden orbs hovering precariously above their fallen, rotting siblings.

From Locust Valley the sound of a little league game floats up to them on the breeze, children's voices riding the warm air. A seagull circling somewhere above lets out a long cry.

'Pay attention, Elodie.' She turns to see Ingrid's eyes upon her. But instead of bowing her head to her books, she gets up and moves to the open window, breathing in the summer smells.

'Sit down, Elodie. What on earth's got into you this afternoon?'

'Where is my mother, Ingrid?' she asks.

In the silence that follows, a wasp flies into the window-pane with a tiny thump. She turns and looks over to where Ingrid stands, a piece of chalk held frozen in mid air, her mouth a little 'O' of shock.

'I said: where is my mother, Ingrid? Who is she?'

Somewhere, down the hill, a dog barks. Elodie turns back to the window.

When Ingrid speaks her voice is quick and flustered. 'Your mother doesn't want to see you, Elodie. I'm very sorry, but there it is. I've tried my best to persuade her but she has a new life now.'

She does not see Ingrid's face when she speaks these words, and in fact, cannot bear to look at her while they float around and around the room. Instead she continues to stand, silently looking out at the perfect, blue sky.

'The truth is, Elodie, your mother is an alcoholic,' Ingrid continues in the strange, brisk voice. 'Her life is not really suited to taking care of a child and we don't even have a fixed address for her anymore . . . ' her voice trails off, but still her words remain, embedded like shards of glass.

Moments later, Ingrid is beside her. 'Oh darling. I'm so sorry.'

But still Elodie does not look at her. She continues to stand, quite still, at the window. She can feel Ingrid's fingers clasping her arm, the faintly musty smell of her breath, so close to her. 'Don't cry, Elodie, please don't cry. You have me, now, darling. We have each other. You'll always have me. I love you so much.'

At last Elodie turns to her and smiles. 'I love you too,' she says.

★　★　★

It's a few weeks later that Elodie begins her secret flights from High Barn. The first time she escapes is early one evening at the end of summer. Ingrid is out, and Claire has just left for the day. She's standing at the foot of the stairs, one ear cocked towards Robert's study, when suddenly she finds herself staring at the front door. As soon as the idea enters her head she feels her heart begin to thump with excitement, her palms start to sweat. She listens again for Robert, but hearing nothing, creeps closer to the

118

door and very quietly, tries the latch. It opens noiselessly, easily. The sweet, dewy smell of grass beyond it fills her nostrils. Deftly, she slips out, closing the door behind her.

That first time, she doesn't venture very far. Just to the edge of the garden, where she stands in the gathering shadows, breathing the smell of the trees in the copse below. The pleasure she feels at being out of the house and in the world alone is so great that she lingers in the last moments of the day, luxuriating in the fresh, warm air, staring up at the vast sky. Soon though, fear of being discovered drives her back towards the house. Reluctantly she opens the door and slips back in and up to her room. That evening she notices that the tight feeling in her chest and lungs has loosened, just a little.

At first she's content to keep to the boundaries of the garden, but over time she grows bolder, and the more often she manages to slip away from the house, the further she ventures. Keeping to the shadows she moves along the edge of the garden to the path that leads into the trees. Sometimes she remains there, breathing in the scents and listening to the furtive scurrying of animals; other times she follows the path right down the hill, until it reaches the road. And there she stops, not quite daring to go any further, not yet. But each time she returns to the house she feels a quiet elation, a sense of power and control that's entirely new to her.

★   ★   ★

And then, one night, she lingers too long beneath the stars. She emerges from the edges of the lawn with a sinking heart to find the familiar car in the drive and Ingrid herself standing on the step, panic in her eyes.

'Elodie,' she cries, as soon as she sees her. 'Oh thank God. Thank God! I was about to call the police.' Rushing forward she pulls Elodie to her and for a moment she thinks that it's going to be OK, that Ingrid will somehow understand. But then Ingrid pulls away and in a voice that chills her says, 'Go up to your room now, Elodie.'

On the front step she meets Robert, his wounded expression echoing his wife's. Wordlessly she passes him and climbs the stairs to the top floor.

$\star$ $\star$ $\star$

'Anything could have happened to you,' Ingrid tells her later, when she comes to her room. Her voice is tight with anger and she shakes her head in exasperation. 'Do you understand, Elodie? You have no idea, no concept of how to take care of yourself out there.'

Elodie doesn't reply but her fists are clenched so tightly that she feels the nails cutting into her palms.

Ingrid crosses the room in quick strides. Reaching for Elodie's arm she says in a pleading tone, 'Where were you going, Elodie? Why did you do it?'

But she shakes herself free and turns away to stare out of the window.

When next Ingrid speaks her voice is icy. 'Until you can be trusted I will keep the door to your floor locked,' she tells her. And without turning or replying Elodie hears her leave, her footsteps receding down the hall, and then, finally, the key turning once again in its lock.

★ ★ ★

From then on, the door not only remains locked throughout the night, but also whenever Ingrid leaves High Barn, regardless of whether Robert's there or not. The world outside recedes, she measures out each day by its predictable landmarks: breakfast, lessons, lunch, lessons, dinner, TV, sleep. Languor grips her, and a kind of listless acceptance. Slowly, she grows accustomed to the whittled down nature of her new life, the predictable, focussed existence in the confines of the top floor. Sometimes, only very occasionally, she will allow her mind to drift to the little girl who used to roam so freely between the forest's trees, but it's the life of a stranger, insubstantial as air, bearing little relation to the person she has become.

From her window she sometimes spies Robert leaving High Barn, his car disappearing off down the hill. At first she believes that he will come for her, will unlock her door and set her free, if only for a few hours. Whenever Ingrid is called away from home she waits for him hopefully, but still he doesn't come. At last a cold, bitter understanding settles upon her: he will not come; he wouldn't dare.

It's a few months after her sixteenth birthday that Anton returns to High Barn. Just as before, she only catches brief, shadowy glimpses of him from her window, but she waits impatiently for a sighting nevertheless, her curiosity roused by his parents' stories of past crimes and outrages. She notices that he has grown taller, but still has the same clenched gait. He wears his hair even longer than before and it falls like a curtain across his features, but still she catches a brief glimpse, once or twice, of the beginnings of a moustache.

Now, when Ingrid comes to the top floor for her lessons, she notices that the old sadness in Ingrid has returned, and that her scratching fingers are busier than ever. She's aware too that the long rumbling arguments have resumed, can smell the resentment and tension in the air and nearly every night is awoken by the sound of her and Robert fighting.

★ ★ ★

Then, one evening at the end of April, everything changes. Ingrid leaves the schoolroom to return downstairs as usual, but instead of the key turning in its lock as it usually does, Elodie realises with a flicker or excitement that Ingrid has forgotten to lock her in. For the next hour she sits alone in her room and listens to the three of them eat their supper below, biding her time. From the open kitchen window the sounds of knives scraping upon plates and fragments of conversation drifts up to her on a light spring breeze and even from where she sits she can detect the careful, forced edge to their voices.

Soon she hears Anton's low tones steadily rising above Ingrid's and Robert's, and at last she hears the sound of a chair scraping across the floor and minutes later the front door slamming so hard that the walls of her room tremble in response. She stands at the window and watches him disappear through the darkness to the end of the drive, and feels a stab of envy.

A short silence follows, and then she hears Ingrid and Robert begin to shout at each other with a renewed ferocity. The aggression in their voices shocks her and she jumps when she hears a plate smashing against a wall, and then the sound of a chair crashing to the ground. She creeps to her door, her fingers clenching and unclenching nervously. The fight crashes on. Another almighty thump, the sound of glass and crockery falling to the floor and then . . . silence. At that moment she hears the front door opening again, footsteps running down the drive, the screech of tires as a car pulls away at speed.

Still she waits. The silence has returned, deeper and more sinister than before. At last she goes to the window, and is surprised to find that the drive is entirely empty. She waits, scarcely breathing, trying to remember the order of the noises she had heard from below. Surely there should still be one car remaining? Either Robert's or Ingrid's? Or had Anton returned during all the fighting and taken one himself?

She goes back to her bedroom door and then out onto the landing. She listens. Nothing. She moves out to the top stair, stops and listens again. How long does she have, she wonders, trembling with excitement at the chance to escape even for a little while. Quickly, she goes to her bedroom and puts on shoes and socks, and then a coat over the sweatshirt and pyjama pants she's wearing. Silently, she creeps downstairs.

Ahead of her, the front door has been left wide open. The black night lies beyond it, thick and silent. She edges closer. Just ten minutes, she tells herself. Just ten minutes alone in the garden, maybe as far as the copse, and then she'll return before anyone even notices. She passes the kitchen. Almost makes it to the front door.

'Elodie.'

At the sound of her name she whips around and gazes into the kitchen. There Ingrid stands. A thin and ghostly figure amidst the wreckage of broken crockery, upturned chairs and scattered cutlery.

They stare at each other.

'Come here,' Ingrid tells her.

Her heart sinks. But with one last glance towards the open front door, she does as she's told. By Ingrid's feet, next to a broken bottle, the eagle lies on its back, red wine dripping from its silver wings.

'Where were you going?' Ingrid asks her in a strange, dull voice.

'I . . . Just. Nowhere. For a walk.' There is a long, tense silence and then her voice rises with a

124

sudden despair. 'Ingrid, please, you can't lock me in here forever.'

But instead of the fury she'd been expecting, Ingrid takes a step towards her and in a small beseeching tone begs her, 'Elodie. Please don't leave. You're all I have.'

Elodie sees again the hunger there, that void she had sensed in Ingrid once before. Hopelessness fills her. 'Ingrid,' she says slowly, backing away. 'Where's Robert? And Anton?'

'I don't know. Gone. There was a terrible argument. I don't know.' She shakes her head and in a sad, plaintive voice tells her, 'You're all I care about.'

They stand there for a moment, surveying each other across the sea of smashed and broken things and then, in one quick movement, Ingrid crosses the room and wraps Elodie in her arms. 'Please,' is all she says as she rocks her.

And in that second, all the pressure and resentment and frustration of the past months engulf Elodie. 'No!' she shouts and, struggling free from Ingrid's grasp, with one, quick shove, sends her reeling from her.

The moment stretches silently, slowly. As Ingrid falls, Elodie reaches for her, snatching futilely at empty air, in an effort to keep her from falling. But fall she does, slipping on the spilt wine and landing with a heavy thump upon the floor.

'Ingrid!' Elodie cries, rushing to where she lies, slumped and motionless on her side. 'Oh Ingrid, I'm sorry!' But it's only when she's knelt beside her that she sees the blood, the silent grimace of agony on her face. Putting her hand on Ingrid's shoulder Elodie gently rolls her onto her back and then she sees it: the silver eagle, its enormous wing embedded between Ingrid's ribs, blood pouring from the wound.

'No,' she whispers. She kneels there, staring dumbly from her own, blood-soaked hands to Ingrid's ashen face, her parted, bloodless lips.

'Ingrid, I'm so sorry,' she screams. 'I didn't mean it!' Gingerly she touches the eagle, forcing herself to attempt to pull it out, but Ingrid's cry of pain is so horrifying that she springs to her feet. 'I don't know what to do. Tell me what to do!' she wails.

In a fog of confusion and panic she backs away towards the door, then gives a sudden scream when she stumbles blindly into someone standing behind her.

'Robert!' she cries when she turns. Relief floods her and she throws her arms around him. 'Oh thank god! Thank God.'

Wiping her tears she watches as he takes a step towards his motionless wife. 'I didn't mean to do it,' she tells him. 'I didn't mean to hurt her! We have to help her, we have to call an ambulance.'

But it's as if Robert cannot hear her. Instead he just stands absolutely still, gazing down at Ingrid, his face a white wall of shock as he takes in the pool of blood seeping from her wound, the silver eagle's wing protruding from her body. From the door, Elodie hears a thin moan escape from Ingrid's lips.

'Robert!' she cries again, the panic rising in her chest. And at last her words spur him into

126

action and she sees him fumbling for something in his pocket. Finally he pulls out his cell phone.

As she watches him stare dumbly down at it, her panic seems to fall away for a moment, and a sudden understanding hits Elodie. She sees the future unfold before her with absolute clarity. The paramedics crowding into the kitchen, fighting to save Ingrid's life like on E.R. She sees the ambulance taking Ingrid to hospital, where the doctors make her better. Ingrid recovering in a white hospital room, surrounded by flowers, each day growing stronger and stronger. And then, fully recovered, returning to High Barn. And everything continuing exactly as it had before.

'Robert,' she says, and watches as he turns to her, his face dazed and startled.

'Yes?' he says.

'Robert, call an ambulance,' she tells him. 'Call an ambulance now.'

'Yes,' he says, his eyes falling to his phone once more. 'Of course.'

She sees his fingers press the phone's power button, sees it jerk into life, sees that he is summoning help. And in that split second, she makes her decision. Turning to the open front door, Elodie runs from High Barn. Through the darkness she runs, down the hill. When she reaches the bottom she flags down the first car that approaches and, still numb with shock, gets in.

PART THREE

14

'Kid? Hey, kid?'

The voice nudges her awake, prodding and poking at her until she opens one eye.

'Hey girl, you got a smoke?'

She becomes aware, bit by bit, of the hard ground beneath her, the stench of rotting garbage, the cramped ache in her limbs. As the first worms of memory slither through her consciousness, she sits up with a start, spies the boy sitting on the low wall she had been sleeping behind, and flinches in shock.

'Relax,' says the boy. 'I ain't gonna hurt you.' He shrugs and squints up at the lightening sky then turns back to her with wide, expectant eyes, 'Just want a cigarette.'

'I don't have any cigarettes,' she tells him, from where she sits between two large trashcans.

'You don't, huh?'

He continues to stare at her while she rubs some feeling back into her hands, wraps her coat more tightly around her, looks down the wide street that's beginning to take shape in the first pale glow of morning, and returns a nervous eye to the stranger, silently willing him to go.

It had still been dark when the man dropped her off on a wide, busy intersection beneath a sudden spattering of rain. 'Queens Junction,' he'd told her with a shrug. 'Far as I go.' She'd felt his eyes watching her through his window wipers as she walked blindly away from the traffic and the noise until she'd come to a narrower, quieter street. She'd moved aimlessly, crossing over to avoid the few people still around at that time of night, keeping to the shadows, her eyes to the ground. In the distance a siren had wailed. On some nearby corner voices were raised in argument.

She had come to a stop outside this low, deserted building, its bricks covered in graffiti and its windows smashed-in cavities. A hand-painted sign above the door read 'Tire Shop'. At that moment, around the nearest corner, a group of men had appeared, moving towards her like a dark, many-headed beast. Their voices had gotten louder and she froze until she heard the crash of a glass bottle shattering on the sidewalk, harsh laughter like slews of ice water. Quickly she'd climbed behind the low brick wall and crouched in the darkness, waiting for them to pass. When she was sure they had gone, she had crawled between two dumpsters and stayed there, shivering, until at last she'd allowed herself to give in to the waves of despair. At some point the rain had returned and finally exhausted she had curled up beneath her coat and drifted into an anxious, shallow sleep.

★　★　★

'Nice place you got here.'

The boy is still staring down at her and she in turn takes in his appearance. He's a few years

132

older than she, and his skin colour and features are like those of Tram, she realises, a Vietnamese nurse from the neurology ward. Unlike Tram, though, this boy is very slender and his thick, black hair is cut and sculpted into the shape of a fin. Around his neck hang several thick, gold chains and his left eyebrow is pierced. His face is quick and delicate, his slanting eyes look like they've been finely carved from stone.

'Where am I?' she asks him, when still he refuses to look away.

He raises an eyebrow. 'You for real?' He wrinkles his nose but doesn't answer. Instead he pulls a bagel wrapped in greased paper from his jacket and begins to eat, looking off down the street while he chews. Mid bite, he turns and notices her hungry eyes on him, her mouth slack with longing. Wordlessly he tears off half and hands it to her, gingerly, as if to a wild dog, watching as she devours it in one greedy gulp. His shrewd black eyes continue to scrutinize her for a few moments. 'Runaway, huh?' he asks.

'Please,' she makes a move to rise from her huddled crouch, 'I — '

'Chill,' he shows her his palms. 'Trust me. I got my own problems.' He sighs then. 'I got to go anyhow.' He jumps down from the wall, stretches and yawns. 'Been a long night.' He gives her another contemplative look, shakes his head and says in a gentler voice, 'I don't know what your story is, kid. But you can't stay here. Go home, girl.' When she doesn't reply, he rolls his eyes and begins to move off, but after a few paces stops again. 'You got money?' he asks.

133

She shakes her head. *Money*. She hadn't had time to think of that.

He pulls some dollar bills from his pocket. 'Here,' he says, passing them to her. He points off down the street. 'There's a shelter two blocks away,' he says, but seeing her blank expression lets his hand fall, shrugs and walks away.

Left alone, desolation wraps its icy arms around her. The sun is higher in the sky now, and she begins to hear the pulse of traffic getting louder in the distance. At last she crawls out from behind the wall and begins to walk. Will they be looking for her yet? She imagines Ingrid in her hospital bed, calling for her. She pulls up the collar of her coat, keeps her eyes glued to the sidewalk, and wanders aimlessly. She has no idea where she's going, no plan of where to head for. Briefly the idea crosses her mind to look for Yaya, but she only knows she lives in a place called Brooklyn. As she walks she thinks of the boy who gave her money; his thin wrists, his delicate black eyes, his fast, sharp way of talking, his weary kindness.

Fear engulfs her. Everything in this world after the rarefied calm of High Barn seems too bright and loud and colourful and fast; unreal, as if she'd stepped into the schoolroom's little TV set and was now walking around inside it with all the dials turned up too high. She walks blindly, concentrating on keeping the panic at bay. She finds herself on a large, busy street lined with small, shabby stores, their wares spilling out across the sidewalk: shoes and clothes and food and electrical equipment beneath colourful

134

awnings and high gaudy signs. Smileys Deli, Checks Cashed, 99¢ Store, George's BBQ, Fried Chicken & Pizza, DeeDees Laundromat, Church of Jesus. She turns into another, larger street, filled with people. As she walks a steady stream of traffic roars beside her. Above her, reams of cables cross each other, holding the sky in a net.

She catches sight of herself in a shop window; a white, thin spectre wrapped in a black, too-large coat. Her eyes huge in her face beneath the mane of red-brown hair, staring back at her like a frightened animal. And then at last her hunger drives her into a fast food restaurant where she has to repeat herself several times before she's understood by the girl chewing gum behind the counter, and whose own accent makes no sense to her, either, but who eventually shrugs and takes her money and gives her a burger and soda in return. The gratitude and relief she feels carry her all the way back to the tire shop, where she crawls once again between the two trash cans and eats her food and waits for the wretched, gnawing fear to return. She comforts herself with images of Ingrid sitting serenely in her hospital bed, nurses tending to her every need, her face rosy with health.

When night falls she notices that on the other side of the wide intersection in the distance, a gang of women begin to congregate. She watches them for a while. Now and then a car pulls up and then away again, taking one of the women with it. The evening is warmer than the one before and on the mild, damp air, their voices and laughter drift over to her. 'Hey honey, you

135

wanna party?' 'Hi handsome, want some company?' Edging nearer to the wall she shivers in her coat and tries desperately to come up with some sort of plan.

A few hours later she's jerked awake by the sound of running footsteps and a volley of aggressive whoops and yells. It's pitch black, save for the insipid flicker of a nearby streetlamp. Carefully she pokes her head above the wall and peers out. Running towards her and pursued by three men is the boy from the night before. She realises that he's heading straight towards her, his face strained and flushed with the exertion of running. Jumping over the wall he crouches next to her, his eyes shining like black glass. He remains there, poised like a cat while he listens to the men's movements. It has all happened within a matter of seconds and she's too surprised to speak.

'Motherfucker! Where'd he go?' the voice behind the wall is very close.

Raising a finger to his lips, the boy motions for Elodie to remain silent.

They hear the men murmuring angrily between themselves. And then, a triumphant, 'There!'

She has no time to think about it. The boy has hold of her hand and they are running through the small lot to the back of the tire shop, over the low wall behind it and into the dark streets beyond, the three men's yells and footfalls just behind them, spurring them on. The boy is agile and quick and seems to know exactly where he's going, running and jumping over fences and ducking between cars. The men are fatter, older and drunk. Even with Elodie gasping and struggling to keep up, it doesn't take long to lose them.

'Here,' says the boy at last, and they turn into a narrow alley lined with the backs of colourful, clapperboard houses, crammed in side by side like the skirted behinds of old ladies, nudging and jostling each other for space. Above them a row of boots and shoes hang by their laces from electricity cables. A dog, tied to a fence, barks at them as they pass.

'Well, we lost them,' says the boy. As they walk she watches him from the corner of her eye and senses that even the tips of his fingers and the black spikes of his hair crackle with anger.

'Who were they?' she asks, timidly.

'Who, them? No one.' He doesn't look at her.

They continue in silence for a while and she realises that she's happy to see him, that her situation feels fractionally less bleak than it did a few hours ago. He is kind, she feels. He will help her.

'What's your name, kid?' he asks after a while.

'Elodie,' she says eagerly without thinking, then anxiously bites her lip.

'Aye-lo-dee, huh?' He stops and holds out a hand. 'Well, I'm Bobby.' She takes it and they shake, but she flinches nervously when a siren's wail erupts around the far corner of the street.

Bobby takes in her reaction, one eyebrow cocked, but says nothing, merely blinks as if storing the information for later. 'Well, Elodie,' he says, 'I guess you could do with some food and a shower. Guess I owe you that much.'

His speech, like that of all the people she has heard in the street, is hard for her to decipher. Unlike Ingrid and the others, whose words were clear and separate from one another, Bobby's all seem to run together, and he often leaves off their endings, or puts the emphasis on the wrong syllables. Also he seems to talk at double the speed to anyone else she's met, and she has to concentrate hard to understand his meaning.

The boy considers her for a moment. 'How old are you anyways? Fourteen?'

'I am sixteen,' she says quietly.

There is a brief pause.

'Talkative little thing, ain't you?' he mutters.

The alley opens onto another wide street. They pass junkyards, parades of shops, small, red-bricked houses with pointing roofs, and wooden ones with stoops and broken furniture outside. The world is lighter now and beginning to stir. Shutters are raised, cars drift past, people emerge from doorways. She moves by Bobby's side in a state of bemused detachment, and once again she feels the strange sense of unreality, as if she has stepped inside the hyper-colourful, too-loud world of a movie. Gradually, the streets they walk through become dingier. Garbage spills from trash cans, old paint crackles over window sills, shop fronts are cramped and uncared for. A plane flies low above their heads.

Bobby smiles, noticing her wide eyes. 'Welcome to Jamaica,' he says. The sky has lightened into a soft blue and the shining sun gathers conviction. Ahead of them some

138

construction workers drop a large sack from a high building and when it hits the ground an enormous cloud of cement dust explodes into the air, the sunlight making it sparkle gold against the blue. For a moment, the dull gnawing in her guts recedes a little and unconsciously she smiles while somewhere, in the depths of her brain, she hears a voice whisper, 'You are free.' She looks up, and is embarrassed to see that the boy is watching her, a strange expression on his face.

She wonders why the men were chasing him and as they walk she considers him from the corner of her eye. His clothes and hairstyle and jewellery are, she guesses, what Yaya would have called 'hip', but she notices that they are worn and made from cheap fabric and there is something about his outfit and his fast talk and jaunty manner that's at odds with the expression in his eyes and something else she senses in him, but can't quite define.

Eventually they come to a stop outside a high red brick tenement. She gazes up at the hundreds of tiny windows and reams of black, iron staircases that hang across the bricks like spider webs. Bobby pushes open a heavy brown door. Inside, the hallway is dark, the walls a graffiti-strewn green. She smells the faintly sour smell of the hot, still air. For a moment she hesitates.

'You coming?' Bobby says from the bottom of the stairwell. She glances behind her, then follows him.

'Elevator's bust,' he explains as they begin to

climb. On each floor a puddle of noise seeps from beneath a line of closed doors: a baby's cry, the thudding bass from a stereo, an unanswered telephone, a child's shriek, TV laughter, the voices of strangers. When they reach the sixth floor, Bobby leads her to a door marked 68. 'Come on in,' he says, turning keys in three different locks.

She finds herself in a narrow hallway.

'In here,' Bobby shows her into a small bedroom. The floor is almost entirely covered by a double mattress. In the corner a small wardrobe overflows with clothes. Next to the bed sits a cassette player and a pile of tapes. Every one of the grubby white walls is covered in posters of the same, small, dark-skinned man wearing a variety of flamboyant outfits. As she looks around her, her legs begin to sway with tiredness and her guts rumble noisily.

'Come on, I'll show you where you can get cleaned up, then I'll make us something to eat.'

She stares back at Bobby and feels a rush of gratitude and relief. 'Thank you,' she whispers.

The bathroom is small and windowless and smells of damp. An extractor fan, its slats covered in a thick layer of dust and little heaps of fluff, chugs feebly into action when she turns on the light. The tub, toilet and basin are a pale pink and around them the paintwork blisters with damp. On the shower rail and over the radiator hang a selection of drying panties and bras and on every surface is piled a dozen different types of half-used tubes of shampoo, razors clogged with rust and hair, greying slivers of soap. Five

140

toothbrushes sit in a dirty cup above the basin. Quickly she undresses and stands beneath the shower, letting the hot water wash away the grime of the past couple of days and nights. She stands under it for as long as she dares, but the evidence of strangers frightens her and she hurriedly dries herself with the towel Bobby gave her and gets dressed.

Her clothes, now that she's clean, are revolting to her; stained and stinking of the dumpsters she has just left. Looking in the small dirty mirror she notices with horror that her sweatshirt is stained with blood and she does her best to wash it off, using all her strength to force from her mind the image of Ingrid as she last saw her, prone and bleeding upon the floor. Opening the door, she darts quickly back across the hall.

In Bobby's small bedroom she tries to cover the washed-out blood stain with her hand but too late, he sees it, and just before he turns away their eyes meet for a second. But, 'Here,' is all he says, throwing her some baggy cotton pants and a T-shirt. 'Put these on.'

For a moment she hesitates, suddenly self-conscious.

'Oh, don't mind me,' he tells her. 'Trust me, honey. You ain't my type.' He winks and leaves the room, closing the door softly behind him.

When he returns a few minutes later he's carrying a plate of sandwiches. They sit on the mattress together to eat.

'You like Prince?' he asks her after a while, seeing her eyes scanning the posters as she crams a cheese sandwich into her mouth. She shrugs, and his jaw drops in amazement. 'You don't know Prince?' His voice is scandalised. 'Where you from, girl? Mars?' Within seconds he's on his feet and pressing a button on the tape player. Music fills the room, a man's high falsetto over a fast beat. 'Man, I love this one.' He begins to hop up and down and gyrate his narrow hips to the music while he sings along, *'Just need your extra time and your — ba-da-ba-da boom — KI-ISS!'* He puts his hands behind his head for a final thrust of his pelvis and despite everything, Elodie laughs.

Bobby stops dancing and stares back at her. 'Wow. You're actually quite something when you smile. You know that?'

He turns the tape off, and takes the plate from her while she stifles a yawn.

'Go on,' he tells her. 'Lie down and get some sleep.' He goes to the window and pulls the heavy blue curtains across the glass, shutting out the sunshine. 'Go ahead,' he nods. 'It's cool. We'll work out what to do with you later.'

She lies down, telling herself that she'll just rest for a moment. In the silence of the strange dark bedroom she remembers the toothbrushes and the underwear hanging in the bathroom and feels again a stab of anxiety at the thought of strangers sleeping on the other side of the thin, grubby walls. She closes her eyes tightly and curls up beneath the pink blanket Bobby had thrown over her, trying with all her might to push any thought of High Barn from her mind. At last she falls into oblivion.

* ★ *

Hours or minutes later the glare of a lamp shines in her eyes and Bobby is sat beside her in the bed. She struggles up with a start, suddenly anxious to have been asleep in the same bed as this stranger. After a few moments Bobby rubs his face and yawns, and then, turning and seeing that she's awake, says mildly, 'Hey, how're you doing?'

She smiles and nods, drawing the blanket under her chin. 'Good, thank you,' she tells him, and he smiles back at her sleepily.

Bobby scrabbles around next to the bed for a while and eventually locates a pack of cigarettes and a lighter. It is only then that she notices with a flush of embarrassment that he's naked from the waist up, and takes in his thin back, the fine, pale-brown, hairless skin, the bumps and spikes of his spine, his delicate neck as he bends to dip his cigarette into the flame. Across his shoulder is a large tattoo of a dragon, its wings moving as if to take flight whenever his muscles flex.

'Bobby?' she says tentatively.

He looks back at her. 'Yeah? What's up?'

'I just wanted to say thank you. I don't know what I would have done if — '

He exhales a long stream of cigarette smoke. 'Speak real nice, don't you?' He smiles. 'That's OK, kid. Couldn't just leave you there for those assholes to find.' A long moment passes in which he considers her seriously. 'Who're you running from, anyhow?'

Before she can answer they hear a door open

143

and close somewhere in the apartment, followed by a woman's voice, a clatter of crockery and a stereo bursting into life. Bobby gets up and stretches. 'Well, come on, you might as well meet the others.'

★ ★ ★

The woman standing by the kitchen table is vast and black and in her twenties. Everything about her is extraordinary to Elodie: her hair, which erupts from her head like molten lava in a million deep-red coils, her breasts, straining beneath tight, hot-pink Lycra, the three gold hoops hanging from each ear, the make-up in splashes of neon upon her dark-brown skin. She's wiping down the table when they walk in, and every movement she makes sets off slow ripples of flesh and a jangle of gold bracelets. Her nails are three inches long, elaborately varnished, their tips encrusted with tiny gems. She wears a diamond stud in her nose.

'Hi honey!' she calls to Bobby when she spots him. Her enormous voice is low and deep. When she spies Elodie hovering nervously in the doorway her hand pauses in mid-wipe and eyeing her from beneath turquoise lids she asks, 'Who's this?' Elodie can only stand and stare in amazement: it's as if an exotic bird of paradise had just swooped down from the sky and begun to make conversation with them.

'Elodie,' Bobby tells her. She notices with alarm that the woman's smile reveals a gold tooth like a pirate in one of the books Yaya used

144

to read to her. 'Elodie, this is Shanique,' says Bobby. 'And that's Darnel,' he adds, jerking his head towards the corner of the room.

It's only then that she notices the short black man wearing nothing but his underpants sitting in a chair by the window. He glances at her disinterestedly for a second before returning to a basketball game playing silently on a little TV on top of the refrigerator. As he watches, his head nods along to music playing on the stereo, a man shouting angrily above a repetitive beat. One hand rests upon the bulge of his belly and his fingers clasp a large, messy cigarette that emanates thick, yellow smoke, and Elodie recognises the sour, pungent smell as the same one she'd smelt when she first walked into the apartment.

And then, just as she's beginning to feel entirely out of her depth another girl walks into the cramped little kitchen. Shoving past Bobby she goes over to the refrigerator where she rummages bad-temperedly among its shelves. She is dressed in a short, silky nightdress and is small and slim but for her breasts which are perfectly round and high and entirely without movement. Her skin is a pale, creamy brown and her long dark hair is pulled back into a ponytail, away from her feline little face which, despite wearing a perpetually displeased expression as if the whole world smells bad to her, is the most beautiful Elodie has ever seen. At that moment she swings around and spots her for the first time. 'Who's that?' she demands, her pretty nose wrinkling in distaste. To Elodie it sounds like, '*Hoo dat?*'

'This is Elodie,' says Bobby. 'She's going to stay for a night or two.' There's something in his tone that tells Elodie he doesn't like the girl much.

She raises one delicate eyebrow. 'Oh yeah? Says who?' The ways she looks at Elodie makes her suddenly conscious of Bobby's too-large clothes, her messy hair and bare feet. 'Last time *I* looked the shelter was four blocks away.' Her voice has a scratchy, metallic quality that reminds Elodie of the noise a mosquito makes when it hits the blue neon bars of a Bug Buster. 'Where'd you find this one anyway? We ain't got room for your skanky waifs and strays.'

'Shut your mouth, Kiki,' snaps Bobby.

'Fuck you, we ain't got space.'

'She's staying in my room, so it ain't your business.'

The girl snorts. 'You into pussy now or something?' she mutters.

'OK,' Shanique says wearily, turning to put a dish into the sink. 'Quit it, both of you, or you'll wake Tyra.'

Elodie hovers nervously in the doorway, almost as terrified of Kiki as she is of being sent back out on the streets again.

Suddenly, however, Shanique smiles kindly at her. 'Why don't you come and sit down, honey?'

Darnel continues to stare mutely at the TV screen, sucking on his foul-smelling cigarette. Eventually, Kiki goes over to him and after shooting one more poisonous glance at Elodie, settles down to watch the game.

146

While Elodie perches nervously at the table Shanique grabs hold of Bobby and wraps him in her massive arms. 'Where'd you go last night, baby?' she asks him.

Bobby's muffled voice replies from somewhere deep between her breasts, 'Oh, you know, girl: Dancing, romancing. Getting laid . . . getting paid.' He frees himself and pulls out a roll of dollar bills from his back pocket. 'Getting rent.'

'Good boy.' She takes the roll of money and kisses him on the cheek. Just then, they hear the sound of a baby crying and she hurries away. Moments later, Darnel slowly lumbers to his feet too, grunts something indecipherable, and slopes after her.

When Shanique returns she has a plump little girl of about two tucked under her arm. The child has the same rich brown skin as Shanique and her hair is pulled into a dozen little sausages, each wrapped with a different coloured band. She picks up the child's podgy little fist and waves it at Elodie. 'Say hello, Tyra,' she says, while a phone begins to ring somewhere. 'Here,' she turns to Elodie and thrusts the baby at her. 'Hold her for a second will you?'

Elodie is so surprised to have a baby sitting on her lap that for a moment she can only sit and stare at her. Tyra stares back, her big brown eyes considering her gravely while she sucks determinedly on a pacifier. In her little lobes are tiny gold hoops. She's dressed in a diaper and an orange dress with Versace Baby written across the front in diamante studs. Tentatively, Elodie puts her arms around the child and pulls her closer, surprised at how comforting it is to hold the little warm body and breathe in her sweet, milky scent.

When Shanique returns she watches Elodie with her daughter for a moment. 'Hey, you're a natural. You mind holding her while I make up some formula?' She turns to Bobby. 'That was Wanda, she can't sit tonight.'

He rolls his eyes. 'You staying home?'

She sighs distractedly. 'I don't know. I gotta work, Bobby. I need the cash.'

He nods. 'Yeah, me too.'

They both turn to Kiki, who is humming to herself and gazing out of the window. Suddenly she turns and sees them looking at her. 'No way,' she snaps. 'You're both tripping if you think I'm staying home tonight.'

Elodie keeps her eyes on the child as Kiki stalks past her and out of the room. While Shanique and Bobby murmur together, her mind drifts back once again to her last moments at High Barn. An image pops into her mind of Ingrid lying slumped upon the floor and she closes her eyes for a moment against a dizzying wave of anxiety. *She'll be OK*, she tells herself. *Ingrid will be OK. Please, let her be OK.*

Just then, she's dragged from her thoughts by the appearance of a large, pale girl with stringy yellow hair walking into the kitchen and yawning extravagantly. 'Hey, Princess,' Shanique calls to her.

'This is Lorraine,' Bobby tells her, 'Only, we call her Princess, as in Princess Di, on account of her being from England.'

148

Princess turns her slow, watery gaze to Elodie for a moment, smiles vaguely, then says in a British accent to no one in particular, 'I just had the funniest dream.'

Her voice is thin and nasal and as she recounts her dream to the room the words seem weightless, drifting through the air without consequence. Her tone is monotone, the story endless. She seems to take no pleasure in the telling of it, as if she's compelled to let the stream of sounds emerge from her thin lips, each word so insubstantial that Elodie feels she's unable to hold on to any one of them. On and on and on they go. Unlike the quickfire of Bobby's speech, a rally of words that he seems to throw like a fistful of pebbles for you to catch, or the sonorous depths and shallows of Shanique's, or even Kiki's blistering outbursts, Princess's speech is like a puff of tepid air.

It takes some minutes for her to finish, which she does without any apparent climax to the story and with a slightly surprised expression, and as soon as the last word is out of her mouth, Elodie finds she cannot remember any part of what she's told them. The others, too, pause blinking and baffled in the silence that follows, before almost all at once they jerk back to life as if from a deep sleep and begin to talk again as if nothing had happened. After a while Princess gets to her feet and lumbers from the kitchen.

'Why don't you go and take your coffee to my room for a while?' Bobby says to Elodie then, gently lifting Tyra from her lap. 'Go ahead,' he says, smiling at her reassuringly.

* ★ ★

At first she sits obediently on the bed, sipping her coffee, aware that her fate is being decided on the other end of the hall. She tries to think clearly about what she'll do if they tell her to leave, but is incapable of picturing herself in the world alone. She puts her head in her hands and for a moment lets the fear wash over her. Her life with Ingrid had not prepared her for self-sufficiency. For all her yearning to be free from High Barn, it had been a vague, impractical longing without any real idea of how she'd actually survive by herself. Restlessly she gets up and pulls the curtains back from the small, dirty window. Below, the city reaches as far as she can see, a vast sea of roads and buildings and traffic, a world full of people living lives that have no place in them for her.

At last anxiety forces her to the door and softly opening it a few inches she puts her ear to the crack. The stereo has been turned off and the kitchen door is still open and she can just make out Bobby and Shanique's voices as they talk together at the kitchen table.

' . . . just sitting there behind a wall, a few blocks from the Junction,' she hears Bobby say.

'You think she's on the stroll?'

She hears Bobby's yelp of laughter. 'What do you think?' he says. 'You saw her Shan, she look like a hooker to you?'

'Well what you going to do with her? Kiki's right, there ain't no room here.'

There's a brief silence in which she feels her heart sink. At last she hears Bobby's voice again. 'She's just a kid,' he says. 'She'd last five minutes out there and if I take her to the shelter she'd be pimped out by Wednesday. We can put her up for a week can't we? Till I persuade her to go on home? Hey, she could even sit with Tyra tonight.'

'Oh, well, I don't know . . . '

The kitchen door is closed suddenly and she can hear no more. Dejectedly she returns to the bed and when Bobby at last comes for her, she keeps her face turned from him, not wanting him to see her desperation. 'Come on,' is all he says.

Back in the kitchen, Shanique spoons orange mush into her daughter's mouth. 'Sit down, honey,' she says. And then, her large brown eyes fixed upon her, asks, 'So, what's your story, girl? You gonna tell me what you're doing on the streets?'

Elodie looks down at her hands and doesn't answer.

Shanique shifts her enormous buttocks in her chair and says gently, 'What happened, kid? Something bad? Police after you?'

She shakes her head.

'Come on,' Bobby says. 'We ain't stupid. I see how you jump every time you hear a siren.' He raises his eyebrows at her. 'I see the blood all over your shirt, too.'

She stares back at him. 'I — ' she begins, but the prospect of reliving it all is too much for her. She stares helplessly back at him.

'OK,' he sighs after a long silence. 'Well, I got to take you to the shelter then.'

'No. Please, Bobby.' She feels the panic rise in her chest, sure that Ingrid will have called the police by now, certain that if they find her she'll be sent straight back to High Barn. Perhaps they'd even put her in prison for a while to punish her.

'OK, OK. Calm down. But you got to tell me what you're running from, Elodie. I can't help you otherwise.'

When she doesn't answer he sighs and goes over to the window and stands with his back to them, staring out at the sky.

Gently, Shanique reaches over and takes her hand. 'What happened, honey? Your daddy been messing with you?' Elodie stares back at her. 'Had a fight with your momma?' Shanique persists. 'Got yourself in trouble? Come on, angel, you can tell Shanique. You in the family way?'

Elodie has no idea what she's talking about, but there's something in her tone and expression that reminds her so much of Yaya that suddenly she can't hold her tears back any longer. She drops her head and begins to sob. After a moment she feels Shanique's arms around her. A comforting smell of coconut butter and cherries fills her nostrils. 'OK now,' the older woman says. 'OK now honey. That's all right. Come on now. You'll be OK.' For a few minutes they stay like that, the two of them, Shanique rocking Elodie in her arms. 'Why don't you tell me from the beginning?'

And so she does. She tells her everything. She tells her about the forest and how she'd found the man dead and ran all night until she reached the road. She tells her about the children's hospital and about coming to America and being taught to speak. She tells them about Ingrid and Robert and Anton, about the arguments, about Ingrid's anger and jealousy, and Robert's hatred for his wife, about the feeling she'd had of slowly suffocating, and how she had longed to escape from it all. She tells them because she has nothing left to lose.

Shanique and Bobby are staring at her open mouthed. 'Go on,' Bobby urges her. 'What happened next?'

'I didn't mean to do it,' she begins, her voice so quiet that they have to lean in closer to hear her. And then, taking a deep breath she describes her last moments at High Barn. How she'd walked past the kitchen and heard Ingrid call her name, how Ingrid had put her arms around her, begging her to stay. The overwhelming revulsion that had made her struggle from her grip, pushing her away. Ingrid falling backwards, slipping on the wine, Elodie reaching for her, snatching at empty air. The sight of her slumped and bleeding on the floor. Robert returning, and, then, finally, her decision to run.

'Shit,' whispers Bobby when she has finished. 'That's the most fucked up thing I ever heard.'

'I *saw* you,' says Shanique with hushed awe. 'On TV, I mean. Years ago. There was a special about you on the Discovery Channel. Shit girl. That was you?'

Mutely, Elodie shrugs. 'She'll be OK, won't

she?' she begs them then. 'The doctors at the hospital, they'd have taken care of Ingrid, wouldn't they?'

And then, her hand flying to her mouth with the sudden shock of realisation, Shanique speaks. 'Oh honey,' she tells her. 'That lady? Ingrid? Honey, that lady died.'

Dimly, as if from very far away, she hears Bobby ask Shanique something and then a distant, muffled response — some story about a radio at the hair salon. But she doesn't listen. *Ingrid is dead.* The sorrow fills her, clinging to each bone like black oil. Dimly, the idea of prison — what she knows about prison from the television — sends thin tendrils of fear snaking their way through her grief. After a while, she becomes aware that she's gasping for breath, feels the room swoop and rock and then a plunging dizziness. Somehow, suddenly, Bobby's arms are around her, lifting her up, pulling her back from the darkness, his voice calling her name. She is back, seated on her chair, the kitchen slowly easing its sickly dipping. At last her vision clears and she sees the worried faces of Shanique and Bobby gazing back at her. 'Oh please,' she whispers. 'Oh please, no.'

From very far away, she hears Shanique's voice talking to her. 'Listen, girl. You've got to get a hold of yourself,'

'I killed her,' she whispers.

'You pushed her,' replies Shanique firmly, putting one large, talloned hand on her shoulder. 'Hell, I'd have shoved that creepy bitch too if it'd

154

been me. You didn't mean to kill her. It was an accident. She slipped and fell and that ain't your fault.'

'But I didn't stay and help her,' says Elodie, her voice rising.

'Well, didn't I hear you say her husband was there?'

A silence falls heavy upon the kitchen, as each of them pursue their separate thoughts.

'Are you going to call the police?' Elodie asks at last, in a small voice.

'The police? Here?' Shanique chuckles and returns to her own seat. 'No, honey, me and the police ain't exactly on speaking terms.'

She and Bobby say nothing for a while longer, just continue staring at her as if she'd grown an extra head. But at last, Shanique rouses herself and all at once is brisk and businesslike. She gets up and fills the kettle.

'OK,' she says decisively. 'You can stay in Bobby's room for a while until we work something out. You can help mind Tyra for me until I find someone to replace that pain in the ass Wanda.'

'Really?' She feels a vague hope trickle through the darkness.

'For a little while at least. Shit, I can't send you back out on the street after a story like that.'

'What about the others?' Bobby asks Shanique.

She sucks her bottom lip for a while. 'Well, Kiki and Darnel never read a paper or watched the news in their lives, and Princess, she don't know what day of the week it is half the time.

Don't you worry,' she says firmly. 'You leave them to me.'

'Thank you,' Elodie whispers.

'Just for a week though,' Shanique warns her. 'I'm serious.'

15

But a week passes and then another. The fact of
Ingrid's death is like a stone lodged permanently
beneath her windpipe and each night she wakes
from shallow, jittery sleep, alert with panic, her
last moments at High Barn replaying in
sickening clarity over and over in her mind. Once
again she feels herself pushing Ingrid away,
watches her teeter, lose her balance, slip then
fall. By the second week, when yet again she
wakes, gasping and sobbing into the darkness,
she finds the light shining suddenly in her eyes
and sits up with a start to see Bobby kneeling
next to her, his eyes grave.

'Girl, you got to stop this,' he tells her.

She rolls away from him. 'I killed her,' she
moans into the pillow. 'I killed her, I killed her.'

At first Bobby doesn't reply, but after listening
to her cry for a while longer he turns the light off
and gets back into the bed next to her. At last he
begins to talk, his voice in the darkness quiet but
emphatic, and as her sobs subside, she begins to
listen.

'Elodie, there ain't one person living in this
apartment who hasn't done something they
regret,' he tells her. 'Trust me, we sure as hell
wouldn't be living like this if something hadn't
gone seriously fucking wrong somewhere down
the line. But the thing is, you got a choice. You

157

either let it eat you up and destroy the rest of your life, or you accept there's not one thing you can do about it now. You hear what I'm saying, Elodie? Don't keep doing this to yourself. The lady slipped. She's dead and nothing's going to change that now.'

In the darkness Elodie lies awake for a long time, thinking about what he's said. And little by little she feels the burden of her guilt begin to change. Gradually, she feels the painful obstruction in her chest loosen, and from that moment the fact of Ingrid's death and her part in it becomes instead like a poison in her bloodstream; an integral and permanent part of her. 'She's dead, and nothing's going to change that now,' Bobby had said. When moments later he puts his arm around her and tells her to go to sleep, she finds that she can. And when she wakes the next morning she's touched to find that Bobby's arm's still there.

★　★　★

At first she keeps to Bobby's room, but as the days wear on and she finds herself looking after Tyra more and more, she begins to venture out from the tiny bedroom, creeping into the kitchen or the living room when she's sure that she's alone. The world of the apartment is soporific and unchanging, as if suspended in its own reality. It floats, high above the streets, warm and cramped and a little smelly, held snugly between the apartments on either side, the noises of unseen lives seeping through the walls. She is encased, secure, hidden. And yet, each day she waits for disaster, for the moment when she'll be asked to leave.

At last she steels herself to talk to Bobby, only for him to wave her concerns away dismissively. 'You any idea how much childcare costs these days?' he asks. 'And it ain't like you eat much.'

Perhaps, she thinks, she'll be allowed to stay here forever, buffered from the world, suspended forever in midair, high above the consequences of what she's done.

She soon notices that the others seem to work the strangest hours, leaving at nine or ten at night and not returning until five in the morning, when they disappear into their rooms until the afternoon. At these times she'll often take Tyra with her to the small living room, where together they play with building blocks or the child's cuddly animals, one eye always on the TV.

Every evening, before they leave, Shanique, Princess and Kiki emerge from their bedrooms and begin the intriguing process of preparing for the night ahead. As the weeks pass, Elodie begins to look forward to these nightly routines, often sitting quietly in the kitchen with Tyra on her lap while music pumps from the stereo and the three of them run back and forth between their rooms and the bathroom, creating a stink of hairspray and perfume, singed hair and deodorant. When at last they are preened and dressed in Lycra and stilettos, they congregate around the kitchen table with their cosmetics and their vodka, setting about

159

the business of making up their faces.

Elodie sits, watching from her corner of the kitchen as they transform their faces, soaking up with wide-eyed envy the camaraderie between the three women. Even Kiki, who usually reminds Elodie of a wasp caught in a jar, loses some of her spikiness and joins in the party atmosphere, refilling glasses and lending her mascara. Elodie always feels a little sorry for Princess however, who never seems to achieve quite the same end result as the other two. Whereas Kiki and Shanique, when they're finally ready, look to Elodie like beautiful, exotic creatures straight from a television ad, Princess somehow manages only to accentuate her plainness. On her pasty, spotty skin the make-up seems to slide and gather in little blotchy pools of grease, and her wide thighs and lumpen flesh seems to squirm unpleasantly beneath her miniskirt. It's clear, though, that Princess doesn't share Elodie's concern, always studying her reflection with a beatific smile, the same one she always wears.

And Elodie is careful, always, not to draw attention to herself. Kiki rarely acknowledges her and Elodie understands that she must, for some reason, have accepted Shanique's decision to let her stay, but every so often she'll look up to find Kiki's cool, assessing gaze upon her, and she'll hurriedly turn away, an uneasy, shivery feeling creeping up her spine.

'Kiki doesn't want me here,' she confides to Bobby one evening.

'So what?' he replies. 'She's got no say in it

160

anyway. This place's in Shanique's name.'

'She hates me,' persists Elodie, flatly. 'And I don't know why.'

'She hates everyone,' replies Bobby in a bored tone. 'Quit worrying about it.'

Elodie drops the subject, but something tells her that Kiki's dislike comes from a deeper instinct she can't begin to fathom. And so she continues to keep out of her way, and hope that Kiki never acts upon it.

★ ★ ★

Every night, once the three women are finally ready, they leave the apartment in a flurry of last-minute phone calls, lost purses and hurried goodbyes. At some point just before or after they go, Bobby always leaves abruptly on his own, announcing he has business to see to and giving a distracted wave. It's strange, the quiet and stillness of the place after everyone has left. She busies herself with bathing Tyra, feeding her and putting her down for the night the way Shanique has taught her, and then she waits for the silence and emptiness of the apartment to descend.

At first, thoughts of Ingrid refuse to let her be, returning like a flurry of hungry crows to peck and peck away at her mind at odd and unexpected moments. Or else she'll be hit, suddenly, with a flashback so vivid it slams into her with the force of a punch, leaving her shakey and sick. Alone in the apartment she forces these images from her mind and ponders instead the lives of the strangers she has so unexpectedly

161

found herself amongst.

She puzzles over where it is they go to at night. She often hears them mention a place called Pinkies, and wonders if it's perhaps a restaurant — a strange sort of restaurant that's open all through the night. She wonders too about Darnel, whose role in the apartment and relationship with the others she can't quite determine. Bobby has told her that he's Tyra's father, but often she'll see him shuffling bleary-eyed from Kiki's bedroom, sometimes from Princess's. Wherever he goes he's followed by the pungent smell of the green herbs he rolls into his cigarettes and his eyes are perpetually half-closed and slightly bloodshot. When he speaks, which isn't often, it's in a slow, quiet mumble, as if he's always just on the verge of falling asleep. But still, Elodie detects a quiet intelligence there; something sharper lying beneath the outward show of sleepiness.

What fascinates her most is the subtle way in which the others change whenever he's around. It's as if they become less, somehow, she notices. Like colours left out too long in the rain. The very essence of Shanique — her loud, rich voice, the way she seems to fill a room all by herself, her physical brightness — fades. When Darnel is nearby, everything in her is focussed on him. She fusses around him, fixing him snacks, fetching him cushions, massaging his shoulders, her voice taking on a sing-song, soothing tone, 'You OK, baby, anything I can get you baby? You look tired, why don't I fix you a sandwich?' Sometimes Elodie half expects her to pick him

162

up, throw him over her shoulder and burp him, the ways she does with Tyra.

Kiki, too. When she speaks to Darnel it's as if she's poured a thick layer of syrup over her voice. Her corrosive tongue, mocking eyes and tightly coiled demeanour are concealed beneath a cloud of fluttering eyelids, sickly-sweet smiles and flirtatious pouts. As if she, too, has left the point of herself in the next room, along with her cell phone, purse and cigarettes.

Even Bobby who ordinarily is never still — continuously drumming his fingers on the table, swirling Tyra around the kitchen, dancing along to the stereo, fighting with Kiki — is subdued when Darnel's around. Only Princess remains the same, the dazed eyes never changing, nor the meandering, dreamy voice. And through it all, Darnel remains impassive, sucking on his reefer, staring with half-closed eyes at the TV screen, accepting their attentions like a flame accepts moths.

It is these things Elodie ponders when she's alone in the apartment at night.

★　★　★

'They're hookers,' Bobby tells her, when she asks one afternoon.

Hookers. Elodie mulls the word over for a moment or two.

'Prostitutes?'

'Oh,' she says. 'Prostitutes.' She has learnt about prostitutes from the TV.

The two of them are in his room, listening to

David Bowie, whom he likes almost as much as Prince, while Bobby gets ready for the night ahead. He glances at her and, putting down his tub of hair wax, sits next to her on the bed.

'See, Darnel's their . . . manager, yeah? He owns Pinkie's, which is where they all operate from. Well, Kiki works in a titty bar in Manhattan too, which is why she thinks the sun shines out of her crack, but mainly they all work for Darnel.'

He gets up again, and peering into the mirror, resumes applying wax to his hair, teasing it into stiff peaks with expert precision. 'Shanique's his babymomma, so she's his number one, but it don't mean much.' He turns and looks at her seriously. 'The thing you have to remember with Darnel is, he ain't as stupid as he looks. He ain't bad, trust me, he's an OK guy compared to most, but you wouldn't want to fuck with him, put it that way.'

She takes it all in, or at least, tries to. 'And you?' she asks politely.

He doesn't look at her. 'Oh, kinda, you know . . . I dance at a club down town,' he tells her vaguely. 'It don't pay too well, though.' He shrugs, avoids her eye. 'Sometimes I need to find money other ways.'

She nods at this, aware by his tone that he's hinting at something else, but has no idea what it is. 'Oh,' she says vaguely.

'I'm saving up to go to classes, though. Dancing and acting, that sort of thing.' He turns and looks at her. 'This ain't what I'm going to be doing the rest of my life.'

'You're a wonderful dancer,' she tells him, glad to be on firm ground again.

He smiles. 'You think so?' he asks her.

'Yes,' she says, 'I really do.'

★ ★ ★

The weeks pass, and still, no mention is made of her leaving. At first her gratitude and relief is so great that she ignores the first soft tendrils of doubt. When she tries to imagine her future, she finds that she cannot. Sometimes, waking in the morning and faced with another day stretching ahead of her in the confines of the small apartment, some of the old claustrophobia and hopelessness of High Barn returns.

'Do you mind me staying in your room?' she asks Bobby.

'Nope. I'm hardly there.'

'What about Shanique? Do you think she wants me to leave?'

Bobby smiles. 'Look, don't worry about it. We like having you here. Tyra's crazy about you and anyway, Shanique's never happier than when she's saving someone's ass, trust me.'

Elodie smiles too at this. Even during the short time she's known them she has come to love Shanique and Bobby. Her favourite times are spent alone with them in the kitchen, drinking coffee, playing with Tyra and listening to them talk. She enjoys the closeness between them, and it touches her how generously they include her in their friendship.

The first time she sees Shanique laugh, she

165

can only stare in open-mouthed amazement, and no matter how many times she witnesses it again, the sight, she is sure, is something she'll never tire of. It begins with the faintest quiver of the lips, a gentle flaring of the nostrils, followed by a low warning gurgle. As the sound crescendos, the lip-quivers are joined by shoulder tremors and chin wobbles, her chest heaving and falling until at last she throws back her head, her breasts and belly undulating, her shoulders and arms shaking and jiggling and finally, with tears streaming down her face, she gives herself up to an almost deafening, tooth-rattling Wuh-ha-ha-ha-ha-ha-ha that fills every corner of the apartment and has the neighbours banging on the walls.

But sometimes, the way Bobby and Shanique talk to each other confuses her. It's like a rapidly flowing river that's impossible to keep up with, full of slang and private jokes, innuendos and nicknames, and everything said at double speed. She notices that Shanique sometimes calls Bobby 'Girlfriend' or 'Miss Thing', or 'Roberta', even though he's a boy. She says these things in an affectionate, jokey kind of way, and yet, Elodie is sure, she doesn't say them to Darnel. There's something she doesn't understand, something being said that she doesn't grasp and she watches the two of them with a perplexed frown, wondering what it means.

★　★　★

166

The part of the day she least enjoys are the hours when they're all in bed, locked in the private world of sleep behind their bedroom doors. Often, Shanique will take Tyra in with her and Elodie will wander listlessly between the living room and the kitchen, killing time until they all wake again. Sometimes even the living room is out of bounds to her, as she'll suddenly stumble upon Darnel passed out on the couch, his fat, sleeping fingers trailing on the carpet, his wet farts escaping into the warm air, the grunts and groans of a pornographic film competing with his snores.

Sometimes Elodie whiles away her afternoons in Princess's bedroom, tucked up with the fat English girl beneath her lilac comforter, surrounded by her collection of cuddly toys and watching a British TV show called EastEnders on BBC America.

'That one's Pauline, and that one's Pat,' Princess tells her, helping herself to another pill from a large jar on the bedside table and absent-mindedly passing one to Elodie. 'And that's the Queen Vic.'

Elodie smiles and shakes her head at the proffered pill.

'That's Sharon,' says Princess, perking up and pointing to a large blonde girl. 'Pretty, ain't she?'

She turns to Elodie and says, 'My dad says I look like her a bit, but I don't think so, do you?' She eyes Elodie hopefully. 'Do you think she looks like me, Elodie?'

'A little,' Elodie lies and is rewarded with a delighted grin.

'Want one?' Princess asks her, once again passing her the jar of assorted capsules, tablets and pills.

'No, thanks, Princess,' Elodie replies, for the seventh time that day.

Mostly though, she spends these lonely hours staring out of the kitchen window, across to the tenements opposite, or at the lone figures trailing across the scrublands far below. At night she'll wake at 3 or 4 or 5 a.m., and listen to the sounds of the city below. It calls to her. She lies on her back and looks up at the ceiling and listens to the roar of other people's air con, music from car stereos, strangers shouting to each other in the street, their voices floating up towards her window like pieces of burnt paper. She watches as distant headlights illuminate the ceiling like the flashing eyes of some great, purring, waiting beast.

At last she stops Bobby just as he's about to go out one evening. The girls are still getting ready, Tyra gurgling happily in her high chair.

'Take me with you,' she says.

'What? No way, Elodie, you know I can't. Shanique don't want the police spotting you and following you back here, sticking their noses in Darnel's business.'

'Please, just to the corner of the street? I'll come straight back, I promise.'

'No. Maybe the police are looking for you, maybe they ain't, but it's not worth the risk.' Bobby shakes his head and puts on his jacket.

She looks back at him, her eyes pleading.

At last he sighs. 'Jesus. OK, OK.' Bobby runs

his fingers through his black fin of hair and casts a critical eye over her. 'Not like that, though.' He turns and rummages through his closet. 'Here,' he says, flinging an oversized, hooded sweatshirt at her. 'Put this on.' He goes to his chest of drawers. 'And these,' he passes her a pair of sunglasses.

She puts them on, the hood pulled down low, the enormous, 70s-style lenses half obscuring her face.

Bobby surveys her, 'Well,' he says with a smile, 'you look like a flicking bug, but at least you don't look like you.'

She smiles back, excitement nudging through the strange, deadening languor that has crept over her during the past few weeks.

'You can walk me to the subway, and then you gotta come straight home,' Bobby tells her as they leave the apartment and make their way down the six flight of stairs.

Emerging into the street she feels a sudden rush of relief, as if she'd been holding her breath for a long time without realising it. As they move away from the apartment blocks and past rows of houses and shops she breathes in the warm, sweet-smelling May air and smiles. Walking close to Bobby she watches as the passers-by rush home beneath the darkening sky, the storekeepers shutting up shop for the night, groups of kids gathering around their cars, music blaring from their stereos. She and Bobby talk little as she stares around her, wide-eyed behind the dark glasses, anxious not to miss a thing. Too soon they come to the subway and reluctantly she says goodbye to Bobby, watching him disappear into the station before turning and slowly making her way back home. She takes her time, drinking in every detail: the rust on a fire hydrant, the face of a child sitting on a step, a scrap of paper drifting across an empty basket ball court, the vibrant green of a passing truck.

From then on, the world outside calls to her like an impatient child. Every evening she dresses in Bobby's sweatshirt and glasses and walks him the few blocks to the subway. Gradually they begin leaving earlier and earlier, taking a longer, more circuitous route each time.

And soon she begins to look forward to being alone with Bobby as much as she does the chance to escape the apartment. She likes to listen to him. He never talks about his past, or where he's going to that night, instead he tells her about his plans for the future, his dream of being famous one day, of being rich and buying a big house in Beverly Hills. 'Like they have on Cribs. We could all live there together,' he tells her, his eyes bright. 'Me, you, Shanique and Tyra.' He shakes his head. 'Fuck, man,' he says wistfully. 'Wouldn't that be fierce?'

She likes to watch him when he talks like this, and thinks how handsome he is, his face so animated, his huge black eyes so bright beneath their long lashes. Over the weeks she feels something strengthen between the two of them she can't quite put her finger on, something that has started to linger there in the gaps between their words. 'I like talking to you, Elodie,' he tells her often. 'You make me feel, I don't know, calm

170

or something,' he laughs. 'Feel like I could tell you anything.'

One day, to her surprise, she finds herself wondering what it would be like to touch the soft dark skin of his neck. These thoughts startle her, and she pushes them away. But she likes to watch him and see the quiet stillness at the heart of his nervous energy, and sometimes, when he looks back at her, she feels almost as if she were touching him after all.

Occasionally when she's alone and holds their friendship to the light, her blood quickens, just a little; her heart beats a little faster. And sometimes she will look up and find his eyes upon her and she will see something mirrored there, as light and fine as spider's silk. For only a second their eyes will meet and in that moment the air between them will thicken, quicken, before they both glance away, and talk of other things.

Often on their daily walks he'll tell her stories about the others. 'Princess?' he says one day. 'She came over from England with big dreams and some dumbass guy who dumped her as soon as her feet touched JFK. Thought she was going to be in the movies, but instead she wanders from one shitty bar job to the next. Thing is, she starts getting a little too free and easy with the party powder. Sooner or later she runs out of money, can't even get the plane home to mommy.

'Then one night, some guy at the bar she works at tells her how she can make a few bucks, if you know what I mean. Then this same guy tells her he's going to be her manager, tells her he's going to take her to Hollywood, but she's just got to turn one more trick first, so as to get the bus fare and all.' He snorts with derision. 'So she borrows some money off him to get herself set up, then a little more so she can buy a bit of coke to make it bearable, then she has to give him a cut of what she earns. Sooner or later she's in too deep, owing money all over the place, and Hollywood? Hollywood's forgotten.' They turn the corner. 'She's clean now, though,' Bobby continues. 'Shanique won't allow that shit around Tyra, so instead Princess spends her life popping pills instead. 'Ludes, Valium, Ritalin. You seen her jar of candy, right?'

'But couldn't she have just run away from the man?'

Bobby snorts. 'Run away? These motherfuckers have friends all over the city. She ain't got the brains to dodge them and they'd kick her black and blue soon as blink, or worse.' They cross the street, the subway just in sight. 'Anyway, Princess's guy gets sick of her eventually, and sells her onto Darnel, which is probably the best thing that's ever happened to the poor dumb bitch, but now she has to work off the money Darnel spent buying her. And so it goes, Elodie honey. And so it goes.' He shakes his head. 'Funny thing is, she's Darnel's biggest earner. Bigger than Kiki, even.' He shakes his head and smiles. 'Turns out she's got some talent after all.'

And then, one day to her surprise he says with sudden, anxious frankness, 'You know I'm just like them, don't you Elodie?'

She looks back at him blankly. Watches him colour and shift his gaze before finally mumbling, 'I go with men for money too.'

She frowns. 'Go where?'

'Jesus, Elodie.' They walk in silence for a bit. Eventually he tries again.

'You know about hookers, right?' he asks.

She shrugs, nods, and he looks away as he tells her, 'Well, men do that too. With other men.'

She thinks about what she knows of sex. The pornographic films Darnel watches and which she views only in quickly stolen glances, brief snapshots of a mechanical clarity that both excites and terrifies her. She thinks about a TV show she watched once, where two men kissed and held each other's hands. She thinks about the nameless longing she had felt at High Barn. She looks up, and notices that Bobby is watching her expectantly, his eyes worried.

'Oh,' she says. 'OK.'

She smiles at him, and holds his gaze until he returns her smile then ducks his head once more.

Whenever they part, he touches her lightly on the shoulder and says goodbye. She feels his fingers there long after she has returned to the apartment. Sometimes she'll be sitting in the kitchen, playing with Tyra and realise with a start that she has spent the last ten minutes thinking about his eyes.

★ ★ ★

Occasionally, when the others are asleep and Tyra is safely tucked up with Shanique, and she can no longer fight her impatience to be outside, she'll creep out of the apartment alone. Each time, she ventures a little further, unable to resist walking just one more block. When she returns to the apartment the city seems to call plaintively after her as she loiters on the sidewalk for as long as she dares before reluctantly turning to the heavy, brown peeling door and allowing the dark hot walls to claim her once more.

One day she returns from roaming the streets to find Shanique and Tyra sitting in the kitchen waiting for her. Two sets of disapproving brown eyes watch her as she takes her place at the table. Her heart sinks. She knows that Shanique hates her leaving the apartment by herself. 'What if you're recognised?' she has asked her more than once. 'Trust me, that would not go down well with Darnel. He has certain . . . business concerns he don't want the police sticking their noses into. If the cops spot you walking down the street and follow you back here, we're all fucked, for real.'

'Hey, Shanique,' she says weakly now. 'Everything OK?'

But instead of the dressing down she'd been expecting, Shanique gets up with a heavy sigh, and, putting Tyra in her highchair, goes over to Elodie, takes her chin in her hand and surveys her critically with narrowed eyes.

'Well,' she says at last, 'if you must keep running around outside all the time, we'd better

174

do something about this hair of yours.'

Ten minutes later, she finds herself sitting with a towel wrapped around her shoulders, while Shanique stands behind her with a pair of scissors in one hand, a fistful of her hair in the other, and a determined look on her face.

Princess, Bobby and Tyra sit across from them, watching wide-eyed.

'I don't usually like white-girls' hair,' Shanique tells her thoughtfully, letting a long strand fall between her fingers. 'Always thought there was something kinda . . . droopy about it.' She strokes Elodie's with a look of wonder on her face. 'But this is beautiful.' She picks up another handful. 'And the colour! Man, the colour's fierce. Like leaves in fall, or something.'

'Very poetic,' observes Bobby dryly. But, when Shanique raises her scissors to make the first cut, Elodie notices him wince and hide his eyes behind his fingers.

Elodie stares at her reflection in the little mirror Princess has propped up for her on the table. 'Cut it!' she whispers urgently, her eyes focussed on the blades. As Shanique makes the first snip and she sees one long, auburn chunk fall to the floor, she feels a surge of exhilaration.

'I can't watch,' says Bobby, his head sinking to the table.

An hour later Elodie emerges from the bathroom with Shanique, the stench of peroxide still in her nostrils, a towel draped over her head. Bobby and Princess eye her expectantly.

'Let's have a look then,' urges Princess.

Elodie and Shanique turn to each other and

175

smile. 'You ready?' Shanique asks her. When Elodie nods, she leans over and snatches the towel from her head with a flourish.

'Holy shit,' whispers Bobby.

'Blimey,' says Princess.

Elodie picks up the little mirror and stares back at her reflection, gingerly putting a hand to the shorn, yellow locks. Shanique's face looms behind her.

'Your eyes look enormous,' she says thoughtfully. 'Bluer.' She smiles. 'You look cute, honey. Like a cute little boy.'

At that moment, Kiki walks into the kitchen. Spying Elodie, she stops in her tracks, her customary sneer replaced by a pantomime display of incredulity. 'Hell,' she says. ' '*Boy*' is right.' She cackles spitefully. 'Damn, Elodie, you better watch your back when Bobby's around,' she nudges Shanique with her elbow, hugely enjoying her own joke. 'Might not be able to keep his hands off you.'

She goes over to the refrigerator, still laughing, while Shanique sucks her teeth disapprovingly and tells her to shut up. Nobody notices the look that passes between Elodie and Bobby then; the fraction of a second where their eyes meet like an electric shock, the way they hurriedly drop their gaze again.

★ ★ ★

Elodie wakes the following morning with an impatience in her belly that she can barely contain. That afternoon, when she walks with

176

Bobby to the subway as usual, she stops him just before he turns into the station's entrance. 'I want to come with you,' she tells him.

'Oh god, don't do this to me.' He shakes his head. 'It ain't safe. Queens is one thing, but . . . it just ain't safe.' He catches her look of disappointment and continues more gently, 'Look, Elodie, we don't know if the police are after you or not. Chances are they'll know that what happened to Ingrid was nothing but an accident. But it ain't worth the risk. Plus they'd put you in care. Trust me, honey, you go on back home.'

'Bobby,' she stares back at him, tears of frustration in her eyes. 'I spent nearly four years locked up in that place. I did nothing without Ingrid's say-so, saw no-one she didn't want me to see. Please. I need to do this. I need to see further than the same four blocks every day. Take me with you.'

She holds Bobby's gaze until at last he sighs and rolls his eyes in defeat. 'All right, already,' he says. 'Jesus.' He puts an arm round her and together they walk into the subway. 'Thought *I* was the drama queen around here.'

*   *   *

From then on, she and Bobby ride the number seven train into Manhattan every day, parting company as soon as they emerge from the darkness onto the sunlit sidewalk. She knows better than to ask Bobby where he goes each evening, and he always disappears swiftly, without a backward glance, leaving her to navigate the surging streets alone.

She soon discovers something extraordinary about the faces that she sees in the flashing yellow gloom of the subway train, or lost among the sea of other faces beneath the looming Manhattan buildings: they all share the same, blank, inward-looking gaze; the same unseeing eyes. Nobody, not one, gives her a second glance. With this realisation comes a surge of exhilaration. She especially loves the subway ride into Manhattan, the way the train soars high above the various districts of Queens before rumbling down beneath the streets. At first, when she emerges from whichever subway stop they have chosen that day, she never ventures further than a few blocks, anxiously memorizing each landmark so she can find her way back again. Gradually though, she casts her net wider as the corner of another block, and then another, calls to her. Slowly, piece by piece, she gets to know the city, finding that she has an instinctive sense of direction, an innate ability to find her way.

Blocks and blocks she walks that long, hot, close summer, the whole grid, from Greenwich Village to the Upper East Side, from China Town to Liberty Harbor, the roar of the subway escaping from grilles beneath her feet, her nostrils filling with the smells of the city. Along the Hudson, over Brooklyn Bridge. She walks with such certainty it's as if she's back there in the heart of the forest again, the skyscrapers her trees. At Times Square she stands and gazes up at the glass and steel, the neon signs floating in the soft twilight. She walks the length of Broadway to Central Park and wanders beneath its leafy ceiling, the trees filled with birdsong, the perimeter edged by patient skyscrapers which gaze down at the green undulating bowl like beasts around a lake.

Fall arrives, abruptly seeing off the summer warmth. One morning just before dawn, Elodie is woken by Bobby returning as usual from his night out alone in the city. She's used to him waking her like this, to stirring from her sleep while he carefully and quietly slips beneath the covers to lie next to her, his breathing almost instantly becoming slower and deeper as he sinks into unconsciousness. But recently, something new has crept into the space between them and more and more often now they'll lie awake for a while, side by side, without touching, their eyes closed, each pretending to be asleep; each pretending not to listen to the other's breathing.

This particular night Bobby is noisier than usual when he comes in. She listens to him undress, hears a sharp gasp of pain when he pulls himself free from his T-shirt. When he crawls into bed next to her he lets out a sudden whimper.

She sits up and turns on the lamp. 'Bobby,' she says, blinking in the sudden glare. 'Are you OK?' No sooner has she said the words than her eyes take in properly the state of Bobby's face. He stares up at the ceiling while she itemises the damage, the bruised cheek, the bloodied lip, the half-closed eye that's already turning a deep and angry purple.

'What happened to you, Bobby?' she asks, dismayed.

He doesn't answer, but a tear slides out of the corner of his swollen eye.

'Bobby,' she repeats, 'please tell me! Are you OK?'

When he speaks, his voice is tight with anger. 'Got jumped,' is all he says, and still he won't look at her. 'Happens, sometimes.'

Gently she lifts the pink blanket and gives a little gasp. His ribs, too, are covered in bruises. She lies down next to him again, her eyes fixed anxiously on his face.

'Why, Bobby?' she whispers. 'Who did this to you?'

He turns on his side, his back to her. 'Fuck, Elodie. I'm so sick of this. I'm just so fucking sick and tired of it.'

She switches the lamp off and reaching over, begins to stroke his hair. He starts to cry, then. She moves closer to him and after a moment's hesitation, puts her arms around him. After a while he begins to talk.

'I'm nineteen next month,' he tells her. 'Which makes it four years since I been working the streets.' He turns on his back and stares up at the thin sliver of moonlight squeezing through the curtains.

'When I was fourteen I got into drugs pretty bad. Been drinking with some older guys for a while anyway. Pretty soon I got to like getting high so much I couldn't ever seem to steal enough to pay for it. Then one day, this guy I know offers me fifty bucks for a blow job. Fifty bucks! All that money for what my stepdad had been taking for free anyway. I didn't need to think too long about it. Pretty soon I got a nice little collection of customers. I looked young for my age, even then — you get more work that way.'

Elodie doesn't say a word, just continues to stroke his hair.

'Pretty soon I'm high on everything I can get my hands on — coke, crack, you name it — and letting strangers fuck me every day just to pay for it. After a while my mom cottoned on to what I was doing and threw me out. So I started living on the streets. I was fifteen — getting picked up by the police every week and sent off to care. Each time they picked me up, I just ran away again. One day Shanique finds me half bleeding to death behind a dumpster after some local fag-haters decided to teach me a lesson. I'd known Shanique all my life, since we were kids, but she left the neighbourhood before me. She was already one of Darnel's girls, hooking for him, so she brings me home with her, gets me off the drugs. If it weren't for Shanique I'd be dead by now, most likely.' He turns onto his side so that he's facing her and they stare at each other for a long time. 'One day I'll get out of this,' he tells her seriously. 'I've been saving up. Going to start going to auditions, maybe join some classes, you know?'

She nods, and they continue to lie there, not speaking or moving. At last she reaches over and very gently strokes the soft skin of his cheek, then lets her fingers trail slowly over his jaw, hovering over the fresh growth of stubble there, before moving on to trace the outline of his lips. She hears her name catch in his throat and her fingers halt for a moment, a clear current passes between them, the moment glimmers and fills the room. She doesn't think about what she does next. Very slowly she leans over and puts her lips to the skin next to his swollen eye, then to his bruised cheek, and finally to his cut and bloodied mouth. For a second, just for a second, it seems that he won't respond, and then at last with a sudden, swift movement he pulls her to him.

His lips are hot and soft; surprising and thrilling, and when his tongue touches hers it brings electric shockwaves of something dark and terrifying and almost unbearably exciting. Soon there's no thought; only the need to feel his naked skin next to hers; his body in her hands, and her urgency is matched by his. When he pulls her free of her shirt she shudders with relief. They lie for a long time, their lips and fingers exploring each other. And then his slim hips are moving with hers, her fingers stroking the bumps and hollows of his back, urging his small, slender buttocks closer until she feels the sudden sharp shock of pain, and then, at last, the surprise of him moving inside her, the building pleasure of it, the final release. Finally they fall apart, their fingers still entwined and it feels as if her whole, breathless body remains filled with the scent and touch of him and a lingering amazement. Bit by bit their sweat cools, their breath slows, and he raises her fingers to his lips.

'Elodie?' he whispers after a long silent moment.

'Yes?'

'You ever do that before?'

'No,' she says.

He doesn't say anything else, for a while, until, 'Me either.'

They smile in the darkness.

16

It's a few months later that Kiki finally makes her move. Christmas and New Year have passed and Elodie has been at the apartment for almost a year. She's woken one night by the bedroom door opening, light and music and voices flooding in from the hall. She sits up, blinking at the figure silhouetted in the doorframe.

'Kiki?' she asks, shielding her eyes in surprise.

'Wakey wakey, Elodie.' Kiki takes a step further into the room, where she stands for a moment, swaying slightly.

'Kiki? What are you doing in here? Is Tyra OK?' Nervously Elodie flounders around until she finds the lamp, and switching it on, takes in Kiki's dishevelled appearance, the make-up smudged across her face, the cat-like eyes unfocussed and glittering.

'Come on, Elodie, pretty little Elodie.' She smiles and stumbles closer to the bed. She bends and with a sudden swipe manages to grab hold of Elodie's wrist. Sharp nails dig into her skin as she's yanked up out of the bed. 'Got some friends who want to meet you,' Kiki slurs in her scratchy voice.

'Kiki, let me go.' As she's dragged across the hallway she hears Tyra begin to wail. 'Please, Kiki,' she begs, 'let me go.'

But Kiki drags her into the living room, where

184

Elodie finds herself in the presence of four men, two sprawled on the couch and two in the armchairs, bottles of beer around their feet, the air heavy with smoke. Music blasts from the stereo while one of Darnel's porn movies plays on the TV screen. She stands in the doorway, desperately tugging at her T-shirt with her free hand to pull it further down over her hips. She tries to back out but Kiki gives another violent yank on her wrist and pulls her into the room.

'This is Elodie,' announces Kiki as she shoves her onto the couch between the two men. She goes over and seats herself on the lap of one of the others, picks up a bottle of vodka and takes a long gulp. Her glinting eyes are fixed on Elodie's face. 'She's going to party with us a while. About time she found herself a boyfriend, ain't that right, girl?'

Sitting stiffly on the couch, Elodie nervously looks around the room. The two men sat next to her seem, thankfully, more interested in a little pipe they are passing jealously back and forth across her. It seems to be made from a little glass bottle, filled with a white sickly-smelling smoke that twirls within the glass until it's inhaled by their eager, sucking lips. As each one takes a hit, the other waits impatiently for his turn, one eye fixed all the while on the sweating, heaving bodies on the screen in front of them.

But, like Kiki, the other two men don't take their eyes off Elodie.

'Kiki, I've got to go and see to Tyra.' She makes a move to get up but the venom in Kiki's voice pins her to the spot.

'Quit whining. You ain't gonna be impolite to my friends, are you?'

'She one of Darnel's?' asks the one Kiki's not sitting on.

Kiki laughs. 'No, she too good for that, ain't that right, Elodie?'

Elodie shakes her head. 'No.' The man continues to eyeball her while he slugs from his bottle of beer, so she turns away from him, and notices that Kiki's man has eased the strap of Kiki's dress down to expose her left breast, which he's now pummelling with his fingertips. Kiki, her eyes still on Elodie, begins to kiss him. Next, the man slides his hand up her thigh until the skirt rides up over her hips. Elodie lowers her gaze to the floor.

After a while Kiki stops kissing him and, smiling sweetly at Elodie, says, 'Why don't you go keep Kenny company?' She jerks her head at the other man.

Elodie shakes her head and the room is silent for a few moments.

Then the man called Kenny says to Kiki, 'No. Why don't *you* come over here and give me some head?'

The two men on the sofa laugh loudly at that. There's a brief, fraught pause while Kiki looks over at Kenny as if he'd just thrown his bottle at her. But quickly pasting a smile back on her face, she replies lightly. 'No thank you, honey, I got my man right here, ain't that right, TK?' But beneath her sweet, sing-song tone there's the faintest hint of uncertainty. And now it seems to Elodie that the temperature in the room has just

186

dropped several degrees.

The man, TK, lets out a short bark of laughter before shoving Kiki off his lap. 'Get off me, bitch. You heard him.'

Standing marooned in the middle of the room, all eyes upon her, Kiki looks in that instant much smaller and younger than before and Elodie feels a tug of pity for her. But with a short, brittle laugh Kiki shakes off her crestfallen expression and walks toward Kenny, who takes a swig from his beer and guffaws. She shoots a look of pure hatred at Elodie as she passes, making her scalp prickle, but worse than that is the resigned humiliation that replaces it, just before she gets down on her knees between Kenny's legs.

While the two men sitting next to her watch Kiki bleary-eyed, Elodie stares at the floor, steeling herself for the moment when she will get up and leave, acutely aware now of her own nakedness beneath the inadequate covering of her T-shirt. With a start, she looks up and notices that TK is staring over at her. 'You going to come here and be friendly?' he asks.

Slowly, Elodie gets to her feet. 'Good girl,' he mumbles approvingly, already fumbling with his zipper. He doesn't notice that she has begun to back out of the room until she's almost at the door.

'Hey!' he calls to her, a look of hurt bewilderment on his face.

At the door Elodie turns and runs, making it to Shanique's bedroom within a matter of seconds. Tears of relief fill her eyes as she slams the door shut and turns the lock. For a moment she stands in the darkness, wishing desperately for Bobby. The sound of footsteps in the hall outside spurs her on again and going over to Tyra's cot she lifts the child out and rocks her gently for a while, in an attempt to calm her tears. The door handle rattles, and TK's voice shouts angrily from the other side. At once, Tyra's snivels turn into frightened wails.

Quickly, Elodie goes to the phone by Shanique's bed and with shaking fingers dials the number for Pinkies. 'Come on, come on,' she whispers into the mouthpiece as the handle on the door rattles more violently. Finally someone picks up.

'Yeah?'

'Can I speak to Shanique please?'

'No, she working.'

She looks in desperation down at Tyra's distressed face.

'Please. Please get her. It's an emergency,' she urges. 'Tell her it's about Tyra.'

The woman on the other end sucks her teeth in annoyance and Elodie hears her drop the phone with a clutter. At last she hears Shanique's voice squawking urgently back at her.

'Shanique, you've got to come back,' Elodie tells her against the noise of banging on the door.

'Why? What's happened? Is Tyra OK? She hurt?'

'No, Tyra's fine, it's Kiki. Will you come back? I don't know what to do, I'm scared, Shanique.' She's barely started explaining when she hears the line go dead. She sinks down onto the bed and sits hugging the child to her.

There's no more banging at the door now, but the music has been turned up loud, and there's the sound of something heavy crashing to the floor, and Kiki arguing with one of the men. She hears the panic in Kiki's voice now and Elodie holds Tyra even closer, willing Shanique to hurry. Just then, she hears another loud crash, an eruption of male laughter, and the sound of Kiki's cry.

It seems to take forever for Shanique to arrive. At last though, she hears the front door open, her name being called, and the sound of footsteps hurrying into the hall. She is surprised to hear Darnel's voice next. Abruptly, the music stops. Dizzy with relief, Elodie puts Tyra back into her crib, turns the key and creeps out into the hallway. When she gets to the living room she stops in her tracks.

The four men are standing now, their hands raised in the air, their faces blank with shock. Darnel is pointing a gun at TK's head. 'Get out,' he says, his customary mumble forgotten. Behind him, Princess and Shanique stand, frozen. The four men begin to edge out of the room, and as the last one leaves, Darnel taps him sharply on the back of the head with the barrel of his gun, making him stumble forward and then run from the apartment.

They all gaze silently down at Kiki for a moment, as she crouches half-naked on the floor amongst the upturned ashtrays and empty bottles. On the TV screen behind her, the pornographic film plays on. In the seconds before Darnel strides over to her, it strikes Elodie how sad the expression on her face is. What Darnel does next happens so fast that Elodie hardly has time to scream. First he slaps Kiki with such force that she falls backwards onto the floor. Next, he begins to kick her. 'Stupid bitch,' he shouts as he slams one foot and then the other again and again into her ribs and Kiki rolls back and forth beneath the blows.

'Stop!' Elodie screams. 'Please stop!' She turns to Shanique and Princess, but they both stand passively, their eyes on the floor. At last it's over. Darnel is panting and looking down at her, his face a wall of fury. 'Dumb fucking bitch.' He shakes his head, wipes the sweat from his brow and walks out of the apartment, slamming the door behind him.

There's silence for a moment or two, while the three of them regard Kiki lying on the floor, rolled into a ball now, her arms still hugging herself in a feeble effort at self-protection. At last Princess goes over to her. 'Come on now, love,' she says soothingly, helping her up. 'Upsie daisy, that's the ticket. Let's get you cleaned up shall we?'

They shuffle slowly towards the bathroom, Kiki whimpering and bent almost double. When they've gone Shanique turns on her heel and heads to her own room. 'Go to bed now, Elodie,' she mutters.

That night she lies awake for a long time, staring up at the ceiling, watching the room gradually lighten as she wonders just how, and when, Kiki will take her revenge.

The strangest thing about Kiki's absence from the apartment is the fact that nobody talks about it. Even Bobby, when she pushes him on the subject, is unforthcoming. 'Heard she cracked a few ribs,' is all he'll say about it. 'Think she's staying with her cousin for a while.' He shrugs and adds vaguely, 'She'll be back, though. Unfortunately.'

They are lying together in his bed, the sweat on their naked skin slowly cooling. Since that first night their hunger for each other has grown by the day. 'I love you,' Bobby tells her once, and his words hang like startled gnats in the silence that follows. Abruptly she rolls away from him and thinks of what she knows of love. She thinks of Ingrid, she thinks of the man in the forest. She turns back to Bobby without answering, covering his mouth with her own.

A week passes, and then another, and Elodie waits anxiously for Kiki's return. But to her surprise, when Kiki finally does breeze back into their lives, she behaves as though nothing at all had happened, flirting with Darnel, quarrelling with Bobby and ordering Princess around exactly as she always had. Elodie she steadfastly ignores as usual, and though grateful for this, Elodie still can't quite shake the suspicion that Kiki's outward display of disinterest is merely an act. Payback, she's sure, must be only around the corner.

Three weeks later, she's proved right. Elodie is sitting in the kitchen with Shanique when Kiki saunters in, fanning herself coquettishly with a rolled-up newspaper.

'Well,' she says with casual sweetness and to no one in particular. 'Look what I found on the subway today.' She throws the paper on the table and makes a show of studying her nails while Shanique unfolds it. Even before Elodie sees the large, black-and-white picture of herself, she instinctively knows, with a dull, awful thud of certainty what this means.

'The Mysterious Disappearance of Little Bird,' Shanique reads aloud. 'Still no leads on the whereabouts of Elodie Brun.' There's a horrible silence as they both look up from the page and exchange a single, bleak glance of comprehension. Shanique passes the paper to her and she takes it with trembling fingers. Next to the picture of herself, is a smaller one of Ingrid.

Elodie looks at the words beneath her photograph, but in her shock they are indecipherable to her. At High Barn, her slow grasp of reading and writing had been a source of constant irritation to Ingrid, and as she stares at the words she is transported for a moment back to the schoolroom, the tedium and frustration of having to go over and over the same simple sentences instantly returning to her.

'You read it,' she says, passing it back to Shanique.

'Police are anxious to talk to Brun in connection with Klein's death,' Shanique begins. 'The search for the missing teenager continues.'

Elodie grips the table as cold panic sluices

over her. Dimly she hears Shanique reading another part of the article, and then commenting in a puzzled voice, 'Says here that Mr Klein came home and found his wife dead, and you missing.' She looks up at Elodie 'But that ain't right, is it? The lady was still alive when that Robert guy come home, that's what you said, ain't it?'

Elodie nods dully, barely listening. If the police wanted to question her, that meant they blamed her. She feels sick with fright.

Across the table, Shanique shrugs. 'Huh. Well, papers got that wrong for a start, didn't they.'

Elodie's eyes fill with tears. 'Oh Shanique,' she whispers, 'what am I going to do?'

Before she can reply, Kiki, her eyes wide and innocent, says in a breathless voice, 'I never knew we had such a celebrity in our midst.'

'Kiki . . . ' Shanique begins in a warning tone. 'This ain't none of your business.'

She sniffs. 'Ain't it? Sure is police business though.' She smiles then, and walks daintily from the room, softly closing the door behind her.

In the silence that follows, Elodie continues to sit motionless, her throat and mouth slowly filling with the dry, metallic taste of despair. 'Shanique,' she whispers again, 'what will I do?'

'It just says they're looking for you, honey. Not that they hold you responsible,' she says weakly, but her lack of conviction is palpable. Finally she gets to her feet. 'I'll talk to her,' she says. 'Try not to panic. I'll talk to her.'

She hears Kiki's door open and close and then the sound of raised voices: Shanique's pleading remonstrations, Kiki's stubborn refusals. She hears it all and knows it's pointless. It finally hits her how stupid she's been, pretending for all these months that she had escaped it all, fooling herself that she could live a normal, happy life. She gazes around the kitchen: this was not her home; she didn't have one. This had merely been a temporary reprieve. Stupid, how stupid she'd been. At that moment, a painful, intangible longing fills her for the mother she has never known.

At last Shanique returns, slumping into her chair and not meeting Elodie's eye. She rubs her temples with her fingertips and finally speaks. 'She says you've got a week.'

'A week?'

'Uh-huh. Get out of here or she'll go to the police.'

After a long, silent moment Shanique reaches across the table and takes hold of Elodie's hand. 'Look, darling,' she says, 'the fact is it ain't safe for you here no more. Kiki will go to the police, you can rely on that.' She looks at her hands, before adding, 'And I can't have the police sniffing round here, Elodie. I just can't.'

Elodie nods, ignoring the tears that have begun to fall.

Shanique gazes back at her, her face lined with pity. At last she gives her hand another squeeze. 'Don't worry,' she says. 'Leave it with me, I'll think of something.'

★ ★ ★

194

'We'll take off together,' Bobby says to her as they lie together in bed that night. 'I'll look after you, I promise, Elodie. It'll be OK, you'll see.'

'Maybe . . . maybe I should go to them. Tell the police what happened. Tell them I didn't mean to hurt her.' She eyes him hopefully.

'Elodie,' Bobby's voice is stern, 'you stay away from the police. What if they don't believe you? What if they decide it was your fault she died and put you in prison? And even if they don't, they'll put you in care, they'd take you away from me.'

She lies there thinking about his words, the thought of being locked up in a cell too awful to contemplate.

He shakes his head. 'They won't find us. We could go anywhere. Fuck it, we could go to Hollywood!'

She lies back upon the pillow, hugging Bobby closer to her, letting him continue with his plans, knowing all the while that it's impossible. She remembers the feeling of unreality she'd had when she first arrived in New York, like being inside a TV set, but Bobby's fantasy is even more unreal. She's overwhelmed by the hopelessness of it all. She tries to focus her mind on Shanique's promise that she'd find a way to help her, and hopes desperately that it's true.

★ ★ ★

To her alarm, Shanique spends much of the following two days away from the apartment, returning only to lock herself in her bedroom with Darnel, where their voices rumble steadily behind the closed door. Elodie loiters in the hallway trying in vain to make sense of their words, but they never rise above an urgent, indecipherable whisper. Once, she passes Darnel in the hall on his way to the bathroom and he eyes her thoughtfully before continuing on his way. She returns to Bobby's room, and, in an agony of uncertainty, waits.

At last Shanique calls Elodie into the kitchen, where she finds the two of them staring gravely back at her. She closes the door and takes a seat.

'I think we've found a way to help you,' Shanique begins.

Elodie listens carefully while Shanique talks and Darnel keeps his eyes fixed upon her. 'It's up to you, honey,' she says when she's finished. 'It's a risk. It's a huge risk. But as far as I can see, it's your only way out.'

Elodie sits and thinks for a while. 'When?' she asks.

'He's coming tonight.'

★   ★   ★

Although he's very large, the man, Gomez, moves with the dainty elegance of a ballerina. He sits at the kitchen table, his enormous bulk seeming to fill the small space, while a slim, silent, very black man stands blank-eyed and motionless by the door. There are two more men, she knows, who have remained outside the apartment keeping guard. But from where she sits Elodie cannot tear her eyes from Gomez's

196

wide, blunt face, his moist, delicate little mouth. A quiet menace seems to rise from him like steam off manure.

Elodie can tell by the thin sheen of sweat on Darnel's brow how nervous he is. Shanique too: she speaks very little and continuously swallows, licks her lips and twists her fingers together. Darnel, after having his one, timid offer of a beer declined has also lapsed into a tense silence beneath an anxious, sycophantic grin. When Gomez speaks his voice is very quiet, his eyes expressionless, his face blank. He doesn't move at all apart from the two index fingers of his neatly clasped hands, which follow the rhythm of his sentences like a conductor controlling an invisible, miniature orchestra.

At first Gomez doesn't look at her while he speaks but when finally he does, she feels the temperature drop acutely and her hands and legs begin to tremble. Between long blinks Gomez holds her in his steady gaze.

'Stand up,' he says at last. She glances at Shanique, who nods back at her. He looks her over carefully for a long time, finally nodding his satisfaction and gesturing for her to sit down. When she's seated again, he keeps his eyes on her as he talks and an instinct tells her suddenly that he knows everything about her, more, even, than she'd told Shanique and Bobby, more, even, than she perhaps knows herself. The thought makes her infinitely uncomfortable. He talks for many minutes, not inviting opinion or comment, merely telling her what will be expected, and what she will receive in return.

When, finally, he leaves with the thin silent man, the three of them exhale with such a loud release of tension, that they laugh and smile foolishly at one another, as if the worst bit was over — as if the most terrifying part wasn't still to come.

★ ★ ★

'I'm scared. I'm so scared, Shanique,' she says, when they are alone, later.

'I don't know what else you going to do. It's your chance for a new life, Elodie. Your only chance. You couldn't have stayed shut up here forever anyway.' She thinks for a moment, shakes her head and says again, 'I don't know what else you can do.' Unhappily Shanique fiddles with one of her bangles. Elodie has noticed that since Gomez left it has been hard for Shanique to meet her gaze. 'You'll be OK, honey. It'll be OK.'

Elodie nods and blinks back her tears.

After a while, Shanique reaches over and takes one of her hands. 'What you going to do if you stay, honey? End up like us? That what you want? No one's going to give you a job — you got no papers, nothing.' She squeezes her hand emphatically, the long, colourful talons stroking her wrist. 'You go to England, honey. You take that money and you start a new life for yourself. Get some learning and don't end up like us,' she smiles sadly, looks over at Tyra and murmurs, 'don't you end up like us.'

Elodie squeezes her hand back and suddenly she finds herself in Shanique's arms, wrapped in her large rolls of flab, her head upon the

198

enormous chest, a faint smell of coco butter and cherries in her nostrils.

★ ★ ★

Her last evening arrives too soon. She and Bobby lie together on his mattress and listen to the sounds of the streets below. There is nothing left to say now. She holds him tight, long after the tears have dried on his face and his breath has deepened into sleep at last. She stays awake for a long time, and waits for the morning to come.

17

Heathrow, England, 12 March 2000

Cocooned within the cabin's static yellow interior, she hurtles between two continents, two lives; suspended between her past and her future. She is ambushed by a nameless terror, by memories she has no words for, from before words existed and when once before she was inside a metal bird roaring to the sky. And somewhere below, her suitcase waits in the hold, nestling malevolently amongst the innocent holiday luggage of her fellow passengers like a poisonous, pot-bellied toad.

Through the little oval window on her left she watches as the plane scales clouds edged with a blinding red light from a sun she can't see. On and on and up and up they soar, through white then red then blue while to her right, frozen-faced stewardesses glide through the aisles, depositing then taking away again little trays of food. The lights dim, the air cools and all around her, people fall into open-mouthed unconsciousness or stare sore-eyed at the flickering TV screens while their headphones whisper and snicker beneath the air conditioner's chilly drone. And still she sits and waits, her back rigid, her hands clenched in her lap. For six hours and twenty minutes she sits, watching the blackening sky.

★ ★ ★

At last the plane begins its steady fall. The
engines roar to their crescendo, wheels hit then
bounce across tarmac and at last come to a
shuddering halt. Outside, all is dark. She has
imagined this moment a million times. In the
airport she follows the stream of crumpled,
sleep-dazed passengers through freezing corridors and up and down escalators and finally to
Passport Control where she falls in line behind
an elderly couple and grips her papers tightly.

Ahead of her is a row of desks behind which
sit unsmiling men and women in suits. Beyond
them security officials with bullet-proof vests eye
the swarm of new arrivals. Everything is as
Gomez told her it would be. Finally, the couple
in front are beckoned through and then at last
the man behind the desk glances up and it's her
turn. Her throat thickens as she approaches and
deposits her passport and disembarkation forms
into his outstretched hand. Beneath his turban,
two brown eyes flicker across her face, swift but
sharp as needles. Second after second after
second passes, each one heavier and longer than
the one before.

A cold, dead weight sits in the pit of her
stomach. Out of the corner of her eye she
glimpses a policeman murmuring something into
his walkie-talkie. Cold sweat prickles her brow.
For the thousandth time that hour she hears
Gomez's voice reminding her to smile and what
to say. The man in the turban continues to stare
down at her passport. Finally, after what feels

201

like several minutes, he looks up. 'Welcome to the UK, Ms Townsend,' he says in a thin British accent. 'How long will you be with us?'

Her smile is painful. 'Two weeks.'

A child in the queue behind her emits a long, slow wail. And then, suddenly, time shifts on a notch; the world continues turning, and the man is at once all brisk indifference. He stamps first her passport and then her papers. 'Have a nice trip.' He blinks his dismissal and looks past her to the next in line. Dizzy with relief, she follows the signs towards Baggage Reclaim, adrenalin shooting through her veins, her heart knocking in her chest.

At the luggage carousel the euphoria gradually fades, as one by one, each bag and suitcase emerging from the flapping plastic strips is lifted from its doleful circuit and taken by its owner towards the door marked Customs. Finally, when there are only three or four groups of stragglers left, she almost cries out with relief when she sees her case finally appear and begin its slow, lonely passage towards her. She lifts it down, unhooks its handle and pulls it behind her, raising her chin an inch and staring straight ahead as a couple of policewomen with large dogs pass by. Her tongue feels thick and bloodless in her mouth.

A stream of passengers from another flight joins her as she begins the slow trudge through the corridor marked Nothing To Declare. To her right, a row of men and women behind a long table watch as she passes, her eyes straight ahead, the case trundling on its wheels behind her. Ahead of her she sees a set of wide double doors marked Arrivals, just beyond them she glimpses a crowd of people gazing in with pale, expectant faces. It is all she can do not to run towards them. She forces her pace to slow as hope begins at last to seep through her fear. *Nearly there.*

And then a sharp voice barks, 'Excuse me!' She freezes, as her brain dislocates itself from her body and she turns towards the group of uniformed men. But *thank God, thank God,* they are looking past her to a man walking just behind her, who is already sighing resignedly and dragging his case over to the inspection table. She moves on, through the door marked Arrivals.

★   ★   ★

On either side of her are railings flanked by waiting people with expectant smiles, or holding up cards with names scrawled on them as they watch the stream of people emerging with her into the large, bright space. A couple of teenage boys carrying skis are greeted warmly by a middle-aged couple. Two young children call excitedly to a smiling woman. And there, at the end of the railings, just as Gomez had promised, stands a man holding a sign on which is written in careful blue letters: Kate Eaves.

Outside, the sky is pitch black. She follows the man to the car park, and as he lifts her case into the boot of his car she feels vomit rise to her throat and heaves and shudders while bile splashes onto the tarmac. The man waits patiently for her to finish. When at last she is sat in the back and they pull away the rain picks up and begins to thump against her window. She gazes out, but can see little apart from flashes of fuzzy yellow light, blue road signs indicating the distance to places she has never heard of, and lone cars speeding past. She stares at the back of the driver's neck, which remains rigid as he silently navigates the car along the black, windswept motorway.

Half an hour passes, then another. The car is silent apart from the rain that is now pelting hard on the roof, and the whine and thump of the windscreen wipers. On either side of the motorway stretch empty fields. At last she gives into the tense exhaustion and for the first time in almost twenty hours she feels her eyelids grow heavy, and she falls into an uneasy sleep. Suddenly — she doesn't know how much time has passed — she's jerked awake by the bumping and juddering of the car across rough terrain, hedges scraping against glass.

They come to a halt. The driver gets out and slams the door behind him. She hears him open then close the boot, then silence. She peers through the rain-splattered windows but can see nothing, only black, empty space. Just then her eyes are blinded by the headlights of another vehicle shining at full beam. As she raises her hand to block the glare her door is opened abruptly and she flinches in shock. The driver, her suitcase in his hand, peers in at her, and says, simply, 'OK.'

She follows him, slipping and sliding across muddy grass to a large car with blacked-out windows. She is shuddering uncontrollably. The driver opens the nearest passenger door and tells her to get in. Then he passes the case in after her, and shuts the door. In the back of the car sit two men. She perches on the seat opposite them, the case resting on the floor between them. She is dizzy with fear.

The older of the two men, after glancing at her once, turns to stare out of the window, though she continues to feel his eyes upon her, reflected in the black glass. The younger man looks at her without blinking for several seconds before abruptly snapping into action. From his coat pocket he pulls a small screwdriver, and sets about removing the tiny bolts that ring her case's interior. Finally, he lifts the hard plastic lining away from its frame. Then, as she watches, he pulls out dozens of silver bricks, one after another. By the time he has finished, there's a pile of sixty on the seat next to him.

He hands one of the bricks to the older man who takes a small knife from his jacket pocket and makes a small incision in the foil. She watches as he scoops out a tiny pile of white powder and brings it, still on the knife's blade, to his face. Lizard like, his tongue darts out and collects half of the powder on its tip. He closes his eyes and nods. Then, he brings the knife to his nose, inserts it in his nostril, and takes a long, hard sniff. He stares ahead, his face expressionless, motionless, except for a small vein that pulses on the side of his forehead.

Finally he sighs, nods, then returns his gaze to the black window. The younger man loads the silver bricks into his briefcase, then reaches into his inside jacket pocket and pulls out an envelope and hands it to her. 'Please,' he says. He watches her expectantly. She opens it and pulls out a British passport and a sheaf of papers, including a birth certificate. All the documents are made out in the name of Kate Eaves. Next he hands her a large jiffy bag. Inside are wads of pink notes. She gazes up at the man. 'Twenty thousand,' he says, and she nods.

Minutes later, she is back in the first car, the suitcase and the envelopes on the floor beside her. The driver throws his cigarette out of the window, eyes her in the rear-view mirror and asks, 'Where to?' She pulls from her pocket the tiny piece of paper that Princess had handed to her before she left. The handwriting is round and childlike, the ink pink and glittery, the 'i's dotted with love hearts. She passes it to the driver, who squints at it, nods, and starts the engine.

18

Kingsbury, north-west London, 14 March 2000
The sky is a hard, flat white. It's 6 a.m. and a
fine drizzle has just begun to fall over Burlington
Road, London NW10. She stands with her case
on the pavement and looks with mystified eyes at
the long curve of 1930s semis, at wheelie bins
and net curtains, pebbledash and daffodils.
Above her, a flock of birds falls through the sky
like black rocks, before swooping upwards to
form a perfect V. A cat eyes her coldly from
behind double-glazed glass as she drags her case
towards number 45.

'You must be Kate?' The woman who answers
the door looks so exactly like the Yorkshire
Terrier she is holding that for a moment Elodie
can only stand and stare. Princess's mother is
short with frizzy hair the same colour as her dog.
They both peer out at her with small, round eyes
from below their yellow fringes. 'I'm Bev,' the
woman tells her.

In the living room Princess's father stands, tall
and vague in a navy jumper. 'This is Alan,' the
woman says. He had been looking in a slightly
baffled way at a large caged bird in the corner of
the room when Elodie entered, and now his
expression remains perplexed. 'Pleased to meet
you,' he says, smiling absently. Rain-coloured
tufts of hair slide in puddles across his scalp. The
bird squawks loudly, and the dog, now

earthbound, scuttles towards it, yapping. The man is so exactly like Princess, her doughy features and sweet, affable expression mirrored in his middle-aged face, that she feels a sudden pang.

'It's very nice to meet you,' she tells him. The room is spotlessly tidy, the radiators belt out heat, a smell of furniture polish hovers in the air. 'Nice to meet you! Nice to meet you!' cries the bird, while the dog howls.

When they are seated and drinking tea, and after Bev and Alan have asked about her journey and they have all talked about the weather, Bev follows Elodie's exhausted gaze to a large, framed photograph of Princess above the fireplace. The three of them consider for a while the slightly stupid smile and watery blue eyes.

'Are you a waitress too, dear, like Lorraine?' asks Bev after a pause.

Elodie shakes her head, remembering suddenly Princess's real name. 'No. I was more of a . . . childminder,' she tells them.

'A nanny!' Princess's parents marvel silently for a moment.

'Still,' Bev continues, 'Waitressing is just to tide her over until she gets a part, isn't it?' She smiles at Elodie hopefully. 'Always going to auditions, isn't she?'

Elodie sips her tea, and nods. Her head aches with tiredness.

'Well,' says Bev brightly, then. 'You must be shattered. Why don't I show you upstairs?'

★ ★ ★

208

They stand in the doorway and survey the small, pink bedroom for a while. 'We've kept it exactly as she left it,' Bev tells her, and they stare with hushed reverence at the fuchsia carpet and curtains, the single bed laden with soft toys. Photographs of Princess cover the walls, her lumpen, blotchy, prepubescent form squashed into tutus or leotards as she high kicks or pirouettes upon a stage. More pictures show her as a podgy teenager, dressed in sequins and satin while a spotty, tuxedoed adolescent whirls her around a dance floor. 'Those are her medals for Ballroom,' explains Bev, pointing proudly at a shelf laden with small silver trophies. 'And those are her certificates for Ballet, Tap and Jazz.' She smiles with satisfaction. 'Such a talented girl.'

And then, finally, Bev leaves her, closing the door gently as she goes, and beneath Princess's pink duvet, the case on the floor by her side, Elodie sleeps at last.

★ ★ ★

The days pass. At first Elodie spends them trailing Bev around the house, lending a hand in the energetic and systematic cleaning from top to bottom of the already immaculate house. Scrubbing, vacuuming, dusting and polishing everything in sight, Bev chats to her in the same cyclical, meandering manner as her daughter once did, her voice as cheerful and unremitting as the patterns on the wallpaper that hangs in every room. She rarely expects a response, so Elodie is free to pursue her own thoughts while

209

she smiles and nods and passes Bev the feather duster.

Alan on the other hand is a largely silent man. Often she will rise early to find him already up and dressed and sitting with a slightly surprised expression at the kitchen table, looking about him as if he's not quite sure how he came to be there. Bev's habitual manner towards her husband is one of weary resignation, treating him rather like a piece of furniture to vacuum around or shift out of the way in favour of something else that might need cleaning. Sometimes Elodie half expects her to spray him with Pledge and rub him with her cloth. 'He's only just retired,' Bev whispers confidingly as they watch through the kitchen window as he pokes absently at a rose bush. 'Doesn't know what to do with himself yet.' She squirts some Fairy into the washing up bowl and seizes a dishcloth. 'Wish he'd bloody well find out though.'

But mostly Alan seems content just to listen to his wife's endless monologues, for his part contributing every now and then with one or other of a long selection of favourite, well-worn sayings: 'Waste Not Want Not,' he'll say. 'Never Rains But It Pours. Each To Their Own. Less Haste, More Speed. Live And Let Live.' He nods while he speaks, as if anxious to be agreeable. Elodie has no idea what these things mean, or what relevance they have, and they are usually entirely ignored by Bev, but the phrases seem to comfort him, the words worn smooth as pebbles with repeated use and said with quiet relish.

Only Percy, the caged minor bird seems to take any real interest in Alan, mimicking him malevolently whenever he opens his mouth. 'Never rains but it pours!' he'll hector. 'Waste not want not!' he'll sneer, while a frenzied Brandy yelps and yaps and tears around in circles beneath his cage.

In the evenings the three of them watch the television with their dinner trays on their laps. Bangers and mash, pizza and chips, spaghetti bolognaise. Coronation Street. Inspector Morse. Who Wants To Be A Millionaire? Outside, the darkness falls and the street lamps buzz insipidly beneath the never-ending drizzle.

★   ★   ★

Little by little, Elodie begins to discover the world that lies beyond 45 Burlington Road. At first she embarks on tentative explorations under the cold, white April sky. Wrapped in Bobby's sweatshirt, the hood pulled down low out of habit over her eyes, she drifts past row upon row of identical square houses, through little parades of shops, past dusty, shabby Halaal food stores, the boarded-up banks, the kebab shops and off-licences and pubs that constitute this corner of suburbia. Trees sprout from between paving stones, torn carrier bags snagged on their twigs like strange fruit. She thinks that it is very different to Queens. Her memories of New York have already taken on a surreal, dream-like quality, but she remembers the city as being either very hot, or very cold. Here the climate

211

seems to be perpetually indifferent; tepid, waiting. Sometimes, as she moves, a faint smell of Bobby rises from the fabric of his sweatshirt, the sweet, musky scent causing the memories to slam into her, his voice and touch and face suddenly unbearably vivid, a nameless pain catching in her chest making her sick with longing.

Every day she walks a little further; to Stanmore, Sudbury and Southall. Here at least a restless energy bubbles between the mosques and market stalls, selling spice and jewellery and Bollywood DVDs. In Harrow she wanders past bookies and bowling alleys, past fashion boutiques and fast food joints, travel agents and tanning salons, supermarkets and cinemas. She slips through automatic doors into the shiny, overheated worlds of shopping centres where people glide with single-minded purpose over faux marble floors.

She walks home past kebab shops glowing blue in the falling dusk, past pubs gurgling orange, emitting short bursts of laughter and music. The streets are empty but for lone figures who drift ghostlike along pavements, their gazes shifting to their feet as they shuffle past her in the gloom. She turns into quiet, residential streets, the front gardens cement squares, their rooms alight with flickering plasma screens. In one house she spies a fat ginger boy punching his fat, ginger sister. In another an elderly man sits alone, eating cereal from a box. On the corner of Burlington Road a lamppost marks the scene of a traffic accident, festooned with bouquets of flowers, shiny plastic and bows wrapped around the rotting vegetation. She thinks of Shanique, Kiki and Princess, she thinks of Bobby. I am Kate, she tells herself. I am Kate Eaves. Through the tepid air she walks.

⋆　⋆　⋆

After a few months she takes some of the money that is still stashed away in her suitcase beneath Princess's bed, and, remembering Shanique's advice enrols at a nearby college, paying in cash for classes in literacy, reading and writing. This has been her plan — her only one — and she follows it through with a kind of numb determination, unable to think how else to fill her days. Before her first class she waits outside as the daytime students come flooding out and pour down the steps towards her. They wear low-slung jeans and shiny trainers, have studs in their eyebrows, hair that is dyed and waxed and shaven. She stands alone, clutching her books and trying to make sense of their accents which seems to make everything they say end in 'ar': 'Nar man', they say. 'Remem-bar?' they ask. 'Yeah,' they shrug, 'whatev-ar.'

But the students who attend her classes are very different from these chattering, laughing, shrieking teens. Her fellow classmates have been at work all day, and have an air of weary determination. They are Albanian, Bosnian, Chinese, Somalian. And when the teacher begins to speak, they listen avidly, hanging with intense concentration on each word. In silence they study their grammar and spelling, their verbs and adjectives and nouns.

At first, Elodie sits at the very back and stares tensely at the blackboard, feeling a mounting panic as she listens to the teacher's instructions. Each time she tries to focus on the lesson, she finds herself transported to High Barn, experiencing again the familiar anxiety; the fear of blundering, of disappointing always present. By the end of each class she is shaken and flustered and finds she can't remember one thing. But slowly, day by day, she begins to relax. Gradually, and with increasing confidence she begins to make progress. Soon she enrolls in more classes — computer studies, secretarial skills, introduction to mathematics — amazed by her growing abilities, the speed and ease with which she learns, relieved to have found something at last to take her mind off Bobby, whom she misses with a constant, physical ache.

Sometimes, when she's watching the TV with Bev and Alan or wandering the streets between her classes, it strikes Elodie that the limbo she experienced on the plane, of being suspended between two lives, has not yet left her. When she tries to imagine the future, she finds that she cannot. When she thinks about her past she finds she can't quite grasp it, so far removed is it from the life she's leading now. At night she will wake at one or two or three o'clock, shaking with fear and drenched in sweat, the fading remnants of Ingrid's voice still lingering, barely.

One evening as she's leaving the college to go home, she looks up to see Tomas, a Polish student from her class falling into step besides her. She has noticed him before, his eyes that stare at her when he thinks she isn't looking, his grave silence. He doesn't look at her as they walk, and she in turn doesn't say a word as they turn off the main street into a narrow road she has never ventured down before. She follows him unquestioningly, sensing instantly what he wants. For the next few weeks after class she goes with him, back to his tiny, bare-walled bedsit, where they undress silently in the dark, while outside, in the corridor, doors slam and footsteps hurry past. Afterwards, he turns from her and mutters in his own language, sometimes he cries. And when one day Tomas doesn't turn up to class and there is no word from him, she doesn't mind. Kate, she tells herself. My name is Kate. Each night she dreams of Bobby. The weeks pass, and then the months. I am Kate Eaves.

19

Kingsbury, north-west London, May 2001
The blue screen glows softly in the darkness, a quiet drone floats just above the silence. The computer room is empty. She takes her seat and logs onto Google. Her hands hover above the keyboard for a few seconds, and then, in the box marked Search, she types the words 'Elodie Brun' and hits Return. Almost immediately a list of sites appears. Her fingers fly to her lap as if burnt. Fear sits heavy in her stomach. She had not planned this; had not known that this was what she would do until she found herself here, and now she sits, too afraid to move, poised between ignorance and knowledge. A part of her wants only to run. But finally she clicks the mouse and begins to read.

The first article is dated 1996. Her eyes fall to a colour photograph and she flinches in shock. The child who stares back at her has a small pale face with huge, wildly staring eyes below a mane of red-brown hair. She is a ragged sprite in a white, hospital-issue gown, flanked by two, kindly looking nurses in a cheerful looking room with children's pictures on the walls. In her hand is a little carved wooden bird. There is something about the set of the child's jaw in the picture, the almost slack-mouthed smile, the peculiar posture, the extreme nakedness of her gaze, that is utterly arresting. It is an extraordinary picture.

Like looking at two incongruous images superimposed upon one another, each one from different eras, different worlds.

She studies the faces of the nurses. Is there something else behind their smiling eyes, besides the kindness? The faintest whisper of unease, perhaps? There in the computer room Kate turns to the window and examines her reflection in the glass: the eyes that stare back are reassuringly guarded, contained, controlled, the hair short and neat and blonde, the face a little plumper, softer. And yet she cannot quench the disquiet that the picture has provoked in her.

She turns back and scrolls down to the second photo. She barely notices her tears as she gazes at the familiar face. The caption beneath it tells her his name is Mathias Bresson. He is younger than when she knew him, but still she recognizes the deep-set, haunted eyes, the hunted expression. Now that she has other faces to compare his to she sees how strangely intense his was, how different to anyone else's she's seen since. Very gently she reaches over to the screen and with her fingertips traces the features of the face that she had loved so much.

Her eyes fall to a tiny, inset picture and she freezes in shock. She leans in closer, at first unable to believe her eyes. It is the woman in the green dress, the same photo that Mathias showed her on that final evening in the forest. There, after all this time, is that strange, unforgettable half-smile, the mysterious dark eyes glancing downwards beneath the heavy fringe. She scrolls up to the beginning of the article and begins to read.

'Tragic loner who caged Little Bird,' the headline announces in large, heavy type. 'Little is known about the man who held Elodie Brun captive for ten years in a remote forester's cottage in Normandy,' she reads. 'A mute since birth and abandoned by his mother aged six, Mathias Bresson spent the rest of his childhood in various care homes. Records from the time describe a shy, introverted boy with severe behavioural problems, and attempts to assign him foster parents were short-lived. Eventually he was sent to a children's home in Rouen where he was to remain until he was seventeen.

'After that, little is known about Bresson's whereabouts, but it seems he lead a reclusive, nomadic existence, occasionally employed as a labourer in nearby farms but often living in hostels or on the streets of Rouen. When he was twenty-eight he was admitted to the city's hospital after a failed suicide attempt and ironically, it was whilst undergoing treatment on the psychiatric ward here that Bresson found happiness at last with fellow patient Celeste Duchamp (pictured inset).

'Both Bresson and Duchamp made good progress under their doctors' care and were eventually discharged. The couple set up home and eventually married, settling down in a quiet village where Bresson found work in nearby woods as a forester. A neighbour from the time, Jean Petit, remembers the couple well. 'They were nice,' he says. 'Quiet, decent people. They kept themselves to themselves, mostly, but

Mathias was a good man. He helped me tile my roof once. I liked him — everyone did. They seemed very happy, especially when Celeste became pregnant. We were all pleased for them in the village and Mathias seemed delighted.'

'But tragedy soon struck when Celeste developed antepartum psychosis, a mental illness that, if not properly treated can lead the expectant mother to experience terrifying hallucinations and thoughts of suicide. When she was seven months pregnant, Mathias returned home one evening to find that she had hanged herself.

' 'It was terrible, dreadful,' recalls Petit. 'We hardly saw him after that — he barely left the house. And then, one day, he just wasn't there anymore. Clean disappeared, and we never saw him again until ten years later when he was in all the papers.'

'Petit continued, 'He wasn't a bad man. He was gentle. I don't think he'd ever had hurt a fly. I was shocked to the bone when I heard he'd taken that young kid. Who knows why he did it? Perhaps he was just trying to replace what he'd lost.' '

She is unable to read any more. Her head sinks into her hands and for a long time all she can do is let the sadness sweep through her. She closes her eyes and casts herself back to the forest. She is sitting outside the little stone house. It's twilight and the birds have begun their evening song. The air is soft and hazy, and the man is sitting on the old bench, smoking his pipe and smiling down at her. There in the college's computer room her fingers stir in her lap as they remember the touch of the little carved bird, how perfectly it had fit inside her palm, how she had carried it with her always, her fingers stroking the familiar, smooth curve of its head, the grooves of its wings. His gift to her. At last she opens her eyes and kissing her finger, places it on Mathias's forehead.

Outside in the corridor, a security guard rattles his keys. 'Thirty minutes, love,' he warns her. She exits the page and opens the second article on the list. The six-page feature that appears next is from an English colour supplement dated 1999.

'Where is Little Bird?' the headline asks. 'Six months after the disappearance of Elodie Brun, the police still have no leads on her whereabouts. We investigate the extraordinary mystery that began in a sleepy market town in northern France, and ended in tragedy fourteen years later on Long Island . . . '

The piece is illustrated with several photographs. The first, slightly blurred and yellowing, is of a young woman about the same age as Kate is now. She has dark auburn hair and blue eyes and is looking at the camera with a shy, lopsided smile. Kate gazes at it confused: it is both her, and not. She reads the caption and her hand flies to her mouth as realisation dawns. 'Thérèse Brun, mother of Elodie, was just 19 when her daughter was abducted,' it says, and her heart rockets to her mouth. 'Mother of Elodie,' she reads again, and the three words begin to swim before her eyes. The rest of the world seems to disappear, for a long time all she is aware of is

Thérèse's face and the loud beating of her heart.

At last she drags her gaze away and eagerly turns to the article, desperate to discover everything she can. But soon her excitement gives way to bitter disappointment. The writer tells her nothing she doesn't already know: that Thérèse had been a young, single mother, struggling to cope, that after Elodie's abduction she had turned to drugs and alcohol, and after living in a squat for a while had finally disappeared, assumed dead. It was exactly as Ingrid had told her. Kate turns back to the photograph, wanting to remember each strand of hair, each freckle and eyelash, every pore and line. She prints out the photograph, folds it up and puts it in her pocket.

'Are you all right, love?' The college security guard is standing in the doorway, staring in concern at her white, tear-stained face. Without answering him, she turns off the PC and runs from the room.

★   ★   ★

She has been sitting in the dark, staring out of Princess's bedroom window for over two hours now. Bev and Alan have long since turned off the TV and gone to bed. Outside, above the small neat back yard, the moon floats in milky blackness. Somewhere a fox screams and she hears Brandy whimper a sleepy response from the kitchen below.

Turning from the window she goes to Princess's dressing table and sitting down, stares at her reflection in the little gilt-edged mirror. Her mother's face returns to her. Who had she been, this stranger, Thérèse? This woman who had named her, made plans for her, loved her? And who would she herself have been if Mathias had not taken her that day? Elodie Brun. She must begin again. She looks around her at the pink walls of someone else's childhood. Kate Eaves. She thinks of the girl standing on the stage at the conference in New York, Ingrid by her side. She thinks about the girl who, in a split second of anger, had pushed Ingrid to her death. 'Kate Eaves,' she whispers, staring at herself. 'Elodie Brun.'

★　★　★

A week later, she spies on the college notice board a square white card advertising a flat to rent a few miles away in Kilburn. The next day she pays in cash the deposit and first month's rent, and moves out.

20

Kilburn, north London, November 2002
It creeps up on her, London. To begin with, as if comparing it to a past lover, she finds the city lacking; not up to the power and passion of her first infatuation. Compared to New York, London is cramped and oppressive; the dark brick buildings press down on her, the sky is shrunken and pale. But then, slowly, freed from the cloying drear of suburbia, she starts to look about her with new eyes. Kilburn, with its run-down pubs and bingo halls, its shabby energy and seedy bluster, seems to her as volatile and unpredictable as a drunken old man: charming and flirtatious one minute, embittered and hostile the next. She begins devouring the city in the way she once consumed New York. And inch by inch, step by step, brick by brick, it claims her.

Wild, cramped, fast, dark and sprawling, turning the corner from ugliness she will suddenly find beauty. From Hampstead to Hammersmith, Clerkenwell to Canning Town she roams, the aggression and glamour of the West End, the eerie, waiting hush of the Square Mile at night and every alley and square and dead-end street in between beginning to edge its way beneath her skin.

Even the climate, which she'd once dismissed as insipid, begins to seduce her as she witnesses

223

the city's mutability beneath each season's spell. The smell of the pavements after rain, the frozen hush of a January dawn. The shimmering neon of Piccadilly Circus beneath snow, the blossom trees of an Islington square in spring. The scent of the cold, black streets in winter, the hazy glow of Hyde Park in summer where once she spies parakeets flying between the trees. It seeps into her soul.

But something else, something even more beguiling than the city begins to make its claim. Wherever she goes she loiters on the corners of strangers' conversations, catching words like falling leaves, sifting through other people's dialogue like a tramp scavenging through bins. In Mayfair words flutter like butterflies from beneath Arab housewives' veils. At bus stops schoolchildren bat them back and forth like ping pong balls. In Newington Green elderly Turks slide them across cafe tables like pieces on a backgammon board. In churches they rise in prayer like dissipating steam. Words as currency, as intimacy, as love or reassurance. Words of anger or persuasion. Words that are curled with tenderness, or scorched by anger, that spit and fizz or slice and wound, words that warm and nourish. She collects them all.

A flurry of voices on the Tube: The next station is Moorgate. You're probably looking at about four-fifty for a decent two-bed these days. Will passengers in the rear carriages please make their way to the front of the train. I mean, he didn't even know how to pronounce Goethe for fuck's sake. Pronounced it gotha. Fucking peasant. Moorgate will be the next stop. I feel awful. Like my brain's going to explode. Will passengers for the Hammersmith and City Line please change here?

Sitting on a park bench she listens to two old women's conversation: Go to the cinema did you then, last night? Nah, didn't fancy it. Stayed in and watched that thing on ITV, the one with the paedophiles. Oh yeah, I sky plussed that. Any good? Nah, bollocks.

A boy on the bus, his cap pulled far down over his eyes, his acne-rimmed lips almost devouring his mobile: Sometimes you just pop into my head and I can't breathe, he says.

On Primrose Hill, one very hot June day, two lovers lie upon the grass. The girl leans over and whispers something to the man, murmuring words like caresses into his neck, and Kate watches as his face is transformed, is flooded by a kind of light, so that she wants to run to them and ask, 'What, what did she say? What caused you to look like that? What was it, what was said?'

And sometimes she will study people who are alone, will just stare as their faces gently undulate like a field of corn beneath the breeze of their own, silent monologues. A middle-aged man in paint-splattered overalls, sucking on a cigarette and staring at his shoes. A woman glaring at a boy carving his name on a nearby bench. An elderly lady walking painstakingly slowly amongst an impatient crowd of commuters. What words shape their thoughts, she wonders.

One day on Clapham Common she watches a young girl sitting on a bench, while her baby sleeps in a pram by her side. She's about sixteen, has a black eye and her hair is lank and greasy. She puffs nervously on a cigarette and stares into space while absentmindedly jiggling her pram back and forth, to and fro. But a soft mewling snaps her from her reverie, and the girl bends down to gaze at the child within. At that moment, an expression of such love transforms her face that Kate is reminded suddenly of something that happened one day long ago on Long Island.

When she first began to speak, she would point at things at random and say to Ingrid, 'This!' Sitting on Clapham Common, Kate smiles to herself at the memory. 'This!' she would demand, urgently, pointing at a cat, a car, a box, a ball, until Ingrid had provided the word she was looking for. Her hunger had been limitless. One day they had walked to Oyster Bay. It had been early evening, and nobody else had been around as they'd watched the sun drop slowly over the horizon. Gradually before her eyes, shade by shade, the sky and the sea had filled with pink, gold, red and purple light. She had tugged at Ingrid's sleeve. 'This!' she had said, pointing at it all. 'This?'

'Sky,' Ingrid had replied.

'NO!' she had protested, because she already knew the word for sky, and that hadn't been what she meant. Nor did she mean, when Ingrid offered them, 'Sunset', 'Ocean', or 'Red'.

Seeing the mother with her child, Kate realises

that the word she had been searching for then was not simply 'beauty', just as the word she wanted now, was not simply 'love'. And just as that vast sky had made her feel suddenly so small, now the expression in the woman's eyes as she gazes at her baby fills her with an immense sadness.

★ ★ ★

She has been living in Kilburn for over two years when she finally plucks up the courage to visit the shabby offices of Nelson and Fisher employment agency on the High Road. As the morning of her first assignment draws near — a six-week placement where she is to file, type and answer the phones for a small accountancy firm in Willesden — her nervousness increases. Although she has spent her time in London watching and listening closely, perfecting the art of blending in, of observing mannerisms and accents, she nevertheless feels acutely, always, her difference. On the afternoon before her first day she cuts and dyes her hair again and buys a selection of nondescript office clothes. That evening she stares at her reflection in the mirror. 'Hi,' she says, with a brief, noncommittal smile in her quiet, accent-less voice. 'I'm Kate Eaves. Pleased to meet you.' She stares back at herself doubtfully.

She needn't have worried: in the accountancy firm in Willesden, and then later in her next post — a call centre near Wembley — and indeed in every job she's subsequently assigned to, it soon becomes clear that her carefully bland exterior is like a mirror for all but the very shrewd to gaze into. Other people, she realizes, will always prefer to talk about themselves, given half a chance. With the more inquisitive of her colleagues she soon becomes skilled in the art of deflection. So, too, are after-work drinks or office parties easily evaded, with tales of fictional waiting boyfriends or appointments with non-existent friends.

There is a certain peace in this new life she has constructed, an enjoyment to be had in the uncomplicatedness of her days. She finds that she can float upon the surfaces of other people's lives quite contentedly. Sitting quietly at her desk, her eyes on her computer screen, she'll listen avidly to her colleagues' chatter, inhaling their families, friends and lovers, their plans for the weekend and next summer's holidays. She collects every banality and big deal — first dates, engagement parties, squabbles with the in-laws, interfering neighbours, husbands' promotions — taking them home to her flat at night to sift through when she's alone.

And it's almost enough for her, this safe, vicarious way of life. Almost. Because in the streets and on the Tube, in the café where she buys her lunch, in the aisle of the supermarket, she sees them. The strangers whose hungry eyes slide over her breasts, hips and legs like oil, or hover greedily over the surface of her face like mosquitoes. And she in turn watches them. A body next to hers on the Tube, the line of a stranger's back or the flash of bare skin beneath a T-shirt's hem. Even a hand gripping a rail or the curve of a mouth will be enough. It is the physical pull of these slivers of masculinity, the naked desire in their faces that triggers her own longing, a compulsion to touch that once ignited becomes impossible to fight. And so, in bars or cafés, in the street or on the Tube, in the supermarket (once, even, at a bus stop), the connection will be made. It's easy once she begins: they always seem to know instantly what she offers, these hopeful strangers, and they rarely turn her down, following her gratefully back to her flat.

And afterwards, as soon as the sweat has cooled, the sheets are smoothed, the door has closed on another departing back, the search begins all over again — the next second glance across the bar or street, the next enquiring smile, the approach, the always accepted invitation.

Once they've gone she sits and smokes in the dark and listens to the sounds of Kilburn below. One night a heavy burst of rain thuds abruptly upon her bedroom skylight, bringing with it an unexpected memory of the forest, transporting her instantly back there with a sudden overwhelming vividness. It had always seemed to rain twice in the forest, she remembers now. There would be the first, heavy release from the sky, followed by a sudden silence, and then would begin the second steady, slow, drip, drip, drip from the leaves. Standing by her bedroom window in Kilburn she hears once again the raindrops thudding on the trees, the long pause, the second ponderous falling, the gradual slowing towards silence, and then at last the birds' resumption of their evening song. She has not thought of the forest for a long time, and the speed and power with which she is returned there leaves her reeling. Abruptly she puts out her cigarette and switches on the TV, turning the volume up higher and higher, keeping her eyes fixed upon the screen.

But in the coming weeks, the unexpected memories keep returning. More and more frequently the forest begins to encroach upon her dreams like ivy twisting through her sleeping mind. One Sunday she walks across Hampstead Heath and passes through a copse of trees. It had been raining heavily that morning and after a while she stops and inhales the smell of damp bracken, wild garlic and toadstools. The memories return with such vividness that she has to reach out for a trunk to steady herself. There she is again, suddenly, in the forest, and it is so real that ahead of her she can almost see the little stone cottage, the smoke curling from its chimney. To her right is the river where they used to fish. She cranes her neck, searching for him, longing for him. And then, as instantly as it fell, the spell breaks. Ahead of her, two men emerge from behind a tree, giggling and holding hands. They look at her curiously as they pass and she staggers away, running out from beneath the trees, back the way she came, towards the road and the low roar of traffic.

★　★　★

It's half past six, and most of her colleagues at the insurance firm in Dalston have left for the evening. She looks at the words that she's just typed into the search engine. 'Little Bird'. Taking a glance around her to check that nobody can see her screen, she hits Return.

It's not the first time that she has made this search in recent weeks and as usual, a number of articles are thrown back at her. 'Who is Little Bird?' 'Disturbed Loner who Caged Little Bird.' 'Snatched tot Elodie is Bird Child of Normandy.' But she has read these accounts before. Scrolling down through the pages she finds at last what she had been looking for, the name of a site that had caught her attention a few nights before. Taking a deep breath she double-clicks her mouse. And there it is.

The site offers such an embarrassment of riches that at first she doesn't know where to start. There they all are, her fellow savages. A freaks' hall of fame that spans the globe and offers more than two centuries' worth of cases. 'An anthropological and sociological examination of feral and socially isolated or confined children,' the sites intro promises. She looks at the long list of names, from Kaspar Hauser, to Victor of Aveyron to the Wolf Children of Bengal. Clicking on it at random, she begins to read their stories.

First is Genie, a Californian girl locked up by her family until age thirteen, half-feral and without speech when she was rescued. Next is Oxana, a Ukrainian child discovered roaming the streets with wild dogs, running on all fours, barking and howling and eating scraps from the floor. The list is endless: children living in chicken coops and found pecking and squawking like hens, children raised by monkeys, or locked up by their families in cellars, attics or sheds. Attached to each case is evidence of the media frenzy it attracted: links to documentaries, TV news coverage, endless press reports.

There in the little Dalston office the minutes tick by and still Kate reads on. It is the photographs that fascinate her most; the combination of vulnerability and wildness in the children's eyes that inspire in her both repulsion and recognition. And gradually it dawns on her that they all share one thing: not one of these rescued children had been successfully rehabilitated, not entirely. Every one of them remained dependent in care homes and institutions, staying forever in the public consciousness as figures of wonder and fear.

Finally, as she knew she would, amongst this sad, unsettling catalogue she finds herself. 'Elodie Brun: Little Bird,' she reads. The first article she clicks on is from a science journal and mainly illustrated with pictures of her brain. Each caption explains the neurological changes and developments that took place as she acquired language. The only photograph is the one of her standing next to Ingrid on the stage at the conference. With furrowed brow Kate works her way through the complicated text, reading about neurological lateralisation, hemispheric specialisation and a hundred other technical terms that she doesn't understand. Throughout, Ingrid's work is described as 'groundbreaking', as having 'huge scientific significance'. She feels a stab of shock when she discovers that she has been the only such child to have ever successfully been taught to speak and that, had she been taken earlier by Mathias, or left the forest later, she would never have learnt to do so.

She magnifies the photograph of herself at the conference. She can tell by her half-open mouth that she's in the middle of delivering her speech, and once again she feels the hot spotlight on her face, her sweating hands clenched in fear before the sea of faces staring back at her. At her side, Ingrid, her eyes blazing with pride as she stares triumphantly back at the crowd in front of them. Kate stares and stares at the photograph, and with a sudden start of recognition she realises that what looked like a tiny circle on the lapel of Ingrid's blouse is actually the little cat brooch, the one with the missing stones that had been Ingrid's favourite. Her eyes prickle with tears as the familiar guilt and sorrow engulfs her. Switching off the computer her head sinks to her hands. After a long time she looks at the clock and is amazed to see that it is ten o'clock. Stiff from sitting, she gets to her feet, picks up her bag and at last goes home.

⋆   ⋆   ⋆

'I am not like them,' she reassures herself as she lies in her bed that night. She thinks about the

233

faces of those animal-children who had staggered half-naked from out of the wild, or the snarling freaks locked up alone for years. 'I was never like them,' she says. She turns over in her bed and looks at her neatly ironed blouse hanging on the back of her door, the polished shoes sat side by side on the floor, ready for another day at the office.

But the next evening and for the rest of the week after that when everyone else has left for the night, Kate remains at her desk, scouring the internet for more stories of these strange, wild creatures. The next weekend she visits her local library, pouring over every book she can find on the subject. Soon she gets into the habit of buying a newspaper each day, combing them tirelessly for news of recent cases. 'I am not like them,' she tells herself over and over as she searches. And yet still she cannot stop herself from thinking about the forest, how it was the last place that she felt she belonged, nor rid herself of the thought that, no matter how carefully she tries to imitate the people who surround her every day, she never truly feels that she is one of them. Often she will take out the computer printout of her mother's face and pour over every detail of it, staring at it until the colours and lines and shadows blur.

One morning she reads about a Romanian boy found living in the Transylvanian countryside, running wild with a pack of stray dogs. When discovered he had been eating one of the very animals that had taken him in as its own. The story horrifies her. She feels a churning in her stomach as she comes to the end and is about to fling the paper from her when suddenly the by-line catches her eye. With a pang of recognition she realises that the writer's name is the same one she had seen beneath dozens of similar articles and features she had read in recent weeks. Tentatively she looks around her to check that none of her colleagues are looking, then copies the name into the search engine.

The picture on Martin Chambers' website shows a serious looking man in his forties with a beard, glasses, and kind, intelligent eyes. She stares at his face for a long time. The site tells her that he is the author of the book *Wild Children: A Study of Human Nature*, and she frowns, certain that she had already read everything her local library had to offer. Her eyes return to his face and as she stares at him the faintest beginnings of a fantasy begin to brew inside her brain. She wonders what it would be like to meet this man. Her head spins with a thousand questions she would ask, the fears that he might be able to put to rest. But even as the thoughts take shape, she knows that it would be impossible: he would be bound to recognise her.

Just then, as she is about to exit the site, a little box headed 'News' catches her eye. The book will be out next week, she reads, and Martin Chambers will be signing copies at its launch the following Saturday. Her eyes land briefly upon the address. She will not go, of course: the risk would be too great. She exits the site and gets on with her work.

The hood is pulled far down over her eyes. She walks slowly but deliberately as if the little bar on Upper Street were emitting some kind of magnetic force. She had not meant to come, and will only stand outside for a little while, she tells herself, once she gets there. She will look through the window and then return to her flat. To another night alone in front of the TV. Or perhaps on the way home she will call in at a bar, perhaps she will meet a man there to spend a few hours with. There in the street she loiters in the shadows and stares through the window. People mill about inside holding little plastic glasses of wine and talking noisily to each other. She edges closer for a better look. Just inside the door an elegantly dressed woman sits with a clipboard, ticking off people's names as they enter.

At the far end of the room, Martin Chambers sits behind a desk, a pile of books in front of him, a pen in his hand. He is looking hopefully around at the chattering, wine-drinking guests, but they are ignoring him. She sighs, and is about to turn when she feels someone jostling behind her. 'Sorry, excuse me, are you going in or not?' The voice is imperious, impatient. She looks up to see a smartly dressed middle-aged couple behind her. Before she knows what's happening, she is being bustled in, the woman with the clipboard is looking at her doubtfully but waving her in alongside the couple and a plastic glass of white wine is being thrust into her hand. And there she is, standing alone amongst the chattering people, only metres away from Martin Chambers and his hopeful pile of books.

It is only then that she notices the photographs. On every wall, in various shapes and sizes, of various quality and age, in black and white or in colour, some of them actual paintings or sketches, the faces of the 'wild children' that she has now grown so familiar with stare back at her. There they all are: Genie, Oxana, Kaspar, Amala and Kamala, Victor and the rest. Around thirty of the most famous cases. Their wary eyes, their odd, discordant grins or grimaces. Few of them are looking at the camera, indeed it is as if the lens has just snared them like a net, plucking them from their natural habitat with a savagery of its own. Her heart twists with pity to see them there, pinned against the wall while the people chatter and smoke below. And then, suddenly, she sees it. She takes a step forward. There it is, her picture, the one taken outside the Rouen hospital. There she is for all to see, displayed upon the wall amongst all the other children. The room begins to rock and lurch around her. She feels ice cold.

A dull rage builds inside her. She doesn't notice when her hand crushes the plastic cup with a snap, is oblivious to the wine pouring over her fingers and the mutters and curious looks around her. But wasn't he right, this Martin Chambers? Wasn't he right to compare her to these others? Hadn't she, after all, proved her savagery the night of Ingrid's death? At last she turns and stumbles from the bar.

Breaking into a run, she hurtles along Upper Street, barely conscious of the Saturday-night stragglers as they jump, startled, from her path. She runs until she gets to the station where she almost throws herself down the escalator, and makes the train just before the doors close. In the bright lurching glare she sits, hunched, oblivious to anything but her own thoughts. When at last she reaches her stop she flies towards Kilburn, not stopping until she reaches her flat where she slams the door behind her and finally gives into her fury, kicking and punching the walls, hurling everything she can pick up before at last she falls to her bed.

After a while she gets up and goes to her window. Below her, in the street, a couple, hand in hand, hurry beneath a brief splattering of rain. A group of teenagers laugh and shriek drunkenly; a woman emerges from a car carrying a sleeping child in her arms. She thinks about their lives, and about the lives of her colleagues; their families, husbands, friends. As she stands there, the street below her gradually empties, the cars pass less frequently until they all but stop. A hush falls over Kilburn. And at last she comes to a decision.

★   ★   ★

It is a few weeks later that she sees the tall, quiet man playing records in the corner of the Mermaid pub in Dalston. He touches her: his slight stoop, his air of quiet calm, the shy hunger

238

in his eyes. And when she wakes next to him the following morning and hears herself promising to return, she watches, mystified, as the smile breaks upon his face like sunshine. She will not be like them, she promises herself.

21

Anton Klein stood beneath the painting of Kaspar Hauser and sipped his warm white wine. Opposite him hung the photograph of Elodie Brun, and he hadn't taken his eyes off it since he arrived. By the door, a prim girl with a clipboard cast him furtive, hungry little glances, tiny missiles of longing bouncing ineffectually off his skin, while the wine waiter standing next to her stared with a more naked admiration. He ignored them both. Slowly the room filled and he felt a familiar deadening ennui. He wasn't sure why he had come; he could have bought the book online. He would take a copy for his collection, he decided, then leave. He drained his glass and looked around for somewhere to deposit it, steadfastly ignoring the waiter's eye.

It was only then that he noticed the girl standing a few metres away from him, staring at the same photograph of Elodie that he had been looking at. She had her back to him — an out-sized, faded red sweatshirt, the hood pulled over her head — but it was her air of focused stillness that held his gaze. She stood as if transfixed, leaning slightly forward, entirely oblivious to the people who milled around her. He waited for her to relax, to move on, but she remained, still.

He examined her more closely. He couldn't

see her face. Just a few yellow feathers of hair escaped the hood. She was dressed in a shapeless cotton knee-length dress or skirt, legs bare and on her feet she wore simple white plimsolls with short, childish red socks. As he watched, he was startled by a loud crack of splintering plastic and noticed with confusion that wine was pouring over her fingers and onto the floor. People were glancing over at her curiously, but still she didn't move. He took a step towards her, feeling an urgent desire suddenly to see her properly and at that same moment she turned, dropped her ruined cup and shouldered her way through the bodies and out of the bar.

And in that split second, he had seen her face. The hood still half obscured it, revealing only a narrow oval of eyes, nose and chin, but still he was sure. Her hair was different, her face a little plumper, older, but it was her, he was certain: it was Elodie. A hot excitement gripped him and within seconds he was pushing his way through the bar, past the disappointed gaze of the waiter and door girl and out onto the street where he spotted her steaming through the Saturday-night crowds of Upper Street. She ran fast and he was out of breath before he caught up with her, just as she was disappearing into the entrance of Highbury and Islington station.

He tore down the escalator and leapt onto the train moments behind her. He took a seat at the end of the carriage furthest from where she sat, rigidly and on the edge of her seat, her hands two tense balls in her lap. Her hood had slipped, revealing the yellow cap of hair, the delicate features, the huge, dark blue eyes, now aglow with a kind of anguish. His gaze lingered over her lips for a while and an intense loathing filled him. He savoured the feeling: it was the first tangible emotion he had felt in some time.

His eyes fell to the curve of her bare legs. A memory snaked its way beneath his hatred and for a moment he was pulled back to High Barn, to the last time he had seen her. He had been sixteen, creeping up the stairs to the top floor, the forbidden key clasped in his hand. He had loitered outside her bedroom door, hatred brewing even then in his jealous adolescent heart. He had put his eye to the crack, the noise of her TV drowning out the floorboard's creek. And there she'd been, his mother's precious project. There she was, lying naked upon the bed, her fourteen-year-old body sliced by rays of light streaming through the window, her long hair gold-red against her pillow. Her beauty so absolute that for a moment it had stopped time, held him in its light, snaking its way into the clenched fist of his heart, a tantalizing glimpse of something as yet unknown. As he'd watched, her fingers had trailed across her breasts then slowly down over her belly and he had given a low involuntary moan in response. And though he had been suddenly and brutally snatched from his trance by the sound of his mother moving dangerously close below, the image of her lying there would be seared across his mind forever. There in the train he reddened with shame at the memory of how this girl, now so hated, had once been the fodder for so much subsequent

242

energetic teenage fantasy.

The train pulled into West Hampstead station and the sudden distraction of her getting to her feet broke him from his reverie. He followed her from the train; careful to keep at a distance he trailed her out of the station into the street, breaking into a run when she began to sprint down Iverson Road. At last, on reaching Kilburn, she turned off the High Road into a narrow, grubby street. The road was poorly lit and he remained concealed by a tree on the opposite pavement when she stopped finally and let herself into one of the tall shabby houses.

Anton waited until, after a brief pause, a light appeared in one of the windows on the top floor. He sheltered beneath the sycamore's branches, his mind returning, as it often did, to the night his mother had died.

There had been an argument over dinner — the usual, pointless bullshit. Eventually he had bolted, sneaking back later to steal his mother's car keys.

What he hated most about his mother, what he could never forgive, was the way she manipulated his father. If it hadn't been for Ingrid poisoning his mind, Robert would never have agreed to him being sent away. Never. His father loved him and the blame was entirely on his mother's shoulders, of that, he had always been certain.

He remembered that he could still hear his parents yelling as he'd slid the keys from her purse. For the rest of the night he had driven aimlessly. At last he'd pulled up in a deserted car park and rolled a joint, the heady effects of the weed mingling with his anger and self-pity. Mulling over his younger self's futile claims on his mother's attention, he saw failure; tantrums and disobedience evolving over time into more serious misdemeanours, and still nothing. He remembered when he had hit her, the satisfying, terrifying sensation of her cheekbone beneath his fist, his own triumph matched only by hers.

Dawn had just begun to bleed over the roofs of High Barn when he returned. He had been surprised to find the front door wide open. Perplexed, he had stood staring dumbly at it for a moment or two, had even looked around him suspiciously as if expecting someone to appear from behind one of the trees. An eerie quiet had contributed to his unease; a strange sense that he was being awaited. At last he entered. And then he had walked into the kitchen. On the threshold he had frozen, taking in the awful sight, a cold disbelief pinning him to the spot. His first reaction had been an involuntary gasp of laughter. 'What?' he had asked the empty room, half thinking it was some bizarre kind of joke. 'What?' he had said again, his hand flying nervously to his mouth.

On the kitchen floor, in the gloom of the cold blue half-light were overturned chairs, broken crockery, puddles of wine and food. And amongst it all, his mother's body. He had crept closer, adrenalin sluicing queasily through his veins, his skin prickling and hot, and he had felt an overwhelming desire to run. There she lay, slumped on her side, a pool of blood already congealing beneath her. Her skin was white, her lips blue, her eyes glassy and blank. 'Mom?' that was what he'd said, just like a little kid. 'Mom?'

And it was only then that he had noticed his father. A tiny noise had made him turn and there he'd been, just sitting at the table. He did not look at Anton when he spoke, his voice so quiet that he had had to strain to hear, 'She killed her,' was what his father had said, 'Elodie.'

There in the Kilburn street, he saw her suddenly appear at the window and he took a couple of steps back into the shadows. It began to rain. A couple clasping hands ran past him followed by a shrieking zig-zag of drunken teens. A little way down the street a mini cab pulled up, ejecting a woman carrying a sleeping child. Still he stayed, still she remained.

At the time, Anton had been surprised by the depth of his grief. Hadn't he, after all, wished his mother dead a million times before? He had not been prepared for the gnawing, guilt-edged sorrow that had attacked him like a sickness. Instead of returning to England he had abandoned his plan to retake his A-levels in favour of staying with his father. The two of them, he had thought, would keep each other company. Perhaps this might bring them closer, he hoped.

But something strange had begun to happen to his father. Over the following weeks he had remained peculiarly distant, refusing to talk about Ingrid's death or even meet his son's eyes. Instead he had kept to his study, often locking the door and refusing to answer Anton when he called him. But the confusion and dismay he felt was nothing compared to the moment when Robert had finally emerged to make his announcement. He had looked out of the window as he'd spoken and Anton had noticed that his hair was much greyer, his face more gaunt and lined. In a quiet, unfamiliar voice he had informed his son that not only had he put High Barn up for sale, he'd accepted a new job in Boston too — he would be moving to a one-bedroomed apartment the following month. Before Anton could even digest this news, he had then been told that all the proceeds from the sale would be his, along with his mother's money, including his grandfather's estate. Robert would be taking nothing. 'Go back to England, Anton,' was all he would say in reply to his son's increasingly desperate questioning. 'I'm sorry, but it's for the best.'

And so, aged nineteen, Anton had found himself in London, wealthy but entirely adrift. His father kept in touch only intermittently; a card at Christmas, a vague email here and there. It was then that the hatred he had once felt for his mother, left floundering in mid-air since her death, had landed squarely upon Elodie's shoulders. She was to blame for this. For all of it. His mother's death, what could only be described as his father's breakdown, the fact that he was now entirely alone in the world. And once his hatred found its home, it flourished, expanding daily until it filled his thoughts, becoming the focus of all his energy and self-pity. Over the years he'd speculated endlessly on Elodie's whereabouts, puzzling over the police trail that had gone so mysteriously cold in Queens. He had brooded over photographs of her face, collected every piece of literature he could find on her. And now, here she was, delivered into his lap like a gift.

There, in the chilly north-London street, four years after she had murdered his mother, Elodie Brun moved away from the window of her flat. Pulling his coat more tightly around him against the cold, Anton went in search of a taxi.

★ ★ ★

In the living room of his central London home he looked at the books, newspaper clippings, internet print-outs and photographs spread out before him on the floor. Taking a seat on the sofa he picked up a small cardboard box from the coffee table and lifted off its lid, pulling out a small, intricately carved figure of a bird. It fit neatly into his palm, and as his fingers stroked the wooden curve of its head he looked over at one of the photographs of Elodie, and smiled.

22

Deptford, south-east London, 20 February 2004
They lay on the floor of Frank's living room, a
bottle of wine between them. 'Auvrey,' Kate said,
staring at him, her fingers lightly stroking his
wrist while she rolled the name around her
tongue. 'Auv-rey.'

'It's French,' Frank told her. 'My dad was
— still is, probably — French.'

'I would like to go to France one day,' she
said.

He saw the intense sadness pass over her face,
and felt a familiar stab of anxiety; the sensation
once again of glimpsing, as though through a
crack in a door, something dark and painful. For
a moment, just a moment, he hovered outside,
debating whether to push the door open and go
in. He felt unsure, inept. Instead he lent over and
kissed her. 'We could go together if you like.'

She smiled. The moment had passed; a key
turned in its lock. 'Do you speak French?' she
asked.

'Yeah,' he shrugged. 'My old man used to
speak it to me. When I was a kid I would pretend
it was our secret language that nobody else could
understand.' He smiled. 'Stupid, really. I kept it
up though, after he left. It's the only lesson at
school I was any good at apart from Music. And
Joanie — Dad's sister — used to speak it too.'

He stared up at the ceiling, remembering how

after his dad left, he would return home from school full of the day's news to find his mum sitting in the fading light, staring blankly out of the window. He would retreat at once to his room, guiltily stashing away the day's triumphs or successes the way a shoplifter secretes his stash about his person. After a while he'd started going round to his aunt's house after school instead. He smiled at the memory. When the house had been Joanie's it had smelt of cats and air freshener. Radio One had blared all day while sunlight shone on brown linoleum. She used to dye her long, curly hair pillar-box red to match her lipstick. She wore dangly earrings and low-cut blouses and always smelt of Diorissimo and cigarettes. By the time he was eleven she had taught him how to make her the perfect gin and tonic.

She was a dressmaker and most afternoons would see Frank standing on a chair with a biscuit in his hand, draped in whatever dress or skirt she was making at the time, while he chatted about his day and she crawled around him, humming along to the radio through a mouthful of pins. Sometimes though, when she opened the door to him, she would announce, 'Bonjour mon petit! Ce soir, nous parlons seulement en Français!' He'd liked that, it had made him feel as if he was still, somehow, talking to his dad.

Frank had been twenty-one when Joanie had got cancer. For the seven weeks before she died he'd visited the hospital almost every day. In the end she'd left him her house; to his mum she'd left her collection of ceramic ducks with the handwritten message, 'For the love of God, dear, CHEER UP!!'

'Say something in French to me,' Kate said, pouring them both more wine.

So he said, 'Je crois que tu es belle. Et je t'aime.'

'What did you say?' she asked eagerly.

'I said that I think that you're beautiful.'

After that she made him talk in French all the time, repeating the words back to him, holding each one lovingly in her mouth: fleur, nuit, cœur, quelquefois, nous, peut-être, merci, demain.

To say that she was unlike any other girl he'd ever known was something of an understatement. There was so much about her that fascinated him: her extreme independence, the way she would go walking the streets alone for hours, her innate ability to find her way wherever she was, the strange, shadowy wildness he glimpsed in her sometimes when her guard was down. The complicated mind games that had seemed to be such an inevitable feature of his previous relationships seemed entirely absent from Kate's psyche. There were no subtexts to decipher, no frosty atmospheres to navigate, wondering what it was he'd done wrong. In fact, she seemed to be always disarmingly to-the-point. ('Why are you so angry with her?' she'd asked soon after they met, when he had been sure he'd been referring to his mother in the friendliest of terms.)

And whenever he saw her, he would be overwhelmed by his need to touch her. Within a few moments his fingers would be itching for her. In bed, he felt as if every shred of feeling in his body rose to the surface of his skin, that every part of him was focussed in the sensation of touching her. They would make love everywhere, anywhere; there, in the hall before she'd barely dropped her bag, on the stairs, in the kitchen, on the sofa, in the bath. Her small legs wrapped tight around him, her lips kissing every part of him, her deft hands urgent, her steady eyes on his.

And as the months passed, little by little he began to feel surer of his place in her life. The words had been bubbling on his tongue for weeks before he finally allowed himself to say them. 'I love you.' The first time he'd said it, she had stared back at him for a long time, until finally she had repeated back to him, carefully, thoughtfully rolling the words around her tongue, 'I love you.'

She moved into his place by almost imperceptibly small degrees. Gradually, more and more of her belongings filled the few, small rooms of his little Deptford house. After a while, she returned less and less frequently to her Kilburn bedsit, until, one day, Frank came back from the record shop where he worked to find her standing on his doorstep, a small suitcase in her hand. 'Lease ran out,' she'd said simply, her dense, petrol-blue eyes on his. 'Can I live here, with you?' And he'd felt his heart leap to an entirely new level of happiness.

At night they would take a bath together in the small, cramped tub. It was old-fashioned and had taps with six knobbly prongs that she said were like his toes. She would sit in the front, her small buttocks wedged between his thighs, his long legs wrapped around her, while the hot tap leaked a slow, steady drip, drip, drip and he massaged soap into her narrow back, tracing her spiky spine with tender fingers until the water ran cold. He was blissfully happy.

★ ★ ★

For those first six months Frank immersed himself so entirely in his new life with Kate that everything else was forgotten. He would go to the record shop where he worked every day as usual, but afterwards he would rush home, every part of him tense with a strange doubt until he saw her again, until he had reassured himself that she was still there, that she really existed, that she was his. So when, in January, an exasperated Jimmy sent him a text telling him to meet him at the pub that night or he'd come round and burn his record collection, he reluctantly kissed Kate goodbye, and set off for the Hope and Anchor.

He was surprised, when he saw Eugene and Jimmy sitting at their usual table, how pleased he was to see them. At the same time it was oddly disorientating finding them so unchanged, when as far as he was concerned everything was different — the whole world was new. He had missed them, he realised.

'It was the Big D peanuts bird that did it,' Jimmy was saying when Frank had got himself a pint and sat down at their table. 'Remember when you'd go to the pub with your old man, and you'd keep asking for more and more nuts, just so the barmaid would get to the ones on her tits? Fucking brilliant!'

'No way,' said Eugene, shaking his head. 'That teacher at Morden, Miss Townsend. Remember her? She fell over and flashed her knicks once, dirty bitch. Now that was the first time Little Eugene came out to play. Serious.' A brief glint of happiness shone in his eyes.

'Bit young for you, weren't she?' asked Jimmy. He smiled at Frank. 'You know he's knocking off Jackie from the Feathers, don't you? She's got to be pushing forty.'

Frank laughed and shook his head.

'Yeah, but I'm doing the daughter as well,' protested Eugene. 'Here mate — ' he turned to Frank ' — couldn't lend us a score, could you?'

'Fuck's sake,' said Jimmy. 'You only had one off me a couple of days ago.'

Frank shrugged. 'Sorry. I'm potless. You still owe me fifty quid anyway.'

They sipped their pints and glanced around the Anchor. By the bar, a couple of thirtysome-things in stripy Gap jumpers talked loudly above the juke-box.

'I mean, it's not the ideal place to raise the kids,' the first one was saying earnestly. 'And, you know, Crouch End had more restaurants and stuff. But, what with the East London line and the Olympics and that, Isobel and I really think New Cross was such a sound investment.'

His friend nodded enthusiastically. 'Bottom

line? There's nowhere else so central you can buy period family homes for these sorts of prices.'

'Besides,' said the first one, 'there's so much character around here. Look at this place. It's so, you know, *London*. I love it.'

His mate nodded, and glanced around him. 'Yeah,' he said, doubtfully. 'Me too.' They finished their drinks in silence.

Jimmy caught Frank's eye and laughed. 'Good to see you mate,' he said.

Frank smiled. 'Yeah. Sorry it's been so long.'

'Kate OK?'

The name sounded odd on Jimmy's lips. He shrugged. 'Yeah, she's great. Things are great. I'll bring her out one night, let you meet her properly,' he trailed off, the idea of it making him feel a bit strange.

Jimmy held his gaze for a beat or two. 'Good idea.'

Frank glanced across to the table opposite where an old man sat alone. He had perfectly parted yellow-grey hair and was dressed in a shirt and neatly-pressed trousers. He had a bulbous, purple nose and thick, horn-rimmed spectacles. Frank's eyes drifted to his feet. They were clad in grey slip-ons, carefully polished, placed neatly side by side and slightly pigeon-toed. Frank raised his glass at him and the old man nodded back. He had sat there, in the same place, every single night that Frank could remember, always carefully dressed in his ironed slacks and shirt, always alone.

'Look,' Eugene interrupted, 'I'm sorry to be a

cunt and that, but seriously, you sure you can't lend me a score?'

'Fuck's sake.' Irritably, Jimmy pulled out a couple of notes and handed them over.

'Thanks. I'll give it you back next week.' Jimmy and Frank watched as Eugene hurried to the other side of the bar, to a grimy looking man with adult acne and a stained FUCK Me T-shirt standing shiftily by the pool table.

Frank raised his eyebrows at Jimmy, who shook his head. 'It's getting worse. He's off his tits most nights. Booze, coke, spliff, you name it. That Jackie from the Feathers, can't believe her luck, can she, so she's giving him handouts left right and centre. Not to mention all the other birds he's scrounging off at the moment.'

Eugene returned looking pleased with himself. He nodded at Jimmy and jerked his head towards the toilets.

'Nah,' said Jimmy. 'Have a word: it's Tuesday night.'

'Yeah, yeah.'

Jimmy and Frank sat in silence for a while. 'Work all right, is it?' Frank asked.

Jimmy smiled broadly, 'Good as gold, mate.' Jimmy had set up his own business a few years ago buying and selling second-hand cars. Now he had his own garage and a two-bedroom flat around the corner.

'Still seeing that Amy?' Frank asked next, referring to a nurse Jimmy had been going out with off and on for six months or so.

'Nah,' Jimmy raised his eyebrows and laughed. 'Nah, mate. You know how it is. You go out with a girl for a bit and it's all — ' he put on a high falsetto giggle ' — Oh Jimmy, you're so funny, Jimmy you're such a laugh, let me suck your knob Jimmy. Before you know it you're walking round Tesco's with a hangover, she hasn't touched your dick for two weeks and she's not talking to you because you can't be fucked to go to her best mate Gemma's engagement party.'

Eugene had returned. 'Why is that?' he asked.

'Why's what?'

'Why are birds' best mates always called Gemma?'

The three of them puzzled it over for a while, and Frank realised that he hadn't ever actually met, or even heard Kate mention, any friends of her own. 'Dunno,' he said.

At the other end of the pub, the barmaid was setting up a karaoke system and a hum of expectation buzzed through the regulars. A few tables away an overweight, defeated looking man a few years older than them was sitting with his girlfriend, a sour-looking woman with an expression of bored indifference on her face. The man looked over and gloomily raised his glass at them before continuing to stare at the table.

'Fucking hell,' said Frank, nudging Jimmy. 'That's John Bennet over there.' Jimmy and Eugene glanced over at the man, before looking embarrassedly away. John had been a god at Morden Comprehensive, a cross between Pele and James Bond. When they were kids nobody had doubted for a minute the glittering future that lay ahead of him. The three of them sat in silence for a few moments, staring into their pints. 'Christ,' said Eugene at last, getting up, 'I'm going for another line.'

A woman in her fifties with a face full of make-up started singing My Heart Will Go On along to the Karaoke machine and Jimmy nudged Frank. 'Look at those two,' he said. Watching the singer on the other side of the pub were two girls in their early twenties. Goldsmiths students slumming it most likely. Frank grinned as one of them — a short, attractive blonde — turned and shot a disdainful look at Jimmy, who sniggered and went to get more drinks.

After a while Eugene returned and started telling them at double speed about one of the regulars at the Feathers. ' . . . so this bloke's starting to feel ill as fuck yeah, and he can't work out why. Everyday he comes back from work, makes himself dinner, goes to bed, gets up, goes to work, comes home, has his dinner, goes to bed'

'Sounds like a right laugh,' interrupted Jimmy.

'Yeah, well, so anyway, every day it's the same as normal, but suddenly he starts feeling a bit gyp and he can't work out why. A week later his old lady goes round and finds him in bed, dead as a dodo.'

'Jesus,' said Frank. 'What'd happened to him?'

Eugene lit a fag. 'Pigeon had flown into the water tank hadn't it? Got stuck, carked it, then started decomposing. Geezer's drinking his water and getting poisoned.' He looked at Frank and Jimmy and laughed. 'Straight up!'

'Death by pigeon,' Jimmy grinned, shaking his head. 'What a way to go.'

It was 10.30. Frank stood up and put his jacket on. 'Sorry lads, but I better get back.' He didn't meet Jimmy's eyes as he added, 'got some early deliveries in the shop tomorrow.' He waved a hand at his two friends and headed for the door. As he left he turned and saw them make a beeline for the two students.

The night was freezing. He turned up his collar against the wind and set out along the deserted New Cross streets. He passed the blackened bricks of the Venue club, the elaborate porticos and turrets of deserted Victorian pubs, grafittied chipboard covering their smashed-in windows. Cafs with handwritten menus blu-tacked to the glass, cab offices with iron grilles to keep out the lunatics and robbers. He passed Afro-Caribbean hairdressers and nail bars, second-hand furniture stores and Cash Converters. Each one was in darkness; the only light in the black streets came from the pubs and off-licences glowing orange on every corner.

He hurried on towards Deptford and his thoughts turned to Eugene. Maybe Jimmy was right: it had been some time since he'd seen Eugene not half out of his head on something or other. He speeded up as he got closer to home and mentally shrugged it off. Eugene had always been a bit nuts, and he and Jimmy had always looked out for him: lending him money, putting him up, helping him get work. He always sorted himself out eventually. He'd probably be fine in a week or two.

When he got home he found Kate sitting on the back step to the garden, smoking a cigarette. She never seemed to feel the cold for some reason. The light from the moon and his kitchen bathed the small bricked-in space in a pale glow. She seemed deep in thought and didn't hear him approach and for a moment, just for a moment as he looked at her it struck him, inexplicably, that he was looking at a complete stranger, and he felt a sharp chill of fear. But then she turned, saw him, and smiled. Relief flooded him. Hugging his coat tighter to himself he sat next to her and she leant her head on his shoulder. They sat in silence for a while.

'I really should do something about this garden,' said Frank at last, looking at the mess of overgrown weeds, the rotting carcass of an armchair he'd dumped out there the summer before and then forgotten about, the dead twigs poking out from moss-covered terracotta pots. 'Used to be Joanie's pride and joy, this.'

'We could make it nice again,' said Kate, reaching for his hand. 'Grow new things.'

'Yeah,' said Frank, pleased with the idea. 'I used to quite like helping her out here when I was a kid.' He laughed, embarrassed. 'Always fancied myself as a bit of a gardener actually. A butch one, naturally.'

He stared out at the small, bricked yard. 'We could have honeysuckle over that wall,' said Frank, 'and a magnolia over there. Then, in that bed we could plant loads of wild flowers and stuff, maybe some hollyhocks . . . '

And as he talked, Kate kept her eyes on his lips, softly repeating the names of the flowers under her breath. 'Honeysuckle, magnolia, camellia, rose.' They sat in silence for a while and rather than the dark, cold yard, they saw their garden in bright sunlight, overflowing with flowers in full bloom on some distant summer's day.

23

London, April 2004
Such a gentle start to the nightmare. Such a quiet beginning to it all.

★   ★   ★

The Soho Picture Library takes up two floors of the offices on Brewer Street. Kate stands on the pavement outside. She's used to the small, brown-carpeted shabbiness of high-street insurance firms and solicitors, and though she had asked her agency for a placement more central now that she'd moved south, she'd not expected anything like this. Newly pointed yellow bricks and real sash windows, a discreet flower box on each sill. She passes through the large glass doors and into the foyer with its fat, expensive sofas and curvaceous vases of plump flowers. A skeletal blonde eyes her suspiciously from behind the reception desk. 'Courier?' she asks.

'No,' says Kate. 'I'm — '

'From the agency?' She doesn't wait for a reply. 'Through that door, second on the left.' The blonde jerks her head towards a large, glass door, fires a brief, appalled glance at Kate's shoes, and returns to her magazine.

★   ★   ★

261

The thirty or so people gathered with her in the small, plush room are students, mostly. Foreigners and students, the majority of them young — cheap labour for mundane work, brought together here by chance to graft for a few months, for a few quid. They are being addressed by a middle-aged man with an earnest, tired face and a soft Birmingham accent. 'Welcome to SPL. I'm Stuart,' he says, and begins to tell them about the 'special project' they have been 'selected' for. But though his audience stares politely at him, they are, Kate knows, barely listening. *Just get on with it, man. Tell us what the fucking job is and we'll do it, if you pay us.* Only Kate listens intently, as she always does.

At last he leads them down a flight of stairs to the library's basement, through a door marked 'Archives'. It's a long, low-ceilinged room, warm and dimly lit and each wall is lined with filing cabinets. Groups of tables with scanners and computers run the length of its centre. In the far corner are stacked several hundred cardboard boxes of what turns out to be photographs. A few people shuffle and cough while Stuart inducts them into the task of sorting, scanning, categorizing, sub-categorizing, labelling, numbering, cross referencing and filing the contents of the boxes.

It's Kate he singles out first, probably because he has noticed she has been paying such close attention. He smiles at her. 'You,' he says, 'and you, please — ' carelessly he points to the girl standing next to her and beckons them over. He

262

takes them to the boxes, and picking two, hands one to each of them. 'Architecture,' he says, reading from their labels. 'That should do you for starters.' Next he leads them to the nearest workstation, spends a few minutes explaining the computers, then moves on to the others.

Left alone, the two smile shyly at each other. 'Hi,' says Kate after a pause. Her co-worker is in her mid twenties, tall and slightly mannish with very short hair and large hands. Kate had noticed her earlier, tripping over her feet and dropping her bag on the way down to the basement.

'I'm Daisy,' she says, offering a clumsy handshake.

They look down at the boxes in front of them. 'Well, I suppose we'd better get on with it,' says Kate. They grimace and smile, and turn to their Macs.

★ ★ ★

Her first day passes quickly enough: the work is easy and absorbing, the low gloom of the archive room peaceful, soporific. That evening she emerges somewhat dazedly onto the scuttling pavements of Soho, taken by surprise by the sudden surge of dark energy. Turning down one furtive little alley she finds a narrow, cobbled street lined with sex shops and strip bars, their secretive entrances and windows lit by neon letters: Peep Show, Sex Toys, DVDs, XXX-Rated. Groups of leather-jacketed men huddle in doorways

263

while young women shiver behind counters staring out with swift, blank eyes. Two German tourists with backpacks whisper furiously in front of a movie theatre. A group of excited lads push past her, shouting and swaggering and swigging from cans. And amongst it all a steady procession of tired office workers head home.

Turning a corner she passes open doorways with handwritten signs: 'Sexy Swedish, 19', 'Naughty Teenage Model', 'Big Black Beauty'. Arrows in marker pen point towards narrow staircases lit by naked bulbs. She looks up and sees a net curtain twitch then part to reveal a pale face staring down at her. On the other side of the street, from a parked car, a man hisses then calls to her, 'Hey sexy girl. Yeah you, Beautiful! You like black cock?' She ducks her head and hurries on, past the mocking smile of a girl in apple-green hot pants standing beneath a sign that says MASSAGE. At last she cuts down Rupert Street and heads for Charing Cross.

Every lunch hour Kate slips from the library to wander the Soho Streets. Leaving the sex shops and alleyways behind, she roams through Berwick Street market up Wardour Street, Old Compton and Frith, down Poland Street, Broadwick and Lexington. Discreet silver plaques shine at her from doorways, alluding to the mysterious practices within: 'Post Production', 'Design Boutique', 'Animation Suite' she reads. Only the young and attractive inhabit this world. Gleaming with entitlement they prowl the streets, mobile phones glued to their murmuring lips.

Sometimes she'll spy one of her fellow basement dwellers shuffling past and clutching a sandwich, blinking bemusedly, as if dazzled as much by the passing glamour as by the sun's cruel spotlight. They are incongruous blemishes upon these chic streets and it seems to Kate over the following months that, as if by silent agreement and in recognition of their subterranean inferiority, they each begin to turn up for work in steadily gloomier outfits, pawing at their cardboard boxes in clothes the colours of shadows, of stains.

She has been at the library only a week when Stuart gathers them all together and introduces the new addition to their team. 'His name got left off the list somehow,' he explains, scratching his head and gesturing to the young man by his side. 'Still — ' he brightens ' — not to worry, you're here now, aren't you?' The newcomer smiles and nods his agreement, while Stuart surveys the long, low room. 'You, um . . . Kate, is it?' he says. 'And, er . . . Daisy. Looks like there's room on your table. Can you show Steven the ropes please? Well done. Right, good.' He nods and smiles vaguely, then hurries away.

The man, Steven, is a few years older than she, Kate guesses. Stocky and muscular, he has almost shaven blond hair and very pale eyebrows. She realises detachedly that he is extremely good looking, and yet there is something a little brutal in his looks, she decides. His physical presence a touch too obtrusive — his jaw a little too square, his muscles a little

265

too large. A solid brick wall of a person, through which no chinks of light can shine.

Back at their workstation Daisy can only stare in mute, pink-faced admiration at their new colleague so it is left to her to explain the simple requirements of their job. He smiles pleasantly as he listens and when, a few minutes later he wanders off in the direction of the toilets, Daisy turns to her with excitement. 'Oh my gosh!' she says. 'How gorgeous is he? He looks like that film star! The one married to what's her name. Did you see his muscles?'

Kate returns her smile vaguely. A film star. Maybe that's what had caused the unsettling twinge of recognition when she had first looked at his face — perhaps she has seen his double on TV.

The afternoon passes peacefully enough. Their new deskmate is a quiet, steady worker and he talks politely to Daisy about a TV show they both watched at the weekend. Morning drifts into afternoon and bit by bit Kate grows used to his presence. It is not until they are approaching the end of the day that she glances up and finds his gaze upon her. There's something so penetrating in his stare that she freezes instantly, like a criminal caught in a searchlight. His green irises gleam back at her in the basement's gloom. She hugs her arms around her in an unconscious, defensive gesture and looks away. When next she turns back he is staring innocently at his computer screen again, the moment has passed: he is just a stranger, like everybody else.

The Anchor is nearly empty when Kate arrives, with only a few regulars dotted here and there. Frank is sitting at a table in the corner, chatting to Jimmy and Eugene over half-finished pints. It's the first time she's seen his friends since the night at the Mermaid, and when she reaches the table she stands awkwardly for a moment, waiting for Frank to notice her. 'Hey,' he says, looking up, and he pats the stool next to him. She smiles as she sits, seeing how pleased he is to see her.

'This is Jimmy,' he says and Jimmy gets up and giving her a clumsy half-hug kisses her enthusiastically on the cheek. 'Hello,' he says warmly. 'I was a bit of a state last time we met,' he laughs and assumes an unconvincing expression of repentance. 'Good to meet you properly at last.'

'And this is Eugene,' adds Frank.

He is in fact more beautiful than she remembered, the golden darkness of his skin, the enormous brown eyes causing her to pause for a second, momentarily dazzled. However, as she smiles and says hello, she notices something that she hadn't seen before: a dark, unhappy quality that can't quite be disguised by the charm of his good looks. He waves at her from the other side of the table, with a smile that fails to reach his eyes.

'How was it today?' Frank asks Kate.

'Fine', she says. 'It was — '

'Here she is, my little blonde bombshell!' Kate

267

is interrupted by Jimmy shouting across the pub to a fair-haired girl with enormous breasts making her way towards them. She sticks her tongue out at Jimmy, pulls a stool up next to him and, helping herself to his pint, takes a long swig.

'This is Mel,' says Jimmy, grinning widely. 'We met in here a few weeks ago, doing Karaoke.'

'What can I say?' she tells them, her accent broad Yorkshire. 'I never could resist a fat piss head singing Eye Of The Tiger.' She smiles back at Jimmy. There is an easy directness about her pretty face and Kate watches how she and Jimmy banter and flirt, seeing how much Mel likes him, that behind her confident front she's anxious to impress.

Just then she notices Eugene drumming his fingers impatiently on his empty glass and frowning at the progress of Frank and Jimmy's pints. 'Does anyone want a drink?' she asks, reaching for her bag.

'Yeah, ta,' Eugene's answer is immediate.

'No, I'll get them, love,' says Jimmy. 'My round.'

When Jimmy is at the bar Kate watches Frank and Mel talk, and feels a rush of affection for him. This is my life, she tells herself. Here, having a drink after work with my boyfriend's friends. She puts her hand on Frank's knee and smiles. The evening passes, and more and more drinks are ordered. Kate watches the three men together, listening to the stream of private jokes and well-worn anecdotes. At one point Jimmy and Frank throw their heads back and laugh long and hard in unison, speechless with hilarity at some shared memory, but instead of the chill of exclusion she usually feels amongst others, she finds herself catching Mel's eye and joining in their laughter.

Just before closing time the five of them become distracted by a commotion on the other side of the pub. Over Frank's shoulder she sees a middle-aged black man shouting drunkenly and incoherently at the barmaid. The few regulars at the bar begin to move away, raising their eyebrows at each other and shaking their heads. The barmaid is talking to him tight-lipped, her arms folded across her chest.

Suddenly he looks wildly around. Spotting the group of them in the corner, he staggers slowly towards their table. Kate and Mel have not noticed how strangely still and silent the others have become, and they watch his progress with curiosity. He seems to be more booze than man, literally held together by alcohol: he's about as ruined as a man can get and still stand upright. When he reaches their table she can see his eyes are bloodshot red. He thrusts his face an inch from hers and she recoils from him, sickened by his rancid breath. His face is ravaged, slack-jawed and unfocussed, his coat reeks of stale wine and urine, is covered in stains and fastened by a length of string. His shoes don't match. He is shouting: an unintelligible barrage of words Kate can't make sense of, can only hear the underlying self-pitying rage of the terminally alcoholic.

At last Kate notices the strange thick silence that has fallen over the others. Frank is watching Eugene with intense embarrassment while Eugene stares hard at the table, his eyes boring through the wood, his body rigid.

The man stops flailing and yelling as he notices Eugene for the first time. 'Yoooooo!' he says pointing at him. 'Yoooooo!'

And finally Eugene looks up, and with a voice laden with disgust says simply, 'Hello, Dad.'

'Yoooo! Yer fuckin . . . yer fuckin . . .' he looks wildly around, searching for a name before finally, triumphantly shouting, 'Cunt!' He staggers a few feet with the effort, reeling round as if to appeal to an imaginary audience. 'S'my son!' He points at Eugene, swaying on the spot for a moment. His voice instantly turns wheedling. 'Fuckingbuyusadrinkson.' He reminds Kate of the slop-drenched rag the barmaid mops the tables with.

'Go home, Dad,' says Eugene. His voice is quiet, calm, but Kate notices that every part of him is clenched with anger.

'Naaaahdonbelikethat!'

Kate glances at Mel, who is gaping open-mouthed, her wide eyes swivelling between Eugene and his father. The smell emanating from him is beginning to make her feel nauseous. Finally Eugene's dad realises he's getting nowhere and, quick as a flash, turns ugly.

'Fuckinsnivellinglittlepieceofpissfuckoffthen-youuselesslittlecunt.' The words are a babble of fury spat at Eugene. Phlegm and a stench like rotten meat fly from his broken-toothed mouth. The pub is silent now: even the juke box seems to hold its breath in horrified fascination. Kate looks at Eugene whose chin has dropped nearly to his chest, his eyes opaque with humiliation. Suddenly his father makes a lunge towards him, his fist raised, and at that moment in a reflex action the tall, muscular young man who could've flattened his paralytic father with one slap, cowers in fear, shielding his face with his arm. A split second passes as his friends gape at him in shock. And then in a flash Frank is on his feet, grabbing hold of the drunk's collar and pushing him towards the door, where, pulling a tenner from his pocket, he uses the note to persuade him, finally, to leave.

★ ★ ★

Despite everyone's best efforts, the mood around the table struggles to recover. Each conversation fizzles out within minutes, as each one of them finds it impossible to drag their watchful gaze from Eugene who, after disappearing to the toilet for some mintues now seems hell-bent on getting as drunk as humanly possibly, ordering more beer and finishing each pint with a large whisky chaser. After his fourth he slams one hand on the table and says, 'Right then, let's get walloped. Who's up for it? Come on, let's make a night of it.'

'Thought you were skint?' asks Jimmy carefully.

'Not a problem mate,' Eugene fishes a small wrap of paper from his pocket. 'Got this on tick yesterday. Want some?'

Jimmy shakes his head and says apologetically, 'No, man, I can't tonight. I — '

'Yeah OK, whatever.' It's only when he gets up and disappears to the loo again that the others notice how drunk he really is, and they watch in silence as he weaves and staggers towards the gents, knocking a chair flying as he goes.

When he returns, his eyes wide and staring, a layer of sweat on his forehead, he takes a swig from Mel's half-drunk pint and turns to Jimmy excitedly, 'C'mon Skinner, let's go out. What d'ya say? Go up town or something? Find some decent fanny for a change.'

Mel's head swivels sharply round at him in surprise, and Jimmy puts a placating hand on her arm. 'Sorry, Euge,' he says, 'I've got stuff to do tomorrow, and — ' he gives Mel a wink ' — this one's on a promise and I'd hate to break her heart.'

Eugene frowns into space for a moment, then turns to Frank. 'Come on Frankie. It'll be like old times, let's just get in a cab and have a few drinks somewhere. Get the fuck out of this dump. Come on Auvrey, what d'ya say man?'

Frank shakes his head, 'Look, Euge, I would but I've got an early start tomorrow, why don't we go out this weekend, yeah? Do it properly?'

At this Eugene springs to his feet and says, 'Well fuck you then,' and with a brief smile to let them know he's joking, adds, 'you useless cunts.'

* ★ *

On the way home Frank and Kate walk hand in hand in silence for a while but she can feel Frank's agitation through his fingers. At last he stops and says, 'Fuck it. I should have gone with him.' He shakes his head. 'It's just — what can I do? Watch him get wasted again? With those wankers from the Feathers? It was all right when we were kids but it gets boring, you know? It gets really fucking old.' He turns to Kate who squeezes his hand but doesn't answer.

'I'll phone him tomorrow,' he says after a while, walking on decisively. 'He'll be all right.'

Inside the door of Frank's little terraced house, Kate reaches for him and they stand in the narrow hall for a moment, her head resting against his chest, his arms around her. And as usual, a sudden and almost overwhelming desire to tell him everything grips her. 'I'm not who you think I am,' she imagines herself saying for the thousandth time since they met. But no sooner has the thought formed than fear engulfs her and she forces it from her mind. She closes her eyes and breathes in the leather smell of his jacket. She has found too much, she tells herself, to risk losing it all now.

The phone rings and Frank breaks free of their embrace and makes for the stairs. 'Can you get that,' he asks her. 'I need the loo.'

She reaches for it quickly, half-wondering if it might be Eugene. But the person on the other end doesn't reply when she answers. Instead

273

whoever it is listens silently for several seconds to her repeated 'Hellos', and then very carefully, very slowly, hangs up.

★   ★   ★

Such a gentle start to the nightmare, such a quiet beginning to it all.

24

Clerkenwell, east London, 1 May 2003

For the past three years Frank had worked at East Side Soundz, a record shop on the Clerkenwell Road that, until Frank had turned up had been teetering on the verge of bankruptcy. As its new manager however, Frank had managed to turn the shop around, building good relations with suppliers, stocking up on records people actually wanted to buy, organising its website and slowly but surely giving the shop a half-decent reputation amongst London's DJs and vinyl collectors. Its owner was Timothy Rimington, a 26-year-old west-Londoner with a fast-dwindling trust fund who lavished upon Frank the sort of doglike devotion and gratitude he usually reserved for his coke dealer. Tim often popped by the shop to hang out, chew the fat and generally get under his employee's feet and that afternoon Frank looked up from the stock-take to see his boss emerging through the door with a pleased smile on his face. 'Whap-nin, bruv?' he said, offering a fist for Frank to touch knuckles with, which reluctantly, Frank did.

Frank had long since given up trying to work out why the white son of an investment banker should want to talk like a fifteen-year-old black kid, so he smiled non-commitedly and tried to turn his boss's attention to the week's takings.

'Tim, I'm glad you're here because we really need to — '

Tim eyed him warily. Frank looked suspiciously like he was going to start talking shop, and Tim really, really hated it when that happened. Luckily though, he remembered just in time why he had popped round in the first place: he had exciting news to share. He held up a silencing hand. 'Thing is though, bruv, I'm thinking of selling up. Me and Jago are going into business together — club promotion and stuff — and for that we need the readies, you get me? No use asking my old man, he's fucking well angst at the moment. So I might have to sell this place just to get us going and that.' He beamed at Frank, and wondered vaguely why Frank didn't smile back.

When Tim had finally driven off in his Audi TT, Frank stuck a new record on and stared moodily as a group of Gilles Peterson wannabes wandered in and made a beeline for the Jazz. He mulled over Tim's bombshell. *He* had done this, he thought, as he gazed around the shop. It was down to him that East Side Soundz was now starting to make a profit — nobody else. If it was his shop he could turn it into something really special, he was certain. Little by little the seeds of an idea began to formulate in his brain.

Since he'd met Kate a new Frank had begun to emerge. Where once he'd been content to just drift along, collecting music, living in his aunt's old house, ballsing up the odd relationship, getting pissed with Jim and Eugene, and generally living his life as if he were watching it on TV, lately he'd started to feel a little differently about things. Something odd had happened to him that morning while he was shaving. Staring into the bathroom mirror he'd seen, once again, his father's face in his own, but instead of depressing him like it usually did he had experienced one of those rare flashes of understanding when the world seems to suddenly snap into focus, and he'd realised with a jolt of surprise that he was now more or less the same age as his dad had been when Frank had been born. Ten years later he'd walked out, but that was his choice, his life.

Staring into his own eyes Frank felt in charge of his own destiny in a way he never had before. He didn't know if this was down to Kate, or his success at the shop, or because time had just happened to roll on to the right moment, but somehow he didn't feel ten years old anymore, waiting for his dad to come walking back through the door. He felt like a man with decisions of his own to make.

The record came to an end and while choosing another he began to play around with the idea of buying Tim out. He had a house with no mortgage in an up-and-coming part of London. All he had to do was get a loan and he could make Tim an offer and take charge of the business himself. Or, failing that, he could open a shop closer to home: south-east London was crying out for a decent vinyl store. He was engrossed in this fantasy when he felt rather than saw someone hovering in front of the counter. When he looked up, it took him a second or two to recognise the face staring back at him.

'Euge!' he said at last, delighted. 'What the fuck are you doing here?' Within seconds he was in front of the counter and slapping his friend on the shoulder. 'Bit far from home, aren't you?' he grinned.

'Jus, you know . . . ' Eugene trailed off and tried to focus his eyes on Frank's before quickly giving up and pretending to riffle through a box of seven-inches on the counter. Frank took in his friend's appearance. When they were kids, he used to worry about what was the right thing to call people like Eugene. His mum and Aunt Joanie used to say 'coloured', while some kids at school said 'halfcaste', and then a teacher had told them they should say 'mixed-race'. But when he met Eugene he'd privately thought of his friend as 'golden', because that was the real colour of his skin, which, together, with his slanting topaz eyes seemed to glow with a purity cruelly lacking in the pasty complexion Nature had inflicted on him and most of his other classmates.

But there in the shop, the state that Eugene had got himself into finally began to sink in. Perhaps it had been a slow transformation over many months, he realised, which is why he had not really understood before how bad things had got. Perhaps he just hadn't wanted to see it. Whereas once Eugene's good looks had been the first thing anyone noticed about him, today, if you didn't know him, it would be the general air of grimy hopelessness that struck you first. He had always been slim but well defined and muscular — now his clothes hung listlessly off him, and Frank could see his shoulder blades poking through his T-shirt. With a pang of guilt, he realised that three weeks had gone by since the ugly scene in the Hope and Anchor, and that he had never, in fact, got round to calling him. The weeks just went so fast, he reflected. They went so damn *fast* these days. There had been a time when he and Euge had seen or spoken to each other every day.

He peered more closely at Eugene's face. The once-golden skin was now tinged with grey and it seemed slack in places it hadn't been before. The cat-like, pale-brown eyes were red-rimmed and dull with dark shadows beneath them. Frank took a step nearer to him. Up close, Eugene's clothes looked like they'd been slept in for a number of nights, but it was the smell that struck him most. He'd always had a whiff of grass and beer about him, but the smell now was a strange, sickly, chemical one that permeated the dank pong of unwashed clothes and skin. It was a smell he dimly recognised, but couldn't quite place. He reached over and put a hand gently on Eugene's shoulder. 'You all right, man?' he asked, softly. 'Because I've got to tell you: you look like shit.'

Eugene finally looked up from the box of records and Frank tried to quell his sense of unease. He watched as Eugene tried, slowly, to arrange his face into a smile. 'Yeah,' he said. 'I'm sweet. Just fucking tired, you know? Not sleeping at the moment, you know how it is.' Frank smiled vaguely back at him. Then, in a rush,

Eugene said, 'Look, man. I've come because I've got a favour to ask, yeah?'

Frank shrugged. 'Course. Anything.'

'I need some money, Frankie. I'll pay you back and I wouldn't ask but I'm desperate. I need a couple of hundred.'

Frank felt a childish stab of disappointment as he stared back at him. He felt stupid at how pleased he'd been to see his friend, assuming that he had come out of his way just to say hello. 'Er, that's a lot of money, Euge,' he said, playing for time. 'I'm not sure if . . . '

'Please, mate? I wouldn't ask but I owe some money, and the thing is, I'm in a bit of a hole.'

'You owe money? Who to?'

Again, Eugene attempted and failed to put some conviction into his smile, and his eyes remained desperate and strange. He waved his hand dismissively, 'Oh, no one, just a bit of rent and stuff. Look Frank, please?'

Frank could bear the awkwardness no longer. 'Sure. OK.' He found a scrap of paper and wrote 'I owe you £200' on it, and swapped it with a handful of £20 notes from the till, making a mental note to draw the money out and replace it later, and trying not to think about how short of cash he'd be for the rest of the month. 'Here you go.'

Eugene grabbed it gratefully. The two didn't meet each other's eyes as he said, 'Thanks mate. You're a lifesaver. Give it back in a week or so, yeah?'

Frank nodded, and they shuffled about uncomfortably for a moment or two before

Eugene said, 'Well, look, anyway. Appreciate it, yeah? Gotta run, though. See you around?'

And he was gone.

Moodily Frank watched a couple of white kids come in and make for the Grime records. They talked and walked like gangster rappers, even though Frank suspected that their mums came from Surrey and wore navy-blue tights. It came to him, suddenly, how desperate for the cash Eugene must have been to have come all the way to Clerkenwell — it was rare that he left Deptford these days. He thought about when they'd been kids and had spent their weekends, the three of them, skateboarding under South-bank and then pegging it across the river in the rain to spend hours pawing through vinyl in Soho record shops before trying their luck at getting served in West End pubs. He tried to remember the last time he'd seen Eugene really laugh, and couldn't.

★　★　★

On his way home, Frank ducked into Sains-bury's, planning to buy food for dinner. He wanted to make something nice for Kate — she'd been weird lately. The barrage of silent phone calls they'd been getting in the past few weeks only irritated him, but they seemed to make her jumpy and nervous as hell and he knew she hadn't been sleeping properly. Also, she'd started working later and later in the library.

As he traipsed around the aisles he felt

depressed thinking again about Eugene. He brooded about the scene a few weeks back with his dad. When they'd been at school Eugene had been in and out of the local care home. There had been rumours that his mum was on the game and everyone knew his dad knocked him about. During the brief periods when Eugene was allowed back home from Eglington Lodge (dark weeks or months in which they watched their friend withdraw into himself, tense and miserable), he and Jimmy had pretty much taken care of their friend between them. During those times Euge had practically lived at Jimmy's house and Frank had often sneaked him into his own bedroom after his mother had taken her Mogadons and passed out for the night.

Eugene had never had any real friends apart from him and Jimmy; he didn't seem to like or trust anyone else, but he treated the two of them with unfailing loyalty and affection. And despite having a temper, he'd always been good company: reckless, a bit crazy, but with a good heart. Although Frank and Eugene were both closer to Jimmy than they were to each other, Frank had always felt that there was something indefinable but fundamental that they recognised in each other: a certain, unspoken understanding about the world that Jimmy missed.

In the dairy aisle he snapped out of his reverie when he spotted that a crowd had gathered and were staring up at the high ceiling of the supermarket. Following their gaze he saw that a sparrow had flown in through the wide glass doors at the front of the shop and was now trapped inside. Frank watched the tiny bird repeatedly nosedive various products on the shelves. It swooped down to peck frantically at the top of a Müller Light yoghurt, or a Nestlé chocolate mousse, then hurtled back up to the ceiling to re-aim and swoop again. A shelf stacker came along and started waving his arms at the bird, successfully chasing it away from the dairy aisle and to the far end of the shop. Just before he turned away, Frank saw the sparrow fly full-speed at a window and fall to the floor like a stone.

* * *

On the way home Frank made a detour via Jimmy's car lot and found his friend reading a paper behind his desk while surreptitiously eyeing up a blonde who was checking out a second-hand Renault in the forecourt. His face broke into a wide grin when he saw Frank. 'Hello mate! Nice surprise!' he leapt up and gave Frank his customary bear hug. 'What you doing here?'

Frank dumped his shopping bags on the floor and sat down in one of the orange plastic chairs in front of Jimmy's desk. 'Just passing. Look, I saw Eugene today. He came into the shop.'

Jimmy sighed, his grin instantly disappearing. 'Oh yeah?'

'He needed money, so . . . '

'Don't tell me you gave it to him?'

Frank nodded ruefully. 'Two hundred quid.'

'For fuck's sake.' Jimmy slapped the table in

exasperation. 'I gave him a hundred two days. ago.'

The friends stared at each other for a moment. 'He was desperate, what was I going to do?' asked Frank defensively. 'He said he owed rent.'

'Rent, my arse,' snorted Jimmy.

'No thanks,' joked Frank, weakly.

'Owes his dealer more like,' Jimmy continued, ignoring him. He put his head in his hands for a moment. 'I'm worried about him. You know he's lost his job at the site?'

Eugene had been working on a building site in Erith, Frank remembered. 'What's he living on?' he asked.

'Signing on and sponging off his mates by the sound of it, and spending it on drugs.'

'He's not that bad, is he?'

'Mate, he's been on a bender since last year. You just hadn't noticed.'

Frank knew Jimmy hadn't meant it as a dig, but the comment stung him anyway. He'd been so wrapped up in Kate he'd barely seen Eugene since he met her.

'I offered him a job here, didn't I?' said Jimmy. 'Fucker never turned up. Seriously, I think we need to go round there and see if he's all right. What you doing tonight? Fancy taking a few beers over to his?'

Frank tried to quell a stab of disappointment at his dinner going to waste. 'Yeah, OK,' he said.

'Nice one, see you round his at eight then, yeah?' Jimmy relaxed and smiled. 'How are you, anyway? Kate OK is she?'

'Yeah, fine. Really well. Everything's great.' He

thought for a moment, then said, 'Actually, I've had a few ideas lately I wanted to talk over with you. Tim wants to sell the shop, and I thought, well, why don't I buy it?'

Jimmy looked at him in surprise. 'Really?'

'Yeah,' said Frank, unable to hide a smile of excitement. ''Cause, you know the house is probably worth a few bob now and there's no money owing on it. I was thinking of getting a loan and buying him out, or even just starting up a new shop round here.'

'Yeah,' said Jimmy, nodding. 'Sounds like a plan.'

'I could even sell the house completely if it takes off, buy somewhere else, maybe move to a new part of London or something, you know? Try somewhere different . . .'

Jimmy raised one eyebrow and coughed. 'Yeah? Where to?'

Frank shrugged; this part of his plan had only occurred to him in the past few seconds. 'Dunno. Anywhere. Could go north or something.'

He was interrupted by a roar of laughter from his friend. 'North London?' he spluttered. '*North London?*'

'Why? What's wrong with that?'

'Oh, nothing mate.' Jimmy shook his head and burst out laughing again. 'You going to start supporting Spurs next, too?'

'Yeah, well, it was just a thought.' Frank tried to swallow his irritation and changed the subject. 'How's things with you, anyway. Still seeing that Mel?'

Jimmy raised his eyebrows and pulled a face. 'Oh, you know. Fucking birds, getting a bit bored to be honest.'

'Why?' Frank was still smarting from Jimmy's sarcasm.

'No reason,' Jimmy squinted through the glass at the blonde who was still checking out the Renault. 'Just, um, you know what birds are like. Bit clingy to be honest.'

'Yeah?' Frank felt his guilt over Eugene and his irritation with Jimmy's earlier piss-taking spill into his voice. 'So you're not going to give her a chance, then? Thought she was really nice.'

Jimmy frowned at Frank's tone. 'Really?' he said, his voice decidedly less jovial.

'Well, don't you get bored with it?' snapped Frank. 'Just, you know, pulling birds and getting pissed all the time, living in the same old place? Don't you want something else, ever?' Frank knew full well he sounded like a wanker, but couldn't seem to stop himself.

Jimmy continued staring at him coolly for a moment. 'Thanks for the advice, but some of us don't want to live under our bird's thumb 24-7.' He turned back to his paper. 'And not all of us are destined for the bright lights of Stoke fucking Newington.'

'Whatever, Jimmy.' Frank got up, gathered his shopping bags together, and headed for the door. 'I'll see you at Eugene's, yeah? I've got stuff to do.'

As he walked home, his bad mood increased. *Fucking piss-taking wanker*. He hated arguing with Jimmy, which is why they'd only had about three rows in the fifteen years they'd known each other. *He just wants me running around in his shadow for the rest of my life, because he's the big man, and I'm the fucking loser and that's the way he likes it.* What really troubled Frank though, was the sneaking suspicion that Jimmy might be right. He'd been a loser for twenty-five years — what made him think he could stop now?

Eventually his thoughts drifted back to Eugene. Suddenly he remembered the strange smell he had noticed on his friend earlier that day, and in a flash it came to him where he'd smelt it before. A year or so ago the stairwell of his mother's block of flats had been used by the local crackheads as a place to hang out. That was the smell he'd recognised: the distinctively sickly, chemical pong of the crack pipe. He felt his heart sink.

★ ★ ★

As he turned the corner into his street he saw Kate in the distance approaching from the far end. The day had turned to twilight now, and she seemed to stand out against the hazy dullness of the sky as if her yellow hair and red T-shirt had stolen all the colour from the world. He waved and called out to her. He didn't notice the silver Mercedes that had turned into the street and stopped at the corner behind her. At the sound of his voice she looked up and smiled, and began to cross the road to meet him. Jesus, that smile. He would never get used to it. He raised his hand and waved, and then he heard the screeching of tyres.

Later he would look back on those next few seconds as if they were a series of disjointed images, as if a slide projector were flashing them across his mind: Kate crossing the road. The silver car speeding directly at her. Kate's face freezing in shock. Her head snapping back to look behind her. The car a metre away from her. Kate, in that final second jumping from the car's path, falling to the ground. The car speeding on past. Again and again he would replay those images. No sound of screeching tyres, or his own terrified shout, no smell of burning rubber — just a silent reel of frozen pictures.

As the car sped past him, Frank thumped the roof with his fist, ducking his head to get a brief, blurred glimpse at the maniac behind the wheel, before running over to Kate.

'Jesus fuck, are you OK?' he asked, kneeling down to where she lay on the tarmac. He helped her to her feet and pulled her towards him, crushing her against his chest in relief. Finally he examined her more closely. 'Fuck! Are you hurt? Are you OK?'

'Yes,' she said, patting herself down and examining a large, bloody graze on her elbow. 'I'm OK, I'm not hurt. Just . . . I can't believe that just happened.' She began to shake violently.

'That *wanker!*' he said, reaching for his mobile. 'I'll call the police.'

'No,' interrupted Kate. 'No. Don't.' There was a sharpness in her voice that surprised Frank into clicking his phone shut again.

'But . . . but he could have fucking killed you!' said Frank incredulously. 'He tried to *kill* you, Kate.' He thought of the face he'd seen behind the wheel as the car flashed past, the expression in the man's eyes. 'Are you crazy?' he asked, walking Kate to the house, 'he tried to run you over, I *saw* it with my own eyes.' Frank broke off, too upset to continue, remembering how his insides had seemed to plummet several feet at the moment the car had accelerated. The horrible flash of terror at the thought that Kate might be killed.

'No,' said Kate, more agitated than he had ever seen her. 'I'm sure it was an accident. There's no point calling the police.' Her voice was very tight and strange. 'We didn't get his number plate, and they'll never catch him now.' He heard her catch her breath. When she spoke again her voice was calm. 'Please, Frank? Can we just go in and sit down? I'm feeling a bit shaky.'

'Yeah, of course.' He looked doubtfully from the phone in his hand to the end of the street where the car had long since disappeared. He put his arm around her, opened the front door and took her into the lounge. He pulled her to him and felt his heart knocking against hers.

'I still think we should call the police,' he said, after a while.

'No,' said Kate, shaking her head. They were sat on the sofa, and, cupping Frank's face in her hands, she softly kissed him. After a few moments she picked up his hand and led him up the stairs. All thoughts of Eugene, and his arrangement to meet Jimmy, were forgotten.

25

London, April 2004

Securing a job at the library had been easy. 'You want to work down there?' the blonde receptionist had said, her face aghast, 'with them?' as if they were sewer rats.

Anton had laid the public-school accent on thick. 'I saw the advert.' His gaze held hers until she'd blushed and looked away. 'Just forgot to answer it.' He rolled his eyes at his own absent-mindedness then reached over and lightly touched her on the arm. 'What's your name, anyway?'

'Nicole.' Running a hand over her thin, flat hair.

'Pretty.' A wistful smile, then, 'Oh, come on, Nikki — ' lowering his voice and leaning in close, his eyes fixed on her lips ' — You're not going to make me beg . . . are you?'

And that had been that. A phone call later and the guy Stuart had been summoned and persuaded. Turned out he could use all the help he could get.

'Bye, Steven,' the girl whose name he'd already forgotten called after him as he followed Stuart through the double doors. 'See you later?'

* * *

Back at his flat that evening he'd had to sit in absolute silence for over two hours just to recover from it all. It had been exhausting, his first day's work. Being in close proximity with others for any length of time always exhausted Anton, he usually avoided it as much as possible. And yet he had stayed in that godforsaken basement until six, making conversation with that half-wit Daisy, and standing so close to her — Elodie — that he could touch her, should he have wanted to. He leant back in his chair and closed his eyes. Everything was progressing beautifully.

His life had changed dramatically over the past six months. Since he had found Elodie his days now had a sense of purpose to them they hadn't had before. For the first time in his life he awoke each morning brimming with excitement. Previously his existence had been one endless round of visits to the gym, scoring increasingly larger supplies of prescription meds from his dealer, drinking beer in front of the TV or standing next to one of the speakers all night at some subterranean techno club, numbed by a cocktail of Xanax and vodka. Occasionally, for a change, he would go home with some nameless, faceless body. But now he was a man with a goal, an objective. Now he was somebody who had plans. He was like a character in a film he reflected; shadowing his target with the professional skill of a secret agent, learning her routines, waiting for hours outside her home, following her to the picture library, finding out where her idiot boyfriend worked. Planning down to the last detail exactly how he would repay her for what she'd done. Life was so much richer now — he would almost miss her when she was gone.

★ ★ ★

The days, the weeks ticked by. Her daily close proximity both sickened and thrilled him like the strange, adrenalin-fuelled onset of sunstroke. By the end of each day he would be gasping for air, desperate to get away from her, unable to contain himself a second longer. And yet, once home he would be left floundering with a restless anxiety that could only be soothed by taking out her photographs or calling her up on the phone.

It was his fourth week at the library; a hot, airless Tuesday. The afternoon stretched on ahead of him. She was sat so he could watch her from the corner of his eye without her noticing. She stared at her computer screen, completely absorbed in what she was doing. Suddenly, not taking her eyes from her work she swiftly removed her sweatshirt and hung it over the back of her chair. As she'd raised her arms he had caught the briefest glimpse of her bare midriff. Beneath her sweatshirt she wore a pale red T-shirt, scoop necked, quite loose over her slender frame. Her short blonde hair curled around her small ears and there was something about the curve of her neck that caused a strange discomfort in his chest and he could feel the warnings of a tension headache. Mentally he checked on his supply of Vicodin. In a sudden movement she lent forward to dip into her box of photographs and he caught a glimpse of the swell of her naked breasts before she straightened up again. He had looked away, his heart painful in his chest.

The sweatshirt stayed there on the back of her chair when she left that night, and again the night after. On impulse, on the third day he snatched it up as he left and took it home with him. He discovered, lying on his bed, that it had different layers of scent; a faint whiff of washing powder, another vaguely sweet smell that was possibly body lotion, and then another, muskier odour beneath the armpits.

He lay on the bed, the sweatshirt to his nose, and for no reason at all, thoughts of his old boarding school drifted into his head. It had been a dismal, bottom-end institution somewhere outside Wigan. He had hated it with a passion. Hated the masters, hated the rules and the ugly, comfortless surroundings, and above all hated his classmates and fellow boarders. The feeling was mutual. His dark, brooding moods had been interspersed with sudden rages, and the biting sarcasm that characterised his rare lighter periods had not endeared him to the other boys. Bursts of insomnia had blighted those years. At night, alone in his dormitory he would think of his father who, whenever they spoke on the phone, would, like his mother, be increasingly full of talk of *her*.

★ ★ ★

He had meant just to sit in his car outside her house for a while. He did that sometimes, when he had nothing else to fill his evening with, or when he felt a sudden need to see her. At about seven she emerged to go to the Spar on the corner. When she returned the lanky prick that she lived with suddenly appeared at the other end of the street. He smiled and waved at her and she raised her own arm in response, began to cross the road to meet him. And something in the way she quickened her pace to go to him, the unthinking certainty between them had filled him with a sudden and overwhelming fury. In another moment they would be touching. Almost before he knew what he was doing his foot was on the accelerator. Moments later he was speeding towards her until, at the last instance, he swerved and ploughed on past down the road. Minutes later he was parked a few blocks away, sweat pouring down his face, huge jagged gasps catching in his throat, his heart thundering. *Stupid stupid idiot* he punched the dash with his palm. That was not how to go about it. That was not part of the plan.

The following Sunday evening he sat on his sofa and stared at his phone. He was tempted to phone her — he enjoyed making those little intrusions into her home. There was something so intimate about talking on the phone to her — not that he talked, of course — but just hearing her voice on the other end was pleasurable, that rally of scared hellos. Her quick, fearful little voice. It was almost as if they were lovers, as if he were her boyfriend, he thought. Calling her up on the phone, her whispering into his ear, hello, hello, hello?

But he didn't call Elodie. Tonight was the night that Mike was coming round.

Since he'd met him two years ago in a club in Shoreditch, Mike had been supplying him with a variety of pills. Mike, a large and largely silent Lithuanian, was a reliable and reassuring presence in his life, turning up at his door at the drop of a hat, with whatever Anton needed. When he had mentioned the gun, Mike's narrow little eyes had not even flickered. 'OK.' A brief nod, his face expressionless as ever. 'I bring next time.'

Anton had had to quell a stab of disappointment. He'd had visions of meeting the gun dealer in person, of perhaps going to a dingy East End pub with an envelope full of unmarked notes. Talk of 'shooters' and 'hits' — that sort of thing. But Mike had been confused when he'd suggested an introduction. 'I just bring to you, yes? No problem, OK? I bring.'

The phone rang: that would be him. 'Mike?' he put the mobile to his ear, his heart thumping pleasurably. 'You're outside?'

Twenty minutes later the 9mm Glock was in his hands. He felt elated as he stared at the shotgun's neat, blunt shape, felt its satisfying heaviness. For the fifth time in as many minutes he unloaded then reloaded the bullets the way Mike had shown him. Going to his window he aimed it at the heads of various passers-by for a while, making happy little shooting noises as he imagined picking off each one. He chuckled to himself as he returned to the sofa to stare at it some more. *This* was living.

26

Soho, central London, 5 May 2004

Spring has washed over London at last, and the city emerges from the receding tide of winter yellow-tinged and victorious. Kate walks the journey from Charing Cross to Soho and the faces that she passes turn pleased but suspicious eyes to the fresh blue skies like crabs peering from beneath rocks. Through Leicester Square she walks, then along the edges of China Town, where boxes of exotic vegetables are unloaded from vans by men in white aprons. She crosses Shaftesbury Avenue into Wardour Street, stopping for a truck that washes away last night's excesses from gutters with bubble-gum scented spray, past pub cleaners come to unlock doors on the ghosts of yesterday's drinkers, on overflowing ashtrays and empty glasses, before she cuts into Brewer Street and passes through the entrance to the library.

Down she goes, down two flights of stairs to the basement, through the door marked Archives, into the long, low-ceilinged room that already by 9.33 a.m. is humming with a quiet industry. She relishes the secret, underground safety of this place, but for the past few weeks she has moved through each day with anxiety snapping at her heels. Since that first, strange phone call there have been several more, on each occasion the person on the other end listening silently to her fearful hellos or to Frank's irritated interrogation before finally, gently, hanging up. (And what menace, what cold, hard menace is held within that silence before the receiver is replaced.)

It has been five days since the car tried to run her down outside Frank's house; five days of scanning every passing face, of jumping at every sound. Five sleepless nights spent reassuring herself over and over that it was just a stranger on the other end of the line, a random maniac behind the wheel. Who else, after all, could it possibly be? And yet a niggling doubt refuses to release her. Now, like an infected wound expelling a splinter, memories of her last night at High Barn rise to the surface of her subconscious with horrible regularity. She cannot shake the idea that someone has found out who she is, that somehow, someone who knows what she did has tracked her down. But, with grim determination she tells herself that she's mistaken. Her fears are irrational, she is sure. No one could possibly have found her out, not now.

Down in the basement she hangs her jacket on a hook by the door and makes her way to the furthest workstation where Daisy and Steven are already turning on their Macs and delving into cardboard boxes. They look up and greet Kate as she approaches, in the manner that has already become so familiar to her: Daisy with her pleased, Labrador eyes, Steven with his quick, flickering smile, his quiet 'Hello,' the brief, penetrating gaze. She greets them both with relief. It feels good to be here again; swallowed up in the comforting yellow gloom.

Over the weeks the Archive room has settled into its patterns, friendships and routines. It is an easy, relaxed camaraderie between people who are used to the random, transient existence of the temporary worker. Only Kate, Daisy and Steven's workstation, stuck at the far end of the room, has a certain self-contained aloofness to the rest. The three work quietly, diligently together, paying scant attention to their fellow 'archivists' (as Stuart likes to call them during his rare trips to the basement). For the first few weeks their talk is restricted to the job in hand: 'Pass the sticky labels will you?' 'What's the server password again?' 'That's European cathedrals done with.' And Kate is grateful for her two colleagues' unobtrusiveness, enjoying the luxury of not having to dodge the usual innocent enquiries into her past.

Their work is repetitive, uncomplicated and so engrossing that often entire mornings can pass in silence, punctuated only by Daisy's occasional habit of embarking on a sentence, randomly and from nowhere, her eager eyes darting between Kate and Steven, her words tumbling out in a breathless rush while her two colleagues smile at her enquiringly until, overwhelmed, she dissolves into nervous laughter before lapsing once again into silence, and they tactfully drop their gaze.

And as the weeks pass Kate feels an odd kind of kinship grow between the three of them. Sometimes it occurs to her that it's not just the physical position of their workstation that separates them from everyone else, an instinct tells her that the three of them share a wider sense of being somehow cut adrift in the world. She gets used to sometimes glancing up and finding Steven's thoughtful gaze upon her, almost as if she were one of the photographs he was holding up to the light. And though occasionally she will feel herself blushing beneath the beam of those green eyes, if sometimes she finds her heart beating a little faster when he speaks to her, she will stubbornly ignore the strange tension between them, pushing it firmly to the back of her mind.

But one day something happens to mark a change between them. Kate returns from lunch a little earlier than usual and, finding the archive room empty, makes her way to the storeroom to fetch a fresh supply of labels. The room is large with high shelves stacked with boxes of stationery, and it's while riffling through one of these boxes, hidden behind a shelf at the back of the room, that she hears the voices of Clive and Adrian, the two men who share the nearest workstation to theirs. Their voices are loud and clear within the storeroom's musty quiet. Kate stops rummaging and holds her breath, waiting for them to leave. It's some moments before she realises that it's she who is the subject of their conversation.

Clive is in his early thirties, a large man with dyed black hair and a ginger goatee and habitually dressed in army fatigues. Kate has heard him explain, loudly and often to anyone who will listen (and frequently when they will not), that he is in fact an artist, merely working in the library to fund his latest project, an instalment piece upon which he has been working for the past seven years. Kate, and indeed everyone else in the archive room, knows an awful lot about Clive already. She knows that he is a member of the Socialist Workers Party, that his favourite film is The Matrix and that he has an exhaustive knowledge of conspiracy theories. Adrian, his co-worker, is a limp, translucent man of about twenty with womanly hips who, despite being the butt of Clive's frequent mood swings and constant ridicule, clearly worships the older man from the tip of his flaky scalp to the soles of his Scholl-shod feet.

Clive and Adrian share their workstation with Marcella, an Italian foreign language student with a beautiful face, a large bottom and a rudimentary grasp of the English language. That both her co-workers would do pretty much anything to have sex with her has been clear to everyone for some weeks. Marcella has recently taken to wearing her iPod while she works, and throwing beseeching looks to the neighbouring tables.

Today, in the storeroom, she hears Adrian's voice first, 'That one on the next table, what's her name? Kate. She's all right, isn't she? Seems nice, like she'd be, you know, nice. Quite fit too, really.'

Clive's voice, when he answers is aghast. 'Her?' he snorts. 'Well, each to their own, mate.'

'No no,' Adrian backtracks rapidly. 'I just meant that she seems OK — didn't say I wanted to fuck her or anything.' The word 'fuck' rings unconvincingly through the room, but Clive laughs obligingly.

'No,' says Clive, after a few moments, and with the air of a man who knows a thing or two about women, 'not my sort at all. I like my ladies with a bit of meat on them. Tits and that. And anyway, something a bit stuck up about those three. The thing about women, Adrian my friend, is the quieter they are, the more mental they usually turn out to be. Girls like that Kate, they might look all nice and quiet on the outside, but inside that little head of hers, mark my words: it'll be like a fire in a pet shop, I guarantee it. Anyway . . . she's got fuck-all arse.'

They talk on for a few minutes before finally their voices drift away and Kate hears the door closing behind them. She exhales, at last, and continues her search through the shelves. Suddenly, a faint noise from a neighbouring aisle causes her to look up and peer through a gap in the shelf. Her heart lurches when she realises that she is staring into the pale-green eyes of Steven; that he has, in fact, been standing there for some time.

Within the few seconds that they hold each other's gaze a variety of emotions flood Kate: embarrassment that he has overheard her being discussed in such a way, self-consciousness that she has been observed by him without her knowing it, shyness at being alone with him for the first time, and something else; something she cannot quite put her finger on, but that makes her drop her eyes in confusion. When she raises them again Steven is still staring at her, but now his eyes are lit with amusement. And all at once, the tension of the moment, of the past five weeks, breaks, and, still holding each other's gaze, they burst into laughter.

Something alters between Kate and Steven from that moment. An unspoken shift in the atmosphere; a barely perceptible loosening. At first, Kate registers this but doesn't give it much thought, so preoccupied is she with other things. But when, one morning, Steven interrupts the quiet progress of their work and casually suggests that the three of them go to a nearby café for lunch, she is, nevertheless, slightly surprised at the flicker of excitement she feels in response.

'Sure,' she says, matching the nonchalance of his tone, and looks at Daisy who is staring at Steven with transparent delight.

It's the first of many lunchtimes the three of them will spend together. When one o'clock comes they head somewhat self-consciously to the door, emerging with shy smiles into the bustle of Brewer Street. The day is warm and the pavements are full of office workers baring white flesh for the first time that year. Steven breaks the silence first, as they trudge in the direction of the nearest sandwich bar. 'I thought it was about time we had a team outing,' he jokes awkwardly, a touch of apology in his tone.

'Oh, absolutely,' Kate rushes to reply. 'Good idea, yes.' They lapse into silence again and, when Daisy trips over a paving slab and scrabbles to pick up her bag, they catch each other's eye momentarily before dropping their gaze to smile at their feet. In the café, they sit at the only empty table, placed in the noisy, busy restaurant by the door to the kitchen, and the hubbub of the surrounding tables only serves to highlight the silence that is now weighing rather heavily between the three of them as they settle into the seats and pick up their menus. Kate opens her mouth to speak, mentally groping around for a topic of conversation. She feels anxious, suddenly, that Steven shouldn't regret his invitation. Before she can utter a word, however, Daisy begins to talk.

And it is as if Daisy has waited her entire life for this moment. As if she has been storing a lifetime's worth of words for this particular Tuesday lunchtime. Because, once she has opened her mouth and begun, it seems that she is incapable of ever closing it again. Steven and Kate can only listen dumbly while, as they read the menu, order and then eat their meal, Daisy talks, and talks, and talks. Within that first hour Kate and Steven learn that she is twenty-six and a Taurus, that she has three rabbits, Billy, Tilly and Bob, that she lives with her mother in a flat in Neasden. They learn that her favourite TV show is Vets In Practice ('or anything to do with animals really, I don't mind'), that her mother has ME, and on Saturday nights she goes to the pictures with her next-door neighbour Haley. She tells them that she's a vegetarian and that she doesn't like to take the Tube and that one day she wants to live in the countryside with her mum, maybe in Sussex because she went there on a school trip once and it was nice.

Not once during that first lunch together do Steven and Kate exchange a word. As Kate stares at Daisy's evermoving mouth, she finds herself becoming steadily lulled, almost hypnotised by the endless stream of words, by their unceasing flow. It's only when she becomes slowly aware of a strange heat upon the side of her face that she glances up to find, once again, Steven's eyes upon her. But there's nothing unreadable in his expression now; nothing negligible in this stare. His desire for her is so naked that she feels herself burn red beneath its beam.

His eyes hold her, refusing to let her look away, and trapped within their glare she feels the first flickers of an instinctive, physical response. She sees that he sees it, and she's aware of a faint mockery in the curve of his lips, a hint of invitation in one slightly raised eyebrow. And there is something else, something else lurking below the sexual current — something dark and frightening that makes her catch her breath. The moment swells and fills the room, she feels that she could almost touch the air between them and wonders how Daisy can just talk on through it, oblivious; why the whole café doesn't turn and stare. Finally, abruptly, he looks away, releasing her, and she hears herself sigh with relief.

When they have finished eating and they get up to leave, Daisy, slapping a hand over her mouth, looks at them both in wide-eyed horror.

'Oh my goodness, I've done it again, haven't I?' she asks.

'What's that?' asks Steven kindly, holding the

door open for them both.

'Oh, my mum's always telling me,' she wails. 'I'm always doing it: going on and on and on. What must you think of me? Going on and on like that all through lunch.'

'Not at all,' Kate and Steven assure her at the same time, and continue to do so all the way back to the library, where, once safely ensconced in the depths of the archive room again, Daisy finally stops apologising, closes her mouth and, her face abject, doesn't open it again for the rest of the afternoon.

That evening as she walks amongst the hurrying crowds towards Charing Cross, Kate's thoughts return to Steven. Unbidden, memories of her old London life flood into her mind, images of the many different strangers in her bed, the transient comfort of their bodies, the brief reassurances they offered. And it occurs to her that sometimes when Frank holds her and tells her that he loves her she will find herself wondering, with a shock of fear, who it is he means. A cold sadness threatens her, and as if to escape it she quickens her pace, gripped by an overwhelming need to see Frank's face.

⋆ ⋆ ⋆

As suddenly as they began, the phone calls stop. A week passes, and then another, and still the strange new silence persists. Gradually, hope begins to build within her. Could it possibly have been, as Frank said, down to a crossed line? A fault with the phone, and nothing more? Yes, she tells herself: yes — it must have been. A mistake, that was all, her imagination getting the better of her. The calls, the car, a horrible coincidence: her mind playing tricks, that was all.

Since that first lunchtime together Kate is careful to avoid Steven's gaze. And when the following week Daisy suggests another trip to the café she deliberately keeps her eyes firmly on her food while she eats, refusing to look up when she feels his eyes upon her again. After a while, she notices that he does the same.

One lunchtime, sitting at their usual table in the corner of the café, Daisy asks Steven about his childhood. He stirs his coffee intently for a moment or two, without answering. He looks up with a smile. 'Nothing too exciting, I'm afraid,' he tells them mildly. 'Only child — mum and dad both teachers. I grew up in Hove, near Brighton. Fairly ordinary upbringing — all a bit middle class and boring, to be honest.' He shrugs and takes a bite from his sandwich.

Kate opens a packet of crisps, and tries in vain to imagine Steven as a small child. When she looks up it is to find the other two gazing at her expectantly. 'What?' she asks, although she knows what's coming.

'Well, what about you?' asks Steven. The intense, piercing stare has returned, and to her surprise she thinks that she can detect a sliver of dislike behind it.

'I, well,' she flounders for a second, momentarily forgetting her stock answer. She looks away and at last recovers, saying with a light smile, 'I grew up in New York. My parents died in a car

307

accident when I was a teenager, so I came over here to live with my aunt in Kenton.' She gives her usual end-of-conversation smile, and pretends to study the dessert blackboard over Steven's shoulder.

'Wow,' says Daisy, impressed. 'How romantic! I always thought you had a slight accent.' She stops, a hand flying nervously to her mouth, 'I mean, oh my gosh, I'm really sorry, Kate. That must have been terrible. I'm so sorry.' Miserably, Daisy picks up the sugar bowl and immediately drops it, causing its entire contents of cubes to cascade across their table.

Kate checks her watch, smiles brightly, and says, 'Well, maybe we should be getting back.' She doesn't look at Steven as she helps Daisy find her bag, which has somehow managed to wind up under a chair two tables away. But as she puts her jacket on her eyes flicker across to Steven, who is still looking at her with his cool, assessing gaze. She ducks her head and not waiting for the others, makes for the door.

★　★　★

May drifts towards its final days. June and July come and go. London sulks beneath vague skies, a grey, flat summer after the first bright promise of spring. In the basement of the Soho Picture Library the mountain of boxes has dwindled to a small pile. A holiday atmosphere has begun to creep into the archive room as the weeks of filing and data-basing finally crawl to an end. Across their workstations people chat loudly to one another about the trips they plan to take, the universities they will be returning to, the next tedious job their agencies have lined up.

One Friday, a few weeks before they're due to finish at the library, Steven does not arrive as usual. As she chats to Daisy, turns on her computer and picks up one of the final boxes of prints, Kate's eyes dart frequently towards the door. Finally she hears it open and turns to it expectantly, but it's only Clive, late as usual. She turns back to her work, and when Daisy asks innocently, 'I wonder where Steve is?' she hears herself snap irritably, 'How on earth would I know?'

More minutes pass and when he has still not arrived at ten, Kate, remembering that the following Monday is a bank holiday, is disturbed by the disappointment she feels at the thought of not seeing him for three whole days. At that moment, however, the door swings open again, and she sees his familiar form making its way towards her. She turns back to the computer screen, hiding her face, and says to him causally, 'There you are. Daisy was beginning to worry.'

'Fell off my bike,' he explains as he takes his seat. 'Fucking bus pulled out right in front of me.' She keeps her eyes on the list of numbers on the screen as he rolls up one of his sleeves to display his wounds. When she hears Daisy gasp appreciatively, she cannot resist letting her eyes drop to the bloody mess of cuts and grazes that almost covers his left forearm.

'Ooh,' says Daisy. 'You should put something on that. Might get an infection.'

'Yeah, suppose I should,' he says, disinterestedly. 'What do you think, Kate?'

She doesn't know what it is about his ruined arm that touches her so, only that the sight of it makes her catch her breath, and it's all she can do not to reach over and trace its bloody terrain with her finger tip.

'Kate?' The sound of her name snaps her out of her reverie, and she stares into his questioning eyes. 'Well? Do you think I'll live?'

She smiles, at last, says, 'Probably,' and turns away. 'Maybe you should stick some Savlon on it though.' She knows that he is still watching her, as she opens the nearest box and pulls out a handful of prints to work on.

She hears Daisy say helpfully, 'There's a first-aid kit in the kitchen.'

Then: 'You go with him, Kate, you know how clumsy I am.'

Her eyes meet his for a fraction of a second. 'Great,' Steven says, jumping to his feet. 'Come on then, Nurse Kate. Heal me.'

She follows him slowly to the tiny kitchen at the end of the archive room, and finds him with his arm under the cold tap. She hesitates by the door, until he looks up and says, 'Think the stuff is in one of the cupboards.' He holds his arm out to her in a gesture that's half childlike, half mocking. There is something in the tone of his voice, and in the odd way in which he's looking at her that makes her turn quickly away to search for the first-aid box.

Gently she takes his arm and with a paper towel dabs the water from the wound. Her fingers circle his wrist and keeping it steady she rubs some antiseptic cream onto the graze with her finger. She doesn't look at him, but her bowed head is inches from his, and she can feel his breath on her cheek. The room is entirely silent as she fumbles for a plaster, and places it gently on his arm. Slowly she smoothes the pink fabric over his wound, the tip of her finger touching, then, the fine skin of his wrist. She can feel his eyes on her, and at the moment her eyes meet his, a noise behind them breaks the silence, and Marcella breezes into the kitchen, murmurs hello, and begins to make some tea.

★ ★ ★

At home that night she takes a bath while Frank cooks dinner. She can hear him singing along to the radio as he bangs pots and pans around in the kitchen. She relaxes in the warm soapy water, her toes on the prongs of the taps, her hand massaging soap into her skin. Suddenly, unbidden, the scene with Steven earlier returns and she shakes her head as if to dislodge his image from her mind, firmly ignoring the dark warmth that spreads over her naked skin as she recalls his breath on her cheek. Just at that moment the telephone rings. Instinctively she sits bolt upright, sending water cascading over the edge of the bath. It has been some time since the last silent call, but nevertheless the sound of its ring continues to make her jump.

She waits, motionless, until at last on the seventh ring she hears Frank finally make it to the hall and pick up the phone. She waits for his exasperated fire of 'hello-hello-hello?' For him to shout, 'Look, who is this? What do you want?' then bang the receiver down in annoyance. But none of this happens. Instead, she hears him murmur calmly into the phone, and then replace the handset, already humming to himself again as he returns to the kitchen. She lets out a long breath, and relaxes back into the water.

★ ★ ★

Later, wrapped in Frank's dressing gown, a towel around her head, she finds him putting the finishing touches to the meal. She watches him for a few moments as he stirs a pot on the stove. On impulse she goes to him and hugs him tightly, feeling along his back with her hands, burying her nose into his chest, smelling his familiar scent. He hugs her back, kisses the top of her head then turns back to the stove.

'Who was that?' she asks after a moment or two, when she's seated at the table.

'Huh?' he asks vaguely as he turns the heat down on the oven.

'On the phone,' she says, rubbing her hair with the towel. 'Earlier,' she adds.

'Oh,' says Frank. 'No one. Wrong number. Can you pass me that spoon, please?'

She stops, her towel poised in mid rub. 'Wrong number?' she repeats, her voice suddenly sharp.

'What? Oh yeah, don't worry. Not our mystery caller this time. Just some old duck. Some lady asking for, uh, Emily, Elodie or something. Elodie Brown, I think she said.' He turns to the sink to drain some pasta, and doesn't see Kate's face empty of colour, doesn't hear her as she whispers, her voice faint, 'Elodie. Elodie Brun.' She puts her head in her hands, and feels the blood rush to her ears, the vomit rising in her throat.

★ ★ ★

That night she lies awake, staring wide-eyed at the ceiling while Frank sleeps peacefully by her side. In the moonlight she watches his body fall and rise, slow and calm with untroubled sleep. He had asked her again and again what the matter was, until finally she'd said she wasn't feeling well and had gone to bed early, pretending to be asleep when he'd come in. Who had tracked her down? Who had found her? As she watches Frank sleep, panic rises in her chest. Tenderly, carefully she reaches over and strokes a strand of hair from his face.

At last, just before dawn, she falls into an uneasy slumber heavy with dreams. She's on a crowded bus, hemmed in by strangers, their coats sodden with rain, the air hot and damp. Just as she is about to push her way through the bodies they press against her and she can't move. She tries to shout but no sound comes, she tries to move but her legs won't work. And then, finally, the driver turns to face her. But it is not the face of a stranger. It is Ingrid.

She screams, then, and tries to get up, to run,

to pull the emergency lever — anything to get out. And then she realises that the faceless person by her side is Frank. 'Don't try to run, my darling,' he soothes, his fingers tightening on her arm. 'We love you, Ingrid and I. We all love you so much. Stay here with us, stay: there's nowhere left to go now.'

Repelled, she writhes away from him and turning to the window sees Steven standing on the pavement below, looking up at her with calm, steady eyes. Then, suddenly, he turns and hurries away, disappearing through the crowded street, until soon it is as if he was never there at all. She tries to call after him, desperate for him to stop, but she can't remember how, her mind is empty of words and when she opens her mouth no sound will come. And then she wakes, her body drenched in sweat, her heart ricocheting off her ribs, and she lies curled on one side, staring blindly at the radiator until at last the shriek of the alarm clock slices through the silence.

★ ★ ★

Later she pretends to sleep while Frank gets up and leaves for work. When she hears the door close behind him she dresses and frantic with sleeplessness and anxiety tries to decide what she should do. As she moves around the house there begins to creep over her the sensation that she's being watched. She sits at the kitchen table and tries to calm down. But still the queasy sense of hidden, spying eyes persists.

From the other side of the thin wall that

314

divides Frank's terraced home from the one next door, she hears the neighbour's child begin to play the piano. With one finger the unseen little girl plays the same nursery song over and over, finally adding her voice to the tune. It's very soft, but she can just make out the words.

Run rabbit run rabbit run, run, run
Run rabbit run rabbit run, run, run.
Bang, bang, bang, bang goes the farmer's gun
So run rabbit, run rabbit, run, run, run.

Over and over the child sings the same simple verse, until it seems to fill Kate's head like a persistent, nagging ache. She sits with clenched fists, willing it to stop until she thinks she might go mad with it. And then, suddenly, it ends as abruptly as it begun, and Kate exhales with relief.

The doorbell breaks the silence and she jumps. Staring down the hall she's aware that she can be seen through the frosted glass of the front door and instinctively she shrinks out of sight of the dark form silhouetted there. After a moment whoever it is begins to bang the knocker insistently: a noisy barrage of brass on wood. Craning her neck she peers nervously again at the door, and it's with a flood of relief that she recognises the blue uniformed outline of the postman. Dully, she gets up and white-faced, takes the package he hands to her, barely responding to his cheerful greeting as she closes the door in his face.

It's not until she's seated once more that she turns without interest to the small, square package in front of her and her eyes fall upon the address label. A swift, dark terror grips her when she reads the precise, black print there. Miss Elodie Brun, it says, and unconsciously she raises her arm and swipes at it, knocking it flying across the floor. In horror she gazes over at the small package sitting so innocently on its side in the corner of the room but she can no more bring herself to approach it than she could a ticking bomb.

And then, in a sudden desperate fury she rushes over to it and tears apart the packaging. Inside, carefully wrapped in tissue paper, is a small, wooden carving. Her legs grow numb beneath her, her hand flies to her mouth and slowly she sinks to the floor. It is the bird, her little wooden bird, carved for her so lovingly all those years ago by Mathias.

Lifting it from its nest of tissue she slowly caresses the fine, smooth curves, her fingers instinctively finding again the familiar grooves of its wings, the dips and hollows of its eyes and beak, its small body fitting as naturally as it always did into the palm of her hand. The seconds, the minutes pass unnoticed as she crouches there, on the kitchen floor with the bird. Gradually the room melts away, and bit by bit her senses become flooded with memories of smells, tastes and sounds: the low gurgle of the river, the wind lifting the branches, the smell of burning wood in the hearth, the profound peace at the heart of the forest the like of which she has not known since. She doesn't even notice her tears.

The telephone's ring wrenches her back to the

present and she leaps to her feet, backing away from the noise into the furthest corner of the room. It continues to ring and ring, filling her ears until she can bear it no longer. 'Who are you?' she screams back at it. 'Leave me alone!' But still it rings, goading her, louder and louder until at last, dropping the bird and pausing only to snatch her bag from the hall, she runs from the house, slamming the door behind her, while the phone shrieks on.

She isn't thinking clearly, knows only that she has to get as far away as possible. Blindly she heads for the station and jumps on a waiting train just before it pulls away. The journey passes in a blur as she perches tensely on the edge of her seat, oblivious to the other passengers. At last the train pulls into Charing Cross.

In the library's basement Steven and Daisy watch curiously as she takes her seat and turns on her computer.

'There you are,' says Daisy, after a pause. 'We were starting to worry.'

Kate stares dumbly back into Daisy's smiling face, and watches as her expression turns to one of concern, and it dawns on her how awful she must look with her swollen face and red-rimmed eyes.

'Are you OK, Kate?' asks Steven.

'I'm fine. Just . . . a bad night's sleep, that's all.'

The day passes. The conversation between Daisy and Steven grows gradually more subdued until finally they lapse into a troubled, watchful silence. She barely registers them. Numbly she

317

goes through the motions of her work as she tries to get her frantic thoughts into some kind of order, but always they return to the unknown menace that has crept into Frank's home, infecting her hard-won happiness like a lethal gas.

When six o'clock arrives, one by one people start to leave the library. The lights are movement activated and as each workstation empties, the bulb above it eventually flickers out until at last all that is left is the one shining above their desk. 'Well,' says Daisy reluctantly, like a child who's been sent to bed early, 'I suppose I'll be off.' She hesitates and says, 'Mum will be wondering . . . '

It isn't until she hears Steven say goodbye that Kate looks up and understands she's leaving. To Daisy's surprise she finds herself suddenly clasped in her arms.

'Bye Daisy,' she says. 'Take care of yourself, won't you?'

'Sure. Of course. I'll see you on Monday.' Daisy stares with puzzled eyes at Kate for a moment, shoots a perplexed glance at Steven, then not knowing what else to do picks up her bag and leaves them alone.

When Kate turns to Steven his eyes seem to gleam at her in the gloom. 'Are you sure you're all right, Kate?' he asks, quietly.

'I — ' She struggles for a moment to answer him. 'I,' she says again, unable to take her eyes away from his.

'Would you like to go somewhere to talk? For a drink or something?'

318

At first she is too surprised to reply but at last she nods. Frank, she knows, will be working late tonight, doing a stock-take at the shop, and the thought of sitting in the house alone fills her with dread.

Outside, they walk in silence for a while. She doesn't question or even notice where they are going, only follows him blindly up Wardour Street, lost in her own thoughts. On the other side of Oxford Street he leads her down a narrow side road and stops outside a pub. She looks up, dazed, as if surprised to find that they are no longer in the library basement, and then she passes wordlessly through the door he is holding open for her.

The pub is almost empty, too small and old-fashioned and out of the way to attract the hordes of Friday-night drinkers thronging the trendier bars nearby. She sits at a corner table while he fetches their drinks. When he's sitting opposite she regards him for a moment or two. And then, without even knowing that she's about to say it, she looks him in the eye, takes a deep breath, and begins to speak. 'When I was two years old,' she says, hearing the words as if listening to a stranger's voice, 'I was kidnapped.'

While Steven listens in absolute, unblinking silence, she tells him everything. The forest, High Barn, Queens, London, Frank, the phone calls, the car, and finally, the carved bird. The words pour from her and as she speaks the relief is overwhelming. On and on she talks, her mouth moving as if by its own free will, and as she tells her story her heart grows steadily lighter. It is only when she reaches the part when she must describe Ingrid's death that she stops, finally unable to continue. 'I thought the house was empty,' she begins, 'but then I heard her call my name from the kitchen. And then . . . and then . . . ' she flounders, unable to meet his eye.

'What, Kate?' his voice is very quiet. 'What happened then?'

She shakes her head. 'It was an accident. A horrible accident.' She cannot look at him. A heavy silence falls.

'You are Little Bird,' he says quietly.

She nods.

The silence stretches on.

At last he says, 'And Frank knows nothing about this?'

She shakes her head, almost feeling now as if she were waking from a dream, astonished that she has told her story at last, that it is Steven she has told it to. Sadness fills her. It should have been Frank. She turns to Steven, searching his face to see what affect her words have had. He is not looking at her, is staring as if unseeing, at the empty air in front of him. But when, suddenly, he turns to her, she feels the breath catch in her throat, her heart thudding now to be looking into the eyes of someone who knows the truth finally, who sees at last who she is. But his face is unreadable, devoid of expression as if he has retreated somewhere deep inside himself. And then a strange thing happens: bit by bit she sees his face become infused with pain.

She moves to the seat next to his. 'Steven?' she

asks, reaching out and touching his arm. 'What is it?'

And with that touch, everything is lost. Their eyes lock. Reflected in his irises she sees twin versions of herself, as she has seen herself reflected in so many men's eyes before his. Slowly, very slowly, hardly aware of what she's doing, she reaches over and puts her fingers to his face. She sits and looks at her hand upon his cheek as if at an object entirely detached from herself. He does not for a second drop his eyes from hers. And then, in a sudden violent movement he pulls her towards him, his fingers gathering her hair tightly in his fist as his lips hit hers and she feels the heat spread across her body, her hands gripping the knotted muscles of his back. Desire slams into her.

And as abruptly as he'd seized her he pulls away and regards her for a moment (a flash of something she can't read; the shadow of something swooping past his eyes). From their separate chairs they survey each other, their breath shallow and quick. 'Kate,' he says, 'will you come with me?' A moment passes, and then another. She nods, and together they leave the pub.

Outside in the street, dusk has just begun to fall. The low thunder of Tottenham Court Road can be heard in the distance, but this street is empty and still. As she moves by his side she feels entirely detached from the world, as if the real her is still back in the kitchen, holding the little carved bird, while this person, following Steven, is a dream version of herself.

They have barely walked more than fifty yards before he stops and says, 'Here. I live here.'

'Here?' The tall, slim town house in the middle of central London is the very last place she had imagined him living.

He points to the top floor, the small attic windows. 'Up there.' He smiles at her confusion. 'Long story. I'm flat sitting.' He delves into his pocket, bringing out a key. 'Come on.'

★ ★ ★

Inside the small low-ceilinged flat she gazes around her at the bare magnolia walls. There is nothing here; no clue to tell her anything about Steven's life. She takes a step back towards the front door but just at that moment he takes her hand and leads her silently to the bedroom. Like the hall this room is empty and bare but for a mattress that is lit like a stage by a lamp on the floor.

Silently they lie down together on the bed, quickly they undress. She watches the monstrous shadows of their bodies thrown by the lamplight across the bare walls; and turning her eyes to his face she finds his intent stare upon her still. She closes her eyes tight shut and in the end, it is Frank's face that she sees.

★ ★ ★

Afterwards she is on her feet in seconds, his sweat still mingling with hers, her breath like jagged glass. She dresses as he watches and without looking back at him or uttering another word she runs from the flat, down the steep stairs and out into the street.

All the way to Charing Cross she runs, through the Friday night crowds in the clammy August heat. And in the packed train she holds her head in her hands and tries in vain to stem her tears. When the train finally pulls into Deptford she runs the few blocks to their home. Tearing open the door, she calls for Frank, but realising that he is still not home, she sinks to the floor and begins to cry.

At last she reaches her decision. She will tell him everything. Tomorrow she will tell him everything.

27

Deptford, that same night

It was 4 a.m. when Frank's mobile rang. Still half-asleep his outstretched fingers fumbled on the floor beside the bed while Kate murmured and shifted in the darkness next to him. There were only four people in the world he would take a call from at that time of night: Kate, his mother, Jimmy, or Eugene. His eyes still closed, he found his Nokia at last and brought it to his face as he slowly cracked open one eye. The little screen glowed blue as it continued to bleep and vibrate. Illuminated letters spelt: Jimmy Mobile.

Frank was wide awake suddenly. He hadn't spoken to Jimmy since they'd argued in the car lot a week ago. He'd been meaning to ring and apologise for not turning up at Eugene's that night, but somehow he'd never got around to it. He pressed a button on his phone. 'Hello?'

'Frank?' Jimmy's voice sounded very loud and unnaturally high in the silent room. Frank sat up in bed, rubbing his face.

'Yes, mate. You OK? D'you know what time — '

'He's dead, Frank,' said Jimmy in the strangely shrill, too-loud voice. 'Eugene's dead.'

* * *

Later, he would remember every detail of those first few hours after Jimmy called. It took less than a couple of minutes to dress and get into his car. He would remember exactly what Jimmy had said, and what he, himself, had told Kate when he finally hung up the phone. He would remember driving around to Eugene's bedsit. He would be able to recall in minute detail the scene that awaited him there: the ambulance and police cars on the street outside, faces peering from the windows of surrounding flats, the door open, the brightness of the hall. As he made his way to the third floor, he saw Jimmy's white, frightened face peering over the stairwell while the paramedics carried down the stretcher that bore their friend's dead body.

He remembered because, after an initial, brief lurch of horror, he had felt so peculiarly calm. It was as if he'd spent his entire life waiting for tragedy and now that it had arrived, he was strangely unable to react.

★　★　★

The police needed Jimmy to make a statement, so Frank rode with him in the police car.

'What happened?' he asked. His voice sounded high and thin, like a recording made long ago. Jimmy, who had been staring out of the window, opened his mouth to speak, but no words came.

'I don't know,' he whispered at last. 'I don't know.' He shook his head.

'Was it . . . I mean, did he . . . top himself?'

whispered Frank. It was a conversation belonging to a film, to someone else's life.

'Top himself?' repeated Jimmy, his voice so loud in the silent car that one of the policemen in the front whipped his head round sharply. '*Top* himself? Course he didn't fucking top himself,' said Jimmy, ignoring the copper. 'What's the matter with you? It wasn't on purpose, was it? Course it wasn't. Too many drugs, accidental overdose, heart attack or something. I don't know, do I? You fucking twat. I mean why — why would he kill himself?'

There was something in the way Jimmy asked this last question that was so unspeakably sad that somewhere in the very depths of himself Frank felt a cautionary nip of pain, like a distant solitary cloud before a hurricane, a warning of the devastation to come. He quenched it, and put a hand on Jimmy's shoulder. 'OK, man. I'm sorry,' he said. 'I'm sorry, I just. Fuck. I can't believe this. I just can't believe it. I mean, *Euge?* What the fuck . . . '

Without warning Jimmy started to cry. His body shook with great, convulsive sobs and Frank gripped his shoulder until they gradually subsided. He realised with a start that in all the years he'd known Jimmy, he'd never once seen him cry. As they drove through the empty Deptford streets he began to tell Frank what happened.

'My phone rang around midnight. I saw Euge's number so I picked up.' Frank nodded, the words, the police car, everything unreal. 'There was music in the background, really loud,' Jimmy continued, 'but he didn't say anything. I thought he was in a club or something. I kept shouting his name, but he didn't reply.' He gave a bitter snort of laughter, the tears spilling from his eyes again. 'I was a bit hacked off to be honest, I was about to hang up on him, but then he started talking.' Jimmy put his head in his hands for a moment, and took a few ragged breaths.

'What was he saying?' asked Frank, not sure that he could really bear to hear it.

'All kinds of crazy shit.' Jimmy shook his head. 'A right load of old nonsense. I'd never heard him like that before. I mean, at first I thought he was just a bit stoned, you know? But he was really weird and confused. Started talking about when we were kids. Asking me if I remembered the day we all met, stuff like that. Even started going on about my mum. Then he got really upset. He kept fading out, and the music in the background was so fucking loud I could hardly hear him. I kept asking him where he was, you know? There was something about his voice that just gave me this weird feeling. But in the end, I told him to go to bed and sleep it off. And I put the phone down.'

At this last bit, he turned to Frank, his eyes wide with horror. He clasped his hand to his mouth to stifle a sob. 'I didn't . . . why didn't I go straight round there, Frank? Why the fuck didn't I just go round there?'

'Look, mate,' said Frank, his hand once again on Jimmy's shoulder, 'how were you to know what was happening? You can't blame yourself

327

for this, nobody could have known. Nobody.' Even as he said the words, he had the sick feeling he'd be repeating them to himself many times some day soon.

Jimmy swallowed, then went on. 'I went to bed, tried to sleep, but in the end I decided, fuck it, you know? I thought I'd go round to Euge's and find him blitzed on something or other, thought I'd have a drink with him and try and talk him out of this bender he's been on for so long. So I did. I took the spare key, went round there and when he didn't answer the door I just let myself in.'

★   ★   ★

The funeral was a week later. The court ruled death by misadventure. The coroner had found a combination of crack cocaine, barbiturates, painkillers and twelve times the recommended level of alcohol in his system. Eugene had choked on his own vomit.

★   ★   ★

In the days between Eugene's death and the funeral, Frank got up, went to work, ate and slept exactly as he always had. In the evenings he would turn on the TV, put on a record or pick up a book and the hours would pass the way they always had. Sometimes he would look up from whatever he was doing to find Kate staring at him, but he would smile at her reassuringly, and carry on as before.

On the morning of Eugene's burial, a Thursday, he woke before six. Fingers of grey light had begun to creep furtively beneath the curtains; rain splattered on the window pane, birds squawked testily from a tree somewhere. He didn't know exactly what had woken him, but he knew he didn't want to lie there in the silent half-light for a second longer.

Kate woke as he was finishing getting dressed. 'Frank?' she asked, sleepily, 'where are you going?'

'Just for a walk,' he replied from somewhere behind a pasted-on smile, reaching out to stroke her hair. 'I'll see you at the church at ten, OK?'

Rubbing her eyes she sat up and silently watched him tie his laces. 'Can I come?' she asked carefully. 'Let me get dressed, Frank. I'll walk with you,' she half rose from the bed when he didn't reply.

'No,' he said, firmly then. 'I'm OK. Just feel like a walk, that's all. I'll see you at the church later.' He squeezed her foot beneath the duvet, and left the room before she could reply.

It had stopped raining by the time Frank emerged from the house. He walked with no purpose, and felt no emotion as he trod the quiet, empty streets. He drifted aimlessly through south-east London, from Deptford to New Cross and on towards Brockley, and at last he stopped, surprised to find himself at the gates to the cemetery where Eugene would be buried in a matter of hours.

Brockley Cemetery is a vast place; sprawling,

Victorian, and cluttered with lopsided, crumbling graves etched with high-minded sentiments from a different era. Between the tomb stones run narrow paths overgrown with weeds and overlooked here and there by lichen-streaked stone angels that sink into the grassy verges, their age-worn faces wasting, crumbling, their wings tethered by ivy. One far end however is reserved for the freshly dead, whose plots are marked with mounds of earth bearing browning wreaths of flowers spelling NAN or awash in a sea of carnations, sodden teddy bears or soggy photographs in peeling plastic.

It was on the edge of this section that Frank spotted the two men in yellow bibs with spades taking a fag break besides a half-dug plot. Frank's insides had been cold since the night of Eugene's death; now they dropped another twenty degrees or so.

He used to like this place, had been coming here since a child, when he wanted to escape his mother. Later, as a teenager he would wander around amongst the graves with his Walkman, sometimes he and Eugene liked to come here to smoke a joint or two, sitting on a bench beneath a tree (Jimmy never came, he said the place gave him the creeps). It was a nice, restful place to come and think, amidst the traffic and greyness of London, more atmospheric and peaceful than the overcrowded parks. Now, gazing around, he felt only repulsion for it all.

He arrived at the church before everyone else: he arrived early for everything in his life, a habit that had been with him since childhood when the thought of keeping anyone waiting would send him into paroxysms of anxiety. The rest of the congregation, such as it was, arrived in hesitant dribs and drabs. He watched them from the side of the church, where he lingered in the shadows. First came Jimmy dressed in his best suit, his face raw with grief. By his side walked Mel, clutching his hand, steering him gently as if he were an inmate on day release from the nearest pensioners' home. Her long blonde hair was pulled back into a ponytail, her enormous breasts swaddled in a severe black dress. As Frank watched, he realised that nothing in Jimmy's life up to this point had prepared him for this — even his grandparents were still alive. He mentally examined himself for similar signs of devastation, found nothing; felt nothing.

After Jimmy and Mel came a rag bag assortment of Eugene's acquaintances: a couple of builders from the site he'd been working on, a handful of past girlfriends, some fellow drinkers from the various local pubs. The ex-girlfriends stood apart from one another, staring into space, fiddling with their mobile phones or shooting covert glances at each other from behind clouds of cigarette smoke. In the morning sunshine they reminded Frank of brightly painted marionettes, taken down from some dark and dusty shelf. He wondered why, out of the legions of Eugene's women, these particular ones had decided to show up today. He could be heartless when it came to girls, Eugene, had never really attached himself to any one of them. Frank glanced around for his parents, but there was no sign of them. He saw Kate arrive and join Jimmy and Mel. Taking a deep breath he went over to them too. The girls made their way into the church while he and Jimmy waited on the steps for the coffin to arrive.

★ ★ ★

Later, at the cemetery, when the small, incongruous group was gathered around the grave, Frank watched the proceedings as though through the wrong end of a telescope. Everything — from helping to carry Eugene's coffin into the church, to listening to the brief service, to watching the wooden box containing his friend being lowered gently into the ground — failed to reach him. He looked over and saw Jimmy crying into Mel's hair. Her arms were round his waist as if she was barely managing to hold him upright. He watched his friend with a mixture of pity and wonder, and catching Mel's eye, returned her smile, feeling glad in a detached, vague kind of way that Jimmy had decided not to go through with his plan to dump her. He became aware of Kate's hand gripping his own tightly, and was surprised to remember that she was by his side. He looked down at her pinched, white face and returned the pressure on her fingers, while the vicar murmured from the other side of the grave.

Clouds like yellow dogs chased each other across a sallow sky. Kate's hand slipped from his as the first clods of earth hit wood, and he watched her walk over to a figure standing some distance away beneath a tree. He was stunned to see his mother standing there. She looked up and saw Kate approach her across the clumpy grass. They had met, once, some months ago, when he had taken Kate round to her flat. It had been an awkward couple of hours in which Kate had floundered under his mum's stubborn silence. Today, however, as Kate approached, he saw his mother smile hesitantly, and make a few tentative steps towards her. They each raised a hand in shy greeting, two castaways waving from their separate islands.

He took in his mother's outfit. She was dressed in her smartest clothes, her hands nervously clutching her best handbag. As he peered closer he was amazed to see that she was wearing make-up. It had to be the first time in over a decade she had left her flat. People began to drift away from the grave, and while he and Jimmy thanked the vicar he continued to eye his mother with disbelief. She looked very small, here, in the outside world.

'Mum,' he said, when he finally joined them. A very fine spray of rain had begun to fall, and he watched it mingle with the patches of rouge on her cheeks.

'Thanks for coming,' he said at last.

She pursed her lips and looked self-consciously away to the stream of traffic in the distance. 'Well,' she said, stiffly, 'he was your best friend, wasn't he? Him and that Jimmy.'

'Yes,' agreed Frank quietly. 'He was.'

'Thick as thieves they was,' she said, turning abruptly to Kate. 'When they were kids.'

Kate smiled tenderly at Frank, and nodded.

'I'm sorry, son,' said his mother, unexpectedly. She turned to him sharply and fixed her eyes on his, but she spoke very softly as she added, 'I'm very sorry for your loss.'

Frank nodded, unable to speak. Suddenly he went to his mother and pulled her to him, wrapping his arms around her small, stiff body. He realised then that it was the first time they had touched since he was a child. 'Thank you,' he said. When he let her go, he noticed that the patches of rouge on her cheeks had been completely washed away.

★ ★ ★

The wake was held at the Hope and Anchor and by his second pint Frank was desperate to leave. He stood by the bar with Kate, watching a fight break out between two of Eugene's exes. 'I've got to get out of here,' he whispered to Kate. He looked across at Jimmy, who had been backed into a corner by Jackie, the barmaid from the Feathers, her face a mess of tears and mascara as she wailed on and on incoherently into her third double Bacardi and coke. Jimmy looked over and caught Frank's eye, and within minutes the two of them, Kate and Mel in tow, were edging towards the door.

'You still got the key?' Frank asked when they were safely outside.

By way of answer, Jimmy pulled his key ring

from his pocket and waggled it in front of Frank's face.

'OK, let's go,' said Frank, and the four of them set off in the direction of Eugene's flat.

★ ★ ★

'I didn't want to remember this place the way I saw it last,' said Jimmy, when they were all sitting in Eugene's front room.

Frank stared around at the familiar dark blue carpet, the ugly brown sofa and chairs, the Taxi Driver poster on the wall, the broken coffee table with its overflowing ashtray still full of roaches and bits of Rizla.

Eugene had been assigned this flat when he'd turned eighteen and was kicked out of the children's home, and from that moment on it had been the focus of their social life. It was an ugly, cramped little place but he and Jimmy had loved it. He wondered vaguely how many nights exactly he had spent round here, getting stoned, watching videos, passing out? He wondered how many girls he'd got off with on this very sofa.

He felt very cold suddenly and shivered; all at once he was feeling unbearably claustrophobic, the walls of the room felt oppressive and cell-like, the smell from the ashtray made him feel queasy. He realised with a heart-stopping flash of shock that it must have been here, on this sofa, that Jimmy had found Eugene's body that night, and he jumped to his feet with a start. Shaking his head at Kate's look of concern he hurried across the room to the bedroom, and closed the door.

Sitting on Eugene's untidy bed he put his head in his hands. He let out a long, painful rush of air from his lungs and looked around at the untidy mess of clothes, empty beer bottles and toiletries. Next to the bed, open face down at page six, where it had been for the past five years or so, was a battered copy of *The Celestine Prophecy*, and despite himself Frank smiled. The room still smelt as it always had, ever since Eugene had moved in there — unwashed clothes, stale spliff smoke, a faint whiff of sex.

A photograph propped up on the cluttered mantelpiece caught his eye, and he went over and picked it up. It was a photo he'd never seen before, did not remember ever having been taken, and he wondered how long Eugene had had it. It was of the three of them, aged about thirteen or so. They had their arms around each other's shoulders. Eugene was in the middle, wearing a yellow vest with '33' written on it in big black letters. His hair was in a wild afro like a bubble around his face and he was looking directly at the camera while Frank and Jimmy were turned towards him. The three were laughing about something but it was Eugene's expression that made him feel as though, just for a moment, the world had split in two: his head was thrown back in mid-laugh, his eyes were wide. It was a moment of total, unselfconscious joy captured forever in the photo.

The tears came without warning and still clutching the photograph the grief that had so far refused to show itself escaped finally in a long, wrenching sob. He dropped the photo to the floor and sat, doubled over on the bed.

He barely registered the sound of the door opening, nor the weight of somebody sitting down next to him on the bed. And then he felt Jimmy's arm around his shoulder and he sunk against his friend, sobbing, while Jimmy silently patted his back.

28

Deptford, south-east London, 12 May 2004
Black, wretched days follow Eugene's funeral.
Kate can only watch as grief grabs Frank by the
throat and pulls him under. For a week now
there has been nothing — no surprises in the
post, no silent phone calls, no speeding cars. But
it's coming, of that she's certain. And there,
slithering beneath it all, is the memory of
Steven's touch; of her betrayal. Now the
memories of Ingrid's death return with horrifying clarity. There's no respite from them: asleep
or awake they come, at first in the form of brief,
static images, but then sewage-like they seep into
her consciousness, creeping across her dreams
like ghosts.

At first she calls in sick at the library, fending
off Stuart's polite concern with stories of viruses
and stomach bugs. Every morning she kisses
Frank goodbye and leaves for work as usual, but
instead of heading towards Soho she prowls the
streets of London, riding busses and the
Underground to random destinations: Highgate,
Camden, Kensington, Whitechapel, anywhere
she can walk unseen amongst the crowds. She
roams the streets of Islington, Archway, Fulham,
always hurrying, hurrying amongst the bodies.
And still the memories pursue her, tapping on
her shoulder, treading on her heels. She thinks of
Steven, of the strange, dreamlike unreality of that

338

evening, the sense of relief that had come from the telling of her story, the intense desire that had gripped her, the sensation of reaching for him, but finding nothing there, of ultimately waking from her trance and seeing only Frank's face, the one concrete truth of him, and then the awful realisation of what she'd done.

Finally, in the middle of Kings Cross, she comes to a halt. The time has come. She can feel danger, poised and waiting, ready to pounce. It is time to leave. She will return to the library to collect her final cheque, and then she'll tell Frank everything.

★　★　★

Descending the stairs to the basement Kate feels at last some relief from her lonely wanderings. The comforting yellow gloom of the Archive Room envelops her and she realises that she's missed this peaceful, underground refuge from the world. She passes the row of workstations, returning her colleagues' greetings until, finally, Daisy looks up and notices her with a smile of delighted surprise. Her eyes meet Steven's for the briefest of moments, but she quickly looks away.

While Daisy rambles excitedly on, Kate smiles and nods, her heart twisting uncomfortably to be so close to him again. Guilt wraps itself around her, tightening its grip. She tries to quash a sudden desire to run. She can barely stand to look at him, and when her eyes do flicker over to him she winces, seeing something quite repellent now in the brute force of his good looks, his jaw too square, his skin too rude with health.

Eventually Daisy wanders off to the Ladies and leaves them alone.

'Good to have you back,' she hears him say. She nods dully, staring hard at her computer screen. 'Feeling better, I hope?'

She looks at him then, manages a smile, and says faintly, 'Yes, thank you.' For the seventh time that hour she glances at the clock. The girl in the payroll department has told her she must wait until four to collect her wages. It occurs to her to leave without them, but if she is to start her life somewhere new she will need all that she can get.

'Kate.' The low urgency of Steven's voice makes her look up in surprise. 'I need to talk to you about something,' he says. 'It's very important.'

She's about to shake her head when he persists. 'Please, Kate.' He lowers his voice still further and with a quick glance around the room says, 'It's about what you told me the other night. Something I've found out. Something you'll want to hear. I think that I can help you.'

She thinks for a while, but then nods her head reluctantly, unable to ignore the tiny sliver of hope his words have given her. 'OK,' she says at last.

'Will you meet me after work? At six, on the corner of Berwick Street?'

At that moment Daisy returns to her desk, and Kate only has time to nod.

340

He doesn't notice her approach. Amongst the streams of people — tourists, office workers, shoppers — he stands gazing off into the distance. She takes in the close-cropped shape of his skull, the wide, muscular shoulders. Suddenly every inch of her longs to run, to not have to talk to this strange unsettling man, wanting only to be with Frank, to feel his body in her arms, to smell his scent, to feel his kiss, to beg his forgiveness. But it's too late, too late. When she's only a couple of feet away Steven turns, although she has made no sound. And then he nods and says, 'Let's go.'

Without a word, they set off in the direction of Oxford Street. She has no desire to return to the dingy little pub they went to before, but here in his presence, alone with him, she feels again the strange dreamlike sense of being dislocated from reality.

'Steven,' she begins, finally, after several minutes of silence, 'what I told you the other night, I haven't told anyone. Nobody knows who I really am, except you. Not even Frank — not yet.'

They cross Oxford Street. At last he speaks. 'There's something you need to know, Kate. But wait a moment, wait until we're alone.'

They continue walking, and as they reach then pass the pub she realises they are heading towards his flat. She stops outside his building, not following him when he bounds up the steps and begins to unlock the front door. At last, noticing her reluctance he walks back down the steps and, before she even knows what's happening, is pulling her towards him and kissing her.

At first, shock stops her from reacting and she hangs, momentarily passive in his arms, her lips unresponsive beneath his until at last she collects herself and pushes him away. 'No, Steven, that's not what I came here for.' She stares back at him angrily. 'The other night was a mistake. I'm sorry, I shouldn't have come. I don't know why I'm here.' She shakes her head and backs away and doesn't see the rage that flares then gutters behind his eyes.

'Wait.' He catches hold of her arm, and with a sudden rush of intensity says, 'I'm sorry, Kate. Please stay. Please, please come upstairs with me. Just to talk, I promise. I need to tell you something. I think I've found a way to help you.'

★   ★   ★

The kitchen's magnolia walls are bare apart from an ugly wall clock noisily clicking away each minute. This flat, she sees now, is a still, soulless place, where no one seems to live, where no one has ever lived. On her way in she had briefly glimpsed a living room but he had hurried her past before she could get a proper look. The bedroom door had been closed, and as she thinks of what had once passed between them there, fresh guilt grips her. Stood in the kitchen, claustrophobia descends on her. The kitchen door clicks shut behind them and she jumps.

Steven is standing near the window, watching her. She hears her own voice, thin and nervous in the silence: 'What did you want to tell me?'

But still he stares without answering and she notices a thin layer of sweat now covers his brow, and it seems as if every speck of him is tensed for something. Her unease grows. She looks around her uncomfortably, glancing up at the clock.

Click. Another minute gone.

'Steven,' she says, 'what's the matter with you? Why are you looking at me like that?' When still he doesn't answer, she turns to the door, 'I've really got to go. I shouldn't have come here.' She feels a confusing sadness. The place chills her, fills her with an unnameable bleakness. She is desperate to leave.

He has crossed the room in seconds, has hold of her arm, his fingers digging into her flesh, the same strange intensity she had seen before. She tries to shake him off. 'Steven!' she protests, too shocked and confused to say anything else. And then, to her amazement, he tries to kiss her again, his mouth rammed against hers, his tongue pushing between her lips. With one arm he pins her against the wall while his free hand roams over her body.

In vain she tries to writhe out of his grip. 'What are you doing?' she asks, but his mouth has moved to her neck and with clumsy fingers he begins to unbutton her dress. 'Come on,' he breathes into her neck, his voice thick and strange. He pulls away and looks into her face, a hunger in his eyes, 'Come on,' he urges again.

'No!' Struggling free at last she makes it to the

kitchen door, but before she can cross the hall he is pushing past her. She tries to catch up with him but he shoves her roughly away, sending her sprawling to the floor and she watches as he pulls a key from his pocket and turning it in the lock, imprisons her.

Anger at last gets the better of her fear. 'Let me out,' she tells him, scrambling to her feet. But when he turns back to her his face is chillingly blank. It astonishes her how quickly it can change, the various emotions laying siege to his features, charging around like crazed gatecrashers before abruptly leaving it entirely empty like a suddenly vacated room. As he moves towards her she retreats until she feels the cold wall at her back. Within moments he is in front of her and she feels the dark immediate threat of him as he looms over her. He grasps her arms and she is aware now of his strength. 'I want to,' he says, his voice devoid of emotion and when she struggles, his face fills with a childish, impotent rage.

She feels the danger just before it happens, like glimpsing a missile flying towards her from the corner of her eye. He grabs her wrist, hauling her into the bedroom. 'No, Steven,' she pleads, but, ignoring her, he throws her onto the bed. It is his silence that is so awful now. At first she cries out as she struggles beneath him, but soon she too lapses into a tense silence, and the two of them wrestle mutely on the bed.

He is too strong for her. Effortlessly he pins her down with one hand, while the other reaches beneath her skirt. When she kicks out with her leg he slaps her hard across the face, then fumbles with the zipper of his jeans. He is unrecognizable, as if something fundamental in his chemical make-up has altered to transform him into an entirely different creature. 'Please,' she says, breaking the silence at last, but it's as if he doesn't hear her. Still keeping her pinned to the mattress he tears at his jeans, grunting with the effort as he pulls them down, and she thrashes beneath him in one last futile bid for freedom.

And then, suddenly, abruptly, everything stops. Time halts, the world is still. There, above her, Steven doesn't even breathe. Only his eyes move and in the strange sudden stillness they collide with hers and as she stares back into their pale green vacuum the moment finally breaks, he is pulling his jeans back up over his hips and in her astonishment she just has time to catch a glimpse of flaccid flesh before with a shout of fury he has run from the room, and seconds later she hears the kitchen door slam shut behind him.

She lies on the bed, unable for the moment to make sense of her reprieve. But finally she sits up, her eyes on the locked front door on the other side of the hall. She listens for some sound from Steven, but can hear nothing. Dazedly she wonders what time it is, and how long he will keep her here. She wonders if he will come back and what he will do when he does. Her wrists and face and shins feel bruised and sore where he'd slapped and pulled her and at the memory of his violence she looks again towards the locked front door, cold fear gnawing at her.

Shakily she refastens the buttons of her dress and as she pushes herself up, her hand falls upon something cold. There amongst the wrinkled sheets from where it must have fallen from his pocket is the front door key. Instantly she is on her feet.

The key is in the lock, the door open in seconds, but just as she is about to escape, she happens to glance across to the living room and catches sight of the stacks of papers, books and photographs piled high upon the coffee table. The thought of Steven catching her there impels her to keep moving but there's something about one of the larger photos, something familiar about its colours and composition that has caught her eye and now causes her to freeze, then turn back and take a few steps closer. In a moment she is crossing the room in quick strides and seizing the photograph from its pile. With mounting disbelief she takes in the familiar image of herself, aged twelve, standing outside the hospital in Rouen.

There it is: the strange off-kilter grimace, the wild eyes, the long mane of auburn hair. With trembling fingers she picks up the rest of the photos and riffles through them with increasing agitation and speed, staring in cold astonishment at pictures she'd long forgotten ever being taken. Here she is at thirteen, fourteen, fifteen — in the school-room with Yaya and Colin, or in the neurology ward with Ingrid, Doctor Irving and the rest. Here she is at the conference. And there she is again, standing outside High Barn.

Her throat is dry, her heart pounds. Next she turns to the newspaper clippings; the familiar headlines screaming back at her. 'Who is Little Bird?', 'Monster Who Imprisoned Tot for Ten Years', 'Little Bird Flies to America', her childhood revealed in a series of lurid articles. Besides them is a stack of books and with growing confusion she reads from their spines: *The Science of Language* by Ingrid Klein, *Wild Children* by Martin Chambers, *The Mowgli People*, *Raised by Wolves: Tales of Feral Children*, and dozens more. Picking them up one by one she sees that each of them has been bookmarked at the place detailing her own story.

At last she throws the final book to the floor and running from the living room she bursts into the kitchen and demands, 'Who are you?'

But even through her shock and confusion she feels a sharp tug of fear at the sight of him. It's so strange, the way he's standing in the corner facing the wall like a chastised child. He doesn't turn to look at her and her scalp prickles as she watches him.

It's some time before he answers. Without moving a muscle he says in a quiet, pleasant voice, 'Did you get the little bird, Elodie?'

Her heart drops. 'Who are you?' she whispers now.

It's only then that he turns, only then that she sees the gun in his hand. 'I'm Anton,' he tells her. 'Remember me, Elodie? You murdered my mother.'

'Anton.' She begins to sway within the

spinning kitchen. '*Anton?*'

He raises the gun until it's pointing at her head. There is something utterly unreal about it all: the gun looks incongruous in his hand, unconvincing, like a toy. She sees that he trembles with excitement; that his eyes keep flickering between her face and the weapon at the end of his arm. His eyes are bright, feverish, he has a strange, almost fearful grin, as though he can hardly believe what he is holding, like a boy acting in a play.

'Sit down,' he orders, and silently, her eyes never leaving him, she feels for one of the chairs and lowers herself into it, the table between them.

As she stares at him, an image suddenly appears to her of a tall, awkward teenager spied from the window of the schoolroom at High Barn. Long hair obscuring his face. An air of quiet rage. *Anton.*

'Why are you doing this?' she asks at last.

'You killed her,' he says, his voice tight with excitement. 'You ruined everything.'

'No!' her eyes fill with tears.

His hand stops trembling, his arm straightens and holds the gun still, aiming it squarely at her face.

She will die here, she realises. Here, now, after everything. A dreamlike succession of faces flashes across her eyes. Mathias, Ingrid, Robert, Shanique, Bobby. The grainy pixels of her mother's features. And finally, it is Frank she sees, his face that smiles back at her across the flashing, smoky gloom of the Mermaid.

29

Deptford, south-east London, 13 May 2004
Frank had woken to a new morning. In the week
or so since Eugene's funeral, his days had
followed more or less the same pattern. He
would wake, blearily, from dank, black sleep,
groggily rising to the surface of blissful
ignorance, until all at once the memories would
hit him like a sack of rocks and he'd turn over,
hiding his head beneath the pillow.

On this particular morning however he had sat
up in bed and, waiting for the familiar boot of
doom to come as usual and grind him beneath
its heel, was surprised when, in fact, this time it
didn't. He still felt like shit, certainly; he still felt
the same wrenching sadness, but now something
else began to seep through his misery. He tried
to decipher what it was exactly he was feeling
but try as he might he couldn't quite put his
finger on it. After a while he decided that it could
only be summed up with two words. And they
were: *Fuck this*.

Some days ago, after yet another night of
drinking whisky alone in the dark while Kate
slept upstairs, he had phoned Tim and told him
he was too ill to make it in. Ever since then he
had spent the hours until Kate returned from
work staring up at the ceiling or sleeping, and
forgetting to wash, dress, or eat. When the phone
rang he ignored it. It would only be Jimmy, and

Jimmy would only want to talk about Eugene. And talking about Eugene was something Frank just couldn't face.

This particular morning however he had gotten out of bed, showered and dressed for the first time in a week, and set about clearing up the house. As he worked, his sense of purpose grew. With every passing minute the idea that had been playing around his brain before Eugene died grew more and more tangible. By the time he had finished mopping the kitchen floor he had made up his mind: he was going to take over the shop from Tim. No more fucking about; this time he meant business. He was going to make something of himself. As he shaved, his mind buzzed with plans. He'd need to mortgage the house, get a business plan together, talk to the bank, convince Tim to sell East Side Soundz to him, and work seven days a week if necessary to turn his idea into a reality. But he could do it, he was sure he could.

The more he thought about it the more it made sense, and the more he pushed Eugene's pointless death to the back of his mind. He looked at the kitchen clock: 3 p.m. He would go and call in at the shop, see what a pig's ear Tim had made of it in his absence, then go and meet Kate and take her out to dinner. At the thought of Kate he smiled properly for the first time in days. And then the second life-changing revelation came. He was going to ask her to marry him. He stared at himself in the hall mirror, his face flushed with excitement, his eyes

350

shining. Then, when the shop began doing really well, they'd have a couple of kids maybe. He grinned to himself as he pictured the two of them standing outside the shop, children by their side, who knows: maybe a dog or two for good measure. It would be perfect. He grabbed his keys and remembering that once again his car was out of action, whistled as he began the short walk to the station.

★ ★ ★

East Side Soundz was in chaos when he arrived. Tim was standing behind the counter, trying to decipher the stoned mumblings of a burly supplier with a fat spliff in his mouth, a delivery note in his hand and a mound of boxes by his feet. His face lit up with relief when he saw Frank. 'Thank fuck for that. Barnaby was too hungover to make it in, I wouldn't have bothered opening up but my dad said he might call round at some point to see how it was going and I didn't want to risk it.'

'Sorry for the past week, man,' said Frank, nodding hello to the supplier. 'Close friend of mine passed away.'

'Really? Oh dear. What happened?'

Frank hesitated. How Tim would love this tale of Drugs and Death in Deptford. 'Pigeon,' he said finally, with an I-don't-want-to-talk-about-it air.

Tim's mouth fell open.

'Straight up. Got into his water tank. Decomposed, poisoned the water. My mate got sicker and sicker then one day . . . carked it. Nasty.'

'Really?' Tim was so thrilled he momentarily lost his gangster accent. 'I mean, gosh, Frank, I'm dreadfully sorry.'

Frank almost smiled. There was actually something quite endearing about Tim when he dropped the Rude Boy act.

'Thanks. Do you mind if I shoot off? Got to organise the funeral and stuff. Sorry. I'll be in next week.'

Tim's face fell. 'Yeah, might close up anyway. This place is more trouble than it's worth.'

'What're you doing tomorrow night?'

Tim looked at him hopefully. 'Nothing, why?'

Frank had always suspected that Tim's evenings were not as full as he liked to make out. 'Fancy going for a few beers?' he asked casually. 'There's something I want to talk to you about. Got a proposition for you.'

Tim flushed with pleasure. Frank had never shown any interest in socialising with him before — except for the time he'd come to his girlfriend Fiona's twenty-first and brought that awful person Jimmy along. He shuddered at the memory. Of course, Fifi had promised there'd been nothing untoward happening when he'd come across her and Jimmy amongst the coats on her parents' four-poster, and he believed her. Of course he did. But still, the man had been an appalling, drunken, nuisance. A night out with Frank, however, was an entirely different matter. Frank knew how to behave himself. Perhaps they could swing by the Engineer later, introduce

352

Frank to the chaps. Show them that Tim Rimington was the sort of guy who had friends from all walks of life. 'Awesome,' he said. 'I'll see you tomorrow night then?'

'Great. See you then, Tim.'

★ ★ ★

It was a nice afternoon so Frank decided to walk up St John Street to the Angel and then get the tube to Soho. It should have been a ten-minute journey but thanks to his train getting stuck in a tunnel for an hour, it was nearly six before he made it, sweltering and pissed off, out of Leicester Square station.

He quickened his pace. He would be just in time to catch Kate if he hurried. As he walked, people began to scurry from office doorways. The sun, in one last attempt to make up for its behaviour over the past few months, shone apologetically over the shop workers and media kids who were already congregating outside the pubs and bars, smiling bravely up at the insincere sky, colluding in the sun's half-arsed pretence at an Indian summer. His heart flipped as he imagined Kate's face when he told her of his plans. He pictured himself proposing to her. Should he get down on one knee? Or would that just be embarrassing? He had missed her, he realised, over this past week while he had been too caught up with grief to pay her any attention.

Turning into Brewer Street it was a few minutes past six when he finally reached the Soho Picture Library, but even so, the scrawny blonde behind the front desk informed him snootily that Kate had just left. Emerging into the street once more he looked to left and right until at last he spotted her disappearing around a corner in the distance. Squinting after her, he could just make out another figure by her side; a man, well built with very blond hair. He began walking after them, quickening his stride in an attempt to catch them up. Berwick Street market was just beginning to pack up and the air was full of the calls of tired traders.

He crossed over into Broadwick Street. Where was she going? Charing Cross was in the other direction. He wondered who the man beside her was. Steven, he supposed; he'd heard her mention him before along with a girl named Daisy. Perhaps they were going for an after-work drink, he thought, and felt a pang of irritation as he realised that he had lost them again. He stopped, gazing from left to right, and just as he was about to give up he glimpsed a flash of her hair in the distance and saw them turn into Poland Street.

As he followed, something he couldn't quite put his finger on began to trouble him. He realised suddenly that he didn't have a clear idea of Kate when she wasn't with him — it was like he could only really see her when she was physically standing in front of him. He felt a sharp stab of jealousy at the thought of some stranger — this stranger — seeing something, understanding something, he didn't. Telling himself to get a grip, but feeling strangely like a child abandoned in a busy crowd, he crossed

Oxford Street and was about to call out when they began walking again. Was there something in the way they walked together? A kind of intimacy? But, no — he was being paranoid, surely? And yet they were moving with some urgency. He stopped when they did, an instinct telling him to hang back, baffled, when they paused nearby a house with several bells on the door. He didn't notice the silver Mercedes parked outside.

Kate seemed to be upset, was saying something to the man as he unlocked the door. She had her back to Frank, but he sensed that there was something very wrong. Every instinct told him to go to her, to gatecrash this strange private scene and pull her away. But then, just as he was about to cross the road it happened. As he watched, the man came back down the stairs and reached out and touched Kate's shoulder. And then he kissed her. In that moment the world around Frank seemed to fall away. He watched them kiss.

A hundred images flashed before him as if he were drowning. His parents, Joanie, the shop, Jimmy, Eugene. He saw his own face earlier, staring back in the mirror, his stupid, stupid plans, his idiotic belief that he could make a success of his life, that he would recover from Eugene's death, that Kate loved him. That Kate loved him. As she turned and followed the man into the house he returned, fleetingly, to Greenwich Park, the summer he was ten: saw again the girl with the red hair and the dragonfly eyes sitting beneath the tree staring back at him.

Saw her smile one last time, and then she vanished.

★   ★   ★

Walking, running across Oxford Street, steaming through Soho and Leicester Square to Charing Cross, no coherent thoughts, just pure blank rage. Shouldering his way through the crowds, his fists clenched, trying to hang onto the fury because if he let it go, the pain would floor him and he would have to face the idea of life after this.

Almost unaware of what he was doing he jumped on a train to New Cross, his movements mechanical, conscious only of his anger. On the train he sat and hated the other passengers; a couple with their kids, a drunk man with his can of cider, an elderly lady doing the crossword: hated them, all of them, with their complacent, unknowing ordinariness, their smug smiles, their retarded happiness. When he got home he would put every scrap of Kate's possessions into the garden and burn them, he told himself. But first he would go to the Hope and Anchor and get totally, irretrievably, numbingly, mindlessly drunk.

★   ★   ★

He was on his fourth pint when he looked up and blearily saw Jimmy walking towards him. Vaguely, he remembered that somewhere around pint three, his mobile had rung and he'd mumbled something into it.

'All right, mate?' Jimmy was reaching for his wallet when he got to where Frank was sitting, shooting daggers at the other regulars. 'What you having?' When Frank didn't respond and kept staring grimly into space, his smile faltered, and he looked at him quizzically. 'Well? What's it to be? Piss-weak Fosters or flat Stella? Come on mate, it ain't *Sophie's Choice* is it?'

He sat down. 'I'm glad you're here, actually. I've got something to tell you. Mel's pregnant, isn't she? I only just found out. I'm telling you, Frank, I'm — ' He looked more closely at his friend's face and realised at last that something was very wrong. He lit a cigarette. 'What's happened?' he asked.

'Kate,' was all Frank could say.

'What about her?'

'I saw her, didn't I? Saw her with someone else.' He drained what was left of his pint.

Jimmy stared back at him as he tried to process what Frank was telling him. 'Fuck off,' he spluttered finally. 'Kate? *Kate?* You sure?'

'Course I'm fucking sure,' spat Frank. 'Saw them with my own eyes, didn't I? Jesus . . . ' he put his head in his hands. 'Fucking *bitch*. Christ knows how long it's been going on.' Raging about Kate seemed to make him feel slightly better and gathering his strength he started ranting into Jimmy's astonished face, 'All this time she's been living in my house, telling me that she loves me, lying to my face, laughing at me all along. Well good luck to her. Good luck to

357

the pair of them. Jesus I'm a mug, I should have let that wanker run her over when I had the chance,' he said, recalling the evening when he had pulled Kate out of the way of the maniac in the silver Merc, and not meaning a word of it.

He helped himself to one of Jimmy's cigarettes while Jimmy tried desperately to think of what to say. 'Look, Frank,' he began, 'you must be gutted. But I . . . Frank?' he asked, when an expression of stunned disbelief flew across his friend's face. 'What is it?'

'Jesus,' said Frank. 'The geezer in the car! Jesus fuck, Jimmy — it was the same bloke. The same bloke I just saw Kate with.' He got to his feet. 'That was the bloke who tried to run her down. I'd recognise the fucker's face anywhere.'

'What are you talking about?' asked Jimmy, but Frank had jumped to his feet.

'My car's fucked. Can I borrow one of yours?' he asked.

'Well, yeah. I can drive you wherever, mate, you know that. But — '

'Right. Let's go.'

They rushed out of the pub, Jimmy wheezing a few yards behind Frank as they ran the mile around the corner to the car lot. 'Where are we going?' he asked, but Frank ignored him. When they reached his tiny office, Jimmy fetched the keys to a VW Golf he'd just had repaired, and unlocking the door, nodded at Frank to get in.

But Frank hesitated. It was one of the strange anomalies of Jimmy's personality that he was actually a rubbish driver. Frank didn't have time to waste and as he thought of Jimmy pootling nervously in the bus lane, fannying around at junctions and dicking about at roundabouts, he held out his hand and said, 'Give me the keys.'

'No fucking way,' Jimmy half laughed. 'You're not insured and it's my car and anyway, you're pissed.'

'I'm completely sober,' he said, and realised with surprise that it was true. 'Give me the keys.'

A long moment passed while Jimmy considered his friend from the other side of the car. It was like looking at a complete stranger. Finally, wordlessly, he passed Frank the keys and got in the passenger seat. Within minutes, Jimmy sincerely wished he hadn't. With a screech of burning rubber, Frank backed out of the car lot, spun the VW around and accelerated faster and faster until within minutes they were on the Old Kent Road. 'Jesus Fucking Christ. Slow down!' shouted Jimmy, as Frank cut up car after car to the sound of furious horns. But Frank ignored him. 'Oh God Oh God Oh God we're all going to die,' yelled Jimmy, as Frank steamed through a red light, narrowly missing a bus.

And still they sped on. By the time they had reached the Elephant and were approaching Waterloo Bridge, Jimmy had given up screaming and was instead sitting ashen faced, his eyes screwed tightly shut, his fingers gripping the dash, silently praying for all his worth that it would soon be over.

In central London he almost cried with relief when Frank spotted a police van and at last slowed down. The streets were clogged with traffic and Jimmy eyed his friend in amazement as he repeatedly slammed his hand on the steering wheel, yelling, 'Come on! Come on you fuckers! Move it!' At last, in Wardour Street, after scaring witless every tourist that dared to try and cross in front of him by maniacally revving his engine and blasting on his horn, Frank turned to Jimmy and said. 'Right. Fuck this. I'm getting out.'

'What?' Aghast, Jimmy looked at the double yellow lines and army of traffic wardens on the pavements. 'You've got to be shitting me. You're not just leaving me here. No way. No way, Frank.' But Frank had already opened the door, and to the sound of furious shouts and honks, was beginning to run off in the direction of Oxford Street.

★ ★ ★

When Frank got to the door of the tall, skinny town house he'd seen Kate disappear into earlier he hit every button on the intercom until at last someone buzzed him in. He hammered at the first internal door he got to until it was opened by a surprised Japanese girl. 'Sorry,' said Frank, 'I'm looking for a friend of mine. He said he lived at flat A, but I must have misheard. He's blond, stocky a bit shorter than me . . . '

'Oh! You must mean Steven,' said the girl, pointing at the ceiling. 'The guy on the top floor.' She smiled, 'Such a sweetie. I — ' but Frank was already pounding up the stairs.

★ ★ ★

The door of Flat D was slightly ajar. He hesitated outside for a moment, peering in through the dark crack, waiting for the blood to stop roaring in his ears, his heart to stop banging in his chest. He pushed the door open a little further and listened. Nothing. He went in and stood in the hall for a few seconds, his ears straining in the silence. To his right was an empty bedroom, to his left the half-closed door of a living room. He could see a bathroom ahead and next to it the closed door of what presumably was the kitchen. And still the eerie silence persisted. Was the flat empty? Uneasiness sluiced through him, there was something creepy about the place he couldn't put his finger on.

The thought of Kate in danger compelled him to keep moving. Going first to the living room he silently, carefully, peered around the half-closed door. It was empty. He would try the kitchen next. But just as he was leaving his eye caught sight of some photographs scattered over the table and floor. On impulse he went to them and gathered them up.

The first picture was of a young girl, about ten or eleven, standing outside a large red-bricked building and surrounded by nurses. She had long auburn hair, the strands of red, gold and brown curling past her shoulders. There was something both arresting and disconcerting about her. He stared more closely at the dark blue irises, and his heart dropped to the floor. 'Kate,' he whispered. His mouth was dry and he felt strangely light-headed as he picked up first one and then another of the newspaper clippings. He skimmed them quickly and when he dropped the last page, he felt his legs grow weak and sank to the sofa. Elodie Brun. The name rolled around and around his confused mind. Elodie Brun. Little Bird. Nothing made sense. He picked up more of the photos, stared at the girl there and felt the first lurch of loss.

Just then a noise from somewhere in the flat snapped him from his reverie and he got to his feet. Who was this guy? This stranger who had tried to run her down, who had her here, somewhere, in this godforsaken place? He dropped the photos to the floor and left the room. Within moments he had crossed the hall and was pushing open the kitchen door.

30

Central London, 12 May 2004

'Why now?' Kate asks, staring into the barrel of the gun.

'What?'

'Why now?' she repeats. 'Why didn't you kill me when you had me here before?'

He doesn't answer immediately, and she sees a glimmer of uncertainty flash across his eyes. And something else; something competing with his rage. She is reminded of a summer evening years ago, when, looking out of the schoolroom window she had seen him for the second time, standing alone at the edge of the garden just as dusk had begun to fall.

The world hesitates, someone else peeps out at her from behind the cold green eyes. But quick as a flash time shifts, the door slams shut, the hatred has returned. 'Why not?' he says, with a belligerent shrug. 'I knew you'd be back.' His smile is ugly. 'Why rush these things?'

But she had seen it, his loneliness.

'Anton,' she says,

'Shut up!' he shouts, taking a step closer and once again she's stunned by his quick-fire change of emotions. 'Have you any idea what you did?' he asks. 'What it was like for me?'

Her voice when she speaks is very quiet. 'Tell me,' she says.

'Shut your mouth,' he says. But there's doubt

there. She sees it, holds on to it.

They stare at each other in the failing light. Outside on the street a woman laughs, a car door slams. She watches, fascinated, the struggle behind his eyes.

Finally he looks away.

'Tell me, Anton,' she persists. 'Please, tell me.'

In the long silence that follows she waits to see which part of him will win.

Click. The ugly clock ticks on.

And when he finally opens his mouth his voice is just a fraction above silence, so she has to strain to catch the words. 'I still dream about it,' he shouts, urgent and desperate. 'I dream about it every night.'

She nods, not taking her eyes from him, and scarcely breathing, murmurs, 'Me too.'

He stares back at her, his eyes unseeing. The gun wavers a little, moves a fraction of an inch to the side and she sees that he's not aware of it now, that he's somewhere else entirely. His gun arm drops another few millimetres. If he were to accidentally pull the trigger now the bullet would miss her. The first tendrils of hope begin to unfurl within her.

'I found her,' he says.

'Yes,' she whispers.

'I'd been driving around all night and in the morning I went home and I went into the kitchen and she was there.' His eyes are wet with tears now, and he brings the hand holding the gun to his face and in a childlike gesture wipes them away.

'My father,' he whispers. 'My father . . . there

364

was so much blood.'

But she can bear it no more. 'I'm so sorry,' she tells him in a rush. 'I'm so sorry, Anton. I didn't mean to hurt her, I swear.'

And like silt rising to the surface of a river her voice brings him slowly back to the present. Dazedly he looks around him as if returning from a dream. He stares at her for a long time. And then, '*You're sorry?*' he says at last, his brow wrinkled in confusion. '*Sorry?*' In an instant the anger has returned. 'You ruined everything,' he tells her. 'I have nothing.' His face is red. 'My father . . . my father . . . ' but the words seem to choke in his throat and he looks away. In a matter of seconds, the other Anton is back. A smile pulls at the corners of his mouth and he almost swaggers closer to her. He is in control again. The gun is back where it was, its barrel aimed squarely between her eyes once more. She feels the cold fist re-establish its grip around her heart.

He shakes his head and laughs. 'You know, Elodie, you speak well, don't you?' He considers her, his head slightly tilted to one side. 'She did that — my mother. She taught you everything, didn't she?'

'Anton, I . . . '

But her interruption is waved away. 'All those years she spent on you.' He takes a step closer. 'Turning you into a human being.' He purses his lips, nods philosophically. 'I've read all about it, you know. While I was wondering where the fuck you'd ran off to. And it really is a fascinating subject, isn't it?'

He's enjoying himself now, has seen the shame flare in her eyes and has leapt upon it. 'What was it she called you in one of her books?' he continues. He furrows his brow, pretending to think. 'A savage with table manners?' He shakes his head with a smile. 'Poor little Elodie,' he says. 'Just one step up from a wild animal really, weren't you, until she came along?'

She looks away, her fists clenched by her side.

'How fucking ironic.' His whisper hisses through the silence.

She turns back to him then, and their eyes hold for a long, cold moment. She gets to her feet.

The sudden movement makes him flinch. His mouth hangs open in surprise. She moves away from the chair and takes a step towards him.

He blinks nervously. 'What are you doing?' he asks. 'Sit down.' Uncertainty flickers in his eye.

The table is still between them but in six steps she will have cleared it. As she takes the first, the barrel of the gun follows her, but still she sees it tremble. 'What are you doing?' he says again, his voice almost pleading. 'Sit down!'

She takes another step, and then another. He starts to shout. 'Get back, Elodie, I mean it.'

Three more steps and she's cleared the table. She turns to face him and there is nothing but a couple of metres of air between them now.

'Anton,' she says, her voice calm, her gaze never leaving his. 'What time did you get back to High Barn that night?'

'What?' He stares at her, his face blank with confusion.

'Tell me, it's important. You said it was morning.'

'Yes, so what?'

An image returns to her of Robert standing in the kitchen looking down at his wife. She hears again Ingrid's awful scream of pain.

'Anton,' she says, 'when I left, your mother was alive. I pushed her, and she fell. It was an accident. But when your father came home she was still alive. He promised me he would call for help. His phone was in his hands.'

Suddenly Kate is transported back to that final night at High Barn. She sees Robert standing alone in the kitchen after she had left, doing nothing, calling no one, while his wife begs for help. A cold, awful understanding settles over Kate as she pictures him putting the phone back in his pocket, then taking a seat at the kitchen table, sitting quietly by as Ingrid bleeds to death in front of him. She sees it now, at last, after all those years of arguing and aggression: Robert's silent protest. His passive revenge.

Anton's voice brings her back with a start. 'No,' he shouts, shaking his head. 'No! You're a liar. My father told me you killed her. You're a fucking liar.'

'It's true,' she tells him quietly. 'It's true. It doesn't change what I did. But I thought that she would live. I thought she'd be OK.'

The clock clicks. The world shifts on.

They stare at each other, the gun still pointed at her head, the rage still in his eyes, but she sees it; somewhere, in the depths of him she sees that he believes her. And something else. Somewhere,

367

some buried part of him had already guessed his father's guilt.

But the barrel doesn't flinch. She takes a step towards it. He cocks the trigger and the noise is brutal in the quiet room.

'It's still your fault,' he tells her, steadying his arm.

Another step.

'I'll shoot you,' he says. 'I'm warning you. I'll shoot.'

Another step, and then another, and now she's in front of him, the tip of the gun's nose digging into her forehead. 'Do it,' she says.

Neither of them speaks. A second and then another drips icily by. She doesn't drop her gaze from his.

And then, with a sudden low moan of despair he lowers his arm. Within seconds he is half crouched upon the floor, the gun resting by his side.

For several moments she watches him, and then at last she goes to him, gently takes the gun from his hand and, after putting it on the table, sits down next to him on the floor. After some time she puts a hand on his shoulder. He is whimpering and gasping now. The clock clicks on. At last she gets to her feet. 'Goodbye, Anton,' she says, and there is a question in her voice. She hesitates, looking down at him, waiting for his answer, and after a long time he silently nods his agreement. She walks to the door just as Frank opens it.

EPILOGUE

31

Paris, 25 February 2005
Frank always knew he'd end up there. Even as his first flight touched down in Barcelona, a part of him always knew that Normandy was where his journey would finish. It takes him several months. As he wanders through Europe; on foot, by boat, by train and plane; while he hops from one Greek island to the next, sails through Norwegian fjords, skies down the Swiss Alps, strolls through the bazaars of Istanbul, he knows, in his heart, that every footstep is taking him closer to northern France.

In an internet café near La Gare du Nord he types 'Elodie Brun' into Google, and makes a note of the name of a tiny market town in northern France; a town in a region of Normandy where the forests are so vast it's said you can lose yourself for years beneath their trees.

London, 10 July 2004
The anger comes from nowhere. It catches her unawares, a sudden wave of rage snatching her up and carrying her off in its swell. For three weeks she lies prone on her bed. Mathias, Ingrid, Robert, Anton — no one escapes her fury. Only at night does she stir from her inertia to wander the streets, her fists balled and her teeth gritted

while she paces the cold black pavements, a pale ghost flitting between the streetlamps. But eventually she can rage and rail no more. Slowly, little by little, the waves of anger begin to subside, growing steadily calmer until finally they retreat altogether, leaving behind only a lingering grief for the mother she never knew, like twisted bones of driftwood on a shore.

Hidden at the bottom of her suitcase she finds the picture of Thérèse. Unfolding it she stares once again at the image of the face that is so heart-stoppingly like her own. The girl who looks back at her is a year or two younger than Kate is now; her hair is dark auburn, her eyes a deep blue. She smiles at the camera with a shy, lopsided grin. The familiar feeling of bafflement and grief hit Kate.

★ ★ ★

After they had left Anton's flat she had told Frank everything. In the taxi home he had listened in silence to every word, the shock weighing heavier in his eyes with every passing mile. Back at his house in Deptford they had sat together on the living room floor and talked until the sun had come up. She had left nothing out.

When she had finished he had not said a word for several minutes. His voice was very quiet when he finally spoke. 'Why didn't you tell me, Kate?' he'd asked. 'I would have done anything for you.'

'I was scared,' she told him, shaking her head, searching for the right words. 'I didn't want to be

372

Elodie Brun any longer. I hated her. I didn't want to be that freak, Little Bird.'

He had listened, nodded. 'But you told him — Anton,' he said. 'You told him,' he looked away. 'And then . . . '

'I'm sorry,' she had picked up his hand and kissed it, her tears falling onto his fingers. 'I love you.'

They had gone to bed and made love, woken hours later, still clinging to each other. 'I love you too,' he'd told her.

They had tried, at first, to start again. But they were like survivors of an earthquake, dazedly stumbling around in the wreckage and shooting covert, wary glances at each other for clues of where to go next. When Frank had first tentatively mentioned going away for a while, on the trip he'd always planned to take, she had leapt upon the idea gratefully, some part of her sensing the approaching tsunami, knowing she'd need to weather it alone.

32

Le Ferté-Macé, Normandy, France,
27 February 2005

The woman in the café on the edge of the square is in her sixties. Her inch-thick make-up stops abruptly at her neck, and as she passes Frank his coffee, her wrist rattles with jewellery. Beneath her apron she wears a tight, low-cut blouse, and as she moves, her cleavage glitters with the many gold chains nestled there. Frank sits and drinks his espresso while staring across at the tall, twin bell towers of the church that stands on the far side of the square. It's a pretty town with friendly locals, but the inquiries he's made so far have been met with apologetic shrugs and the shaking of heads.

He is the café's only customer and when the woman approaches with a lipsticked smile and poised cloth she seems eager to talk. 'Here on holiday, are you?' she begins, as she sidles closer.

'Yes,' he says. 'But I'm actually looking for someone. Maybe you know her?'

'Probably,' she agrees, pausing to light a cigarette with a fancy lighter she pulls from her apron pocket. 'I know everyone around here.'

And so he asks her about Thérèse, the local girl whose daughter had been stolen only yards away, twenty years before.

The waitress sucks deeply on her cigarette,

leaving a sticky red ring upon the white filter, before exhaling a long stream of smoke. 'Sure, I knew Thérèse, poor kid,' she says. 'She was from one of the estates out on the road to Flers. Only sixteen when she got knocked up by some guy from out of town.' She pauses and smiles coquettishly, and, patting her platinum-blonde perm adds, 'Of course, I was barely out of my teens myself at the time.'

Frank smiles politely and asks, 'Do you know what happened to her?'

She shrugs. 'After the kid went missing Thérèse just seemed to fall apart. Turned to drink and god knows what else. Used to see her hanging around the square by herself. Last I heard she was living in a squat with some druggies over in Argentan. Haven't seen her for about fifteen years though.'

'Thanks,' says Frank.

'Shocking about that daughter of hers, that woman dying and her just vanishing like that, just disappearing into thin air. They never found her, did they?'

Frank finishes his coffee. 'No. They never did.' He gets up to pay. At the door he stops and says, 'The old bakers shop — Preton's — the one Thérèse was in when the baby was stolen? Is it still here?'

'Yes, love. Well, the shop is, anyway. Old Preton's long retired of course, grumpy old sod. Come to think of it, if anyone knows what happened to Thérèse, Georges would.' She points over to the far side of the square. 'It's over there, handsome. Just there, on the corner. You go and ask the new owners where Georges lives now, they bought the shop off him a few years back.'

★ ★ ★

When Frank knocks on the door of the tiny house in the hamlet of Magny-le-Desert, it's opened by a small hunched man in his late seventies.

'Monsieur Preton?' asks Frank.

'Who's asking?' he replies, his small eyes peering, his lip-less mouth pursed in a thin, suspicious line.

'My name is Frank Auvrey. I wanted to talk to you about Thérèse Brun.'

Two seconds later he finds himself staring at red peeling paint, the door having been sharply slammed in his face. Frank sighs and hammers on it again. 'Monsieur Preton,' he calls. 'Please, sir. This is important.'

The door opens a crack. The small wrinkled face is pinched with anger. 'Can't you people leave her alone?' he shouts. 'Nearly twenty years ago it was.' His beady, yellowing eyes fix Frank with contempt. 'Filling your newspapers with lies and gossip.' He coughs heartily, and shuts the door again.

'Monsieur Preton,' calls Frank patiently. 'You don't understand. I'm a friend of Elodie's. Elodie Brun.'

Very slowly, the door opens a jar, two turtle eyes peer out.

His voice is sharp. 'What did you say?'

376

'I'm trying to find Thérèse, I'm a friend of her daughter Elodie.'

There's a long, silent pause, and then the door reopens and Frank follows the shuffling, stooped old man inside.

The ground floor of the small stone house consists of one large room with a tiny kitchen leading off it. In the centre is a table, with an elderly ginger dog snoring softly beneath it. The walls are bare apart from a couple of pictures of the Virgin Mary and some snapshots of the sleeping dog as a puppy. In one corner a pot-bellied stove sits next to a grandfather clock, in the other, a TV set blares. Slowly, Preton shuffles over to it and switches it off. The place smells of coffee and damp fur.

'This better not be a trick, boy.' His French is so thick with the regional accent that Frank struggles for a few seconds to decipher it. 'Because if it is I'll set Fidel on you.' His old finger points shakily at the geriatric mutt lying prone beneath the table, who raises his eyebrows a fraction, shifts arthritically on his haunches, glances at Frank and thumps his tail, then falls back to sleep with a contented sigh.

'It's not a trick, sir,' says Frank. 'I really do know Elodie. And I'm trying to trace her mother.'

Georges Preton stares hard at Frank, then with a grunt, gestures for him to sit, before disappearing into the kitchen. When he returns he carries a tray laden with coffee cups, a steaming pot, and a bottle of Calvados. 'Is it true, then?' he says with abrupt gruffness as he pours them both a cup of thick black coffee. 'Is it true what I read in the papers. That she ran off and left that Klein woman for dead?'

'No,' says Frank quietly. 'No. That's not true at all.' And, taking a cup from Georges, he begins to tell him everything that had happened to Kate after she was stolen from outside his shop all those years ago.

When he reaches the part where Ingrid told Elodie her mother no longer cared about her, the old man bangs his fist on the table. 'That bitch!' And when Frank tells him about her last night at High Barn, Georges' jaw sets in a hard, angry line. 'The poor kid,' he mutters. Otherwise he listens in absolute, unblinking silence until Frank has finished.

'Where is she?' He asks eagerly then, refilling their cups with Calvados. 'Is she in France? Is she here?'

Frank hesitates, and not looking Georges in the eye, replies, 'No, Monsieur Preton. No, I'm afraid she isn't.'

The old baker considers Frank silently for a moment. 'Why not?' he asks.

And then, to his surprise, Frank finds himself telling the old man everything. The French words seem to come to him like the lyrics of a song he'd thought he'd long forgotten. He tells Preton how they had tried to make things work for a while but in the end it had all just fallen apart. 'She never told me who she was, and what had happened to her, she told that maniac instead. She didn't trust me. She lied to me.' He shakes his head and drains his Calvados. 'And

378

then they — he and she, they . . . '

The old man continues to stare at him for a while and his voice when he speaks is gruff. 'Do you love her?'

Frank stares into his empty cup for a while. 'Yes. More than I can say.'

A long silence follows. The grandfather clock ticks on, the dog snores by his feet, and Frank feels, if not exactly happier, then lighter than he has for some time. Georges says nothing for a while, but at last he looks up, and fixing him in his beady gaze, says, 'Then don't be such a bloody fool, son.'

He gets to his feet. As he passes Frank he puts a hand on his shoulder. 'I'm going to bed now. Make sure you're back here at nine sharp in the morning.' He shuffles over to the kitchen and switches off the lights. 'Oh, and Frank? Take Fidel out for a piss before you go, there's a good lad.'

★ ★ ★

When he arrives at the house a little before nine the next day, Preton is already waiting for him outside in his ancient Citroën. He leans over and unlocks the passenger door. 'Get in,' he says, turning the key in the ignition.

Frank goes over and peers doubtfully through the window. Inside it's more or less the same size as a can of beans. Fidel is squashed into the open truck part. 'Where are we going?' he asks, getting in.

Preton steps on the accelerator and they lurch

forward with a loud splutter from the engine. 'Hang on to your breakfast this time, Fidel,' he yells over his shoulder. 'Where are we going?' he asks Frank in surprise. 'We're going to see Thérèse, of course.'

It's on the forty-minute drive over to Argentan that Frank, still reeling from Preton's revelation, learns the sad story of Thérèse's life. 'She fell apart after the child disappeared,' Georges tells him. 'It was like watching someone die in slow motion. She got in with a bad lot — junkies, no hopers. They gave her drugs and booze, took advantage of her.' He shakes his head. 'I tried my best to help her, but she was hell-bent on losing herself. She wouldn't listen to me — it was as though she were punishing herself for what had happened. By the time Elodie turned up again, she was a bloody mess. Out of her mind on God knows what.' He snorts angrily, 'And then that Ingrid person turned up.'

Preton drives on in silence for a while, but when he speaks again, his voice is still furious. 'She just wouldn't let up. Convincing Thérèse she was unfit to care for Elodie, that the child would be better off without her. Hounding her, bullying her. Promising her that Elodie would be back in a year, that she'd be able to visit her in the States — that it was all in Elodie's best interests. Thérèse is half-English, speaks it fluently, Klein was at the top of her field and it seemed to her like it would be Elodie's best chance to rebuild her life.'

As Frank listens to Georges talk, an image of Kate on the journey back from Anton's flat flashes into his mind; how she'd looked when she'd told him about the mother she'd never known. An intense pity twists in his guts. 'Go on,' he prompts.

'Well, for a while, after Thérèse had signed the papers, it looked like she was going to pull herself together at last. She got clean, kicked the booze and drugs, even got herself a little cleaning job so she could provide a home for Elodie when she returned. It was all she talked about. I was amazed at the change in her.'

'So what happened?' asks Frank.

'What happened is that bitch, Klein, kept putting her off. Saying that it would ruin the kid's progress if she were to return to France, that she just needed a little longer. This went on for months. In the end, she told Thérèse that the kid didn't want to see her. Wanted nothing to do with her. Fed her a load of nonsense about Elodie being happier where she was, that Thérèse was nothing to her now.

'I tried to persuade her to put up a fight, but instead she hit the drugs and booze harder than before. She had always blamed herself for Elodie's disappearance, I guess that's why it was so easy for her to believe Ingrid's lies. When news came through that Klein was dead and Elodie had disappeared, she took to her bed. She's barely left her flat since. It's like she's just given up on life. She blames herself for it all.'

There's a long silence. Finally Frank turns to the little old man, whose eyes are fixed determinedly on the road ahead. 'She's lucky to have you,' he remarks.

Preton shrugs. 'When it happened outside my shop I felt responsible somehow. She was so young. It destroyed her so completely.' He glances at Frank with a grim smile. 'But now she's got a second chance, hasn't she, thanks to you? To put things right.' He turns back to the road. 'And everyone deserves that, don't you think?'

Soon they approach the suburbs of a large town. As the traffic grows thicker around them, Frank's thoughts return once again to Kate. He closes his eyes as he recalls how wounded he'd been at her betrayal, how self-righteously hurt. Her face returns to him now; her smile, and he remembers all the times he'd sensed a darkness there; something secretive and painful beneath the surface that he'd been determined not to confront. As they finally pull up outside a tall apartment block in a dirty, dead-end street, he is gripped by such an intense longing for Kate he can barely get out of the car.

★ ★ ★

The woman who answers the door to them is in her early forties, her auburn hair is flecked with grey, her eyes dull, vacant, and rimmed with shadows. But still Frank can see the girl he loves glimmering behind those dark blue irises. The resemblance to Kate is unmistakable.

'Georges,' Thérèse says faintly. 'This is a nice surprise.' Glancing curiously at Frank she stands aside to let them in.

When the three of them are seated in her tiny

living room Preton takes her hand and begins to talk. 'Thérèse,' he says gently, 'this is Frank, my dear.' He leans forward. 'Thérèse, he knows Elodie,' he says. 'He knows where she is. Do you understand? We've found her.'

And Frank, for the rest of his life, will not forget the expression in her eyes, like a flock of birds returning at last, after a long, cold winter.

33

London, 1 March, 2005
Summer drifts into autumn. The decision to leave Frank's house comes to her out of the blue one morning and the second she has thought of it she realises she cannot bear to remain in his home without him any longer. She finds a flat to rent in Borough; a tiny, pretty place not far from the river, and leaving her new address with Jimmy, she moves in.

A week later she signs on to a new employment agency and accepts a placement in a small accountancy firm in Waterloo. The days, the weeks pass. Her new job is simple but diverting, her colleagues pleasant and unobtrusive. Occasionally one or two of the other secretaries will ask her to lunch or to the pub for a drink after work and she always accepts. She is content; finding peace in the uncomplicated rituals of these days. She misses Frank with a constant, dull ache. At some point she stops dyeing and cutting her hair, allowing the new growth of red and brown to unfurl to the bottom of her neck. 'Elodie,' she whispers to her reflection. 'Elodie Brun'. At night she dreams of Frank, and it is his face she sees, when she wakes.

★ ★ ★

One evening, when Frank has been gone for nearly eight months, she walks home from work along the river, stopping at the South Bank for a while to watch some street performers dance. It's a mild March night, with just a hint of winter remaining in the air. The lights from the embankment cast a yellow glow across the black water. The trees are strewn with hundreds of coloured bulbs. Above her, behind the glass façade of the Festival Hall she can see crowds of people on the brink of their nights out, clutching tickets and talking excitedly to one another.

Along the walkway by the river the booksellers have begun to pack up their stalls and she lingers amongst them, leafing through first one paperback, and then another. Just as she's about to move off, her gaze lands on one in particular that makes the breath catch in her throat. *Wild Children*, by Martin Chambers, she reads. After a long moment she picks it up and searches through it until she finds the old familiar photograph of herself. She stares at it for a long time, waiting for the usual feelings of panic and revulsion to return. They never come. After some minutes, she puts the book down and, hugging her coat around her against a sudden gust of wind, goes to stand at the edge of the walkway, looking down at the black swirling water below. She becomes entirely lost in thought.

'Nice night.' The man standing a few feet away is tall and young.

'Yes,' she agrees.

'Tom,' he says, after a pause, raising a hand in shy salute.

'Elodie,' she tells him with a smile. 'I'm Elodie.'

'I saw you walking past earlier, and — ' he pauses and gives a short embarrassed laugh — 'I'm sorry to be so forward but you're absolutely gorgeous. I'd never forgive myself if I didn't ask for your number.' He stands there, looking back at her.

She takes in his broad shoulders, his hopeful, attractive face. 'No,' she tells him gently. 'No, but thanks anyway.'

★ ★ ★

She walks home through Waterloo, past the station's sweeping steps, the floodlit theatre, the pubs flickering beneath a sudden rain. She wraps her arms around her chest as though to contain the happiness that is beginning to grow new roots, new buds there. When she reaches Borough's twisting little streets a gust of wind sends scraps of litter scuttling around her feet and ivy creeps across some blackened bricks. Above her someone slams a window shut, a streetlamp casts a yellow net. At first, she doesn't see the figure sitting on her step, his rucksack propped against the door; doesn't spot him until she's at her gate and sees his eyes and smile that seems to fill the sky, and reaching for his hand she helps him to his feet. 'Frank,' she says.

author note

My thanks to Dave Holloway, Rachel Pask, Claire Paterson, Alex Pierce, Justin Quirk, Susan Watt and the team at HarperCollins, Anna Way.

www.feralchildren.com

We do hope that you have enjoyed reading this large print book.

Did you know that all of our titles are available for purchase?

We publish a wide range of high quality large print books including:
Romances, Mysteries, Classics
General Fiction
Non Fiction and Westerns

Special interest titles available in large print are:
The Little Oxford Dictionary
Music Book
Song Book
Hymn Book
Service Book

Also available from us courtesy of Oxford University Press:
Young Readers' Dictionary
(large print edition)
Young Readers' Thesaurus
(large print edition)

For further information or a free brochure, please contact us at:
Ulverscroft Large Print Books Ltd.,
The Green, Bradgate Road, Anstey,
Leicester, LE7 7FU, England.
Tel: (00 44) 0116 236 4325
Fax: (00 44) 0116 234 0205

Other titles published by
The House of Ulverscroft:

THE DEAD OF SUMMER

Camilla Way

Following the death of her mother, Anita and her family have moved to a new town, a new home, and a new neighbourhood. The long school holidays are approaching, with summer stretching out before them. Kyle lives across the road from Anita. Cool, surly, laconic, he tells her about the hidden, disused mines: a perfect playground for kids with nothing better to do. But what they don't know is that these mines will be the scene of the most unsettling crime this community has ever known. This summer, everything will change. This summer, the dead days have come home to stay.

THE ELEPHANT KEEPER

Christopher Nicholson

In the middle of the 18th century, a ship docks at Bristol with an extraordinary cargo: two young elephants. Bought by a wealthy landowner, they are taken to his estate in the English countryside. A stable boy, Tom Page, is given the task of caring for them. *The Elephant Keeper* is Tom's account of his life with the elephants. As the years pass, and as they journey across England, his relationship with the female elephant deepens in a startling manner. Along the way they meet incredulity, distrust and tragedy, but their understanding of each other keeps them together.

THE LIFE YOU WANT

Emily Barr

Tansy Harris is a terrible mother: the kind who forgets to pick her children up from school and contemplates an affair with her son's teacher. But when she married Max, they'd agreed it wouldn't change them — they'd still be free do whatever they want, see the world. But they *have* changed, and Tansy can't cope. To avoid the looming meltdown, Tansy decides the answer is India: to go alone, take stock and return a better person. India turns out to be everything she hoped for. However, when she visits an old backpacker friend who's joined a cult in the south, Tansy finds something terrifying and much bigger than her. She realises, too late, that she's in the wrong place at the wrong time . . .

THE GULF BETWEEN US

Geraldine Bedell

Annie Lester's life is quite a challenge. A single mother to three boys, her ex-boyfriend is now an international film star. Whilst tolerating her bigoted brother, she's trying to avoid a dismissive film producer with a mission to annoy her. And Annie Lester tackles all this in the small Gulf emirate of Hawar, where, in 2002, America's invasion of Iraq reverberates. As her life unravels in unexpected ways, Annie has to decide where her loyalties lie. Are her sons defined by who they are, or by what they do? Can a British woman ever be at home in the Middle East? And can James Hartley, the blue-eyed heartthrob adored by millions, really be serious about someone as ordinary as Annie Lester believes herself to be?